The FREE STATE of GALVESTON

J. B. Lifflander

The Free State of Galveston
Copyright © 2017 J.B. Lifflander
Published by AsGold Media
Ridgefield, WA 98642
www.asgoldmedia.com
Artwork by Duncan Long

ISBN 978-0-9711339-7-6
LCCN 2017910574

All Rights Reserved. No part of this publication may be reproduced, stored in a retrieval system, or transmitted in any form or by any means, including but not limited to electronic, mechanical, digital, photocopy, recording, etc. without the prior written permission from the publisher. The exception would be for brief quotations in printed reviews.

Printed in the United States of America

To my wife, Carol, of whom it can be said:

> *The heart of her husband safely trusts her;*
> *So he will have no lack of gain.*
> *She does him good and not evil*
> *All the days of her life.*—Proverbs 31:1-12 (NKJV)

AUTHOR'S INTRODUCTION

Hi, I'm J.B. Lifflander or John Lifflander and I write novels and technical books, and I live in Ridgefield, Washington. The Free State of Galveston is fiction but it also has some semi-autobiographical elements—I grew up in Galveston, Texas, and my friends drove fast cars, and I am a licensed pilot. I went to Ball High School and also lived in Houston and observed the beginning of the hippie movement in the 1960s from that vantage point.

Other similarities between the book and my life are that my father was an historian who specialized in the Civil War, and went to Columbia University, and taught history at Galveston College and Texas A&M, and my mother was Australian, and was a nurse in that country. I also lived in the large, historical house described in the book, and the photograph on the back cover is of that actual house.

The characters in the book are not actual people, but are based on composites of friends and others I have known, and some of the incidents did occur. My prayer is that many will be blessed by this book.

CHAPTER 1

"No, Dad, I'm not tired—I promise you."

"Well, you've been driving for over seven hours, and it is getting late."

"I'm wide awake and I can keep driving," I said, glancing in the rearview mirror where I could see my mother sleeping. "We're getting pretty close to Fredericksburg, and I know you want to visit the battlefield. If we get there tonight, you can see it in the morning. Besides, we need to get to Galveston so I don't miss too much school."

"Paul, somehow I don't think that missing school is the greatest concern you have—perhaps you're excited to see the car you inherited from your aunt?"

"Oh, that's right—I almost forgot about that. You said it may be an old Cadillac. I should be excited about that."

"Don't push it, or I may teach your mother how to drive and give it to her."

"Okay, okay. I'm excited about the car—the truth wins out!"

"Now we have to drive three and a half more hours to get there, and I'm concerned about you falling asleep."

"Dad, I'm not tired."

"Did I tell you about the time your uncle fell asleep at the wheel and only woke up—"

"When he hit the guardrail. Yeah, Dad, you've told me about fifty times now. So I promise you if I get sleepy, I'll tell you."

"Okay, because I'm getting sleepy myself and I can't look out for you."

"Dad, I'm sixteen and I've been driving for two years now."

"Oh, yes, I forgot how mature and experienced you are at sixteen."

"Do I detect some mild sarcasm in that statement?"

"Interpret it as you will."

"Well, have a good rest and I'll wake you when we get to Fredericksburg."

"And you won't speed—you'll watch the speed limit. A lot of these little towns are speed traps—did you know that?"

"Yes, dear Father. You told me previously."

"Don't get smart now."

"I thought you wanted me to be smart and make good grades."

"You are really pushing it now—that's *rebellious* sarcasm."

"Oh, you mean that kind of smart—I'm sorry, I must've misunderstood."

"I don't think so."

"Interpret it as you will."

"Oh, you are chronically incorrigible, but nevertheless I am going to trust you. I'm going to try to sleep now."

"Thank you, and sweet dreams."

We were on our way to Galveston, Texas, to live in a house we had inherited from my aunt, who had died a few years before. The house had been vacant for a long time, because my father had never gotten around to putting it on the market. But that worked out well, because in the meantime my mother began to suffer from chronic bronchitis and our family doctor told her that relocating to a warmer climate than Connecticut would help her condition. Galveston was warm most of the year, and the winters were mild, so we hoped her health would improve there.

My father was a history professor who had stopped teaching and was now writing textbooks, and his favorite subject was the Civil War. He respected the South and its generals even though he was born and raised in New York—which seemed a bit ironic to me. And he seemed to never stop talking about that war—little snippets of history tended to find their way into his conversations about other things. It was almost as if he could find an application to almost everything in contemporary life from some aspect of the Civil War. And, although he was fond of saying, "I teach the past, but I don't live in it," it was clear to me that the opposite was true.

He did live in the past, somewhere between the musty pages of the numerous volumes of history that cluttered his massive library, and somewhere in the minds of the many young, idealistic soldiers that he spoke so passionately of when describing the battles of the Civil War in a way which I've never heard them described before or since. He was not one to recite dates or trite elements from boring textbooks—he would rather quote from the diary of an everyday noncommissioned soldier who had made some unusual or seemingly trivial comment about the war, which nevertheless brought it to life in a way that the didactic recordation of most history books do not.

"We're here," I said, as I pulled into the parking lot of the Holiday Inn, but there was no answer. Both of my parents were sleeping soundly, and I didn't want to wake them, but I knew I had to. I gently shook my father's shoulder and he looked up abruptly at me, a bit confused for a moment.

"Where are we?" he said, and then looked up at the hotel sign. "Oh, we're here—we're already in Fredericksburg?"

"Yes sir—and no accidents, no tickets, and I didn't even fall asleep and hit the guardrail!"

"Okay, good job. Let's check in and wake up your mother once we have the suitcases in the hotel. I want her to get as much sleep as she can."

My mother was Australian and she had little knowledge of the Civil War until she met my father in World War Two, where she tended him as a nurse in an almost classical love story tale. I doubt she shared his boundless fascination for the subject, but she so carefully listened to him expound on it that I could not tell if she was merely being dutiful, or had also developed an inordinate interest. Whatever the case, the next day we visited our third battlefield, where he regaled us with his amazing repertoire of quotes from privates to generals, and reenacted what was said on approximately the same piece of land it was said on. That evening it seemed to transcend just being a quote and he somehow became the soldier who was making the statement. His acting on this occasion was rather extraordinary.

Sitting on the ground next to the Rappahannock River, he started talking softly. "These boys were sentimentalists and they loved to sing, and the thing is that both the Union and Confederate soldiers sang a lot of the same songs. One was called 'Lorena.'"

He then started singing in his deep, melodic voice.

The years creep slowly by, Lorena,
The snow is on the grass again
The sun's low down in the sky, Lorena,
The frost gleams where the flowers have been.

There was a hypnotic effect as he sang, and then he stopped and touched the ground. "One day," he went on, taking a deep breath of the frosty air and watching it wisp away in a white cloud as he exhaled. "One day during the long winter of the Battle of Fredericksburg, the rival armies were camped on the opposite sides of the Rappahannock. The Confederates camped right here, right where we're sitting. The armies were so close to each other that they were talking, comparing notes on rations, what their generals were like, and other things. They'd been fighting a long, hard war and the fields were filled with blood, but they were chatting with each other that night. And that night the Union band came down to the river bank and played beautifully. There was no radio then, and the music was prized and appreciated. The Yank band played rousing tunes like 'John Brown's Body' and 'The Battle Cry of Freedom.'"

"Northerners and Southerners listened and sang those songs, massed in their thousands on the hillsides as the cold, bitter wind blew and the campfires flickered against the black water. When the band stopped for a moment, some Southerners yelled across the river, 'Now play some of ours!' And you know what? Without a pause the Yankee band swung into 'Maryland My Maryland' and then 'Dixie'. Then they played 'Home Sweet Home' and the soldiers sang on both sides of the river. A few weeks later they were ripping each other to shreds."

He then began to sing again in a very low voice.

I wish I was in the land of cotton
Old times there are not forgotten
Look away! Look away! Look away! Dixie Land

I wish I was in Dixie, Hooray! Hooray!
In Dixie Land I'll take my stand
To live and die in Dixie…

Somehow as he sang I seemed to get a vision of those soldiers and I felt emotional. I glanced at my mother and could see tears forming in her eyes, and I knew he brought something of the past to life for her as well. She looked up and noticed me watching her, and wiped her eyes, evidently embarrassed and not realizing that I was similarly affected. She then made an uncharacteristic quip which had the effect of bringing us all down to earth.

"Well, we better not stay in Dixie if we want to move to Texas."

My father turned toward her gradually, his eyes showing that he was still in 1862, but was reluctantly transitioning to the reality of the present.

"Lincoln needed to win, but it didn't happen here. This was the most lopsided battle of the war because the North lost twice as many men as the South. But enough about that—you're right, we better get going."

My mother was awake, but my father was sleeping when I drove across a long bridge that connected Galveston Island to the mainland. We had eaten lunch in Houston, and I thought that the wine my father had with his sandwich had put him to sleep. My father earned most of his money from royalties from textbooks he wrote. Making a living that way had a good and bad effect on him. The good part was that he was able to live the life of a leisurely academic, but somehow the pace of that life got too leisurely and he began spending more time picking out fine wines and less time researching and writing textbooks. The truth is that he had become a drunk, but when one gets drunk on expensive wine, it can sometimes appear more acceptable. However, the effect remains the same, regardless of how sophisticated the drinker may be.

My mother had confided in me that she hoped that he would teach again in Galveston because they had a fairly new community college there. He had taught at regular universities in the past, but not for many years. I knew he was a good teacher, but I also knew that he was always having trouble getting along with university staff. Besides the fact that he was sometimes outlandishly eccentric, I gathered that he wanted to teach in a dramatic way which they did not always approve of. My mother hoped that if he began teaching again it would force him to cut down on his drinking, because he never drank when he taught. But the question was, where would he teach? If he taught in Houston, it was a fifty-mile drive each way, and he did not like driving.

I wondered if he would be open to teaching again as I glanced back at him sleeping in the backseat of our Buick Electra. My mother was in the front seat, and she looked at me, questioningly. "A penny for your thoughts," she said.

"You can have them for free," I answered, but I knew I could not tell her what I was thinking in case he woke up.

"I'm still waiting," she said.

We were driving westward on a main arterial street named Broadway, and I glanced at the commercial buildings on both sides. They looked a little rundown. "I don't see the ocean," I said.

She looked down at a pamphlet. "It says here that it's a top tourist destination, and there are about 67,000 people. It's an island about three miles wide and twenty-seven miles long. I think we're on the wrong side for that."

"Well, at least we are west of the South—Dad won't have any civil war history to lecture me on, I imagine."

Almost as if on cue, he woke up and heard my last sentence. "*Au contraire*! Things happened here during the Civil War. Major General John Magruder attacked the occupying Union troops and expelled them from the island in January 1863 in the Battle of Galveston. But the city also suffered the fate of many waterfront and river cities because in 1867 a yellow fever epidemic killed 1,800 people."

"And this city has a history of firsts in Texas. They built the first opera house in 1870, the first orphanage in 1876, and they got telephone lines in 1878 and electric lights in 1883. By the end of the 19th century, the population was about 37,000, and it was one of the largest cotton ports in the nation. But then in 1900 there was the terrible hurricane that killed about 7,000 people, so they built a seawall to keep the town from flooding in the future, and—"

"Dad…Dad…I'd like to hear all of this, but I'm trying to find the way to the house right now. So can we get the complete history later?"

My father was a little taken aback, but he did realize that I needed to focus my attention. "Yes, of course, the history lesson can come later—but there is a lot more. It's a very interesting island with a sordid past."

The house looked like a mansion, but it was in an older neighborhood in Galveston. Many of the surrounding homes were rundown, but interspersed were a few larger homes that had been kept up. The house had four stories including the basement, and it was made of stone. The top story was a ballroom, which had seen better days, but the rest of the house was in beautiful condition, especially considering it was built in 1895. As we walked in, the sun shone through a stained glass window into the foyer with red and amber hues, creating a somewhat surreal effect. The ceilings were also painted, and my mother commented that she might find a relative of Michelangelo hiding about somewhere in the huge home.

The furniture was covered with sheets to keep dust off it, and we went through the house taking them off. As my mother and I grabbed the end of a sheet covering a couch, my father pulled one off a large easy chair which was covered with green velvet. "That's a beautiful chair," my mother said, walking over to it and touching it. "But we still have our furniture coming and I don't know where we will put everything. We may need to store some things."

My father walked into the kitchen and came out with some keys in his hand. "Okay, you've been patient, and these are the keys, so let's go look at the car."

"Great. Mum, are you coming?" She looked over at me and then back at the furniture. I knew she wanted to finish the adventure of finding out what the rest of the furniture looked like, but she knew I was champing at the bit to see the car, so she acquiesced.

"Yes, let's see the car."

We walked out of the house and to the back, where there was a four- car garage that had an apartment above it. It wasn't as old as the rest of the house—cars were not in use in 1895—but since it was constructed of wood and not stone like the house, it was rundown and needed paint and other maintenance. My father fumbled with the keys trying to find the one that opened the garage as I stood watching, doing all I could not to snatch them away from him. He was undoubtedly very intelligent, but part of his eccentricity was that he was often incompetent when it came to practical things. He was trying each key, but then he would forget which key he had already tried. He stopped for a moment, and then he handed me the keys and I quickly tried each one until I got the right one.

As we opened the door, winged cockroaches flew into our faces and my mother started screaming and pulling at her hair, where one had become entangled. My father tried to get it out but it took a few minutes and when the ordeal was over she looked horrified. "It's okay, dear. It's gone now," my father said, consolingly.

"I knew there were bugs here, but flying roaches!" she exclaimed.

I was too selfish to worry about her reaction and I moved through the garage until I saw the car. It was a ten-year-old Cadillac, and it was coated with dust—making it look gray. The tires had lost some air, and I moved closer and used my hand to wipe the dust off to find out that it was pink. I stood back, aghast, as my parents walked up. "It's pink!" I said.

"Yes, it is definitely pink," my father said, trying to hide a smile.

I looked at him and frowned. "You think this is funny, don't you?"

"Of course not," he said, and then he burst out laughing. "It takes a real man to drive a pink car."

"Oh, you...you!" I said, and then started laughing myself.

"I think it's a pretty color," my mother said, seeming to ignore us. "But it won't do for you, will it?"

"It will have to do for him, unless he wants to take the bus to school," my father said.

I blew off some dust from the driver's door and opened it. "Where are the keys?" I asked.

"Oh, I have them here," my father said, handing them to me. I tried to start the car but the battery was dead. Then I looked at the odometer. "It only has about 12,000 miles on it. Has it flipped over?"

"I don't think so. Your aunt had bad vision and rarely drove and she was in a home for several years before she died," my father said.

"Yes, I think that's all it has. The interior is almost like new. I'm glad the roaches didn't get inside. Can we buy a battery now? There was a Sears on Broadway, I think."

"Can't wait to get to school—is that it?" Dad said.

"You bet. If I get it running I can go tomorrow."

"I think we ought to take a day to clean things up and get settled," my mother said. "It's getting a bit late to go to the store and if we are going to sleep here tonight we need to work on the house together. You can work on the car tomorrow and go to school the following day."

"Please let me get the battery. I'll work extra fast if you let me," I cajoled.

"Okay—but don't drive fast to Sears," my father said.

My mother was on the phone and my father was reading a book when I came down for breakfast.

"So the school has the transcripts. Okay, thank you ever so much, good-bye," she said, hanging up the phone. She turned to us and passed me a plate. "I've made scrambled eggs."

"Thanks, Mum," I said, remembering how I had been teased for calling her Mum instead of Mom when I was in elementary school. I had not realized then that some of her Australian words and pronunciations made my speech stand out.

"The school is on Forty-third and Avenue O. Do you have a map?" she asked.

"No."

"Well, you don't want to be late your first day."

"I drove by yesterday after I got the car running."

"Oh, good. What did it look like?"

"It's big—a pink brick building and it looks pretty modern."

My father had been brooding a little at the table, and I thought I knew why. At times he would get upset over some fine point of history and it would bother him for a few days. He was mumbling unhappily and at first all I heard was "McClellan." I thought I would try to bring him into the current world a little. "Hi, Dad, what are you reading?" He didn't answer, but looked up rather intensely at me, as if he were going to scold me for something.

"It's McClellan again, isn't it?" I asked, not only because I'd heard him say the name, but I also knew that he had a preoccupation with the general who was in charge of the Northern troops at the beginning of the Civil War.

"McClellan was cautious," he began, looking out as if he were looking at the general, himself. "And at one time I could understand that—a little. But last night I figured out how many young men were killed because he wouldn't take the initiative—he would not fight! It's more than exasperating, it's criminal."

"He was probably only doing what he thought was right," I said, instantly regretting my comment.

"What he thought was right? Was he right when he found Lee's orders? He found Lee's position and movements three times and he still would not fight!"

"Easy, dear," my mother interjected.

"Was he right to disrespect Lincoln, when the president came to visit him and he wouldn't even come out of his office to see him? Can you imagine a general refusing to see the president of the United States, his commander in chief, when he makes a personal visit to his house? The war dragged on until 1865 when it might have been over several years earlier if he'd acted. At one time I could forgive him, but…"

"There's not much Paul can do about it now," my mother said.

"Yes, I know," he said, looking up and obviously regretting that was the case. "No one can do anything now—more's the pity."

"You're right, Dad. I didn't know he disrespected Lincoln. That was not cool."

"Yes, it definitely was not 'cool,' that is a certainty."

"Well, I have to get to school. Please don't stay upset about it all day. McClellan was just a man, he wasn't perfect."

"Easy for you to say," he muttered as I left the house.

CHAPTER 2

The Cadillac looked almost like new once I washed and waxed it, but it turned out to be a bright shade of pink and it stood out so much that I wondered if I would have been better off to leave the dust on it. I was hoping no one would see me driving it, but they did. I had gone to a private school in Connecticut and we had a strict dress code where we always wore slacks. So, to make matters worse, I wore slacks that morning. But I would soon regret that decision when I saw everyone else wearing jeans.

The student parking lot was packed with cars, and I drove around until I finally found a space on the outer fringes. The trouble was that this was also where many of the students were hanging out, smoking cigarettes and sitting in their cars listening to the radio. I got out of the car quickly and started walking towards the school when several boys came up to me, smiling. They had seen me get out of the car and one of them whistled as one might at a girl.

"I really like that car—it suits you," he said.

"Thank you for the compliment," I answered wryly and kept walking. I could hear a Beach Boy's song coming from the radio of someone's car and "I get around…" was getting louder as I came closer to an area where a large group of boys were sitting around their cars, most of which were old and beat up. But one stood out—it was a new pale yellow Pontiac GTO with magnesium wheels and over-sized tires. The evident owner sat on the hood with his legs crossed seeming to steep in the regality of his automotive throne.

I noticed that a lot of the boys were wearing light blue jeans, a pale yellow shirt, and brown penny loafers—some without socks. Most of them also had dark suntans. They were the surfer crowd and many of them had blond hair that was bleached with peroxide. The boy on the hood was also dressed that way, but he wasn't as tanned and his clothes seemed to be better fitting and more expensive. I wondered if he was accepted because of his car.

"You want to drag that old Caddy?" a boy with floppy blond hair asked me.

"No, I need to get to the main office to register."

"You're new, huh?" another boy said with a slow Texas drawl, as he stood next to his old woody station wagon (one with real wood on the sides) and spoke as if that meant I might be some strange alien from another planet.

I nodded and another boy stepped in my way. "You can't go there until you get a suntan," he said, and the others laughed.

"Yeah, no ghosts allowed," another one said as he took a Marlboro from his pack of cigarettes, then lit it and inhaled with the expertise of a veteran smoker.

"You really think he's alive?" one of them asked.

"Yeah, man," another said. "He's like a vampire—a queer vampire with a pink car—come back from the dead."

"Yeah, kinda like a new horror film—the walking dead queer."

I looked at the kid in my way and tried to figure out if they were going to gang up on me or if they were just having some fun. They didn't seem too dangerous, so I stepped to the side and began walking away. As I did, two girls got out of a car and were walking in front of me.

"Watch out, he's a dead queer with a pretty pink car," the first boy shouted.

I noticed the girls were laughing at me and I felt embarrassed. I looked back and shouted, "Where I'm from we spot queers because they dye their hair blonde like women." The girls giggled at my retort.

"Come back, queer! No one puts down the great Kahuna," one of them shouted back.

I wanted to skip a week of school and get a tan or at least go home and change into some jeans—but it was too late now.

In the administration office, I spoke to an older lady.

"Excuse me."

"Yes?" she said, finally looking over at me.

"I'm new here. I'd like to register."

"What's your name?"

"Paul Welles. My high school in Connecticut was supposed to send all the information."

"Okay. Well, why don't you sit down over there and I'll have Darlene fill out a card on you while I look for your transcripts."

I took a seat where she pointed and in a few minutes one of the students who was working in the office walked over and took a seat next to me with a clipboard and pen in her hand.

"What is your full name?"

"Paul Winston Welles."

"Can you spell it?"

"I think so...let me see..." I said. She giggled a little and I spelled it for her.

"Height?"

"Six feet."

"Weight?"

"One hundred and fifty-five pounds."

About this time I noticed a few other girls who worked in the office were walking around and glancing over at me.

"Hair color?"

"Brown."

"Eye color?"

"Brown."

About this time one of the girls walked by again and smiled.

"Don't forget to say he's cute," she said, and then swiftly walked away. About this time, the older woman walked up to us.

"I found your transcripts—looks like you were an honor roll student, so keep up the good work."

"I will. Thank you."

"I can't find an equivalent class to your business statistics class, but I can put you into a business math class. It's normally only for seniors. Would that be okay?"

"Yes, that's fine."

"I've also got you in English and biology… looks like we can match everything else except Latin. We don't teach that here."

"That's fine. I've had enough of it."

"Did you bring tennis shoes and gym clothes for P.E.?"

"They're in my car."

"Well, you can get them after this, because I've got you in a P.E. class right before lunch."

The coach was a short, squatty man, and I didn't like the way he looked at me. I suited up and walked onto the gym floor with the rest of the students, and we began a series of exercises, starting with jumping jacks. When that was over, we were supposed to play dodge ball. There were two boys throwing, and they were big fellows. I saw them talking to the coach before the game and it was obvious they were his favorites. I wondered if they had failed a few years because they looked too old to be in high school.

I was trying to figure out how anyone else would get a chance to throw the ball, since they monopolized it. They kept throwing and getting people out, but they always missed me. I was beginning to feel pretty good about that, until I realized that for some reason they weren't trying. Soon there were only five other kids they were throwing at, and then it was just me and another kid, who was especially fast. When he was hit, things became ominously silent, and the two boys throwing just kept bouncing the dodge balls, but they weren't throwing at me. Then someone walked up with an air pump and they filled the balls with more air, until they were as hard as they could make them.

I knew what was coming and braced myself for the first throw, but it missed—then the second one came and missed also. The other students watched gleefully, but the coach was not around. They bounced the over-filled balls hard against the wall of the gym, all the while watching me and savoring their chance to keep me on edge—wondering when they would throw. Suddenly they both threw their balls at me as hard as they could, one hitting me in the face and the other landing on my side and arm. My head was reeling from the hit, and I held my hands up and walked to the side, but they had two more balls and they hit me again.

"You got me, I'm out," I said, walking towards the other boys.

"No, it's a new game now for the new boy," one of them said, hitting me again with a ball.

"It's called initiation," one of the boys in the class said, as another ball was thrown towards me, and I ducked. It hit someone else and I walked off the court. They were going to keep throwing at me when the coach showed up and said "showers" and we all walked into the locker room. I noticed the coach hanging around as I began to take my gym clothes off for a shower. He was staring at me, and I decided to skip it and just get dressed.

"Aren't you taking a shower, Welles?" he asked.

"No, Coach," I said.

"Well you're supposed to," he retorted.

I ignored him and got dressed and walked to the cafeteria. As I was paying, someone walked up behind me and said in a low voice, "Hey, queer." I was so angry about the dodge ball that I turned around quickly, ready to put the tray down and fight, but it was the boy with the GTO and he was smiling disarmingly. "Come on, you can sit with me and I'll tell you all about Ball High," he offered.

I followed him to a table where a few other boys who knew him were sitting. "I'm Gordon Silvers," he said, and held out his hand.

"Paul Welles," I answered, and shook it. Gordon was about five feet eight inches tall, and he had black hair. His eyes flickered with intelligence, and what he lacked in looks he made up for with charisma.

He looked at my arm and head and shook his head. "What happened? You're not white anymore. You're kind of pink like your car."

"A friendly game of dodge ball in P.E. You got some real animals in this dump."

"It's just the first time. They'll leave you alone now. But I can get you out of P.E. forever with a note from my father."

"How can a note from your father get me out of P.E.?"

"He's a doctor, that's how. I've got some of his stationery and I can write what I want."

"You're not kidding, are you?"

"Not about P.E.—that's serious stuff. Just think, for thirty bucks no more jumping jacks, stinky locker room, tiny towels, and running to class half wet from the shower, not to mention the coach leering at you."

"You noticed that also, huh?"

"Yeah—he *really* likes his boys. So instead you can just relax in the study hall because you have, let's say, vestibular balance disorder. See, you feel like you're dizzy when you exercise—like you're floating, kind of like vertigo, you poor thing. You have semicircular canals in your ear which are three fluid-filled loops arranged roughly at right angles to each other. They tell the brain to coordinate things when your head moves in a rotating or circular way, like when you nod your head up and down or look from right to left. And yours are all messed up."

"Sounds bad."

"Oh, it is. So bad that the doctor has ordered you out of P.E. so the condition doesn't worsen. All signed and official—and also a good time for you because you are new and no one knows anything about you yet."

"Wow. You don't sell used cars after school, do you?"

"Very funny. Only thirty bucks. Remember, it's a limited offer."

Suddenly there was a loud noise a few tables away. A chair was knocked down and it skidded across the floor, which got everyone's attention. A tough-looking Mexican kid, wearing khaki pants and orange-brown pointed shoes was just about to sit in it when a big, husky boy kicked it over. "This table is reserved," he said. The Mexican boy touched his pocket and I was wondering if he had a knife in it. He walked up to the big fellow and they eyed each other angrily, each waiting for the other to make the first move. Finally the Mexican kid slowly backed away.

"What was that about?" I asked.

"That's Jim Mahoney, football player, honor student, and all around perfect person—at least in his mind. And only his friends sit at that table."

"Then why did that kid try to sit there?"

"I don't know. Why don't you ask him? Maybe you could do an article for the school paper."

"Anyone ever tell you that you're a smart—"

Gordon grabbed my schedule before I could finish. "What are you doing?" I asked.

"We have chemistry together, and you've got Travis for English, so I have good news and bad news."

"Okay."

"The good news is she's good looking, and the bad news is she's a nitpicky pain of a teacher, although I don't think she will be teaching the whole year."

"How do you know that?"

"Her husband is a medical student. The University of Texas Medical Branch is here and my father also teaches there. When the medical students are in school often their wives teach until they get out. Her husband will be a pediatrician, I think."

"Why won't she be teaching?" I asked.

"I overheard my father say she's pregnant."

All of the sudden our attention was diverted when suddenly laughter erupted from Mahoney's table, where his voice was the loudest.

"Oh he must have told a joke—he always laughs at his own—it can make you sick."

"I take it you don't like him."

"Yeah, he's in love with himself."

"What's the matter, he didn't want to buy one of your P.E. notes?"

"Good one. Okay, Welles, I'll pick you up at 7 PM tonight and show you the town. What's your address, or should I just look for a house with a pink caddy in the driveway?"

"You mean tonight?"

"Yeah, it's Friday."

"Okay," I said, and gave him my address. "But what are we going to do?"

"We're just going to have some fun," Gordon said.

"I guess I'll find out when you come."

After dinner that night I walked to the door of one of the rooms on the first level of the house that my father had made into a study, which he called his library. He was reading, as usual, and I waited until he noticed I was there. He'd already had a few glasses of wine with dinner, and it seemed to make him jovial. He was sipping some when he looked up at me.

"Hi, son. Come in and talk to me."

I walked in and sat down.

"Let me read this poem to you," he said, and I knew I'd have to listen if I wanted any money that night. One of his great loves was poetry, and he seemed to read the same ones over and over.

"It's a wonderful one by Kipling." He read it in a baritone, dramatic voice.

> *If you can keep your head when all about you*
> *Are losing theirs and blaming it on you,*
> *If you can trust yourself when all men doubt you,*
> *But make allowance for their doubting too;*
> *If you can wait and not be tired by waiting,*
> *Or being lied about, don't deal in lies,*
> *Or being hated, don't give way to hating,*
> *And yet don't look too good, nor talk too wise:*
>
> *If you can dream—and not make dreams your master;*
> *If you can think—and not make thoughts your aim;*
> *If you can meet with Triumph and Disaster*

And treat those two impostors just the same;
If you can bear to hear the truth you've spoken
Twisted by knaves to make a trap for fools,
Or watch the things you gave your life to, broken,
And stoop and build 'em up with worn-out tools:

If you can make one heap of all your winnings
And risk it on one turn of pitch-and-toss,
And lose, and start again at your beginnings
And never breathe a word about your loss;
If you can force your heart and nerve and sinew
To serve your turn long after they are gone,
And so hold on when there is nothing in you
Except the Will which says to them: 'Hold on!'

If you can talk with crowds and keep your virtue,
'Or walk with Kings—nor lose the common touch,
If neither foes nor loving friends can hurt you,
If all men count with you, but none too much;
If you can fill the unforgiving minute
With sixty seconds' worth of distance run,
Yours is the Earth and everything that's in it,
And—which is more—you'll be a Man, my son!

"What do you think?" he asked. I'd heard it before, but I didn't remember all of it, and I was not sure how to answer.

"Sounds like something that would be hard to live up to," I said.

"Yes, I think so, but it can be a goal, you see. We need goals in life or we just…we just deteriorate."

I thought he was about to lecture me more on the poem, so I tried to change the subject and it worked. "Are you still mad at McClellan?" I asked, and his eyes lit up as he got the question—evidently he wanted to talk about it.

"I'm glad you asked that," he said very seriously. "Not as much now—he doesn't bear all the blame, you know." As he said it, there was a little flicker of a smile, which I thought was his acknowledgement of his own eccentricity. It was as if he were saying, *I know I go on and on about the Civil War, but it's fun for me to indulge, even though deep down I know there are current matters to contend with—this is what I like to think about.*

"I'm actually angrier with Pinkerton," he continued. "You see, in a way he was just as responsible."

"Who was Pinkerton? Isn't that an armored truck company or something?"

"Right you are. Allan Pinkerton started the company before the Civil War, but at that time it was just a detective agency. McClellan had known him before the war, and when McClellan became a major general he called Pinkerton in and put him in charge of military intelligence, espionage, and counterespionage. Pinkerton built up a large organization of spies and planted them throughout the South."

"So that didn't help McClellan?"

"It should have, but it didn't. It may have been that Pinkerton had an overactive imagination or he was just overly cautious, but he kept over-estimating the size of the Confederate army. He made McClellan think he was outnumbered in almost every battle, when in reality McClellan vastly outnumbered the Confederates. So you see, the blame has to be shared by Pinkerton."

"Yeah, I think so," I said, looking at my watch. Gordon was supposed to be at the house in fifteen minutes. I had to get my father off the subject and on to something closer to the present. "You must miss all the rest of your books."

"Yes," he answered, his mind reluctantly leaving the discussion about Pinkerton.

I looked at my watch again, and then up at him. "You think I could have ten dollars? I spent all my allowance and the other money I had on the fees and stuff at school and I have a new friend picking me up."

"Sure," he said, reaching for his wallet. "Why didn't you say that was what you wanted when you came in?"

"Well, I also wanted to talk to you a little," I lied, as I took the money from him. As I walked away, Gordon, who was a little early, rang the doorbell and my mother answered. He was standing in the living room by the time I got there.

"Hi, Gordon, I see you've met my mother."

"Wouldn't you boys like some milk and cookies? They were freshly baked this afternoon," my mother offered.

"Oh, that sounds wonderful, Mrs. Welles. Thank you so much for the offer, but we have to be somewhere in a little while and we don't have time," Gordon said. "But I'm sure they're delicious and look forward to having some another time."

About that time my father walked into the foyer where we were standing. "Gordon, this is my father," I said.

"Nice to meet you, Dr. Welles."

"And a pleasure to meet you, Gordon."

"Gordon's father is a doctor also—he's a plastic surgeon," I said.

"Oh, that's quite impressive. I'd love to meet him sometime," my father said congenially.

"Well, you boys have a good time, then," my mother said, and we walked outside.

"Boy, you lay it on thick, don't you? I'm sure they're delicious," I said, chuckling.

"I'm just trying to be nice," Gordon said.

"Why didn't you just honk?" I asked.

"I did, several times. I'll bet you can't hear anything in this house, it's so big—I thought it was a museum or something when I drove up. What did you say your father was—an historian? I didn't know it paid that well."

"He writes textbooks now, but he used to be a history professor. But my aunt left us the house."

"Oh, so is that why you moved here?"

"Yeah, my mother needed a warmer climate and it all just worked out."

We walked down the front stairs towards his car, and he turned around and looked at the house again. "This is some house. Too bad it's in such a rundown area. This used to be a rich neighborhood—but that was about fifty years ago. Oh—I didn't mean to insult you."

"Really? I thought insulting me was your new hobby. I know the neighborhood is older—but there are a few old mansions around here like ours. And the Bishop's Castle is a few blocks away."

"Yeah, we toured that before." Gordon stopped, opened the door, and introduced me to his friends, R.J. Crystal and Curt Robinson. "I've reserved shotgun for you tonight," he said, and I got in the front seat.

"I think you better buckle your seat belt," R.J. suggested.

"Okay," I said, but as I began to, Gordon floored the GTO and we went screeching down the street. The inertia threw me back in the seat, making it hard for me to connect the seat belt. As we raced down the street, I noticed a sign above the glove compartment that read, "Do not roll down the windows over 100 MPH." Suddenly we were sliding around a corner and then we approached a four-way stop. But Gordon only slowed down to about twenty miles per hour and then cruised through it.

"Didn't you see that stop sign?" I asked, a little frazzled.

"Calm down, it was a four-way—no real risk," he assured me. "There were no cars at the intersection." I looked back at R.J. and Curt for a minute, and Curt shrugged his shoulders.

"Better get used to it," he said, as we made another hair-raising turn onto a main arterial called Broadway.

"You didn't tell me you were crazy," I said.

"You didn't ask," Gordon retorted as he tailgated a car until it left the fast lane and he flew by it.

"I know we're in a big hurry, but where are we going?" I asked.

"Pelican Island—I do a little racing there."

"No kidding—I never would have guessed."

The light was fading, but I could see that we were on a poorly paved bridge that was taking us to what looked like a barren island. Quickly we were over the bridge, and the island seemed isolated until we reached an area where about twenty cars were parked and some people were standing around.

As Gordon parked, a teenager who was standing next to a souped-up 1955 Chevrolet walked up to us. "Hey, Mahoney and his friends are looking to race you. He's got his brother's new Plymouth GTX with the 426 hemi and he's looking for you…and it's fast, man."

"Where are they now, Jerry?" Gordon asked, looking around as the dusk faded into darkness.

"Well, they were here a minute ago," he said, and just then the Plymouth came barreling down the road and skidded to a stop next to Gordon's car.

"Hey, how are ya, Jewboy?" Mahoney said to Gordon, and then began laughing as if it was just a friendly joke.

"Okay, goyim," Gordon said, trying to hold in his anger. "Your big brother must be home from college."

"Yeah, and he lent me his car so I could cream your—"

"Save the cream for your wounds," Gordon said with confidence. "How much you got to lose?"

"Twenty bucks," Mahoney answered.

"Not worth my time," Gordon said, and he started to drive away slowly. "Welles, how much do you have?"

"Ten dollars," I answered.

"You can double it tonight," he said. "Give it to me."

"But how do you know you'll win?"

"Because I timed him when he was testing it out at Cherry Hill last week. He didn't know what he was doing. He may be a great jock, but he doesn't know how to drive. He can't come off the line right; he's either too slow or he skids too much. I can beat him."

"But you said no already."

"He'll be back. Look, he's coming now."

I looked in back of me and saw Mahoney driving up.

"I've been waiting for this," Gordon said. "How much money do you guys have?" he asked, looking in the rearview mirror.

"I've got five," R.J. said.

"What about you, Curt?"

"I've got five also, but that's for lunch money and…"

"Come on, give it here. I'll double it for you."

"Okay," he said, reluctantly giving in and holding up the bill, which Gordon snatched from his hand.

Mahoney stopped next to Gordon's car again, and one of his friends rolled down the window. "Okay, how much? We have some more."

"Fifty bucks—can you do it?" Gordon asked.

"Naa…"

"Okay, forty."

"All we have is twenty-seven."

"But you got your senior ring early. Make it forty. Twenty-seven cash and the ring for collateral," Gordon said.

Mahoney said something to his two friends, and then nodded. "Okay, we'll take your money. Who's going to hold it?"

"R.J. will hold it. I'll have one passenger, and you can have one."

"Okay," Mahoney said. "R.J., don't run off with my ring or I'll wring your neck, understand?"

"Yeah, you're scary," R.J. said, almost to himself as he and Curt got out of the car.

Jerry, the boy with the 1955 Chevy, waved to another boy and he drove up. "Can you mark the quarter mile? There's a rock there. Park your car by the rock and watch for the winner." The boy nodded and drove off, then the cars got into position. When his friend reached the end of the quarter mile, Jerry stood between us with his hand in the air.

"Welles, look over at Mahoney and make sure he doesn't jump the line."

Engines were revving and the boy dropped his hand, and Gordon leaped in front of the Plymouth. In a few seconds, the Plymouth started to catch up, and was almost equal to us when the GTO started pulling ahead. The race only lasted about thirteen seconds, and Gordon spun his car in a U-turn and went back to pick R.J. up. Mahoney tried to follow, but when he tried to make his U-turn he almost slid into a ditch. After we picked up everyone Mahoney drove up, his face red and twisted with anger.

"Give me my ring, Silvers."

"I will when you give me thirteen dollars."

"It's worth a lot more than that!" Mahoney shouted.

"Look, man, you lost and it's collateral."

"You better not lose it or you're dead meat," Mahoney shouted, and then he floored the Plymouth and started fishtailing, almost losing control of the car.

"Looks like you made a new friend," I said, laughing.

"A slightly sore loser," Curt said.

"That'll teach him to talk to me that way. Okay, you guys can thank me now, I doubled your money. See? I said we would win."

"Now that you've got his ring, does that mean you and Mahoney are going steady?" R.J. asked, but Gordon ignored him.

"We've got beer money now, so let's get some," Curt said.

"You're on," Gordon said, and we drove back over the causeway and were soon at a liquor store in a seedy part of town. He drove around the block where there were a few bums sitting down in an alley. Gordon rolled his window down to talk to one of them. "Sir, may I ask you a question?"

The bum put down a bottle of cheap wine and came up to the window, but said nothing.

"Sir, we have all somehow forgotten our ID's, so even though we are all over twenty-one, we look young and need assistance in purchasing some beer. And we would like to compensate you for your trouble."

"And why should I do that—so you can end up like me?"

"Don't worry, that will never happen," Gordon said confidently.

"Is that right—you know it all, don't you. Well, let me tell you something. 'For none can tell, to what red hell, his sightless soul may stray,'" the bum said slowly.

Gordon smirked and drove his car forward about thirty feet to where another bum was sitting. This one came up without being asked and was eager to help. "What will it be, my boys?"

We waited while he went into the store and bought it for us. "You know that first drunk must have been educated," I said.

"How do you know that?" R.J. asked.

"Well, he quoted a poem—my father likes poetry and I've heard that line before."

"Really?" R.J. said, and it was obvious that no one cared about what I was saying. The drunk delivered the package and earned two dollars, but I really didn't want to drink it, as I had observed my father's problem with wine over the years and had decided that I did not want to go that way. As it turned out, the other three drank it up so fast that no one cared that I only had one can.

Curt had to work at SeaWorld the next morning so we dropped him off and then drove to the Boulevard, which is parallel to the beach and was the main drag where everyone cruised—tourists and locals alike. Hotels and restaurants and other business, mostly for tourists, lined the street. It was the slowest driving Gordon had done since I'd been in the car, and I realized the reason was that he was attempting to drink his malt liquor and look for girls at the same time. As we got near the end of the island, Gordon looked over at me. "Hold this beer, Welles, we need to turn around." At that end of the island was a place called Cherry Hill, and one side of the road went up at about a thirty-degree angle. Once you drove up to the top, there was a flat area to ride on, but Gordon only wanted to turn around.

We started back the other way, and were near the Jack Tar hotel when we saw a car with four girls in it drive out. "That's it—think of something cool to say, R.J," Gordon said.

We pulled up next to the girls, and R.J. tried to speak, but he slurred his words. "Hi, haven't we…seen you…before?" he said.

"No, Bozo, we don't know you, and we don't want to know you—you're drunk!" a girl sitting in the backseat said.

The driver then accelerated and R.J. looked at Gordon. "Aren't you going to chase them?"

"I think it's a lost cause, and you sound terrible. You guzzled more beer than any of us."

"Well...I wasn't sure...sure what to say," R.J. said, still slurring.

"Yeah, I noticed, Roland Jefferson," Gordon said mockingly.

"Don't call me that, Silvers, I hate it—it's R.J. Look, Welles likes the poetic—maybe he can...think of something."

"Well, first let's take you home so you can sleep it off," Gordon said, and we drove for a few minutes until we reached his house, and soon we were back on the Boulevard. Gordon slowed down and looked in back of him. "I think I see a couple of girls," he said, as he watched a car that was pulling out of a drive-in restaurant. "Look—there are girls in the blue Mustang." We had passed them, so he pulled over and waited for them to drive by and then pulled out.

"Okay, Welles, let's see what a Yankee can do," Gordon said, and before I could protest, we were driving beside the girls, with the driver next to my side of the car. The driver was pretty, but she turned away when I looked at her.

"We're not used to such beauty on these shores," I said, and I noticed she giggled a little. Her hairdo reminded me of Shelly Fabares's in the Donna Reed Show. "And you look so much like Shelly Fabares," I continued, which was not far from the truth, but Shelly was better looking.

With that she looked over at me and smiled. "You really think so?"

"Yes, you could be her sister."

"She's my favorite actress. I really like her."

"So where are you from?"

"Dallas."

"Oh," I said, not knowing where that was. "That's a beautiful place," I said.

"Where are you from?" she asked.

"We live here."

"It must be great to live at the beach," she said, and then Gordon had to slow down because of a car in front of us.

"Can you catch up with them?"

"I'm trying, I'm trying," Gordon answered as he maneuvered around a car by going into the other lane. "Dallas is a beautiful place? Have you been there?"

"No, I don't even know where it is."

"You have a good rap, Welles. Your rap and my car are going to be good for hustling."

"Where are they?" I asked, as we got through the traffic in front of us.

"I don't know—they disappeared. I think we better turn around, because she was driving slow, and she must have pulled off. What did her friend look like—I couldn't see her."

"She was alright; I couldn't see her very well."

"Alright, huh? Sounds like a dog."

"No, I couldn't see her—really."

We backtracked, and then I saw the car. "I think that's it—looks like it's at that hotel."

Gordon looked back. "That's the Commodore," he said, and made an illegal, screeching U-turn on the Boulevard that slammed my head against the window.

"Hey, man, would you warn me next time? That hurt!"

"Sorry, I'm in hot pursuit."

We pulled up to the car and Gordon sighed. "They've already gone in—oh well, that's the way the cookie crumbles." As he finished speaking, the driver came out and opened the trunk of the car. "Get out, Welles, she likes you. Come on, hurry before she goes back in the hotel." He seemed ready to push me out of the car.

"Hi, I'm Paul," I said as she closed the trunk. She looked at me quizzically for a moment, and then seemed to remember who I was. "You look more like Shelley close up."

"My name's Debbie," she said, and then her attention went to Gordon, who had gotten out of the car and was walking up to us.

"Do you and your friend want to go for a ride with us?" Gordon asked.

"We'd like to, but we're here with my parents and we're going back to Dallas tomorrow. But if you ever come to Dallas, I'd really like to see you," Debbie said, and she smiled warmly at me. She opened her purse and wrote down her phone number and gave it to me.

"Okay, thanks," I said, and took her number, and her friend came out as I did. She was not attractive.

"Oh, this is Ramona," Debbie said, but Gordon was already getting back in the car.

"Nice to meet you, Ramona," I said, looking over at Gordon. "He's got to get home now—it's past his curfew. Nice meeting you."

I got back in the car and Gordon took off quickly. "Man, what a waste of time," Gordon grumbled.

"You were rude—how do you think that made her feel? You could at least have said hello to her."

Gordon was quiet for a while. "Sorry, Welles, I'm allergic to girls like that."

On Saturday morning my father was drinking coffee at the dining room table by himself. I sat down with a bowl of cereal and greeted him. When he put down the paper for a moment, I cleared my throat and he looked at me. "Dad, I remember you read a poem that said something like 'none can tell to what red hell his sightless soul may stray.' Who wrote that?" As I asked the question, the thought that this might turn into a long lesson occurred to me. But I wanted to know enough to ask, since I heard the drunk quote that line.

"Ah, that is from *The Ballad of Reading Gaol*. Oscar Wilde was imprisoned there—do you want to know how that happened?"

I was surprised he was actually asking me—normally he would just start speaking. "Yes, I do."

"Okay, I have a little time. By the way, I will be teaching again—Texas A and M has a branch here for their maritime students and I'll be teaching them a class in American History."

"That's great, Dad. What does A and M stand for?"

"Agricultural and Mechanical—their main campus is in College Station, Texas. This branch is where they train men who want to be sea captains."

"I see."

"It's just one class and it will not start for a while, but I'm preparing the lesson plan today—need to incorporate more Texas history than I usually would for a different state. This is one state that is really proud of its history. Anyway, back to Wilde. He was a brilliant writer, and famous and lauded in his day. He wrote what many think is the best comedic play ever—*The Importance of Being Earnest*. One day when he went through customs coming back to England, they asked him if he had anything to declare. He answered, 'Only my genius!'"

"Pretty clever, but what about that line—did I have it right?"

"Yes," he said, and quoted that part of the poem.

So with curious eyes and sick surmise
We watched him day by day,
And wondered if each one of us
Would end the self-same way,
For none can tell to what red Hell
His sightless soul may stray.

"You see, you might understand it better if I tell you a little about him. He was married with two children but then everything seemed to change when he turned forty, and he became a homosexual. Or maybe he'd been hiding it before that time. Anyway, within one hundred days of finishing *The*

Importance of Being Earnest, he ended up in real trouble. He had engaged in a homosexual relationship with the son of the Marquess of Queensbury, who was known for the boxing rules he invented. When he was confronted with the truth, Wilde sued Queensbury for slander, but he lost the trial and ended up in prison. If he hadn't sued Queensbury it probably would have blown over, but slander was punishable by two years in prison. Queensbury had to prove that the allegations were true, which he did with several witnesses. The prison was Reading Gaol, and it was a torturous, horrible place. It was so bad that even Queensbury tried to get him out when he found out how badly Wilde was doing."

"But Dad, didn't that poem also have something in it about every man killing the thing he loved?"

"Yes, here is one stanza:

Yet each man kills the thing he loves
By each let this be heard,
Some do it with a bitter look,
Some with a flattering word,
The coward does it with a kiss,
The brave man with a sword!

"And another thing about him—after prison, he was a changed man—something happened to him—he got religious, but today no one talks about that part of his life. Here is a sample of what he wrote about it:

And every human heart that breaks,
In prison-cell or yard,
Is as that broken box that gave
Its treasure to the Lord,
And filled the unclean leper's house
With the scent of costliest nard.

Ah! Happy they whose hearts can break
And peace of pardon win!

*How else may man make straight his plan
And cleanse his soul from Sin?
How else but through a broken heart
May Lord Christ enter in?
...And a broken and a contrite heart
The Lord will not despise.*

"But I still don't understand the part about killing the thing you love. I just don't get it," I said.

"It's probably better if you read the whole poem. It's in a box somewhere with the moving truck that's coming—supposed to be here soon. But I think what he was trying to say was that—" He stopped speaking as my mother walked into the dining room.

"Are you still taking me shopping?" she asked. She did not drive so it was up to one of us to take her.

"Yes, Dear. We'll talk about this later, Paul," he said, as he got up from his chair.

"I don't know if I need the book if you've got it all memorized."

"No, I don't know it all—it's a very long poem—that's just what I could remember from it."

"Not bad from memory, Professor."

"Thank you. Does that compliment mean you want some money?"

"How sad that you think I had ulterior motives! But now that you mention it, I do need some gas money—that Caddy is a gas guzzler."

On Monday morning I went to my first Business Mathematics class—it was first period and I missed it the day I registered. I walked in and sat down, and then a very attractive girl sat down next to me. As soon as everyone was in place, the bell rang and the teacher began to speak.

"We have a new student," he said, looking over at me, and then reading from a card, he said my name. "Paul Welles—please stand up, Paul."

I did and then sat down. "What elective were you taking at your school, Paul?"

"Statistics, so I couldn't continue," I answered.

"Yes, we should have a course in that also, but we don't. Mary, take a few minutes with Paul and show him where we are while I call the roll, please."

I suddenly realized that the pretty girl sitting next to me was the same one he was talking to. Her hair was medium brown, and her eyes sort of sparkled when she turned to me. As I looked at her I realized that it was not that she was just pretty, but she seemed so nice and pleasant when she smiled at me. There was a special charm about her, as if she were glowing with happiness and innocence. She got up and moved next to my desk, and stood over me, and showed me where I should be in the book.

"Where are you from?" she asked, as she turned the pages.

"Connecticut."

"Oh, that's so different—I hope you'll like it here," she said sweetly.

"I already do," I said, looking into her eyes. I had never looked into any girl's eyes as I did that day, and I instantly felt like there was something special between us. I wondered, did she feel it also? Was this unusual feeling, this chemistry, one-sided? I thought it had to be somewhat mutual as I stared at her. Then, realizing what I was doing, I forced my eyes from her and looked back at the book.

"Good. Most of this you've probably had. There are percentages, and different averages and graphs…"

I didn't hear much of what she said, but the roll call was ending and suddenly she closed the book and looked at me—and the look was melting me, and again I wondered if she felt anything or if it was just me.

"We don't have time to do this now. I'm busy tomorrow, but why don't you come over after school on Tuesday and I'll try to catch you up."

I was surprised—pleasantly surprised, but since it caught me off guard it took me a moment to answer. "Sure, great," I heard myself say.

"Good, I'll give you my phone number when class ends," she said, and then she went back to her desk just as the teacher was beginning his lesson. It seemed I could only think of her for the rest of the class time, and I missed most of what the teacher was saying.

At lunchtime, I sat with Gordon and while we were beginning to eat, Mary walked by and smiled at me. "Hi, Paul," she said.

"Hi, Mary, see you later," I said, and she went to sit at a table with some of her girlfriends.

"How do you know her?" Gordon asked.

"She's in my Business Math class, and she's going to be my girlfriend." As soon as I said that, Gordon almost choked on his food, and then he started laughing.

"Okay, okay, what's so funny?"

"Number one, she's a senior and you're a lowly junior. Number two, she's a cheerleader and you just got here, and number three…are you sure you're ready for number three?"

"Yes, Gordon, I'm ready."

"Number three—do you remember that big jock, Mahoney?"

"How could I forget him?"

"That's her boyfriend."

Suddenly I felt like someone punched me in the stomach, but I really thought she was signaling, in a subtle way, that she liked me. "Well, she was super nice to me, man. And you saw her just now—you saw how she greeted me."

"She's that way to everyone—she is very nice and very popular. But she's the kind of girl who'd get upset if you said 'darn' around her. I think she's kind of religious. One of her friends is Ruth Hart, and she's real religious—wears long dresses and her hair in a bun."

39

"Well, she invited me over to her house to catch up on the course."

"That's great. Maybe Mahoney will be there and he can teach you some football."

"Okay, Gordon, I get it."

"I'm sorry, man. I know why you like her—everyone does. I just don't want you to get your hopes up."

"Yeah, I guess I won't after what you've told me—so, whatever."

There was to be a special assembly in the auditorium instead of the next period, so a group of us walked over together and sat down. Gordon was on my right and R.J. Crystal on my left. The vice principal was on a portable stage standing next to a microphone on a stand. He waited impatiently until most of the students had taken seats and then he began to talk.

"We have the honor of a visit from a Houston police detective whom I invited because of the youth problems that are now facing our nation. He is also a personal friend of mine, and I am very pleased that he accepted my invitation to speak. He has some very important information to share with you, so please be courteous and give him your undivided attention. Sergeant Ricstetter, of the vice squad of the Houston Police Department, thank you for coming."

The heavy-set policeman walked to the microphone, but when he began to speak, it came out as a shriek, because of feedback from the microphone. That brought some laughter and giggles, but it was soon adjusted. He had a very twangy Texas accent, which stood out. Most of the people I had met in Galveston did not have such strong accents.

"There's a drug problem going on in Houston and a lot of people are worried that it's also comin' down here. I've seen some sad sights in Houston. I've seen kids from good families become disgraceful 'cause they got hooked on drugs. Nice kids don't know what they're gettin' into, and the next thing they know, well, they're gettin' dragged down to the depths."

He paused for a moment and looked at the audience. "They're some marriage-wanna and L, S, and D addicts we've had to drag out of the gutter 'cause they went plum crazy. They take them uppers to go up and downers to go down and before you know it, they don't know up from down.

"Three weeks ago, I had to break someone's heart. The boy's father was a bank president. I had to tell him that his son was dead. He started on marriage-wanna and ended up on L, S and D. He walked up to a six-inch curb and was afraid to step off—real scared about everything. But he walked to a sixty-foot overpass and jumped clean off. He had been a good student and an athlete, but them drugs brought him down."

He paused for a moment and looked at his notes and then back at the audience. "See, you start with one drug, maybe marriage-wanna, and then you get on the harder stuff and it's a one-way ticket, a one-way trip to a sad, sad world and then maybe death. No, I can't tell you what to do, and I know that. But I want to educate you a little about these things, so you can avoid them."

He held up a hand-rolled cigarette above his head. "This is a marriage-wanna cigarette and you might be at a party and someone might pass one around. That's how it might start. So, if you get a cigarette like this, you call the *po*-lice. If it's burning, it will smell kinda sweet, a real thick smell. So you call the *po*-lice, and you might save someone's life. Imagine that—you might save someone's life. Now I'm here because I care about young people—and your parents care about you. So don't throw your life away for nothing. Thank you."

We applauded as he sat down, and R.J. turned to me. "Is this guy for real?—marriage-wanna—I wonder if he even finished high school."

CHAPTER 3

My heart was beating hard as I looked up Mary Sanderson's address on the map. If I had been in Galveston longer, I would have immediately known that it was only about five blocks away from my house. I debated whether I should drive or walk. If I drove she might be impressed by my car, or she might—well, who knows what she might think since it was pink? But it was in beautiful condition, and I thought it was a plus, so I drove and found her address, which was a small apartment complex. I looked again and noticed that she had written #9 as the apartment number. I looked in my rearview mirror and combed my hair, then took a deep breath and walked to her apartment and knocked. She opened the door and gave me a sweet smile. "Oh, Paul, I'm so glad you could make it. Thanks for coming! It's so good to see you."

Her greeting was a little effusive, but also sincere. I knew by now it was part of her personality. But I also thought it seemed nicer than I would have expected from a girl who was simply helping someone with homework. As I looked into her eyes, I began to freeze up, and I stood there in the doorway at a loss for words. Finally, I heard myself answer, "Nice to see you, too."

As I walked in, her mother came into the living room, and she was dressed in a nurse's uniform. "This is my mother, Paul," Mary said and then turned to her mother. "This is Paul Welles, the new boy I told you about."

"Hello, Mrs. Sanderson," I said, thinking about what Mary had just said—*the new boy I told you about*. What had she said about me? Did she like me enough already to tell her mother something nice about me? I barely heard Mrs. Sanderson's reply.

"Nice to meet you, Paul. I just got off duty at John Sealy—that's the hospital, so I'm going to change now while Mary helps you with your homework."

"Sealy is the name of the street I live on. I wonder if they're connected."

"Yes, John Sealy was one of the richest Texans and his widow opened the hospital in 1890, and the street was named after him. In 1891 it became the University of Texas Medical Branch to teach doctors…but I'm boring you with this," she said.

"No, not at all. My dad's a history professor and I love to hear about the history of things," I said, twisting the truth a little, since I really did get bored with a lot of the history I heard at home.

"Oh, how very interesting he must be to talk to. Well, Mary will help you get caught up—she's an A student." Mrs. Sanderson then walked into the hallway and I heard a door close.

"Let's sit in the kitchen," Mary said, and we walked to the table there and I put my book and notebook down. Her books were already on the table, and I took a seat. She sat down next to me and moved her chair close to me, as she opened the textbook to Chapter One. "We've already covered the first three chapters in class, so those are the only ones you'll need to study. Chapter one begins with simple and compound interest…"

As she spoke she moved a little closer and her body was lightly touching mine. I wondered if she liked me—was she just being nice as Gordon had said—would she have done this for anyone? I moved slightly closer to her and made more contact with her—her side was now touching mine, but she did not pull away.

After we had gone through the chapters, she stood up and walked towards the refrigerator. "Would you like something to drink?" she asked.

"Oh, no thanks. I guess that catches me up, and I really appreciate it."

"It's nothing—I want to make certain you feel welcome in Galveston."

"Well I do—I really do," I said, and turned towards the living room. It was then that I noticed a picture of a man next to a fighter jet. "Is that your Dad?" I asked.

"Yes, he was a fighter pilot in the Korean War."

"Really? I'll bet he's got some interesting stories to tell."

"He would have, he was a great pilot, but he was killed in the war. His jet was shot down."

"Oh, I'm sorry…"

"That's why we live in this apartment. Mom said we had a house before that but she couldn't afford the payments. I was only one when he died, so I never really knew him."

As I was trying to say something else—and was groping for words—a gray and white long-haired cat came from the hallway and rubbed against my legs. Mary bent down to pet the cat and looked up at me, astonished. "Hilary is never that friendly to anyone!" she said.

I petted Hilary, scratching her under her chin, and she meowed and looked up at me. "Oh, this is really unusual. I'll have to tell Mom," Mary said, smiling, as she picked up her cat and hugged it.

"May I use your bathroom before I go?" I asked.

As I walked towards the bathroom, a door to a bedroom was open and the light was on. I thought it was Mary's because her mother was in the other one, and the door there was closed. On the wall of the open bedroom there was a picture of Jesus with this inscription below it: *Behold, I come quickly*. I was wondering what that meant when I spied a book on a bookshelf titled *The Poems of Emily Dickinson*. After I used the bathroom, her mother came out to say good-bye and Mary walked me to the door.

"I had a great time tonight," I said, not really thinking about what I was saying. As soon as it was out of my mouth I regretted it, because it sounded more like we had been on a date. But Mary surprised me.

"I did too—I really did," she said.

I walked out, wondering again—did she like me, or was she just being nice? Did she notice when I moved closer to her, or did it not even register with her?

When I got home, I walked into my father's study and he was reading, as usual. "Hi, Dad."
"Oh, hello, Son."
"Do we have any poetry by Emily Dickinson?" I asked.
He looked surprised. "So you are finally getting interested in poetry—I was wondering when that would happen. I was just reading Kipling, 'Gunga Din.' See, the British had colonized India in those days, and they recruited some of the Indians as water carriers and ammunition carriers—they called them regimental *bhisti*. They were treated poorly, and Kipling uses the low-class cockney dialect in the poem—speaking the way most of the British soldiers would have spoken. Din's uniform was nothing, just a tattered rag, and the only field equipment he had was a goatskin water-bag. When the soldiers were sweating and thirsty they would call out to Din, and threaten to hit him unless he filled up their water bottles quickly.

"But Gunga Din didn't seem to know fear; whenever the soldiers fought, he would be fifty paces behind with his water-skin on his back ready to help. And when this soldier gets hurt, he cries out to Din. He says he can never forget the night when he was struck with a bullet and was 'chokin' mad with thirst.' Gunga Din found him and lifted up his head and gave him the only water he had. Even though it was green and slimy, he says it was the best drink he ever tasted. He remembered his words—groveling on the ground he had cried out, 'For Gawd's sake git the water, Gunga Din!' So Gunga Din carried him away, but Din took a bullet as he helped him. And right before he died he got the soldier inside and said he hoped he had enjoyed his drink. You see, the British looked down on the Indians, but he had great admiration for this brave man. It shows us not to look on the outside of a person—the heart is what counts. Here is a sample:

I shan't forgit the night
When I dropped be'ind the fight
With a bullet where my belt-plate should 'a' been.
I was chokin' mad with thirst,
An' the man that spied me first
Was our good old grinnin', gruntin' Gunga Din.
'E lifted up my 'ead,
An' he plugged me where I bled,
An' 'e guv me 'arf-a-pint o' water green.
It was crawlin' and it stunk,
But of all the drinks I've drunk,
I'm gratefullest to one from Gunga Din.
It was 'Din! Din! Din!
"Ere's a beggar with a bullet through 'is spleen;
"E's chawin' up the ground,
'An' 'e's kickin' all around:
'For Gawd's sake git the water, Gunga Din!'

'E carried me away
To where a dooli lay,
An' a bullet come an' drilled the beggar clean.
'E put me safe inside,
An' just before 'e died,
'I 'ope you liked your drink,' sez Gunga Din.

"That's interesting, Dad," I said, trying not to be too blunt in getting what I was asking for. "Do you also have Dickinson?"

"Oh…yes, Emily Dickinson. Yes, I've got all my books now, and your mother has done me the kind favor of putting them all in order on the bookshelves. They are not by type but are alphabetical."

He began to get up but I walked over to the bookshelves before he got there and found the same volume I had seen at Mary's apartment. I began to leaf through it, then looked up at my father, who was still happy at what he thought was my new interest.

"You see, poems are sort of like music. They speak to the heart—they express something that words in normal conversation cannot express—they often have a deeper meaning," he said, unable to stop teaching. I tried to get a word in when he paused, but just then my mother came in with a sandwich for him.

"So what would be the most famous poem she wrote?"

"Well, she's your mother's favorite, let's ask her," he suggested, as she put down a glass of water and took his glass of wine away. He frowned at her, but she smiled back.

"No, William, you need water also," she said, sounding more like his mother than his wife. He acquiesced and took a sip and again frowned slightly.

"Paul has a sudden interest in Emily Dickinson, and I know you like her. What is your favorite poem of hers?"

"That's easy, it's called 'If I Can Stop'":

If I can stop one heart from breaking,
If I can ease one life the aching,
Or cool one pain,
Or help one fainting robin
Unto his nest again,
I shall not live in vain.

On Friday Gordon called me. "Are you still on for tonight?"

"Yeah, when are you coming?" I asked.

"Well, there is a little complication—I'm stuck with my cousin Benjy tonight. My aunt and uncle are here from La Marque."

"Where is La Marque and why is Benjy a problem?"

"La Marque is a rinky-dink town about fifteen miles from here and Benjy—well you'll meet him. I have to eat dinner with everyone so I'll pick you up about 8:30 or 9."

Benjy was a plump, bespectacled kid who looked a lot younger than his sixteen years. Gordon asked him to sit in the backseat when I got to the car, and I could tell he wasn't happy about it. I said hello, but he only nodded.

"So, what are we going to do, Gordon?" he asked as Gordon accelerated down Sealy Street and then turned towards Broadway.

"I thought we'd go to a movie," Gordon said.

"Oh, I don't want to do that—I can do that in La Marque."

"Okay, what do you want to do?" Gordon asked.

"Let's cruise for chicks on the Boulevard," Benjy said in an excited tone. "I'll bet the chicks love this car."

Gordon looked over at me and smiled. "Okay, we'll cruise," he said, racing up another street towards the beach.

After we drove for about fifteen minutes on the Boulevard, Benjy was getting impatient. "Where are all the chicks—I think we have more in La Marque," he complained.

"Benjy, I can't make the chicks—we just have to keep driving," Gordon said, and suddenly Benjy spied a car with some girls and spoke excitedly.

"There are three pulling out of that hotel," he shouted, loud enough to hurt our ears as he watched the car.

"Okay, okay," Gordon said, looking back at the hotel since we had just passed it.

"No they already took off—they're over there," Benjy pointed to a car that was behind us in the slow lane. Gordon slowed down and their car began to catch up with ours. We looked and saw that there were three attractive girls in the car.

"They do look good," Gordon said as they went by.

"See? I know how to spot them," Benjy proclaimed. "But you're letting them go—you need to catch up!"

"I don't want to be too obvious. Did they look at us, Welles?"

"I don't think so."

They were ahead of us now, and they moved into the fast lane. Gordon pulled over to the slow lane and slowly caught up to them. He watched the girl in the front passenger seat, waiting to get her attention, but she hadn't looked our way. He was about to speak, but before he could, Benjy shouted through the window in a high, squeaky voice. "You want to go for a ride with us?"

The girl in the backseat looked over at him and smiled. "Isn't it past your bedtime?" she asked. Then she said something to the driver and they sped up. Gordon looked over at me and slightly shook his head.

"What is she talking about?—it's only nine o'clock. Come on, Gordon, speed up and we can catch them," Benjy said.

"Naa...I don't think they're the ones for us," Gordon said, smiling a little at me as he spoke.

"Man, Galveston girls are stuck up. In La Marque the girls are real friendly," Benjy said.

"I'll bet," Gordon said, under his breath so Benjy couldn't hear.

"We ought to go to Houston—that's where the real action is," Benjy said.

"Do you have gas money?" Gordon asked.

"Yeah, I just got my allowance and I save it for stuff like this. But can we get some beer, first?" Benjy asked.

"You want to get some beer? If we do, you won't rat on us, will you?" Gordon asked.

"Hey, it's my idea—we get beer all the time in La Marque. There are plenty of guys who will buy it for us. But I want to go to Houston, to Love Street, because that's where the action is."

"Love Street?" Gordon said.

"Yeah, Allen's Landing. It's like a park in the middle of Houston—downtown—and it's where the hippy chicks are that go to love-ins," Benjy said.

"Have you been there before?" I asked.

"Well, no, but I've heard a lot about it—it's hippy heaven," Benjy said.

"Okay, Benjy, we'll go. It might be more entertaining than a movie," Gordon said, as he turned off the Boulevard and headed towards a liquor store we'd been to before. Gordon drove around but there was no one hanging out near the store. "Boy, never a drunk when you need one," he said, exasperated. "Okay, let's try something else. Sometimes you can give these guys a little extra and they'll sell to you." Gordon opened the door to get out but we stayed in the car, and he looked back at us, angrily. "You guys have to come too—I'm not taking the risk by myself."

We got out of the car and walked into the store with him. There were some other patrons there, and as soon as they left, Gordon walked up to the clerk and said something to him, and he nodded, then Gordon came back to us and we walked to the refrigerated case where the beer was and grabbed a six-pack. Gordon gave him an extra three dollars and the clerk looked around and then put the beer in a bag and set it on the counter. Benjy took the bag, but the clerk put his hand on Benjy's to stop him. "One of you boys take it out, that boy don't look old enough to buy bubble gum," he said. And with that Gordon grabbed the package.

It was about ten in the evening when we got to Allen's Landing, and it was bustling with long-haired people, bikers, and straight-looking onlookers. We had to park many blocks away, and we walked up to Allen's Landing, which was also called "Love Street." The landing was a park by the water, and as we walked through it, Benjy stared incredulously. "Are they wearing wigs?" he asked.

"I don't think so," Gordon said.

There were some long-hairs throwing a Frisbee to each other, and one of them was doing cartwheels between throws. Another one was making strange faces as he tried to catch the Frisbee, which he often failed to do. They had on tie-dyed T-shirts and old jeans. There was a three-story building with a psychedelic club at the top, where a band was playing. We could hear the band a little as we walked towards the building. The club had a sign on it that said, "Love Street Light Circus Feel Good Machine."

"Man, there are some really weird people around here—I can see why they call them freaks," Benjy said, as we walked towards the club and he watched them playing with the Frisbee. The stairway was outside the building, and as we walked up to the club, the sound from the band got louder. A girl walked out wearing a translucent top without a bra on, and Benjy turned his head to follow her down the stairs. "Did you see that!" he exclaimed.

"Benjy, maybe she's from La Marque and she'll dig you," Gordon remarked. When we got to the top of the stairs, a man told Gordon that there was a cover charge. He turned away and we walked back down the stairs.

"I'm not paying to see a bunch of freaks," he said, as we reached the bottom of the long stairway. Then we walked through the park, and a very skinny girl with long, stringy blonde hair and dirty bare feet approached me. She might have been attractive if she had cleaned herself up, but her eyes seemed dead as she got closer to me. I backed away as she moved towards me.

"Hey, man. I have some really far-out orange wedge that will get you off for hours," she said.

"Orange wedge?" Benjy said, and she looked at him for a moment.

"Acid, man. LSD. Haven't you ever done any acid? You'll really flip out."

"No thank you," Benjy said, and we walked away.

"Man, she was enough to make you believe in witches," Gordon said.

There were about twelve hippies in a group and some of them were moving around on the grass in a sort of pantomime. We watched them for a moment and one of them looked at us and came up to Gordon. "I've got some heavy grass—Acapulco gold, and it's only ten bucks a lid."

"No thanks," he answered.

His friend gave us a disdainful look. "What's the matter, afraid your momma wouldn't like it?" he mocked.

"No, my Daddy. He's Sergeant Ricstetter, Narcotics," Gordon said in a serious tone.

Looking worried, the hippies shrank back from us and soon they all disappeared. We laughed as we realized they were gone so quickly. We then walked into a "head" shop with black lights, posters, lava lamps, a variety of papers to roll cigarettes with, water pipes, and other such items. Inside there was a pretty girl with dark hair of about twenty wearing a halter top with no bra which showed her firm stomach. She was sort of dancing around as she looked at the black lights—obviously high on something. When she saw us, she came up to me. "Don't you think these are groovy? And I think you are groovy also, straight arrow." I backed up a little and she moved closer and put her arm around me. "You want to come back to my pad..." she began, but just then a long-haired man with a beard walked in and grabbed her.

"Laura, where have you been?" he said, scoldingly, as he took her by the arm.

"Oh, man, you're putting me on a bum trip," she said, reluctantly going with him as he escorted her out of the head shop.

"Hey, this could have been your lucky night," Gordon said.

"Man, she must be one of those free love girls," Benjy said. "Maybe we can find some other ones."

"No, we have to go now. Your parents will be mad at me if we stay out too late," Gordon said.

When we got back to the car, Benjy grabbed a beer and began to open it. "Hey, not here," Gordon said. "Anyone can see you. Wait until we get on the freeway."

Soon we were on the freeway and Benjy drank a beer quickly and then took another one. We were soon out of Houston and had been driving about twenty minutes when Gordon looked back and saw that Benjy was sleeping.

"I think it was the beer," he said in a low voice. "Did he drink all four?"

I looked back and grabbed the paper bag with empties in it. "Looks like he drank four, because I didn't have one and you only had one, and there is still one on the seat."

"Why that little guzzler. I'm stopping at the gas station up here and we'll throw away the empty cans," Gordon said, as he pulled off the freeway. "You want the last one?"

"No, you can have it."

"Nah, we'll save it. I don't want to smell like beer when I get home," Gordon said.

Soon we were on the freeway again. "Paul, look at the speedometer—would you say we are going a hundred and thirty-five? I think it's that much past a hundred and twenty." As he spoke calmly, we passed a car which seem to almost be standing still compared to our speed.

I looked over at the speedometer. "Yeah, that's great. Now why don't you slow down?"

"You're right. I don't want to strain the engine," he said, decelerating to about ninety miles an hour. The speed limit was seventy. "By the way, whatever happened with Mary? Did you go over there?"

"Yeah, she was really nice."

"Oh, I think he's in love! Well, all you have to do is kick Mahoney's…"

We both heard a siren and suddenly a red flashing light was behind us.

"Man, how did he do that? He must have been driving in back of me with no lights on—he's so close he already has my plate."

Gordon slowed down to pull over, and the police car, a Plymouth, pulled in front of us to force us off the road.

"Look, cop, if I was going to run I would've left that dopey Plymouth in the dust by now," Gordon said, angrily, and then he remembered the beer. "Welles, get rid of the beer…"

"I'm doing it," I said, and I opened the door and threw it out as we came to a stop. Benjy was in the backseat, still sleeping. As the police car pulled up Gordon let out a sigh.

"Oh, no, it's the League City police. I've heard about these guys from Mike D'Angelo. He said they always tow your car because the police chief's brother has a towing company, and they keep you in jail until you pay the tow charge and the ticket."

As he finished talking the policeman swaggered up to the car. He was a big, brawny fellow with a twangy Texas accent—and his voice sounded threatening. "All right, get out of the car and put your hands against the roof and spread 'em."

As Gordon and I got out, the cop opened the back door and looked at Benjy, who was still sleeping. "Wake up there, sleeping beauty—the clock has done struck midnight and you're just a punk again." Then he jammed the stick into Benjy's stomach, and Benjy awoke and grabbed the night stick. When he realized what was happening he let go of it. Then the cop walked over to a can of beer that I threw out and picked it up. I wondered how he could have found it, and then I realized that since he was following so closely he might have seen it when I threw it out. He picked up the can and walked back to us.

"Now you boys can do better than that," he said.

"Better than what?" Gordon asked.

"Than throwing this can out of the car," the cop said, moving closer to Gordon in an intimidating manner.

"That isn't ours," Gordon said.

"Oh yeah? Well I think it is."

"But you have to prove it."

As this point he got very angry and he held up his stick. "I might have to prove how far this stick can go up your—"

As he spoke, Benjy threw up and the cop jumped out of the way to avoid the spray. "Can't hold his liquor, huh?" the cop said.

"That's not why he threw up," Gordon said flatly. "You hit him in the stomach."

As Gordon finished speaking the cop walked around him and then whacked the night stick into the back of his left leg, knocking him to the ground. I walked over to help Gordon and he hit me on the shoulder with a glancing blow, since I moved when I saw it coming. He swung again the opposite way and this one landed solidly on my other shoulder. Then he handcuffed us. "Get in the back of the car," he commanded, and after that no one said anything until we reached the police station. When we got there, he ordered us out and jabbed us with the stick as we walked in. The station was filled with cigarette smoke and it also smelled like stale beer.

"What you got there, Bob?" the policeman on duty asked.

"We've got some real smart boys here, Frank," he said. Then he pulled our wallets out of our pockets and handed them to Frank, who took out our driver's licenses.

"Welcome to League City," Frank said sarcastically.

"Book them on DWI, resisting arrest, disrespect to an officer, reckless driving, underage consumption of alcohol, and have their car towed in."

I could see that Gordon wanted to protest, but he thought better of it and stayed quiet. As Bob was speaking, I noticed a paper on a desk next to Frank's. It said that Judge Nathaniel Poindexter would be on vacation until the twenty-second of the month, and that his cases would be handled by another judge. I had to stop reading because Bob moved towards me and used his stick to hold up my chin.

"Now we're going to type a confession and each of you are going to sign it," he said.

"We won't sign anything—I want to call my uncle." Frank gave me a look as if to say, "if that's the way you want it," but before he could do anything else, I spoke again.

"My uncle is a judge and he told me never to sign a confession."

"Yeah, and my uncle's the president. Who cares, punk?"

"But you must know him. His name is Poindexter," I said.

Frank and Bob exchanged glances, and it was obvious that they were concerned.

"What's his first name?" Bob asked.

"Nathaniel, and I don't think he'll be too happy about you hitting us with that stick."

Both of them were quiet for a moment, evidently weighing the situation, and then Bob spoke again. "If he's your uncle, call him up and have him come and get you."

"I would, but he's on vacation right now. He won't be back until about the twenty-second of this month."

Now they seemed worried and they exchanged glances again.

"There's no real damage from the stick—you all feel okay, right?" Bob said, drastically changing his attitude.

"I think we're okay," I said.

"I'll tell you what. We're gonna make this one a warning. And you're not gonna mention anything about it to your uncle, right?"

"Right," I said, and he looked at Gordon.

"Right," Gordon said, and then Benjy said it also, and he took off our cuffs.

"I'll drive you to your car," Bob said.

When we got into the car, Gordon waited for the cop to drive away, and then he looked at me, quizzically. "You have a relative who's a judge?"

"Not exactly," I said.

"So who is Poindexter, anyway?"

"He's a judge."

"Yeah, I know that much, but how do you know him?"

"I don't."

"Okay, Welles, don't drive me crazy. Tell me what just happened in that police station."

"Speaking of driving crazy, if you'll stop doing that I'll tell you," I said, waiting a moment before I continued speaking. "While we were standing there, I noticed a piece of paper on a desk next to the cop who was writing us up, and it said that Judge Nathaniel Poindexter would be on vacation until the twenty-second."

"So you just made up the part about him being your uncle."

"That's right, and that's why we're free."

"Wow, you're getting Texas smart. It must be the humid Galveston air. Nice going."

"So, will you do something for me in return?"

"Sure."

"Drive the speed limit on the way home. I don't know if I can handle any more melodrama tonight."

"Yeah, and he hurt me with the stick," Benjy chimed in.

"What's that got to do with going the speed limit?" Gordon asked.

"We wouldn't have been pulled over if you hadn't been speeding," Benjy said.

Okay, I give up. I'll try to go the speed limit—if I can, it's kind of hard."

"Just pretend your momma is in the car," I said.

"I can't do that—my mother refuses to ride with me," Gordon said.

"I wonder why? Remember, seventy, Gordon," I said, noticing that he was already over the speed limit.

"But my favorite song is on the radio," Gordon protested, as we listened to *Light My Fire* by the Doors. "I always speed to that song."

"Well, light your fire some other way," I suggested.

"Yeah, go seventy, Gordon," Benjy said.

Gordon looked in the rearview mirror at Benjy, a little irritated. "Oh, you guys are pathetic," he said, finally giving in and slowing down to seventy. "My car will probably get all carboned up going that slow."

CHAPTER 4

That night I kept thinking of how I might be able to get Mary to like me and it occurred to me that she would be impressed if I became a pilot like her father. I'd always had an interest in flying anyway, and the more I thought about it, the better the idea seemed. My father was always impressed by the heroics of soldiers, and he included them whenever he could in his history books and when he taught. His favorite movie was *Yankee Doodle Dandy*, which was the story of George M. Cohan, who wrote many patriotic songs. The movie starred James Cagney.

The next morning was a Saturday, and I knew he'd be watching reruns of a documentary series called "The Big Picture." It was mostly about World War Two, which he fought in as a soldier, and he never missed it. I had watched a few of them but had gotten bored with it, so he was happily surprised when I sat down with him to see it that morning.

I considered it my lucky day, because the subject of the show was the P-51 fighter plane. The announcer began:

"The P-51 is arguably the most recognized and celebrated American fighter of the Second World War. It was introduced in 1942, and was designed and flown in a matter of months. It made such an impact that it was considered the war-winning design for the Allies.

The P-51 Mustangs primarily assisted in escorting bombers on long range sorties but were able to attack ground targets with bombs and machine guns and outperform any of the German fighters that were matched against them. The Mustang exuded "Classic Warbird" in every sense of the phrase and went on to be one of the most recognized piston engine fighters of all time."

As the announcer spoke, there were many scenes of the plane in combat and from the airfield. When a commercial break came, I started talking about current aircraft. "You know, Dad, I think the F-4 Phantom is the best fighter jet today. It can fly at mach 2.2—that's over twice the speed of sound."

"Really? I haven't kept up with the new ones," he said.

"It's an incredible plane. It can carry more than 18,000 pounds of weapons including air-to-air missiles, air-to-ground missiles, and various bombs, and it keeps setting speed and altitude records."

The show came on again, and this time the B-24 bomber was discussed. It was a thirty-minute show, and when it was over, I tried to think of what to say next. "Dad, do you think I'd make a good pilot?"

He looked surprised and hesitated before he answered. "Well, I don't know, I never thought about it. Did I ever tell you about the time I flew to Florida and we got in a storm? I thought the wing would fall off."

"But, don't you think I'd make a good pilot?"

"The wing kept shaking and shaking. I never wanted to fly again after that."

"I was thinking about taking lessons."

"Lessons? That's very dangerous. When you take lessons, you just have one little engine—if it goes out, that's it! I think it's too dangerous."

"But Dad, you're the reason I want to learn to fly."

"I am?"

"Sure. Remember all those stories about those brave young lads in the Royal Air Force? One of your favorite movies, *Dawn Patrol* with Errol Flynn and David Niven? We watched that one together whenever it came on TV. You often quoted Winston Churchhill when he talked about the sacrifice the British airmen made—never have so few done so much for so many—or something like that."

He was quiet for a moment. "So you want to be a military pilot?"

"Absolutely—I would really like to fly a jet in the…in the Marines, but I don't know how hard that would be to do."

"It's probably not easy—there's a lot of competition. But you have good eyesight, which is required."

"Yeah, so I thought I might start by getting a private pilot's license, and there's an airport here, but it's fairly expensive."

He sat up and looked at me for a moment, giving me more attention than he had, and I could tell he was now considering what I was saying more seriously. "So you have thought about this? Is this really something you want to do?"

"Yes, I really want to do it. So much that I was thinking that I might use my savings for it—but I'm not sure it would be enough."

"Well, you might not have to. Let me talk to your mother about it."

"Oh, thanks, Dad. That would be great!"

"Now, I just said I would talk to her and I'll think about it. I'm not saying anymore than that. But don't say anything to her about flying for the military—that would worry her."

"I understand," I said, figuring he'd let me since I connected it with patriotism.

"I've decided to take you up on that P.E. letter," I told Gordon at lunch.

"Sure, are you still having trouble?"

"Not too much—I have another reason."

"Okay, I'm waiting to hear it."

"It's personal."

"You mean you won't tell me? Now you really have me interested," he said, partly jesting and partly serious.

"All right, I'll tell you. I'm studying to be a pilot and that would give me more time to prepare."

"Hmm. A smart boy like you needs more study time, huh?"

"Yeah, I need more time."

"Is that the only reason?"

"Okay, Gordon, there is another reason. Mary has a class next to the study hall at that period."

"You mean you're still in love with her—the impossible dream? How did that song go?"

To dream the impossible dream
To fight the unbeatable foe
To bear with unbearable sorrow
To run where the brave dare not go

"Come on, cut it out. Besides, your singing is horrible."
"I don't know if I can do this—I might be responsible for your early demise if Mahoney sees you. How could I ever bear the guilt!"
"Gordon—write the letter. I should have just told you I can't stand the coach."
"But you probably stand a better chance with him than with Mary," Gordon said, laughing so much that he could barely get the words out.
"Oh, you got payback coming now, bud."
"Okay, okay. To show you what kind of a friend I am, I'll do it and I'll even discount it to thirty bucks."
"That's not a discount—that's the same price you told me when we first met," I protested. "And don't forget the drive back from Houston when I saved your…" I stopped talking as Mary walked by with her friend, Ruth. She smiled and walked up to us.
"Hi, boys. Paul, have you met Ruth Hart?" she asked.
"Not really, but I've seen you in the halls," I said, standing up and shaking hands with Ruth. "It's good to finally say hello."
"A pleasure to meet you," Ruth said, and she smiled, but did not seem to want to make much eye contact with me. I noticed that she was an attractive girl, but with her hair in a bun and with her glasses, that was not immediately apparent. Both Mary and Ruth had a special sweetness about them—it was hard to define. But they didn't seem to match—Mary dressed normally and wore a little makeup and her hair was

long and curled. Ruth had a plain-looking long dress and wore no makeup.

"Do you need any more help with the class?" Mary asked.

"Well, I do have a few questions," I answered, even though I didn't need any more help but just wanted to see her again.

"Come by anytime," she said, and they walked away.

"See what I mean?" I said.

"Paul, as your friend—really, I need to tell you something. There's a kid, Joey, in the band that looks kind of like Benjy, but fatter. The band and the cheerleaders were practicing and Mary slipped and fell, and Joey came to her rescue. He helped her up, and ran and got some ice from the cafeteria and wrapped it in a towel and put it on her ankle, and held it there until she felt better. Then he helped her up and carried her books for her. Mary was so grateful that she invited him over for dinner at her house, and whenever she saw him she seemed just as friendly as she did with you just then. Anyway, Joey thought she had fallen for him, and he started telling everyone that Mary was his girlfriend."

"Even with Mahoney around?"

"This was before Mahoney. I don't think Mary was dating anyone. Anyway, Joey kept coming over to Mary's place, bringing her gifts and stuff. Joey's father is a cardiologist and they have some money. But finally it was Mary's mother—at least this is what I heard—it was her mother that set Joey straight."

"Okay," I said, now doubting myself more than ever.

"You can't really blame Joey for thinking that—she actually led him on without knowing what she was doing—at least that's how I see it. She was just being nice to him—but she didn't understand how he would take it. Now look, I know you don't look like Joey and girls like you, but I just wanted you to know about that."

"Thanks for telling me, and I mean that, Gordon."

I appreciated Gordon's warning, but I still could not get Mary off my mind, and I didn't want to give up the hope that she might like me as more than a friend. I was able to visit her again a few days later, and we went over more of the material. When we finished, her mother offered us some homemade cheesecake, and all three of us sat at the kitchen table in the small apartment.

"So how do you like Ball High?" Mrs. Sanderson asked.

"Oh, it's fine—I have good teachers."

"And what are your favorite subjects, Paul?" she asked.

"Well, I like English and science and I like poetry—although that's not exactly a subject." I could tell that Mrs. Sanderson was pleasantly surprised by my answer.

"Really. It seems most boys are just interested in sports these days, and driving fast cars."

"Have you ever read Emily Dickinson?" Mary asked.

I smiled at her and then at her mother, and quoted the poem I had memorized.

If I can stop one heart from breaking,
I shall not live in vain:
If I can ease one life the aching,
Or cool one pain,
Or help one fainting robin
Unto his nest again,
I shall not live in vain.

Mary looked at her mother and then back at me. "Why, that's my favorite poem."

Just then her cat ran out from the bedroom and walked up to me. I petted her under the chin and she meowed happily.

"Why, Hilary really likes you!" Mary said.

Hilary continued to snuggle against my leg.

"You must be a cat person," Mrs. Sanderson said.

My flight instructor was a former military pilot, and since my father arranged the payments, he told him that I wanted to be a fighter pilot. In reality, I just wanted to impress Mary and increase my chances of dating her, but I had to keep up the ruse with the instructor. His name was Mr. Hanson, and he told me on the first day that my training was going to be a lot more intense because of my goal. He said he wanted to see me achieve it, and that he had trained others for military flying. My father had told me that as a former officer he would expect me to call him "Sir."

"When they're on your tail, most say it's over for you," he said as we were taxiing out for my first flight with him. "But if you learn to fly well, you might even beat that death sentence."

"You mean when they're gunning for you?" I asked.

"Exactly. Most pilots give up when that happens, but there are ways to shake them if you know what to do. But that's a long way off for you."

I had already studied the ground school manual and I understood all the instruments, but I was surprised that as soon as we were three thousand feet in the air, he told me to take over on the controls. I struggled to keep the plane flying straight, looking at the attitude indicator which shows the pitch of the plane which is the up and down motion and the bank which is the side motion. After a few minutes of watching me, he spoke. "You keep looking at the instruments, and you need to look at the sky. You can't stay straight because you haven't oriented yourself visually. Flying just with instruments will come later."

"Yes sir," I said, and I looked at the horizon and tried to get oriented.

"You can also tell if you are climbing or descending by listening to the engine. You will hear the RPMs change when the pitch attitude changes. But for now, let's climb to eight thousand feet."

I did as he instructed, and then he looked over at me and tugged on my seatbelt. "Is it secure?" he asked.

"Yes sir, it is," I answered.

"Now turn to the right, then to the left, and then back to the heading I gave you," he said, and I followed his instruction. When we were back to the heading, he looked over at me again. "You know the ailerons and rudder are used when you turn—you understand that operation, correct?"

"Yes sir, I understand it very well."

"So, let's say that we're flying along as we are now, and the controls don't work. How will you make the airplane turn?"

"You mean without ailerons or the rudder, so I have no controls?"

"That's what I mean. I want you to pretend they don't work. What are you going to do to make the plane turn?"

"I don't know, sir," I said, and just as I finished he reached over and opened my door. "What are you doing?" I shouted.

"Keep flying, son. Keep flying."

I wondered if he was going to push me out, but after a few seconds, which seemed much longer, he closed the door.

"Are you crazy?"

"It's are you crazy, sir?" he said, laughing. "Now look at your heading—do you see that you turned?"

"Yes…yes, I do."

"So, now you know how to turn the plane without the controls," he said, and then he opened his own door, and the plane turned to the right. "You open the door and it draws in the air and turns the plane."

I was relieved but a little irritated. "Why didn't you just tell me?" I asked.

"Two reasons. First, now you will never forget this lesson, and second, I got a little idea of how you act under pressure. And you did okay, you didn't lose your head."

"Thank you…sir," I said.

CHAPTER 5

That week I had trouble in my English class. Gordon was right about Mrs. Travis, the English teacher. She was an attractive woman, but she was an annoying teacher. Besides constantly talking about the days when she was a cheerleader at her college in Florida, she was strongly opinionated and found fault with anything that was said in the class that she did not agree with. We were studying the play *Our Town* by Thornton Wilder. Wilder had won a Pulitzer prize for the play, and we had to write an essay about what the play meant to us, which everyone had already turned in, but we had not received the papers back yet. On this particular day, we were discussing the play in class, and she was calling on different students and asking them questions about it. Near the end of the class she got around to me.

"Paul, what did you like the most about the play?"

It took me a while to think about an answer, because I didn't like the play at all. "Well, the dialog seemed to flow well," I finally said.

"And what did you like the least?"

"The play was about what supposedly happens when people die, but since Wilder didn't know, I found that part to be unbelievable."

"How do you know that he didn't know?"

"Well, the idea of someone coming back after they died to experience life as a twelve-year-old again just didn't seem realistic to me. And the part where the woman was counseled by other spirits not to go back and do that—well, I just didn't buy it."

"You didn't buy it?" she said, a little sarcastically.

"No, I didn't."

"Do you realize that this man won the Pulitzer prize for this play?"

"Yes, I knew that—you told us that when you gave us the reading assignment."

"But you didn't *buy* the story," she said. "And what do you mean by that?"

I took a moment before answering. I thought what I said had an obvious meaning, but I also knew that she was unhappy with me. "I explained it in detail in the essay, and…"

"I haven't read the essays yet, so why don't you explain it to the class?"

"Well, his whole idea, it seems to me, was to show people that they ought to make good use of the time we have here, because it's precious."

"Yes, I think that is the basic idea," she said. "Go on."

"But in the play all the dead people—I mean their spirits—are saying that she has to forget everything about the earth life. So, I don't see how this life would be precious if we are supposed to forget everything about it. But mostly, he just made up what he thinks happens when you die."

"Well, it's allegorical. Do you know what that means?"

"Yes, I know what that means."

"Then define it for the class."

I took a breath, wondering why she was so annoyed.

"Well, an allegory is a fictional example of something that symbolizes some concept that the author is trying to express."

"But what you don't seem to understand is that you don't take the allegory as actual truth. It just *represents* truth."

"Well, it represents the thing that the author believes is truth—but that wouldn't necessarily be the truth. It's just his opinion."

"So you can't see the spiritual meaning in this play—that it represents a general truth about mankind? Have you completely missed that?"

I was quiet for a moment, not wanting to argue with her and wondering what kind of a grade I would get on my essay, since I had titled it "Not Really Great," in referring to Wilder. "I didn't miss it, I just didn't agree with it. I think a story or a play is like a menu—you may like something different from what I like just as people have different tastes for food."

"So now you are comparing Thornton Wilder's Pulitzer winning masterpiece to a food dish?" she said, laughing, and some of the other students laughed also.

I was embarrassed and was beginning to get angry. "Yes, and he had a bad recipe, used too much salt and sugar, and burned it so it tasted so bad I had to spit it out!"

That got an even bigger laugh from the class, and Mrs. Travis got red in the face and was about to say something else when the bell rang.

As I walked out, a girl came up to me. I could tell she wanted to say something but was hesitant because she was shy. I smiled at her, trying to put her at ease. "Hi, my name's Rachel, and I liked what you said in there," she said.

"Thank you, but I don't think Mrs. Travis liked it."

"It doesn't matter. You spoke up and that was brave. And Wilder has no clue what happens when you die."

I smiled at her and she kept walking with me.

"But I do, and we can talk about God sometime if you want to," she offered.

"Yes, that would be nice," I said, not really meaning it, but not wanting to offend her.

It was a Saturday afternoon, and Gordon was cleaning up racing on Pelican Island. R.J. was there with his father's Pontiac Grand Prix, and Curt has been riding with him. Curt sometimes drove his father's Toyota Corona, which, needless to say, was not a car he raced. So far, Gordon had won about twenty-five dollars when a couple of men in their twenties drove up in a Ford Galaxie with a four-twenty-seven logo on the side near the front. They stopped close to us, then showed off a little by driving back and forth, spinning their tires and then coming to a screeching stop. I noticed that Gordon was listening intently to their car each time it drove by. After a few minutes, they drove up to where we were, and you could hear the thumping of their racing camshaft. Finally, they shut off the engine and looked around at the twenty or so cars that were gathered there.

"Howdy—I'm Randy and he's Carl—we're from Texas City," Randy sort of announced to everyone. Both of them looked rough, and Randy had grease on his clothing, which made me think he had been working on the car he was driving. I sensed they would be trouble and was hoping that Gordon was getting the same feeling, and that we would have nothing to do with them.

No one said anything and Randy looked around. "Who has the fastest car, here?" he asked.

"So far, I do," Gordon said.

"Ah, a gift from your Momma?" Carl said.

"No—Daddy," Gordon said, matter of factly.

"Well let's race, title for title," Randy said, smugly.

"I couldn't do that if my Daddy's name is on the title—he'd have to sign it, and I doubt he'd agree to do anything so stupid," Gordon retorted.

"Is that a quarter-mile you're running on?" Carl asked, ignoring Gordon's answer as he looked at the strip of road where we raced.

"Yeah, there's a big rock at the end painted red where it ends," R.J., who had just walked up, said.

"I'll race you for fifty," Gordon said suddenly, and I looked at him with a startled look.

"Okay."

"We'll each have a passenger. And there's a kid over there who'll hold the money," Gordon said, and he whistled to get a younger boy's attention. "Hey, Jimmy, come hold the money and flag us off."

"Fifty bucks, huh? The boy must be rich," Randy said.

Gordon ignored them and we got back in his car. When he closed the door, I shook my head. "You want to risk that much? They've got a 427 engine and I could hear the full race cam."

"Yeah, and I could hear it missing out—that wasn't just the cam thumping, his timing is off. Anyway, that car is about four years old and it's heavy. Even the new ones only clock about fifteen seconds, so I should be two seconds faster."

"Okay, it's your money," I said, as we got into position.

"On the count of three," Jimmy said, and he began counting but he had only said "two" when the Ford jumped the line. But they were still smoking their tires when Gordon passed them, and they never did catch up. Gordon drove back to collect his winnings, and they raced back also.

"You jumped the line!" Randy shouted as he drove up.

"No, you jumped it—everyone saw you, and I still won."

"No you didn't—we go again," Randy insisted.

Gordon was quiet for a moment. "Okay, fair enough," he said, and he turned around and lined up with Randy again. Jimmy signaled them to start, and Randy jumped the line again, but this time Gordon turned around and drove back and grabbed the money that Jimmy was holding and drove towards the bridge that would take us off Pelican Island.

As soon as Randy and Carl figured out what happened, they came after us. I was looking through the rear window as we seemed to fly across the bridge. We hit a bump and my head hit the top of the car. "Do you see them?" Gordon asked.

"No, not yet...yeah, I do see them, they just got on the bridge."

Gordon made a fast turn onto Broadway, where there was enough traffic that he thought we might blend in, then he turned off onto a smaller street. "I think we lost them," he said, slowing down a little. "They're from out of town anyway, they don't know the roads like I do." We turned again, and suddenly the Ford was on that road coming towards us. When they spotted our car they sped up, so Gordon did a sliding U-turn as they came barreling towards us. Soon we were at an intersection and a truck was crossing, and Gordon had to slow down. As soon as it passed, Gordon floored the GTO. A song on the radio was playing:

Sue's letters came every day
Gave him the strength to show him the way
To fight for his country and the girl he loved
That's a soldier's only pay...

Then Billy heard no word from Sue
He was worried sick, but what could he do
The bullets were flying as he hugged the ground
And back home, Sue was running round.

"Would you turn that stupid thing off," Gordon shouted as we made another turn but could not seem to shake the Ford.

I turned the radio off, and we approached a busy intersection with a stoplight, but Gordon didn't slow down. "What are you doing? The light is red!"

"Don't worry, I'm baiting them," Gordon said, and just then he threw the GTO into another 180-degree skid at about fifty miles an hour, and the Ford went on through the red light but did not hit anyone in the intersection.

Now Gordon was really driving fast, but as he slalomed around a corner the car stalled. "Don't worry, I think we lost them," he said confidently, but I saw them coming toward us as he spoke.

"They're coming and they're going to kill us," I said.

"Sometimes when you skid like that, gas is thrown out of the carb and…"

"Don't explain it! Oh, God, please help us, please make the car start," I shouted. "Please start!"

Gordon was still cranking the engine with no success as Randy and Carl came out of their car, and both of them were carrying tire irons. Randy ran to the car and smashed the right rear passenger window, and just as he did, the car started and we took off again. They ran to their car but we turned as they were getting in, and then we turned several more times, going faster than Gordon had ever driven with me in the car before.

"We lost them this time," Gordon said, but then we heard a siren and we could see a police car several blocks in back of us.

But Gordon didn't slow down.

"Man, you better stop. You can get in real trouble running from the police," I said.

"Shut up, Welles. I know what I'm doing—they can't read my plate yet." He then made another series of turns, but we could still hear the siren. Turning onto a quiet residential street, he pulled into a house with a driveway that continued from the street to the back of the house, where it was obscured by shrubs and trees from the road. He shut the car off and we sat there, breathing heavily. We could still hear the siren.

"Sorry, I shouted at you, man," he said.

"Don't worry, I think I know why."

"We need to stay here until this dies down. The cops don't have a plate but they have a description of the car. And we need to give those two gubers in that flaky Ford time to give up and go back to Texas City."

As we sat there an elderly woman with white hair looked out of a back window in the house. Then she came out the back door and slowly walked over to us.

"Oh no, we may have to leave," Gordon said, and before she could say anything, he got out of the car. "I'm so sorry, we made a wrong turn. He just moved here," he said, pointing to me. "We're lost." The lady looked at me and then back at him. When she spoke she had a thick accent of some sort.

"It's okay," she said, stopping for a moment and listening to the siren. "It looks like someone had a accident," she added, looking at the GTO's broken window.

"Yes, these young vandals—it's terrible these days," Gordon said.

"Well, I'm Mrs. Rosh. I'm an old lady, and I'd like to have some company and you need some time, I think—to figure out where you are. So come in for some milk and cookies. I haven't baked any, but I have Oreos. Do you like Oreos?"

"Yes, we do," I answered, as I got out of the car. "My name is Paul and he's Gordon."

Mrs. Rosh looked at me and appeared a little shocked.

"You look so much like my late son—he was very handsome like you. See, I have his picture here." She opened a cameo on her necklace and there was a picture of a teenage boy. I suppose it looked a little like me. Then she closed it and we walked into her house.

The house was large and was originally luxurious, with long, flowing velvet curtains and ornate oak woodwork. Although still impressive, it was now rundown and it also had a subtly eerie feeling to it.

"Please sit," Mrs. Rosh said, showing us into a formal dining room. She then left to get the cookies and milk.

"This place has seen better days," Gordon said, looking around.

"It's better than being at the police station," I said, and as I finished speaking she came back with the food.

Gordon bit into a cookie and then spoke in a somewhat self-deprecating manner. "We were so dumb, getting mixed up in that."

Mrs. Rosh answered him in a serious voice. "The whole world is mixed up. That is why the secret order was started, to keep the wisdom of the ages."

"The secret order? What is that?" I asked.

"It is everything that you don't see, because it's spiritual. When I was young, in Romania, we saw so many wonderful things—things you would not believe—people today don't believe."

"What things?" I asked.

"We saw iron become gold. Fire dance on water. I walked on hot coals and never got burned. My mother said I had a special gift. When the Central Powers invaded Translyvania, my mother said disaster was coming. She told me to use my special powers to make us invisible."

Gordon turned to me and pursed his lips. "Central Powers?"

"Germany, Austria, and Hungary—they invaded Romania in 1916," I whispered to him.

"So I prayed to the Great Spirit, and the soldiers ran past us. We were right in the road and they were rounding everyone up and killing them, but we walked for miles and no one touched us—not one saw us. We were invisible—I had the power. The Germans missed us then, but I married later and they killed my son when Romania sided with the Nazis and they were allowed to kill the Jews and the Romas. We were Romas—you say Gypsies. I was not there to save my son—he was out hunting for food when they got him."

"I'm sorry to hear that," I said, and Mrs. Rosh sat down next to me and picked up my hand and looked at my palm. Then she began to read it.

"It's coming…it's coming—a great love. Oh, such a great love. And such a great sadness too. So you need power for this—you need power to get what you want and to survive," she said, and she handed me an ornate star-shaped charm with some foreign writing on the back of it, which appeared to be made of gold. "Take this one thing from me—this amulet."

I looked at it again, surprised that she was offering it to me, and was not sure what to say. "I can't take this," I finally said.

"No," she said, holding her hands so they closed my hand around the amulet. "You are so like my son—but he went into the wonder of eternity so young. I think…I think some of his spirit is in you—this must be why you came. There are no coincidences in life, you know."

"But this looks expensive and…" I began to protest, but she interrupted me.

"Please take it from me. It was made for you. This amulet has power—it can get you what you want. Please."

Gordon was getting restless and he stood up. "Thank you for the cookies, ma'am. We better get going."

We got into the car and as we were driving away, Gordon tried to imitate her accent. "The wisdom of the secret order…here, let me see that." He grabbed the amulet from my hand and put it to his mouth.

"What are you doing?" I said, reaching over to get it back from him.

"It's real gold," he said, after biting it. "That might be worth something."

"Well, your bite mark won't help it," I said.

"I think Dracula already bit it. Man, that woman was batty. There's no such place as Transylvania—it's from the movie—you know, *Dracula*."

"You're wrong. Transylvania is in Romania."

"Oh, it's a real place? How did you know that, and the Central Powers thing?"

"I've gotten a history lesson almost every day of my life."

"Yeah, I guess you have. Well, I always wanted to know someone from the secret order, especially someone with Dracula's accent!" he said, again mimicking Mrs. Rosh.

"Well, whatever she has, she saved our bacon, and I think we ought to go home in case your Texas City friends are still roaming the streets."

"I agree—but since you have the amulet now, couldn't you just make us invisible?"

We got our essays back at the end of class from Mrs. Travis. She passed them out as we were going out of the room, and I didn't look at mine until I got to the hallway. When I opened it up, I could hardly believe that I had made a C-minus. I had always been an A student, especially in English classes, and I had spent a lot of time writing the essay. My title, "Not Really Great," was definitely "over the top" but I didn't realize it at the time. And Mrs. Travis had drawn a red line through it and made the comment "Who do you think you are?" next to it.

I walked back into the class and when our eyes met I could tell she knew that I was surprised at the grade. She turned away, but I walked up to her and waited for her to turn around. "I can't believe this grade," I said.

"Well, you'll have to," she answered.

"I have always been told that my writing is excellent—so I don't understand this."

She looked up at me and hesitated for a moment. "No one said your writing is not good, that's not the point."

"Then why a C-minus?"

"I don't have time to talk to you about this now. You can come by after school and I will discuss it then."

"Okay," I said, and I walked out and went to my next class, which was chemistry, which Gordon also had. I sat down next to him, and he looked over at me.

"Did someone die?" he asked, noticing my angry face.

"Worse than that, Travis gave me a C-minus for a perfectly good paper."

"I warned you—she can be that way."

"Well, I'm supposed to meet her about it after school."

"I don't know if I'd do that."

"What do you mean? Of course I'll meet with her. It's not fair."

"Okay, but if you get her mad at you, things could get worse."

"You mean, like she might flunk me or something?"

"I don't know, but there are certain personalities that she just does not get along with—normally the people who don't bow down to her. So if you go, just don't push too hard—she needs to always be right."

"Sounds like Genghis Khan."

"Was that the Chinese dictator?"

"Yeah, he was brutal. You either joined the Mongol Empire or he massacred you."

"That may not be a bad comparison," Gordon said, and then the teacher started speaking.

After sixth period I headed for Mrs. Travis's classroom. I had tried to calm down because I realized I could make things worse if I was not careful. She smiled a phony smile at me, and motioned for me to sit down at a chair on the side of her desk, facing her. "So what would you like to talk about?" she asked, as if she didn't know.

"My grade. I worked hard on this paper and I don't know why it was so low," I said, holding the paper in my hand.

"Your writing is…well, it is good, as far as grammatical construction, but you have impugned one of the great writers in American literature, almost in a mocking way."

"But don't I have a right to my own opinion?"

"Yes, but an uniformed, uneducated opinion, by someone so immature that they cannot grasp the greatness of Wilder's work, is not deserving of a grade higher than I gave you."

"I see," I said, not certain what else to say, because I was boiling mad but was trying not to show it. "What can I do to bring the grade up?"

She thought for a moment. "Well, you need to begin to understand the greatness of Wilder and the contribution he made to literature and then rewrite the paper accordingly. I want you to learn from your mistake, and try to understand the higher level that he wrote on—he actually writes on several levels, and I think you did not quite grasp the higher levels."

"You mean about spirits coming back to earth?"

She seemed agitated by my question, but then she overcame it. "I mean the significance of what he communicated—not in the literal sense, but in an intellectual sense."

I could see I would get nowhere with more questions, so I stood up and tried to smile and make the best of it. "When do you want the rewrite?"

"Oh, take several weeks if you need to—take the time you need to re-read the play. I won't make this grade permanent, and I'll just hold on to this paper until you're finished," she said, smiling, but I wasn't certain if the smile was because she was trying to be nice, or because she relished the power she had in trying to make me change my opinion of Wilder. It was clear to me that unless I wrote what she wanted to hear and changed what I really thought about Wilder, my grade would not improve. As I walked away from the classroom, I wondered if I would be compromising my integrity by changing the paper, or if I should just play along to get a better grade.

The next day at school, Gordon sat down with me at lunch. "I may have some really great news for you."

"Yeah?"

"Okay—there's a doctor who collects cars and lives in Houston, but he has a beach house here in Jamaica Beach. He knows my Dad, and when he was at our house last week, I mentioned your Cadillac, and he's interested. Since it's in cherry condition I think he'll pay a lot for it—this guy is loaded. Now the other thing is that I know an older guy who got drafted and he has to do something with a Chevelle SS396. It's only a year and a half old, but I think you can get it cheap because he's kind of desperate to sell it. And he never drove it hard."

"How much cash do you think I'd have to come up with?"

"Don't know yet, it depends on what you can get for that Caddy. He'll be here this weekend, and you can show him the car."

"I better get a price before I ask my parents," I said. "Do you think he will mind that it's pink?"

"It may be a selling point—the color was kind of rare, I think."

I started jogging so I would have an excuse to go by Mary's apartment, since it was only a few blocks from our house. One day I saw her getting out of her mother's car, a Chevy Biscayne, and she waved to me and smiled as I went by. She stood there by the door, and I wanted to stop and talk to her, but I was afraid it would seem too obvious why I was jogging in front of her apartment building if I did stop.

Later I met the doctor who collected cars and he gave me an offer on the Cadillac, and it was much more than I expected to get. Afterwards, Gordon helped me negotiate a price on the Chevy. Then it was time to present all of this to my father. I was not certain how to do it, so I just decided to ask him one day after school. He was in his study as usual, book in one hand and wineglass in the other. He looked up at me as I entered.

"How much?" he asked.

"How much what?"

"How much money do you want? I am again anticipating the reason for your visit."

"Actually, quite a bit," I said, and then I told him about selling the car and buying the other one, and what a great deal I thought it was.

"So, how much was that again?" he asked, and I passed him a paper with the numbers on it.

"I've written it down."

"Yes, I see," he said, looking over the paper with a serious look on his face. "So, is this anything like the hot rod Gordon roars up our driveway to pick you up in—well, that's a silly question, of course it is."

"No, it's just a normal car," I lied, knowing he knew nothing about cars.

"So it's an SS396. What does the SS stand for—it's not Schutzstaffel is it? It's not a German car is it?" he asked.

"No, Dad, it's a Chevy. But what did Schutzstaffle stand for, anyway?"

"It would be translated Protective Squad—but it was called the SS. There were several SS groups, the Allgemeine or General SS and Waffen SS, which was the armed SS. The Allgemeine SS was responsible for enforcing the racial policy of Nazi Germany, whereas the Waffen-SS consisted of combat units of troops within Nazi Germany's military. A third SS was the Totenkopfverbände, which ran the concentration camps and extermination camps. They were the ones who killed about six million Jews. I will not buy a car that had anything to do with that!"

"Easy, Dad. It stands for super sports. It's an American car. I promise you. It's made by General Motors."

"Well, let me tell you something about General Motors. In 1934 the biggest auto and truck manufacturer in Germany was not a German carmaker. The biggest one in Germany, and in fact all of Europe, was General Motors. Since 1929 it owned and ran Opel, which made 40 percent of the cars in Germany. And James Mooney, the president of GM in Europe, lauded

Hitler as a great leader. So, are you sure you know what SS stands for?"

I sat there for a moment, not knowing what to say. I couldn't just say that his concern about SS was ridiculous—I knew I would have to deal with him based on history to prevail.

"But didn't you tell me that Henry Ford and J.P. Morgan supported Hitler at first? That was before anyone knew he was killing Jews and gypsies. And you're driving a Buick and that's made by GM."

He looked at me for a moment, trying to come back with something, and then he gave up.

"I still don't like the SS part of this. You never know—"

"Dad, I don't need all the money—I have some I saved, and some I inherited from Aunt Mildred, and I can get a job after school—"

He interrupted me. "Now my question is, do you really need a car like this? All you want it for is to race around and impress girls, and I think that is giving in to an adolescent impulse, don't you?"

"Maybe, but I'm just a teenager—I do have some frailities."

"But that's a lot of money for a car, and if you peel out like Gordon does you'll have to buy new tires every few months."

"Is that youth slang?"

"Watch it now, or I might make you drive a Volkswagen. I know that's a German car, and it's a lot cheaper...and slower."

"I was just joking. I won't peel out. I'll drive sensibly."

"Well, I doubt that, but I'll tell you what—I'll leave it to fate and your education."

"What do you mean by that?" I asked, becoming a little annoyed.

"It means that whether or not you get your 397—I mean 396—will depend on how well you've listened to my history lessons over the years."

"Come on, don't do this to me, just give me a yes or a no."

"Okay then, no."

"All right, all right, I'll play the game."

"That's more like it. There will be five oral questions, and you have five minutes to answer each one. If any answer or part of an answer is incorrect, you will keep your pink beauty. But if you get them all correct, you will get your 397—I mean 396. I would have respected them more if they called it 397—at least that's a prime number."

"But five out of five—if I got four out of five, that would be an eighty—that would be a passing grade."

"Sorry, those are the rules. Are you in or out?" he asked.

"I'm in, I'm in, but I'd like some time to study."

"Study for what? You can't study for this quiz—the questions will be based on an accumulation of all the history I have taught you—either you learned it or you haven't. Nothing will be on the test that I haven't covered—that's fair, isn't it?" he said, smiling at me.

"Yeah, I guess," I said, and at that moment I wished I'd listened more carefully when he rambled on incessantly about history, but it was too late to do anything about that now. He was truly enjoying the fun of this little game, but to me it was serious business. I really wanted that car, especially since I couldn't really drive a pink Cadillac on the Boulevard without being laughed at, and Gordon was fond of reminding me of the rides he gave me whenever he wanted a favor.

"Okay, I'm ready," I said, remembering at that moment that next to war documentaries, my father's favorite show was College Bowl, and I was wincing a little inside as I thought of how hard the questions were on that show. I could actually never remember him missing any of them on the subject of history when we watched together.

"What was the single most important mistake that Hitler made in the war—what turned the tide for the Allies—and how did a lack of historical knowledge influence that mistake?"

"He attacked Russia while he was fighting on other fronts, and when winter came, his soldiers started losing because they could not handle the cold. Their vehicles also got stuck in the snow and mud and some of them even froze to death in the cold weather. The Russians were better equipped to fight in the frigid weather, and they had many soldiers on skis, which made them more mobile."

"But what about the historical part?"

I had to think for a moment and then it came to me. "The same thing had happened to other countries who had attacked Russia in the past, and it had happened to the Germans before in World War One, but they didn't record any of that in their history books. Maybe because they were too proud."

He looked at me, and I thought I could tell that he felt the question was a little too easy. I wished I had taken more time to answer, to make it seem harder, but it was too late now.

"Okay, the next question," he said, thinking about it for a moment. "Name the Axis powers, and the name of the compact they originally made."

"Germany, Italy, Japan—that was the Tripartite pact."

"Yes, you are correct, but who joined them later?"

"Well, Bulgaria, Slovakia, Hungary and…" I stopped talking and tried to remember the last country.

"Are you stumped? Are we finished?" he asked.

"No. You said I have five minutes for each question."

"That I did, I'll just check my watch and wait. You know, since the collector noticed the Cadillac is in excellent condition, a lot of boys would be satisfied…"

"Dad, come on, let me think." Just then I remembered that Mrs. Rosh mentioned that Romania agreed to side with the Nazis and kill the Jews and Gypsies. "Romania!" I said, triumphantly.

"Are you sure?" he asked, and I looked at him, wondering if I was making a mistake.

"Yes, I'm sure."

"You are correct."

"Well, it wasn't fair to ask me if I was sure—that was a little below the belt," I said.

"Sorry, I'll try to only hit you in the face from now on," he said, smiling. "All Queensbury rules from now on. How many times did the Union army find out about Lee's plans in the Civil War but not act on them?"

I knew the answer to that because he had recently talked about it, but I took my time and pretended to think for a few minutes. "Three times," I said.

"You're doing pretty well," he said, and I wondered if he was going to make the next questions harder.

"In 1938, in regards to Hitler, who was the prime minister of England, what did he do, and what did Churchhill say about it?"

"It was Chamberlain, and he visited Hitler to make a peace treaty—the Munich Agreement—which gave the Germans Czechoslovakia. When he came back he said that England now has peace with honor, but Churchill said they would have neither."

"Well, that is the essence of it. More specifically, Chamberlain said he had returned from Germany bringing peace with honor. Churchill said to him, 'You were given the choice between war and dishonor. You chose dishonor and you will have war.'"

"But I still got it right, didn't I? You can't expect me to have memorized it," I said defensively.

"Not to worry, you got it right, and you only have one left."

"Okay, I'm ready."

Again I could tell he was thinking about the question, and I wondered if he was considering the bottles of fine wine that might not be purchased if he gave me the money to buy the car. After a long wait, I finally got the question.

"What was the Dred Scott Decision, and what were its legal implications, and how did it affect the Civil War?"

I breathed a sigh of relief when I heard the question, because he had just been talking about it the other day—and I knew he wrote his thesis on it when he was a student at Columbia University.

"Let's see. It was about a slave—Dred Scott—who escaped to a free state and then went to federal court to win his freedom on the grounds that he was now living in a free state, and therefore should be free."

"Go on, what happened then?"

"Well, they said that just because he was in a free state didn't mean he was free, so he lost, and the acrimony between the North and South increased because of that."

"Is that all?"

"Well, yes. I mean that's got to be right, isn't it?"

"Don't worry, son," he said, slapping me on the leg. "The Cadillac's got many good miles left in it."

"You mean I missed that question?" I said incredulously. "Are you sure you're not cheating?"

"Now, now, let's not get slanderous—accept defeat gracefully. You were almost correct, but remember I said you had to get the whole answer. You see, the Dred Scott Decision stated that slaves were not citizens, and therefore could not sue in the federal courts. It also declared that the Missouri Compromise of 1820, which had forbidden slavery in that part of the Lousiana Purchase, was an unconstitutional exercise of congressional power. So it was the first time that the U.S. Supreme Court made slavery legal in the territories, thus pushing the nation further along towards the Civil War. Thus, the fact that it declared slavery legal was a landmark decision, and that was the most important aspect of the case."

"Now, Dad, I got enough of it right. You're nailing me on complex technicalities and legal issues."

"Treaties have been broken and wars started because of overlooked technicalities and legal issues."

"Okay, I won't say anything more about it," I said, and I stood up to leave the study.

"Where are you going?" he asked. "Sit down." I did and he looked at me with a mischievous glint in his eye. "Who do I make the check out to—what's the boy's name who has the three ninety-five?"

"You mean you're giving it to me, after all?" I said.

"Yes—but only because the Dred Scott question was perhaps a little too difficult. But I also think this will add to your education—and mine, as well."

"How will it do that?"

"You'll find out how many friends an inanimate object can make, and I'll observe you learning. It will be a sociological experiment for us both."

"Thanks. Were you going to give it to me all along?"

"Absolutely not," he said, suddenly acting very serious. "So from now on you better listen very carefully when I give you a history lesson."

"Well, I really appreciate it, and I'm going to get a part-time job and pay you back as soon as I can."

"Don't be too concerned about that, but there is one condition I am making."

"Sure, anything."

"It will be your responsibility to take your mother shopping at the supermarket and anywhere else she needs to go," he said impishly.

My mother didn't drive, and he had always taken her before.

"Oh, no, you know she always takes forever."

"I certainly do," he said gleefully. "And now I can't wait until you get the car, either."

CHAPTER 6

"You won't break that Muncie four-speed if you shift it harder," Gordon said, as we rode in my new used car on the end of the island on Cherry Hill. "If you're gonna race, you need to shift faster and harder."

"Okay," I said, and I slammed the shifter into second, spinning the tires with a screech as we barreled down the Boulevard. Soon we were driving past Stewart Beach, and Gordon spotted two girls walking on the sidewalk. "Slow down! There are two chicks there, and they're both fine!" he shouted. "Can't you see them?"

"Yeah, but they look kind of young."

"Young and fine, the way I like them. Now make the block and when we drive back up to the Boulevard on 10th Street they should be walking right past your car."

"Yes sir, your new chauffeur is following your directions."

We drove up 10th Street, but they weren't there. Soon a car was in back of us and I had to move.

"I wonder where they went?" Gordon said.

"Probably in that shell shop," I said, referring to the tourist shops that sold shells and other things. Actually most of the merchandise, including the shells, was imported from Taiwan and other countries.

"Okay, let's park and go in—any good chauffeur can parallel park, and I think that space is big enough," he said, pointing to the only space that was nearby, which was right on Seawall Boulevard.

"Gordon, I don't really want to chase them."

"Well I do, so let me out."

As soon as we parked, he jumped out of the car and raced to the shell shop. I followed slowly, and by the time I walked in, he was already talking to one of the girls. He didn't see me, so instead of walking up to him, I walked around the side of the shop, and bent down a little in one of the isles and listened to him. As I did, one of the girls noticed me.

"Hi, my name's Gordon. Where are you from?" Gordon asked, and one of them just giggled and moved away from him, and the other didn't respond at all. Then he looked over and saw me. He signaled me to come over, but I stayed where I was, looking at postcards. Exasperated, he walked over to me.

"What are you doing, Paul?"

"Looking at postcards."

"Yeah, well, will you come over and help me out?"

"I thought we were testing out my car."

"I would never let a mere automobile interfere with my quest for love."

"Oh, so it's love you're after—that's touching. But I'm not in the mood right now."

Gordon looked at me for a moment, then smiled knowingly. "Oh, I see. Well she's with Mahoney—probably making out with Mahoney right now, while you eat your heart out and the world is passing you by. Remember, she's with Mahoney!"

"Don't talk about Mary," I said in a serious tone.

"Okay, then tell me I'm wrong. That's what's stopping you, right?"

I looked over at the girls and then back at him. They were walking towards the front of the store.

"Come on, be a friend, they're getting away. You can even have the blonde."

"Yeah, I'm sure, because the brunette is much cuter, and she checked me out when I came in the store."

"Yes, then you must have the brunette. I'll bet it was love at first sight—and she'll even love you more when she sees your car."

As we spoke they stopped to look at some hats.

"Okay, but they sure do look young."

Gordon started singing in a low voice, and he stopped as we reached them. "A younger girl keeps rollin' 'cross my mind. No matter how much I try, I can't seem to leave her memory behind.'"

I don't know if I was the reason, but they were more receptive now.

"I'm Gordon and this is Paul."

The girls giggled again, and then the brunette smiled at me. "I'm Cheryl and this is my cousin, Debbie."

"Nice to meet both of you. Do you girls live around here, or are you from some exotic place where the women are always beautiful?" I asked.

The girls giggled again, and then Cheryl spoke. "We're just from Galveston."

"And we've never seen you before! Do you live nearby?" I asked.

"Yes, we live near the medical center," Cheryl said.

"Do you go to Ball High?" I asked.

"Yes, I'm in tenth grade. What grade are you in?" Cheryl said.

"Paul and I are in eleventh grade," Gordon answered.

"Debbie is still in junior high. She's in ninth grade," Cheryl said, but Debbie made a face, which seemed to indicate she did not want her to say how young she was.

"So let's cruise the Boulevard and get to know each other," Gordon suggested.

"I don't know," Debbie said, looking at her cousin.

"We will just drive on the Boulevard—you won't go anywhere else, right?" Cheryl said.

"Just the Boulevard—scout's honor. But we can drop you off at home if you want," Gordon answered.

"We have to be back here at three—my mom's picking us up," Cheryl said, looking over at Debbie. "Just a minute," she said and then walked with Debbie away from us to discuss it with her.

"Wow, they are both foxes!" Gordon said when they walked out of earshot, but he could see that I wasn't smiling. "Oh, give it up, will you? She's as fine as Mary—I'd say even better."

"It's not all about looks. You probably need to grasp that in your quest for true love."

"You know, you're starting to sound like my mother. But I know what I want to grasp today, and here she comes," Gordon said, as the girls came back towards us.

Soon we were driving along the seawall, and Cheryl moved closer to me on the bench seat of my Chevelle. She was a very attractive girl, but for some reason, I could only think of Mary that day. We stopped at a drive-in and got milkshakes and then it was time to drop them off at the shell shop. Cheryl was nervous that her mother would see us, so we left quickly after exchanging phone numbers.

"Wow, what a great day. 'Something tells me I'm into something good,'" he sang, from the Herman's Hermits song. Then he began to sing the whole song.

Woke up this mornin' feelin' fine
There's somethin' special on my mind
Last night I met a new girl in the neighbourhood, whoa yeah
Somethin' tells me I'm into something good
(Somethin' tells me I'm into somethin')

"Hey, give me a break, will you?" I said.
"Sorry, I'm happy—she's a really nice girl, and she likes me—you saw us making out, didn't you? Or were you too busy with Cheryl cozying up to you? I didn't see you push her away."

The next time I went to my English class, Mrs. Travis wasn't there when the bell rang. I had heard from Gordon that she was close to delivering her baby. After about five minutes, a beautiful dark-haired woman rushed in and smiled at everyone, then sat down at the teacher's desk.

"I'm Mrs. Erickson, and I'll be substituting for Mrs. Travis for several weeks. I'm not certain how long it will be."

She then stood up again and wrote her name on the blackboard, but it was not her name I was looking at but her curvaceous figure—and from the low whistle I heard from the back of the room, I was not the only one. She turned back towards the class, and smiled again, and I wasn't sure if she was ignoring the whistle or smiling because of it. Whatever the case, she didn't seem upset by it.

At the end of the class, she gave an assignment. "Write a paper about something that happened in your life that had an emotional impact on you—perhaps some interaction with another person, something someone said to you, or some event that occurred. It should be at least twenty-five hundred words, and it is due in two weeks...Oh, by the way, will Paul Welles see me after class for a moment?"

I was startled to hear my name, but I walked up to her desk as everyone else was leaving. She looked up at me with her beautiful, sexy brown eyes, and it was hard for me not to blush. Then she handed me my paper on "Our Town," and I saw that it had a new grade on it—an A-minus. "I re-graded this," she said, and I looked at her for a moment, quizzically.

"You re-graded it?"

"Yes, Mrs. Travis left it for me with a note to re-grade it."

I thought for a moment, and decided honesty was the best policy, as my mother was always saying. Also, I knew that Mrs. Travis would find out anyway. "Thank you, but I think Mrs.Travis wanted me to rewrite it."

"Why?"

"Well, she thought I didn't appreciate Wilder and wanted me to change it."

Mrs. Erickson laughed a little, and it was sort of a girlish laugh, then she looked at me for a moment. "Well, I read it and my grade will stand, But a word to the wise, a title like 'Not Really Great,' probably got her back up. You could learn to be more subtle."

"I understand, and you solved a dilemma for me. I was trying to figure out if I would be compromising my integrity if I wrote what she wanted just to get a better grade."

Mrs. Erickson thought for a moment before answering. "I think you could write more neutrally about Wilder and not compromise yourself. I understand you really don't like his writing and evidently Mrs. Travis does. So you could have written more about the play without such a scathing critique."

"Okay, thanks for the advice—and the grade."

At lunch Gordon filled me in about Mrs. Erickson. "She's twenty-four years old and her husband is doing his residency in psychiatry. Her first name is Susan, by the way."

"Man, are all the teachers married to medical students in this town?"

"A lot of the young ones are. Are you complaining? I think she's terrific!"

"I didn't know you had a class with her."

"I wasn't talking about her teaching—I've seen her walking down the hallway—everyone has. And, man, is she hard to miss! She is gorgeous. Now I've done you a favor with all this inside information, right? And also getting you a deal on your Caddy and the 396, right?"

"I'm afraid of where this is going."

"Have no fear—I only want you to ask Cheryl to go to the school dance with you. We can double date. Debbie's parents won't let her go out with me unless Cheryl comes along—they say she's too young to go by herself."

"Oh, I don't know."

"If you go to the dance you will see Mahoney slobbering all over Mary and she won't be resisting."

"Gordon, I told you not to bring Mary up!" I said, my voice rising. Some other students heard me and looked over and I quieted down.

"Sorry, but I've done a lot of favors for you, and I'm asking you to do this because Debbie really likes me, and I've never met a girl I liked more. We talked for two hours on the phone last night, and she only hung up when her mother had to make a phone call."

I sighed and nodded my head affirmatively. "Okay, Gordon—but what if she doesn't want to go with me?"

"Oh, she'll want to go. Cheryl really likes you—Debbie told me."

Mary was not in class for two days that week, Thursday and Friday. I saw Ruth in the hallway and she said Mary was sick, so I made notes on what we covered in class and walked over to her house on Saturday morning. As I rang the doorbell, Ruth drove up with her mother and got out of the car. Her mother drove away, and as she did, Mary opened the door. She was in her pajamas and she looked surprised to see me. Then she saw Ruth.

"I just brought over some notes from the class—I was going to drop them off with your mother. I'm sorry to bother you."

"It's no bother and it's sweet that you thought of me," Mary said.

"Well, I better get going," I said, turning from the door as Ruth greeted Mary.

"No, come in with me and pray for Mary with me," Ruth said. "Mary's mother is working today—that's okay, isn't it Mary?"

"Yes, of course, although I hate for Paul to see me like this."

"I think you still look wonderful," I said, and she smiled and seemed to perk up a little with the compliment.

We walked in and Ruth took a small vial of oil out of her purse and asked Mary to sit down at the kitchen table. "You know God is our healer, don't you, Paul?"

"Yes, I guess so."

"Do you go to church somewhere?"

"We used to go in Connecticut, but we're not going anywhere right now."

"Well, I'd like to invite you to our church."

"Okay, thanks," I said, and she unscrewed the cap on the vial of oil and put some on her finger.

Ruth closed her eyes and began to pray. "Lord, we come to your throne of mercy and grace, believing your Word, which in James 5:16 tells us that the effectual fervent prayer of a righteous man availeth much. And in James 5:14, and I'm paraphrasing, it says anoint the sick with oil and the prayer of faith shall save the sick, and the Lord shall raise him up. And if he has committed sins, they shall be forgiven him. So I anoint you, Mary, in the name of the Father and Son and Holy Spirit for healing from this flu. And in Mark 16 it says that these signs shall follow them that believe, they will lay hands on the sick and they shall recover. So, I ask for healing in Jesus' name. Paul, is there anything that you would like to pray?"

I was taken by surprise at her question, and it took me a moment to answer. When she prayed I seemed to sense something in the room, and I was not sure what it was but it seemed to absorb my attention. I finally got my words out. "No, I think you covered it all, amen."

"Yes, amen," she said, and Mary followed.

"My, I think I feel better already," Mary said. "Paul, thank you so much for the notes. And Ruth, thank you for coming to take care of me, and your prayers always mean so much to me."

"Oh, I love helping my best friend," Ruth said.

"Well, I better be going," I said.

"Thanks for your prayers," Ruth said, and I walked out.

As I walked home I wondered what I had felt in that apartment when she prayed—it felt like something different, but nice. Soon I had walked the five blocks to my house.

The night of the dance there was a band playing which was made up of high school students. Gordon and I were both dancing as they played their rendition of "A Groovy Kind of Love" by the Mindbenders.

...Wouldn't you agree?
Baby, you and me
Got a groovy kind of love
We've got a groovy kind of love
When I'm in your arms
Nothing seems to matter
If the world would shatter, I don't care...

As the song stopped, Cheryl and Debbie headed to the restroom together.

"Why do they always go together?" Gordon asked, rhetorically. "I wonder what they talk about in there."

As he spoke I noticed Mary walking towards us, coming from the restroom. I had seen her with Jim Mahoney from across the room earlier in the evening, and I wondered if she was walking by us to greet us, or we just happened to be on the way back to where she was sitting. Whatever her motivation, she stopped and smiled at me. "Hi Gordon. Hi Paul, are you having a good time?"

"Yes, I am—I mean we are," I answered.

"I would think so. I saw you dancing with your date and she is a very pretty girl," Mary said, and as she spoke I wondered if she was slightly jealous.

Just then the music started playing again. It was a song by the Troggs, called "Love is All Around."

"The evening would even be better if you would dance with me," I said.

Mary looked around for a moment, then back at me. "Well, Jim is with his friends, so I guess that would be okay." The song continued as I put my arm around her waist. As she moved her body closer to mine, it was almost as if I felt electricity. I wanted to hold her even closer, but I restrained myself as we danced very slowly.

I feel it in my fingers, I feel it in my toes
Love is all around me and so the feeling grows
It is written on the wind, it's everywhere I go
So if you really love me, come on and let it show

Without thinking, I found myself singing the last part of the song into her ear as we danced.

You know I love you, I always will
My mind's made up by the way that I feel

There's no beginning, there be no end
'Cause on my love, you can depend

Suddenly someone poked me very hard in the back. I turned around and it was Mahoney with a scowl on his face. "Can I cut in?" he demanded, as he poked me again, even harder than the first time. Mary seemed a little nervous, and we separated quickly, as Jim took her hand. As I moved away, he poked me in the back again. When I turned around, Cheryl was standing about twenty feet away, watching, and she did not look happy. I walked up to her and she turned away from me.

"What's the matter?" I asked, as I watched Gordon and Debbie dancing.

"You really like her, don't you?"

"You mean Mary—she's just a neighbor—we're just friends. She's got a boyfriend."

"Yeah, sure, I saw the way you looked at her."

"No, you have it all wrong. I said we're just friends."

"Oh, I don't believe you, but let's dance," she said, taking my arm and leading me back to the dance floor.

After we danced, Gordon pulled me aside. "Paul, I can't really make out with Debbie here, and we're in my car, so I'm always driving. So I want to go to Stewart Beach after this and park."

I didn't answer him, and he became agitated. "Look, man, one dance with Mary will not change things—anyway, can't you have a good time with Cheryl and not worry about it?"

"I can, but I feel like a…what do they say…a heel. She saw me with Mary and she figured out right away that I like her. She's very perceptive and even though I denied it she didn't believe me. I feel like I'm using her."

"Man, you haven't promised to marry her! What's the big deal? You make out a little and both of you have fun."

"Okay, Gordon. If they want to go, we'll go."

CHAPTER 7

That night when I got home I couldn't shake the feeling I had when I held Mary in my arms for that dance. It wasn't a very long time, but I kept replaying it over and over again. Finally I fell asleep and when I did I dreamed about the meeting we had with Mrs. Rosh. I had forgotten what she said until in the dream she kept repeating it over and over again. She kept saying, "This amulet has power—it can get you what you want. It can get you what you want. It can get you what you want."

Finally I fell asleep, and when I woke up on Saturday morning, there was something shining intensely in my eyes. I closed them and then opened them again, but a beam of light seemed to be blinding me to everything else. When my eyes adjusted, I could see that it was the sun reflecting brightly from the charm she gave me. The whole room was brilliantly radiant from the sun reflecting from the amulet, and rings of light were refracting from the walls in an unusual pattern. As I watched it with fascination, the words she spoke came into my mind again—it has power—*it can get you what you want*. I wondered about that—did it really have power?

"I want Mary more than anything," I whispered, and I felt something like electricity go down my back. Then suddenly I heard my mother's voice from outside the door, and the sun seemed to shift because the reflection from the amulet faded, and things went back to normal. "Do you want breakfast?" she repeated.

"Yes, Mum. I'll be down in a few minutes. Thank you." I looked over at the amulet and chuckled. What a bunch of nonsense—the old woman was probably batty like Gordon said. Just because the sun was shining didn't mean a thing, and it was that dream that made me think something unusual was happening. I was fully awake now, and could see how ridiculous it all was.

After breakfast I began my routine of jogging—and passing Mary's apartment building. I was always hoping that she would come out and see me, but so far that had never happened. As I ran by, she opened the door and her cat ran out to the street. I heard her scream just as I saw a car hit the cat. It was obvious Hilary was dead. I ran to Mary. She was crying and shaking uncontrollably, and as soon as I reached her she grabbed me and hugged me. I walked back into the apartment and tried to get her to sit down. I was happy that she was hugging me, but she was holding my arm so tightly that my circulation was decreasing and I was beginning to lose the feeling in my arm.

Finally she sat down, still crying. "I loved Hilary so much. I don't know why she ran out like that."

"I'm sorry that happened, Mary," I said, still happy that she was holding on to me. Then she took a deep breath and let go of me and reached for a tissue on her coffee table.

"I'm sorry I got so emotional. I really loved Hilary, and it was just such a shock," she said, obviously embarrassed. "But I'm glad you were there."

"I am too. Look, I'll call the city and have them take care of it—where is your phone?"

"It's in the kitchen. Thank you, Paul."

I walked into the kitchen and saw a telephone book there and began looking for the phone number for animal control. Just then the doorbell rang and she got up slowly to answer it. I heard Mahoney's voice as he walked in.

"What a bloody mess—some cat got creamed on the street," he said laughingly.

Mary burst into tears again. "That was Hilary!" she cried, and he got quiet for a moment as he realized that he had said the wrong thing. Then he saw me in the kitchen and he walked towards me.

"What are you doing here?"

"I live in the neighborhood. I just happened to be passing by."

"Well you better happen to leave."

Then he walked up to Mary and tried to hug her, but she pulled away. "Please, leave me alone."

"Okay, I'm leaving, and so are you," he said, pointing at me.

He was looking very angry and I decided that I better go. "Okay, I'll call them to take care of this when I get home," I said to Mary, and I walked outside with Mahoney following. After he closed the door, he pushed me. He was taller and outweighed me by about seventy-five pounds, and I was no match for him.

"I know you're making a play for my girl, and you better stop it or I'll twist your head off, slime," he said, and he waited for me to walk away before he got into his car to leave.

Gordon picked me up on Saturday night, and I told him about seeing Mary the previous day.

"Okay, so her cat got killed and she hugged you. I might hug you also if something bad enough happened to me."

"I hope not."

"What I mean is that some women get emotional and sometimes hug people when they are in distress," Gordon said.

"I know Gordon, I know. But she was holding on to me really tight and she didn't let go for a long time. I think it was more than her being in distress—I think she used that as an excuse. I think it was a turning point in our relationship."

"Yeah, the point where Mahoney keeps turning your head until it falls off. Isn't that what he said?"

"Why are you trying to make this thing with Mary a bummer for me?"

"Paul, I'm not. But you keep looking at it with rose-colored glasses. She's Mahoney's girlfriend and he will beat you to a pulp if you keep going over there. And as much as you run by her house, I imagine you'll see him again."

"What do you mean, as much I run by her house—why do you say that?"

Gordon smiled for a moment, and then looked over at me, knowingly. "Well don't you?"

"Oh, never mind."

"I still think Cheryl is a fox and you're crazy not to like her. And she likes you—she's not the impossible dream."

Then he started singing.

To dream the impossible dream
To fight the unbeatable foe
To bear with unbearable sorrow
To run where the brave dare not go
To right the unrightable wrong
To love pure and chaste from afar
To try when your arms are too weary
To reach the unreachable star
This is my quest
To follow that star
No matter how hopeless
No matter how far

"Stop, stop, stop!" I said, looking for one of his eight-track tapes in the glove compartment. "Did you memorize that whole dumb song?"

"When we went to New York we saw *The Man of La Mancha* on Broadway and my parents bought the record. I think it's a good song."

"I'm sure it is when a real singer sings it."

"Okay, I'll stop singing, even if it does describe you. But since we're picking up Debbie and Cheryl can you get your mind off Mary and on Cheryl? Or do you only like the ones you can't get?"

"I don't like Mary because I can't get her—I just like her. She's sweet and nice, and when I'm around her, even in class, I feel good. I don't feel that way around any other girl."

"I'm sorry I asked, because I wish you liked Cheryl as much as I like Debbie." Gordon started humming and I pushed a tape in his eight-track player to shut him up.

Groovin' on a Sunday afternoon

Really couldn't get away too soon
I can't imagine anything that's better…

"Yeah, that's a good song. And everything has been good since I met Debbie, but I can't let her meet my parents."

"Why not?"

"Paul, she's a *shiksa*—I mean that's not a nice word in Yiddish, but it means a girl who isn't Jewish, and I'm supposed to marry a Jewish girl. And if they find out I like her…well, let's just say I don't want them to know."

"Sounds like you're serious about her."

"I am, and I don't want to worry about tomorrow. You know sha la la la, live for today. I'll figure out how to break it to my parents when the time comes," Gordon said as he pulled up to Debbie's house to pick her up.

After seeing a movie, we went to Cherry Hill and parked near the end where there were no cars. It was very dark there, and we were both making out when I heard a rumble that sounded like a car motor. "Did you hear that?" I asked Gordon.

He was kissing Debbie and didn't answer for a moment, then I heard it again and this time he did also. I looked through the back window but it was dark. "Gordon, start the car and put it into reverse so the backup lights come on—I think the noise is coming from the rear." As I finished speaking, the noise stopped and it was silent.

Gordon reluctantly pulled away from Debbie and turned the ignition on to accessories. Then he put the car in reverse, and as soon as the backup lights were on I saw the blue Ford in the distance in back of us and two men getting out of the car with baseball bats in their hands. Gordon also saw them in his rearview mirror, and he started the car as quickly as he could. When our lights came on the men realized we were escaping and they got back into their car and started it. "It must be the same guys," Gordon said, as he shifted into first gear and took off, tires squealing, but his tires weren't the only things squealing. The girls were shocked and none of us had buckled our seatbelts and as Gordon drove down the slanted road to the main boulevard, we were getting thrown around in the car.

"What is going on?" Cheryl screamed as Gordon shifted hard into third gear.

"Those guys are dangerous," I said. "We have to get out of here."

Gordon was moving faster than the blue Ford, but when we got to the area where the hotels were, traffic was thick and he had to slow down. As he came to the light, the Ford bumped him. Debbie started crying, and Gordon sped up and then made a U-turn in the middle of the Boulevard. The Ford followed, and Gordon pulled off the Boulevard and raced down 23rd Street. Cheryl was also upset and was trying to say something, but couldn't seem to get the words out.

"We'll lose them now. They don't know the back streets," Gordon said as the Ford barreled down on us and he threw the GTO into a 180-degree skid. Then he made a fast turn onto a side street, skidding the whole way. We slid around the corner and the Ford kept going, unable to stop fast enough to follow. Soon we were racing down an alley and then up another street and then through an alley again. I couldn't see the Ford anymore and I told Gordon, but he continued speeding down various streets and alleys until he felt certain that he had lost them.

"I want to go home," Debbie cried.

"There's nothing to worry about now," Gordon said reassuringly. "We've lost them."

Cheryl was also upset but was doing better than Debbie, who was wimpering in fear. "Why were they chasing you?" Cheryl asked.

"Gordon beat them in a race and won some money and they got mad over that," I explained.

"Well, why don't you just give them the money back?" Cheryl asked.

"We would if we could. It's not like we get the chance to discuss it with them," Gordon explained.

"I want to go home," Debbie said again, sniffling. "This is the worst date I've ever had."

"I'm sorry. I was just trying to protect everyone," Gordon said.

"Drive me home!" Debbie said emphatically.

"Okay, I'm going there," Gordon said, and he drove to her house.

Mrs. Erickson asked me to stay after class on Monday, and I was hoping she hadn't changed her mind about the grade she gave me on the paper. Everyone left the class and I waited in the seat next to her desk as she looked for something. It turned out to be my new paper.

"I wanted to tell you something after reading this paper. It was very honest—you talked about how the girl that no one liked came to you, and you said 'her eyes begged understanding' but you treated her just like everyone else did. Was that when you were in school in Connecticut?"

"Yes. Did you not like the paper?" I asked, wondering why she was talking to me about it, and also trying not to stare at her body. She was sitting with her beautiful legs crossed and she uncrossed them as she spoke and her dress rose up past her knee.

"No, I loved the paper," she said, handing it to me, and I looked and saw that it had an A-plus on it.

"Oh, great, thank you."

"It was good—the writing reminded me of a great writer."

"Who do you mean?"

"Thornton Wilder," she said, with a deadpan expression.

I looked at her a moment, confused. Then she smiled.

"Oh, that was a joke," she said, touching my arm gently as she laughed. "Seriously, though, I wanted to tell you that you have a gift. I love the way you write, and if you practice, I think you can become a very good writer. Have you ever thought about that—does it interest you?"

"Well, no, I haven't really. I'm not sure what I want to do."

"I checked your scores in the front office—you can be anything you want to be."

"Oh, thanks, Mrs. Erickson. I appreciate the encouragement."

It was getting late for me to get to my next class, and I was concerned but was trying not to show it.

"I will be interested to see what you do with your life...okay, see you tomorrow," she said.

I smiled and left the classroom, and the compliment made me feel as if I were riding on air.

The next day I saw Mary in the hallway as she was walking towards our Business Math class and she seemed sad, but she tried to smile at me. Normally she always seemed very happy, so this was unusual.

"Hi, are you okay?" I asked.

"Yes...well, no, I'm still bothered about Hilary. I keep seeing her there, dead on the ground and..."

I interrupted. "You need a kitten. Can I take you to the pound after school and we can get one?" She didn't answer for a moment and at first I thought she was going to turn me down. But then she smiled, and I imagined she was thinking of how much fun a new kitten would be.

"Okay, I'll tell my ride that I'm going with you," she said.

I wondered if it was normal for someone to be that bothered about a cat, especially since so much time had passed. But I remembered how upset she was when the incident happened and figured she was just very sensitive.

I was watching to see if Mahoney was around as Mary got into my car after school.

"This is a really nice car," Mary said as she closed the door.

"Thank you."

"Thank you for taking me to the pound. I thought about going, but then I felt that maybe I was being unfaithful to

Hilary if I got another cat so quickly, because I loved her so much and she also loved me."

I wasn't certain how to respond to what she said and was quiet for a few moments. "I'm sure Hilary would want you to be happy—we all want the best for our loved ones."

"Yes, that's very perceptive—I think what you said is true. I mean, if something happened to me, I'd want Hilary to have a new owner—that would be my main concern."

We looked at several kittens, and one light gray one seemed to be especially friendly. "I think I want that one," Mary said.

"It's a male," the attendant said.

"I think I'll call him Freddie," Mary said.

"That will be four dollars," the attendant said, after he put the cat in a cardboard box for us to transport him and told Mary to be sure to have him neutered when he was older.

I took out my wallet and paid him before Mary could even open her purse. "You can't pay for it," she protested.

"But I want to—it's a gift to you."

"Are you sure?" she asked.

"Yes, I am."

We drove to her apartment, and I followed her in with the cat. She had her purse and schoolbooks in her hands, and as soon as she put them down, she opened the box and petted the kitten for a moment. She was smiling and I could see that she was very happy with the new cat. In fact, she seemed to forget I was there for a few minutes. Then she remembered and she looked up. "I'd have you say hello to my mother, but she's working her shift now. Thanks again for the kitten—I love him."

"You're welcome."

"So, now what can I do for you?" she asked.

"Mary, it was a gift—I don't need anything in return."

"But I want to give you a gift, also."

I thought for a moment and got an idea. "I'd like a kiss, then."

"A kiss?" she said, surprised.

"Yes—on the mouth," I said, and then she smiled, and she put the kitten down and pushed out her lips a little.

"Okay, then, close your eyes," I said, and she did so. Then I moved towards her, but instead of giving her a peck on the lips, I put my arms around her and held her close as I kissed her. At first she protested by making a sound, but as I continued kissing her, she gave in and put her arms around me also, and began kissing me back. We stayed in that embrace for a long time, but finally she pulled away, evidently surprised at herself.

"I shouldn't have done that," she said.

"Do you want me to take it back?" I asked, and I moved towards her and kissed her lightly again.

"Take it back? Oh, you're clever, aren't you? But really, I've been seeing Jim for a year now and…"

"But you're not going steady, are you? I don't see his ring around your neck."

"Well, we are, in a way."

I thought about what to say next. I had heard the expression "all's fair in love and war," and decided to mention something I'd heard about Mahoney. "But he's not faithful to you," I said.

She looked at me, and her face changed into a slight frown.

"What do you mean?"

"I mean he's been with Cindy…I can't remember her last name."

"Cindy?" she said, in thought.

"Yeah, the one that has the reputation." I really didn't know who the girl was, but I'd heard that she had been with the football team, and many other guys as well, so I wasn't really lying.

"Oh, that Cindy."

"Yes, that Cindy," I said, and she was quiet for a moment, obviously unhappy. "I wouldn't cheat on you if you were my girlfriend."

She looked around and rolled her eyes. "You're really forward, aren't you—I mean we hardly know each other and—"

"And I've wanted to kiss you since the first day I saw you in the Business Math class. Now tell me—did you like it?"

She looked at me again and shook her head in disbelief. "You seem shy one minute and the next you're trying to kiss me."

"You gave me permission."

"Only the first time."

"I tried to take it back."

"Yes, is that something you use with all the girls? Your date at the dance was very attractive," she said, smiling.

"No, I've never taken a kiss back before," I said with a straight face, which caused her to laugh. "And my date was no one special."

"Neither am I."

"Yes you are—you are very special."

"Oh, and how is that?"

"You are like a ray of sunshine—and when I'm around you I feel good…elated."

"Oh, Paul—don't say those things."

"Okay, let's get back to my question."

"What was that?"

"Did you like the kiss?"

She looked at me again for a long time and then started laughing a little. It seemed from her laugh that she was trying to lighten the conversation, because I sounded serious when I said she was special. "Yes, Paul, I liked it. You're cute and you kiss well, but I have a boyfriend. Thanks for the cat."

"Okay, I'm leaving," I said. "But let me know when he needs to be neutered and I'll take you to the pound."

"That's okay, my Mom will take me."

That Saturday afternoon, I had to work on a paper I was writing for my American History class, so I was home all day. My mother made lunch, and as I sat at the table, I suggested that we find a church to go to. This came as no small surprise to my parents. My father was reading the paper and he put it down.

"When you were twelve you asked us if we really believed it all, and when we said we weren't sure, you declared that you would never go to church again—so has something happened?"

"Yeah, I changed my mind," I said, and of course the reason was because Mrs. Sanderson had asked me about it, and I wanted to be able to tell her that I was a churchgoer the next time I saw her, in the hope that she would like me more and my chances with Mary would increase.

"Well, we are going to church tomorrow for the first time, but I didn't mention it to you because of what you told us before."

"Okay, let me know when I need to be ready."

Just then my father smiled a knowing smile. "Is that girl you keep mentioning, Mary—is she religious?"

"I'm not sure," I lied. "She might be," I added, trying to diminish his victory in discovering my true motive.

"So you might just get a little religious, also?"

"Oh, William, don't look for ulterior motives—let's be thankful that Paul wants to go," my mother admonished.

Gordon picked me up after church on Sunday afternoon, and we began cruising Seawall Boulevard. The seventeen-foot-high seawall had been built after a storm destroyed most of the city in 1900 and killed as many as 12,000 people. Gordon was in a great mood as we drove along, and he put in a new eight-track tape he had recently purchased. I had just told him about seeing Mary the previous day.

"Yeah, that was pretty cool how you got her to kiss you, but it sounds like she made it clear that she wasn't interested," Gordon said, as we drove past the Galvez Hotel.

"But she said I was cute and she liked the kiss," I countered.

"Puppy dogs and kittens are cute," Gordon said. "By the way, we need to take your car from now on when we go out. Debbie is afraid those guys will chase us again."

I was quiet and Gordon looked over at me. "We have a date with them next Friday, remember?"

"Yes, I remember," I said in a low voice.

"Oh, come on, Welles, Mary is still just a fantasy."

We were heading east when Gordon spotted the blue Ford racing up towards us from the rear. "It's them," he shouted and I looked back and recognized Randy and Carl as they sped up to Gordon's car. He accelerated and we were getting away as Gordon slalomed between cars, but there was too much traffic to get past all of it, and the Ford pulled up next to Gordon in the left lane.

"I'll give you the money back," Gordon shouted, and I pulled out my wallet and some bills, but they ignored us and pulled ahead of us, which they could do because there was a car in front of Gordon and he couldn't go any faster. Then they swerved towards us and Gordon also swerved and soon we were driving on the sidewalk. Gordon recovered and we got back into the lane and didn't see them for a few moments. We were almost to Cherry Hill and then suddenly the Ford appeared in back of us, moving very fast. "Those guys are crazy," Gordon said, cussing at them. He sped up, but there were two cars blocking us and soon the Ford was riding beside us again, pushing us to the sidewalk again. The GTO hit a trash can with the right front fender, but Gordon recovered and we drove back on the street.

The Ford went on ahead of us, and as we pulled out it slowed down, evidently trying to get in back of us for another hit, and the slower we drove, the slower they drove. We were now at the end of the island and there were no cars around us.

"Let's get out of here—let's get off the Boulevard," I said.

"If I turn around they'll follow us and slam us again. They won't give up until they've wrecked my car!" Gordon shouted.

"If they want to play chicken, I may as well quit backing down if I'm going to get wrecked anyway."

"What do you mean?"

"I mean, two can play at this game, and I'm not chickening out anymore."

"Are you nuts? You're catching up with them. Let's turn around."

"That won't work. You have to stand up to the bully and punch him in the nose," he said, and his face stiffened with determination. This time as he approached the Ford, he swerved into their lane before they had a chance to swerve into ours. We were heading east and the seawall was to our right. Cherry Hill was unusual because one could drive on the slanting paved area that ran parallel to the Boulevard and at the top it leveled out again. That hill was to our left and to avoid us as we swerved towards it, the Ford went up the slanting side but it was also still skidding sideways.

"Well, look who's chicken now!" Gordon said triumphantly. The Ford still seemed to be out of control, and it careened from one side to the other and then came back down from the hill. I thought at that point the driver would pull out of the skid, but he seemed to make the mistake of turning away from the skid instead of turning into the skid. This caused the car to spin around. Gordon was driving and he couldn't see the car as well as I could, but he could see that it was coming down towards the Boulevard.

"Are they coming after us again?" Gordon asked, but just as the words left his mouth, the Ford continued in an uncontrolled spin and then went over the seawall and crashed into the sand. We were still moving and soon we couldn't see it anymore.

"Man, they really ate it. Did you see that?" I asked.

"Yeah, they're probably all right, but we better go back and help them," Gordon said, and he turned the car around and we headed back in their direction, but just as we accelerated from the U-turn, we could see a ball of fire coming from where the car was. We kept driving towards it and soon we could see that it was their car that was burning, and then there was a second explosion, and a larger ball of fire came from the car. It burned brightly with yellow and orange flames and billows of black smoke were rising from it as we drove past it.

"I can't believe it! You need to pull over," I said.

"I'm not pulling over until we get away from here. I didn't see any other cars around but we need to get away."

Gordon drove carefully until we got to 27th Street and then he turned to the right off the Boulevard until we reached Menard Park. We pulled over there, and he opened the door and threw up.

"You shouldn't have swerved towards them," I said.

"Shut up, Welles."

"I wonder if they're dead—they're probably dead," I said, rubbing my eyes and finding it hard to believe that what had just happened was real.

Gordon took some deep breaths and stopped heaving. Then he closed the door and looked at me. "You know they're dead, and you can't tell anyone about this. You have to swear to me that you won't breathe a word."

"Okay, Gordon, I won't."

We drove in silence and when we were almost to my house, something occurred to me. "Let me off before you get to my house. I'm thinking I'll tell my parents that I was with someone else—just in case."

"Okay."

"And I won't say anything, but if someone did see you, and they saw me with you, I wouldn't be able to deny that."

"Paul, I said tell no one and you swore you wouldn't."

"Yeah, well, this just happened and I've had to think about it. I won't tell anyone, but if we were seen it would be useless for me to deny it. That's all I'm saying."

"Okay—I don't think anyone saw us. There were no cars around."

"I know. I looked around also, and no one was parked up on Cherry Hill. Okay, let me out here and I'll walk the rest of the way."

I got in the house and went straight to my room, and my head was still spinning with what had happened. Later my mother called me for dinner and I told her I wasn't hungry. I wondered if those men could have survived the crash, and I finally went downstairs and found some food in the kitchen left over from dinner. My parents were watching the news on TV and I took some of the food out on a tray and sat with them. I stopped eating when I heard the announcer.

Two men were killed today when their car ran off the seawall and burst into flames. They had apparently been drinking heavily because the bartender at Duffy's Bar and Grill remembers them because they were talking about how fast their car was. He stopped serving them when he realized they were getting too drunk to drive, and he said they became irate and left.

So they were dead. It felt as if someone had punched me in the stomach as I tried to absorb the reality of it. Of course I thought they were dead when I saw the fire, but this...this was the confirmation, and I was feeling dizzy all of the sudden, and I felt nauseous, and then I started hyperventilating and I couldn't catch my breath. My mother ran over to me with a terrified look on her face, with my father behind her. She unbuttoned the top of my shirt.

"Paul, what's wrong?"

"I don't know," I said.

"Calm your breathing. Control it, don't let it control you," she said.

I made an effort to slow my breathing down, and then I started coughing. Then I let out another deep breath and it appeared to normalize.

"Should we call the doctor?" my father asked. My mother had been a nurse, so he looked to her for medical advice whenever we were sick.

"Well, his breathing is normal now. How do you feel?" my mother asked.

"I'm okay, but I feel nauseous," I answered.

"Let's get you to bed," my mother suggested. "I'll call the doctor if it persists."

I walked upstairs with my mother holding my arm, thinking about what the news announcer had said. They were drunk—that's probably why they kept trying to slam us, even when we offered them the money, and maybe why they didn't control their car better. But how much trouble could we be in? Was Gordon at fault for swerving into them? They had been trying to kill us, so what choice did we have? Wasn't it self-defense? Then I remembered a show I'd seen where someone was charged with manslaughter because the driver was negligent and a person in the car he hit died. I wondered how serious it would be if someone did see us. The thought made me start to breath heavily again. "No, control it," my mother said, with uncharacteristic authority in her voice. "You must control it," she said loudly, and she shook me. I got my breathing under control again as my father ascended the stairs.

We walked into my huge bedroom and I sat down on the four-poster bed. My mother gave me an aspirin for the headache and left the room briefly to get our thermometer and I closed my eyes. Soon she was back and she put it in my mouth. When she pulled it out, she seemed concerned. My father was also in the room. "Is it high?" he asked.

"No, it's low…too low," she said. "Open your mouth and stick out your tongue."

I did so and she looked at me, curiously. "Do you have a cut anywhere—even a small one?"

"No, I don't think so. Why?"

"Because a low temperature can be caused by an infection."

"What else can cause it?" my father asked.

"Going into shock, but I don't see any reason Paul would have that problem. It can also be connected with liver failure or kidney failure. I want you to stay as still as you can and try to rest, and I'll check it again in the morning."

So it was shock—that was probably the reason I felt so bad. I tried to get my mind off it but I kept seeing that car exploding over and over again in my mind. I wondered how long it might take for someone to come forward if they saw what happened. I had a vision of the police coming and arresting me at school, and how embarrassing that would be. Mary would really like me then! I could go to the police now and protect myself from being part of this—I thought it was called being an accessory—but I had promised Gordon, and I knew that it would be terrible for him if I did. No, I would not be a traitor to my friend. I'd stay quiet and hope for the best.

That night I had nightmares about the two men. My mind kept replaying when they chased us and broke the window, and then when they skidded off the seawall. I would wake up thinking the whole thing was a bad dream, but then I'd realize that it did happen. It was late when I woke up—later in the morning I was finally able to sleep. I felt better, but I had a headache. I didn't want to go to school, or do anything else.

When my mother asked me, I said I was feeling better but I did feign being sicker than I was. She asked if I wanted to see a doctor, and I told her no, because I was feeling better but thought I just needed rest. The next day I did the same thing, and that evening I talked to Gordon on the phone. He told me no one had mentioned the "thing," which became our code word for the crash, so I was beginning to feel better about it—at least about not getting caught. I was rarely sick and generally went to school even if I was not feeling perfect, so my mother did not question it when I told her I wanted to say home on the second day. I told her I was almost well, but was not quite up to going.

CHAPTER 8

For that two-day period I tried to get the crash out of my mind. I read some books from my father's library, and by the end of the second day, I was finally able to stop constantly thinking about it. I also slept a lot, and that seemed to help. I had to keep my mind off it, and just as my mother told me to control my breathing, I had to control what I thought about. And when it did manage to stay in my thoughts, I constantly reminded myself that they were trying to kill us and they were drunk and it was only an accident. Also, I could not change anything—I had to accept what had happened and move on in life.

I was in bed on Tuesday afternoon when my mother knocked on my bedroom door.

"Come in."

"You have some visitors," she said.

"Visitors? It's not Gordon, is it?"

"No, two young ladies. Mary Sanderson and Ruth Hart."

"Really?" I said. "Well give me a minute and I'll come downstairs." I jumped out of bed and ran into the bathroom to comb my hair. I kept fussing with it until I realized it was taking too much time, so I put on my robe and walked downstairs. When I reached the parlor they both looked up at me.

"Hi, Paul," Mary said.

"Well, hi, Mary and Ruth. What a wonderful surprise."

"I heard you were sick and I made notes from the class we have and I've copied them for you. I thought that might help you catch up," Mary said, handing them to me.

"Oh, that's very nice," I said, still a little stunned about them being there. My mother walked out of the room and I sat down in a chair across from the couch they were sitting on.

"I didn't know you lived in this historic house," Mary said. "I've walked past this place so many times—it's an incredible house."

"We inherited it from my aunt," I said.

"Paul, can we pray for you to get well—would that bother you?" Ruth asked.

"Pray for me? Why of course, that would be fine. Should we close our eyes then?" I asked.

"I don't know if it matters," Ruth said.

"You can if you want to—however you feel led," Mary added.

I closed my eyes and Ruth started praying. "Father, in the name of Jesus Christ we ask you to heal Paul. And more than that, we ask that you would reveal yourself to him and bless him," Ruth said. After a few seconds, when I realized that the prayer was over, I looked up.

"Thank you, that was a nice prayer. But, Mary, to copy all your notes was so much work…"

"I'm happy to do it. I wanted to repay the favor."

"The favor? Oh, you mean the cat—well, you already did that."

"But you took it back," Mary said, smiling as Ruth looked on, perplexed. "It's a silly joke," she added, looking at Ruth.

"Then I guess you did owe me—okay, kitten paid in full," I said, teasingly.

At that point my mother walked back in. "May I get you girls something? We have an upside down cake I made yesterday."

"Oh, thank you, but we can't stay, Mrs. Welles. We just wanted to drop the notes off for Paul."

"Well, that is very nice of you," my mother said. Just then my father walked out of his study, and I thought I could tell by the way he was walking that he had been drinking a little.

"Oh, I didn't know we had company," he said jovially.

"Yes, dear, this is Mary Sanderson and this is Ruth Hart."

"It's a pleasure to meet both of you," he said, and he shook their hands. "I'm Dr. Welles."

"Nice to meet you, Dr. Welles," Mary said.

"Yes, nice to meet you. Do you have a practice at the university medical center?" Ruth asked.

"He's not that kind of doctor. He can't even tie a decent bandage. My mother's the medical help in the family—she used to be a nurse," I said.

"Paul! Dr. Welles is a history professor," my mother said, not liking my sarcastic comment.

"Oh, that's so impressive. History is one of my favorite subjects," Ruth said.

"Mrs. Welles, my mother is a nurse at John Sealy Hospital. I'm sure she'd love to meet you," Mary said.

"I'd like that," my mother responded.

Then my father looked at Mary again, as if he now recognized her in some way. "Oh, you must be *that* Mary—the one Paul keeps talking about." My mother glared at him and I was embarrassed. "Oh, I'm sorry, I let the cat out of the bag—or is it the kitten—didn't you buy her a kitten?"

I ignored him, and Mary said nothing, but as they stood up to leave, she gave me a huge smile, and I had a hard time disconnecting from her eyes. At first I thought it meant that she was beginning to like me, but I couldn't be certain. That was the problem of liking a girl who was always so nice to everyone—you couldn't tell. After they left, my mother touched my forehead and looked at my eyes. "Are you all right now—you look so much better?"

"Yes, I think I'm well," I said.

"Oh, those girls were so nice. I can see why you like Mary—she seems like such a special girl—but so does Ruth. And they are both so sweet and pretty."

"Yes, they were very personable," my father said. "And I did bandage you when you were eleven and you fell off your bicycle."

"And Mum had to redo it when she saw what you did."

My father looked at my mother. "You never told me that."

"You never asked."

"Dad, you embarrassed me in front of her."

"I'm sorry, son. When I realized she was the girl, it just came out."

"And you were rude to your father," my mother said.

"I was just joking about the bandage thing," I protested.

"The tone was unpleasant," she admonished.

"Ann, I wasn't offended," my father said.

"Nevertheless, Paul needs to apologize, and it did offend *me*," she added.

"I'm sorry, I was just trying to be funny. But I realize it could have been taken the wrong way."

"Why can't you be...nicer to her?" Gordon asked, as we drove towards Debbie's house.

"I am nice to her," I said.

"She told Debbie that even when you kiss her, you seem...I think she said, distant." He was quiet for about a moment. "I mean she is a really pretty girl. Don't you like kissing her?"

"Yes, she is pretty and I like kissing her but—"

"But she's not Mary, is that it?"

"Look, Gordon, I'm dating Cheryl so you can see Debbie—so don't push it."

"Okay, okay. But maybe you could kiss her with more passion."

"More passion?"

"Yeah, like you grab her and kiss her like your heart's on fire. You need to burn with passion."

"Oh, give me a break."

I drove into Debbie's driveway and Gordon got out of the car. "Her parents are starting to really like me—but I have to talk to them a little to make her happy—I can't rush out. And she was pretty upset after that wild ride, but I think things are okay now. Anyway, this may take a while, so please be patient."

"How can I when I'm burning with passion?"

"Good point. I'll soon return."

Gordon wasn't kidding about taking a while, and as I waited I thought about Cheryl. It was true that I had my heart set on Mary, but I did like Cheryl. And if I stopped seeing her, it would ruin things for Gordon and Debbie. Anyway, the chances of really winning Mary seemed unlikely I thought, as they finally came out of the front door. We then drove to Cheryl's house and picked her up. We were going to a movie at the Martini Theater. As we drove, Debbie leaned forward to ask me a question.

"Gordon says we can take his car now because those guys won't bother you anymore. Is that true?"

I was surprised at the question, and took a moment to answer. "Yes, there are no more problems with them anymore, everything is fine now. They won't bother us again."

"Do you promise?" Debbie asked.

"Yes, I promise," I said.

"Okay, then, I guess we can go in the GTO now."

"Great," Gordon said, and he pulled Debbie back to the seat and kissed her, but she pulled away.

"No, but you have to drive slower from now on. Your driving has always scared me. Drive like Paul, he's more careful."

"Okay, I'll drive like the tortoise in the front seat, old, slow Paul," he said in a creaky voice, imitating an old man.

"Good, that's what I want, and so does Cheryl."

"But he does drive fast sometimes—I'm teaching him," Gordon added.

"Oh, no," Cheryl said.

"Well, he has to learn—I mean what if someone else was chasing us?" Gordon said, and then realized what a mistake he had made. "I mean, no one will be chasing us again. I shouldn't have said that. I didn't mean that."

"Is there someone else who might chase us?" Debbie said, suddenly concerned.

"No, no, of course not. I was just—"

"Paul, are other people chasing you?" Debbie asked, moving forward in her seat.

"No, there's no one," I answered.

"Then why did Gordon say that?"

"He spoke without using his brain. I promise you no one else is chasing us and there is nothing to worry about—honestly. Ignore Dumbo," I said.

She then looked over at Gordon again and he looked back at her. "That's it—brainless talking," Gordon agreed. "And I'm really sorry."

We watched *To Sir with Love*, or at least we sort of watched it as we were in the back of the balcony doing as much making out as we were watching the movie. "I like you more than any boy I've ever known," Cheryl whispered in my ear. I was not certain how to respond. She kissed me on the neck and then spoke again. "Do you like me that way?"

"I like you," I said, not able to commit to more than that. "I really like you," I added, but I could tell she was not happy with my response—I think she wanted me to say the same thing she said to me.

"Do you want to go steady?" Cheryl asked me as she kissed my ear and neck again.

I didn't answer for a while, and was not sure what to say. I had not given up on Mary, but I didn't want to upset her, but I was also surprised that she was asking me. "Well?" she said, and I knew I couldn't avoid answering.

"We haven't known each other that long," I said. "Let's give it some time." I knew she didn't like the answer, but she seemed to accept it.

"Okay," she finally said, and then she kissed me on the lips so strongly that the only thing I could think of was Gordon talking about kissing with passion. So I kissed her back the same way, and she seemed happy about that. I wondered if I was being a hypocrite—I was really confused and not sure what to do, because my body loved the kiss, but my mind was just not into it. Instead I couldn't help comparing it to when I kissed Mary. That kiss seemed almost electric to me—there was something so special about it. As I was thinking about it, Cheryl kissed me hard again, and I returned it, as convincingly as possible. I felt convicted that I was using her and was not certain what to do.

One day at school that week, I left the class that I had with Mary, and we walked down the hall together, talking about the assignment we had been given. I looked up and suddenly saw Jim Mahoney. Mary smiled at him as we passed, but he stared at me. When she turned to go into her next class, I kept walking to mine, and I was almost there when Jim ran up to me.

"You're dead meat," he said.

"What are you talking about?"

"You bought Mary a cat. Someone at the pound told me, and I told you to stay away from her," he said, doubling his fist up and looking around to see if anyone was watching. A teacher was walking down the hall, so he unclenched it.

"She's just a friend—do you allow her to have friends?" I said, getting a little braver since I saw the teacher was there. Then I wondered what he would have done if he knew I'd kissed her and I felt a lump in my throat. The teacher continued down the hallway and he clenched his fist again and held it up to my face.

"I'm gonna teach you a lesson, Welles. You don't mess with my girl!" he said, raising his voice as he spoke. His face was very red and he was extremely angry and he held his fist back and acted as if he would punch me in the face. I backed up and he looked around and saw some other students walking by, and put down his arm. "Your time is coming, Slime," he said, adding some other names that were worse as he walked away from me.

Yes, I was afraid, but there wasn't much I could do about it. I hurried to my next class and got in just before the bell rang. A girl sitting next to me looked at me and seemed startled, so I guess my face showed how I felt. "Are you okay?" she asked.

"Oh, yeah—fine, I was just running late and had to hurry," I said.

At lunch, Gordon asked me why I was so sullen. I didn't want to tell him, but he kept pushing. "It's something to do with Mary, isn't it?"

I let out a breath with a sigh. "Yes, Gordon, you're right."

"I normally am. I'm learning to read you pretty well, I think."

"Yeah, and you can probably read my mind, also," I said, angrily.

"What is that supposed to mean?"

"It means you're ticking me off with your know-it-all attitude."

He was quiet for a few minutes as we ate lunch. I looked over and could see Mahoney at the jock table, but he couldn't see me. I wondered when I would run into him again.

"I'm sorry, Paul. You're right," Gordon said.

"Yeah, that's cool. The problem is Mahoney."

"How bad is it? What did he do?"

I hesitated for a moment. "He threatened me. I guess he's going to do a number on me when he gets a chance."

"Because of Mary?"

"You got it. He knows I bought her a cat."

"But he doesn't know you kissed her, does he?"

"Gordon, keep your voice down. If he knew that I'd probably be dead by now."

"So what did you say when he threatened you?"

"I said we were just friends—and that is the truth."

"Hey, I didn't say it wasn't the truth. But I think you need to tell him you're sorry and you won't see her again. That's about the only way you may get out of this."

"Oh, grovel before him, is that it? No way, man."

"I'm just trying to help—it's your neck."

The next Saturday morning my parents went to Houston to tour a museum. They wanted me to go, but I told them I had too much homework. That was actually true, because after the crash I had a hard time concentrating and I was getting behind in school. They had just left, and it was about 9 a.m. when the doorbell rang. I was still in my bedroom, in pajamas, so I put on a robe and went downstairs. The front door was huge and it had stained glass in it, but the glass was too high to see out of. I thought of what a mistake that design was as I opened it. Mary was there. Her eyes looked a little red and she seemed very worried. I wondered what catastrophe might have occurred as I invited her in.

"Oh, I don't need to come in. I was going to call, but your number isn't in the book yet," she said, evidently out of breath because she had rushed over to our house.

I looked at her for a moment, and then she held her hand out and steadied it on my arm. "It's Freddy. He's in the tree and I can't get him out. Mom is working so I called Jim, but his father said he was gone and he didn't know when he'd return. I hate to ask you, but would you help?"

I had to keep myself from laughing, since the incident seemed so minor to me, but it was obviously very disturbing to her. A little too disturbing, I thought, as I answered. "Yes, of course. But please come in because it will take a moment for me to change."

For the first time she seemed to realize that I was still in my pajamas and she walked in and sat down on the red velvet covered bench that was next to the front door. "You must think I live in my pajamas, because whenever you visit, I'm in them," I said jokingly. But she was too upset to appreciate any humor, so I hurried upstairs and changed as quickly as I could.

As I walked downstairs I watched her sitting there, and I could tell she was fretting. "It will be all right, Mary. I'll get him down. I think I saw a ladder in the garage and we can get that."

"So you're not sure you have one?" she asked.

"No, I know there is one, I'm just not sure of the condition. We inherited the house from my aunt, and some of her stuff doesn't work."

"Oh, I see," she said, as she followed me outside. We walked to the back of the property to the four-car garage with an apartment above it. The apartment had been for live-in help, but now it was rundown. I opened a garage and found a wooden ladder. It was somewhat rickety, but it was the only one there.

"Do you think this is tall enough?" I asked Mary.

"Yes—I mean it should get you to a large branch, if you don't mind climbing the tree from that point."

"Okay, let's take this old blanket and put in on the roof of my car," I said, pointing to a dusty blanket that was on a shelf in the garage. I carried it to my car and we put it on the roof. Then I put the ladder on the roof and tied it down with some rope that was in the garage.

"Do you think this will hold it?" Mary asked.

"I'm not sure, but it's pretty heavy to carry, so let's try it. Hold on to the rope on your side and I'll hold on to mine when I can, and I'll drive slowly."

When we got to her apartment, I could see Freddy in a tree in the front, and he was meowing louder than I thought a kitten could. I put the ladder against the tree and was able to pull myself up on a strong branch. Then I reached up to get him, but he was scared and wouldn't come to me. "Come on, kitty," I said several times, but he was just out of my reach and appeared to have no intention of moving towards me. Then I heard Mary praying.

"Oh, God, please show Freddy that Paul is trying to help him! Please move him towards Paul. Oh, please God, in Jesus' name."

The prayer sounded a little desperate to me, but suddenly Freddie walked over to me on the thin branch he was on, and I picked him up and moved with him down the large branch to the ladder. When I got to the ladder, I began to walk down the rail, but Mary climbed it and took the cat before I could descend. When she did, the ladder leaned over, and as soon as she was off it, it fell to the side, with me on it. I hit the ground pretty hard and it stunned me.

Mary ran over to me and started crying and held me by the shoulders. I regained full consciousness but was tempted to play "possum" a little longer since she was so concerned and I wondered if she might start mouth-to-mouth resuscitation. I gave in when I realized how upset she was. I could feel her trembling, so I opened my eyes and smiled at her.

"Oh, are you okay?" she said, with great relief.

"I think I'm okay." I got up slowly. My right arm was scratched and bruised and it ached, and my jeans were torn a little on the right side. When she saw the blood she got upset again. "Don't worry, it's not bad."

"We have to get you inside to wash it. You can get an infection," she said very seriously.

"Okay, let's go inside—but I can walk okay. You might want to get your cat in before he decides to climb again."

She looked around, a little surprised that she had forgotten him. I was happy that she had, for I was beginning to wonder who she cared for the most. She took the cat in and I followed. We walked into the bathroom and she started washing my wounds.

"I just feel terrible that I caused this," she said.

"You didn't—it was just an accident. That ladder has seen better days."

"No, I did. I shouldn't have tried to climb it when you were on it. I was too anxious to get Freddie."

"Okay, so you owe me again—does that mean I get another kiss?" I said.

She was quiet for just a moment, and then she answered, ignoring my question.

"Have you eaten breakfast?"

"No."

"Then I will make you a dream breakfast. Eggs, bacon, pancakes...and—what else would you want?"

I puckered my lips at her, and she smiled for the first time that morning. "I mean to eat, silly."

"What you said sounds fine, but you don't owe me anything."

"But I want to," she insisted.

"Okay."

We walked into the living room, and I sat on a couch there, and I could see the kitchen from that vantage point. She walked into the kitchen and began to pull out some pans. "Are you sure I can't help?" I asked.

"Of course not."

I looked out of the window and saw the ladder was still where it had fallen, which was partly over the curb on the street, right in back of my car. "I'll be back in a minute—I need to move the ladder."

"Oh, I can help."

"It's okay, I can do it," I assured her, and got up and walked outside. The kitchen window was over the sink and she could see me from there, but she was busy cooking and not looking in that direction. I walked over to the ladder and bent down to pick it up. As I was rising with the ladder in both hands, something hit me in the back of neck that felt like a sledge hammer and I collapsed on the sidewalk, my head hitting the ladder as I went down. As I tried to get up I got a kick in the face that pushed me over on my side, and I looked up into Jim Mahoney's face.

"Get up!" he commanded, but as I tried to, he kicked me again, with a glancing blow to my ribs. This time I rolled to get away from him and finally was able to stand up. I held my fists up, but I was woozy from his blows and my fall, and he easily landed a punch to my right eye, and then one that hit my left eyebrow, and caused it to bleed. In fact, the blood kept spurting out and it was blinding me. I wiped it from my eyes and then he ran at me like a bull and knocked me down. He started to kick at me again, but stopped because we both heard screaming and turned towards the apartment.

It was Mary and her first scream was unintelligible, but the second one rang out as "Stop hitting him." Then she was suddenly bending down next to me. "What have you done!" she said to Mahoney, who now was trying to play innocent.

"I told him to leave you alone—I was just trying to protect you. I heard you called and needed help with your cat."

"Oh...! Are you all right?" Mary said, holding me. She glanced angrily at Jim and said, "I asked him for help with Freddie—Okay?"

"Yeah, well, I'm sorry. I didn't mean to hurt him."

Mary looked up him at again and was quiet for a second. "I saw you—you were brutal. You might have killed him if I hadn't come out. I never want to see you again!"

"What? We have a date tonight," Jim protested.

"Not anymore," she said, as she tried to help me up. Jim walked over and acted as if he would help, also. He tried to take my arm, but I moved it away from him.

"I meant what I said—it's over between us. I'm so sorry, Paul."

Mahoney didn't seem to be able to take no for an answer, and he lingered there for a while but didn't say anything.

"I need to take you to the hospital," Mary said, and we walked over to my car. "Can you drive?"

"I'll take him," Jim offered, and then Mary really got angry—so angry that it surprised me.

"No you won't. Look what you've done to him! Now get out of here, and I mean it!"

Jim was also surprised, but Mary's resoluteness was very clear. It was the end of that relationship, and as much as I was hurting, I was also thinking that I had a pretty good chance with her now.

He was quiet for a while, looking down as if he wasn't certain what to say. Then he got in his car and took off in a huff, his tires squealing as he accelerated.

"Oh, I'm so sorry this happened," Mary said, bursting into tears.

"It's okay, Mary."

"But you've got to hate me after all this, and I don't blame you."

"Mary, I don't hate you, it was Jim who hit me."

"Yes, but...well, we better get you to the hospital."

126

"I think I'll be all right."

"But…" she began just as her mother drove up.

"Oh, thank God, Mom's back from work."

Mrs. Sanderson got out and gasped when she saw me. "What happened, Paul?"

"I fell out of a tree."

"And then Jim beat him up," Mary added.

"Jim beat you up?" Mrs. Sanderson said, perplexed. "Come inside so we can clean you up."

"Mom, do you think he needs to go to the hospital?"

"I don't know yet. Let's get him inside first."

As we walked in Mrs. Sanderson looked at me curiously. "Why would Jim want to hurt you?" she asked. I was about to answer when Mary spoke.

"He was jealous, Mom." And then she explained the whole thing with Freddy and how she had asked me over to rescue him as she and her mother helped me into the bathroom, where I sat on the toilet seat. There was a mirror nearby and I picked it up to look at the damage.

"Well, I can see why he might be jealous—you're a handsome boy," Mrs. Sanderson said.

"You mean I was?" I said, putting the mirror down, and Mrs. Sanderson smiled at my silly joke, but Mary was still upset.

Mrs. Sanderson gave me some aspirin and cleaned me up and applied some iodine, which burned like fire, but I tried not to react—I didn't want to seem like a wimp in front of Mary. After she was finished she said she wanted me to go to the hospital, but I declined. "I really just want to go home," I said.

"Do you feel well enough to drive?" she asked.

"Yes, I can manage."

"But you never even had breakfast, and your parents will be gone all day."

"I know, but that's okay. I'll be okay, I just want to lie down."

"Oh, Mom, can I go with him? I promised him breakfast and I can take care of him until his parents come home. It's the least I can do."

Mrs. Sanderson looked at her daughter for a moment, in thought. Before she could answer, Mary spoke again. "He only lives five blocks away—it's that huge historic house, remember?"

"Oh, yes, I remember," Mrs. Sanderson said, looking at me warily.

"Can I cook at your house? Would your parents mind? I can bring everything," Mary asked.

"They wouldn't mind, but we have plenty of food there—no need to bring anything."

"Okay, I'll drive over with you and drop you off. But you have cheerleading practice at two o'clock, so you need to be home by one-thirty," Mrs. Sanderson added, looking at me as if she was trying to determine if I was trustworthy.

Mrs. Sanderson came into the house with Mary and was obviously impressed with it. I told them I was going to lie down on a daybed in the parlor, and then she and Mary went into the kitchen. It was a very large kitchen, because when the house was built many people with such homes had help for cooking and cleaning, and I heard Mrs. Sanderson joke with Mary that it must be the chef's day off. They found a tray table in the large pantry area and Mary brought it out to me. Her mother left after a few minutes, and I lay back, and realized that much of my body was aching. I had been so caught up with the idea of Mary coming over to help me, that I had almost forgotten the pain—but now I was really feeling it.

Mary walked in with some orange juice. "I'll have scrambled eggs ready in a minute, but I didn't see any pancake mix."

"Oh, I think my mother makes it from scratch. But I just want some toast—I don't need pancakes."

"Are you sure that's all you want?"

"Yes, but could you turn on the TV?"

"Of course." Mary turned it on and a show called "Hollywood Squares" came on, a game show where different celebrities answer questions in a comical way. Barbara Eden was answering a question about dating.

"Wow, she is so beautiful. She has the perfect figure and the perfect face," Mary said.

"I like yours better," I said, and it made her kind of blush.

"I'll be back," she said, exiting into the kitchen.

After eating, I fell asleep in front of the TV set, and was suddenly awakened by a touch on my shoulder from Mary. She must have turned the TV off. I had been dreaming and it took me a minute to remember what had happened.

"I'm going now—I think you just need to rest," she said. "Do you want to go to your bedroom? Do you need help up the stairs?"

"No, I'm okay. I can go up myself," I said, drowsily.

"I'll check on you later. Do you know when your parents are coming home?"

"No, I'm not sure when."

"Well, call my number if you need anything. My mother is there, and she can help you, and I'll be back from cheerleading practice around 4:30."

"Okay, thank you for taking such good care of me."

"It's the least I can do. I'm so sorry for what happened," she said, and then she left.

I lay there wanting to sleep more, but the pain was great, and the aspirin had worn off. I found some more in the medicine cabinet in a downstairs bathroom, and then I turned the TV on again and watched a rerun of a show about doctors called "Ben Casey." Ben was bawling out some doctor for being greedy, when my parents opened the door. My mother dropped her purse when she saw me, and I explained to them that I fell off the ladder.

My mother insisted that I go to bed. After a few minutes she came into the room and sat down next to me. "It is possible that you have some broken bones, so if you have continuous pain tomorrow, we may want to get an x-ray."

"Mrs. Sanderson mentioned that also, but I didn't want to go to the hospital."

"So who beat you up?"

"What? I said I fell—that's what happened."

"Paul, I was a nurse and I took care of a lot of people, and I know when someone's wounds are from a fight—and yours are. Now tell me the truth."

"I did tell you the truth—I did fall from the ladder, but after that I got into a fight. Or I guess it wasn't much of a fight—I was still hurting from the fall, and he rabbit-punched me when I wasn't looking and it all went down from there."

"And why would anyone want to hurt you?" she asked, but she answered her own question before I could answer. "Oh, it's over Mary. Her boyfriend did it, didn't he?"

I closed my eyes for a moment. "Yes, you figured it out."

"You must really like that girl," she said, and she took my head in both of her hands and started moving it back and forth. "Does it hurt when I do that?"

"No, not too much."

"Now try to move it back and forth yourself—does it hurt when you do that?"

"Yes, it hurts."

"Then don't do that," she said, smiling.

I looked at her quizzically.

"It's an old nurse's joke," she explained.

"They must have a weird sense of humor in Australia," I said, and then the phone rang. She walked over and answered it, and came back to me.

"It's Gordon. I told him you were incapacitated, but…"

"I'll talk to him—I'm supposed to have a date tonight," I said, getting up.

"Wait here, I think the phone will reach," she said, and she brought it over to me.

"Hi, Gordon. I can't go tonight."

"But you have to, you have a date with Cheryl."

"Tell her I'm sorry. I was in an accident and I'm hurt badly."

"That's what your mother said. Did you wreck your car?"

"No, I fell out of a tree," I said, not wanting to tell him anymore.

"You fell out of a tree?"

"Yes—is that difficult to understand?"

"No, but what were you doing in a tree?"

"Gordon, I don't have time to go into this."

"If you're at home and can't go anywhere, why wouldn't you have time?"

"Oh, you are really a pain in the"—I looked up at my mother, then stopped for a moment and finished—"neck."

"Momma must still be there," he said.

"Okay, just tell me what you were doing in a tree—I'm sure Cheryl will want to know."

"I don't think so."

"Sure she will, she loves you. She can kiss it and make it better."

"Hey, man, I'm hurting and you're making fun of me."

"I'm sorry, Paul. But please tell me the story."

"Okay, I was pruning a tree for my mother."

"You mean this has nothing to do with Mary?"

"No."

"Just when I thought I was clairvoyant and I should join the secret order. Seriously though, I'm sorry to hear this. But are you sure you can't go? I'll drive real slow."

"Gordon, I gotta go."

"Okay, hope you feel better. I'm not sure what I'm going to do now about the date."

"I'm sure you'll think of something."

"How about if we come over to cheer you up? That way I could still say we were double-dating."

"Good-bye, Gordon."

"So, can we come?"

"No, let me suffer in peace," I said, and I hung up. My mother walked over to me and rearranged my pillow and fluffed it, but I knew she wanted to say something the way she was hovering over me.

"Paul, I know you're hurting, and I know you want to say whatever is expedient."

"Oh, you heard about the gardening?"

"Yes, I did, and I do not recommend lying. Remember, the little poem I taught you when you were young. 'Oh, what a tangled web we weave, when first we practice to deceive.'"

"Okay, Mum. You're right. I shouldn't have lied. But can I rest now?"

"Yes, of course," she said, and the phone rang again, and she answered it. I heard her say "Mary," and I started waving my arms. She looked over at me, and sighed. "Yes, he can talk to you," she said, and handed me the telephone.

"Hi, Paul, how are you feeling?"

"I'm doing okay, how are you?"

"Oh, Paul, I feel so terrible about this whole thing. I just hope you're not seriously hurt."

"Mum thinks I'm okay, and she used to be a nurse," I said, and my mother began to shake her head in disagreement, pursing her lips.

"We don't know yet, Paul," she said in a low voice.

"Oh, that's good," Mary said. "So how can I help now?"

"How about going out with me when I'm better?"

She hesitated before answering, and I was afraid the answer would be no. But I was wrong.

"Okay, where would you like to go?"

"Do you like miniature golf?"

"I don't know, I've never played it. Have you?"

"Oh, yeah," I lied. "And I can teach you. We can go to the place I saw in Stewart Beach."

"Yes, I've seen it. I would like to try it—it will be fun."

CHAPTER 9

I stayed home recovering for the next few days, and when I came back to school, I happened to see Mrs. Erickson in the hallway as I walked towards my locker. She stopped and looked at me for a moment, not saying anything but looking at the cuts on my face with concern.

"You're probably wondering what happened to me. I fell out of a tree."

"They ought to arrest that lout on assault charges," she said, and then she walked away.

So she knew, I thought, as I walked down the hallway. And throughout the day, I found out that everyone knew. Evidently Mahoney had been bragging about defeating me, although I didn't see what there was to brag about since he was so much bigger than I was. At lunchtime I sat down with Gordon, as usual, and the people at Mahoney's table keep pointing at me and laughing. Finally two of them walked over to our table. "Hey Welles, you make a good punching bag," one of them said.

"Guess you learned at least one thing at Ball High," the other one said.

"Yeah, and maybe Mahoney learned how to lose a girlfriend," I said, and they both looked back at Mahoney, who did not hear what I said.

"Maybe you didn't learn after all," the second one said, and they walked back to Mahoney's table and spoke to him, evidently telling him what I said, because he was looking over at me, snarling.

"Man, are you crazy? You want him to beat you up again?" Gordon said.

"I don't really care," I said, and went back to eating my lunch. Actually I was worried, and I wished I hadn't said anything, but I was so angry at them that I spoke without thinking first.

"Well, you better watch your back when you go out to the parking lot today," Gordon advised.

That evening my mother came up to my room, and asked how I was feeling. After I told her, she lingered and I knew she wanted to say something but she always seemed to take a long time to get to the point. "So, how was school today?" she finally said.

"Okay—but what do you really want to say? I know there is something."

"You'll probably get angry at me for this, but Mrs. Mahoney is on the board of the Galveston Historical Society, and she's been talking to me about doing some photographs of the house and registering it."

"You mean Jim's mother?"

"Yes."

"Okay, and so?"

"So I called her about this matter the day it happened, and I told her that I would be calling the police and pressing charges if her son touched you again."

"Oh, I see."

"And she called me tonight—just a little while ago, and said that you were provoking Jim and I should tell you to stop."

"Yeah, well, his two cronies came by at lunch and started gloating about him beating me up. So they started it."

"Did you say anything to them?"

"Yeah, but I don't want to go into it."

"Well, a word to the wise. Ignore any taunting and be the bigger man by not reacting to it."

"Okay, I will."

"And I hope you're not too angry at me for calling her."

"No—I'm not angry. You're just trying to protect me."

"I'm glad you see it that way."

She walked out of my room, and I thought of how glad I was that she did call his mother. I figured he might have beat me up again if she hadn't.

I called Mary several days later to set up a time for miniature golf on Saturday afternoon, and she asked me to come over for lunch before we played. That morning I spent a lot of time getting ready, wearing my new light blue jeans and a pale yellow shirt, and a tan belt, which was the way so many boys were dressing at that time. I'd resisted dressing like they did up to that time, because I took pride in not being like everyone else, but I'd overheard Mary saying she liked that combination.

Her mother had made roast beef sandwiches and before we ate, they bowed their heads to pray, but Mrs. Sanderson was quiet for a moment. "Paul, would you say grace for us?"

I was taken by surprise, but we prayed at home, so I said the normal prayer. "Thank you for what we are about to receive, amen."

"Thank you, Paul. But just so you know, we pray in Jesus' name."

"Oh, I'm sorry."

"It's quite all right."

I could tell that Mary didn't like what her mother was saying, but her mother was not to be dissuaded when she spoke.

"So how was the church you went to—did you like it?"

"Oh, yes. It was fine."

She asked me which one it was and I told her.

"Paul, I need to tell you that that particular church does not preach the salvation message," Mrs. Sanderson said.

"Oh, really?" I said, not certain what to say.

"Yes, Jesus said in John 3:3 that we must be 'born again' to enter the kingdom of heaven. But that church is…how do I say this?"

"Mom, do you have to?" Mary asked.

Her mother ignored her. "Paul, did you know that vaccinations against diseases often have some of the actual disease in them? They contain a killed or weakened part of the germ responsible for the disease and when the person receives the vaccine, the body reacts by making protective antibodies. The antibodies make the person immune to catching the actual disease."

"Yes, I remember that we studied that in biology. That's very interesting."

"Well, religion can be the same way. You can go to church and get a little of it, but that can stop you from getting the real thing."

"Oh, I see. So our church is like that. I'll have to tell my parents about that."

"Yes, to know Christ you must repent and ask him into your heart—but it's a full commitment."

"Mom…"

"No, that's good advice. I appreciate that, Mrs. Sanderson, and I will think about it."

"Well, if you have any questions just ask me—or ask Mary. She knows the Lord."

"Okay, I will, and thanks for lunch."

"Oh, it's not over yet. I baked some brownies with walnuts in them. But they're still in the oven, so why don't you and Mary sit in the living room and I'll call when they're ready."

We sat down, and I noticed a photo album on the table, and it was open. There were pictures of a male teenager but the photos were brown and faded. "Is that your father?" I asked.

"Yes, that's him when he was in high school."

"So are there more pictures of him in this album?"

"Yes, would you like to see them?"

"I would."

Mary turned the pages and on one page there was a picture of her father standing next to a jet. At the bottom of the photograph, someone had written "Lockheed F80 Shooting Star" and next to that someone else wrote "Fly a Shooting Star Like a Thunderbolt!"

"Is that the plane he flew?"

"Yes, that's the Shooting Star—funny how they give them these beautiful names and they're used for destruction. He was killed in Operation Thunderbolt in 1951. Fly a shooting star like a thunderbolt—it almost sounds poetic," she said, staring wistfully at the photograph. Then she turned the page. "Here he is with my mother at the beach, the summer before he left. See how handsome he was," she added, perking up a little.

"Yes, and he also looks like he was a very nice man."

"I don't remember him, I'm sorry to say. I was too young."

I turned the page and saw him several years younger, also in uniform. "He looks younger here. Was he always in the service?"

"No, but he was also a pilot in World War Two, and then got out, but a general he knew asked him to join again when the Korean War started, and he felt it was his duty. He said he felt like God had called him because he was gifted at what he did. He'd flown many missions in World War Two and was never shot down. But then he died in Korea—so I wonder if that was God's will."

"Here they are, just out of the oven, and they're hot, so be careful," Mrs. Sanderson said, delivering the brownies to the coffee table on a tray with two glasses of milk. We thanked her mother, and she walked out of the room for a while.

I thumbed through the photographs and saw some recent ones of Mary. In one of them, she was at a dance with another girl, who I thought I recognized. "That girl looks like someone I've seen at school. Is she a friend of yours?"

"Yes, she's my best friend."

"Oh, I thought Ruth was."

"That is Ruth, silly. She just has her hair down and curled and she has makeup on."

"Wow, what a difference. She looks very pretty."

"And I thought I'd never hear the end of it. But her parents forgave me and never mentioned it again."

"What do you mean? Why did they have to forgive you?"

"Because I put her up to it. I did her hair and her makeup, and lent her a dress and hardly anyone at the dance recognized her, but the boys were swarming around her."

"So what was the problem?"

"Well, her parents don't allow her to dance or wear makeup, and they didn't even know she was going. She spent the night with me and I talked her into going, and then I did her hair and makeup. After the dance we stopped for a hamburger and just happened to run into her father. So I thought that would be big trouble for both of us, and maybe they wouldn't let us be friends anymore."

"But why don't they let her dance and all?"

"Because they're very devout Christians and they think it's sinful. I mean we're devout also, but they think we're too loose and we think they're too legalistic."

"Oh," I said, getting the gist of it but not quite understanding all of it. "What do you mean by being legalistic? Like you have to follow the Bible word for word or something?"

"Yeah, sort of. It's how you interpret it. Women are supposed to be modest, and the Harts are very strict about that. They also wouldn't let Ruth try out for cheerleading because of the outfits. But don't get me wrong, they are also extremely nice people who would do anything for us—or for anyone, even a stranger. They've taken in people off the street who had nowhere to go. And when Mom was sick Mrs. Hart took care of her for over a week. Not only did she cook, but she washed the clothes, made the beds, and cleaned our home. Mom and I still joke that the apartment has never been as clean since then. I offered to do a lot of it, but Mrs. Hart wouldn't hear of it. She wanted me to have time for school and homework and cheerleading practice—even though she doesn't agree with it. They are exemplary Christians—the kind of people you can trust and rely on, and I couldn't have a better friend."

"Yes, it sounds like it," I said, thinking about what she had said as we stood up to leave. She left the room to tell her mother, and we drove to the miniature golf place. After we paid, I asked her to go first. She tried to hit the ball, but missed. Then she tried again, but it didn't go very far.

"Can I give you a lesson?"

"Sure."

"Okay," I said and I walked behind her and held the golf club with her. My intentions were not honorable—I only wanted to hug her, but I don't think she ever figured that out. We swung at it together, and missed again.

"You need to bend your knees a little," I said, because I had heard that somewhere even though I had never played golf. I took the club from behind her and held her tightly between my arms as we tried again. I could smell some perfume on her neck and the fragrance was lilacs. I hesitated for a moment, because my mind wasn't exactly on the game.

"I'm ready," she said.

We tried again, and hit the ball this time, but it jumped out of the track and into the grass on the sidelines.

"It's your turn," she said.

"Don't you want to try again?"

"No, I want to see how an expert plays."

"Well, I'm not exactly an expert," I said, wondering if she had seen through me. I took the golf club and missed the first time, and also the second time. "I'm not used to these clubs," I said, and she started smiling. Finally I hit the ball and it went into the air and landed on top of Donald Duck's bill. Mary started laughing.

"I think you're rusty."

"No, that's my special shot. Actually it's very difficult to make that shot. See if you can do it."

"Oh, you are so silly. Did you ever really play this game before?"

"Well, not exactly this one, but something similar—croquet."

We finished the game and went for a walk on the beach. It was a beautiful, sunny day, and the weather was not as humid as it often gets in Galveston. As we got near the end of the beach, where cars were not allowed, Mary took her shoes off and ran towards the water. I followed and we walked in the water together. No one else was around, and we were holding hands walking, when she stopped to roll her pants up so they wouldn't get wet. When she straightened up I put my arms around her and kissed her. She kissed me back and then pulled away.

"What's wrong?"

"Oh, I just want to walk right now. And we need to get to know each other a little better."

"But I thought you liked it when we kissed before."

"I did, but you sort of tricked me into that one," she said, and then she kicked the water in my direction, splashing me, and ran away from me.

"Oh, so that's the game we're playing." I chased her and splashed her a little also.

"What a beautiful, wonderful day," she said, and she twirled around in the water a few times, smiling.

"Yes it is," I said, thinking that this was the best time I had ever had with a girl, and wondering if it would last.

"So, what do you think of Galveston—do you like it here?"

"I like it here because of you."

"Oh, you're such a flatterer. I mean, really."

"Really—that's the truth. But I miss the snow a little, and I can't ski here, but I also like the warm weather. It never really gets cold here."

"I guess it doesn't compare to Connecticut, but I think it's cold when winter comes—cold enough for me, anyway, and Mom gets cold easily also."

"Did your mother ever think about getting married again?"

"No, not really. I told her she should and I wouldn't mind at all. But she said she just never met the right person."

"It must have been hard growing up without a father."

"Well, it would have been harder if it hadn't been for Jesus."

"What do you mean?"

"Oh, there's this hymn, *In the Garden*, and it goes like this, she said, and began to sing in a high, delightful voice.

And he walks with me and he talks with me
And he tells me I am his own
And the joy we share as we tarry there
None other has ever known.

He speaks and the sound of his voice is so sweet
The birds hush their singing
And the melody that he gave to me
Within my heart is ringing.

"Jesus made it up to me. He was very real to me when I was young, and I used to sing that song all the time. That's the way he comforted me."

"Oh, that's nice," I said, thinking what she said was a little strange, but she seemed very serious and I didn't know what else to say.

"Of course he's still always with me, but he made the effort to really be there when I was young—because I needed him to be."

I was still thinking about what she said when she splashed me again. "Let's see how fast you can run," she said, and took off.

That evening my mother was working in the kitchen when I walked in and took some food out of the refrigerator. She was rolling out some dough on the counter and I sat down at the kitchen table and began eating some cold chicken. "So, how was the date with Mary?"

"It was fine—she's fun to be around."

"And you played miniature golf, and then what did you do?"

"We walked on the beach and…Mum, if I ask you something, will you promise not to tell Dad?"

"You didn't do something bad, did you?"

"No, nothing like that—I just have a question about religion."

"Well, I don't know if I'm qualified, but I will keep it in confidence."

"Have you known religious people who think that Jesus talks to them? Is that normal?"

"Well, that's a good question, because my aunt—that is your great aunt Ethel is like that—always talking about Jesus as if he were in the room with us or something. My mother thought she was a bit batty, but she was always very kind to me."

"But was she batty? I mean was she off mentally?"

"No, not at all. She was a very talented artist—she taught me how to draw."

"So your mother just said she was batty because of the Jesus thing?"

"Yes, that was it. She annoyed my mother at times because of her religion, but they did get along. We're planning a trip to Australia this summer, so you'll meet her and my mother then, and everyone else."

"You mean you made a decision already? I thought you and Dad were just thinking about it."

"Oh, I've let the cat out of the bag now—it was supposed to be a surprise for you. We'd only talked about it in general before. But I'm so happy for you because you always said how much you wanted to go there. I remember when you got that boomerang for your tenth birthday and you kept throwing it until you learned to make it return. That year you cried because you wanted to go so much and meet your cousins. And you wanted to see the kangaroos and the koala bears. But we just couldn't get away."

"I promise not to cry anymore," I said.

"Oh, you nut, you! Well, I may as well tell you the whole story. We've already told all the relatives and they are excited about finally meeting you. You know I've been sending photos of you to them over the years and telling them what a fine young man you are."

"How long do you think it will take?" I asked, thinking about how it might affect my relationship with Mary.

"Most of the summer, and it's going to be a great trip. I have relatives in Sydney, Melbourne, and Hobart, Tasmania. It will be a little cool there, because the seasons are opposite ours, but the winters are also mild, so it should be quite pleasant."

"Well, let me know when you get the exact dates."

"I will. It's going to be such a wonderful trip. It's expensive, but we'll have a great time!"

I looked at her and did my best to smile. She evidently had no idea that I wanted to be with Mary for the summer, and I wondered what this might mean for our relationship—that is, if we really had one. We had only been on one date, and I wasn't sure if Mary even considered playing miniature golf a real date. In fact, I wasn't sure where I stood with Mary, but I thought I'd try to find out, so I called her that evening.

"Mary, I had a great time today."

"I did too, Paul."

"So can we do it again?"

"You mean play miniature golf?"

"No, let's go out and see a movie?"

"Oh, I don't go to many of those—they're so bad these days."

"But I think I know of a good one that you'll like. Have you heard that song by Lulu, *To Sir with Love*?"

"Oh, I love that song."

"Well it was written for that movie, and I think you'll like it."

"Are you sure there's nothing bad in it?"

"I don't think so," I said, but I really already knew because I'd seen the movie, but I didn't want to tell her. "You'll like it."

"Okay, but it will have to be Friday or Saturday, I'm not allowed to go out on weeknights."

"What about getting together to study? We've got a test coming up."

"That would be okay."

"Okay, I'll come over tomorrow night then?"

"Oh…well… yes that would be okay."

CHAPTER 10

Many days later I saw Gordon at lunch and sat down next to him, but his attitude was different towards me. He started eating and didn't say anything, which was uncharacteristic for him. I stopped eating and stared at him and he finally looked at me.

"What?" Gordon asked.

"That's what I was going to ask you."

"What do you mean?"

"I mean ever since you sat down you've ignored me."

"Yeah, I guess I have because I'm mad at you."

"For what?"

"For breaking Cheryl's heart. She knew you liked Mary, and she thinks you were just using her now that you're not dating her anymore."

"Oh, I'm sorry. I thought you were just using *me* so you could go out with Debbie? Or did I miss something?"

"No, I guess you're right. I just never thought you and Mary would ever…"

"Yeah, I know, the impossible dream. But it has happened."

"I still don't understand how."

"Oh, thanks."

"No it's not that you aren't…oh, never mind. But you never seem to want to go riding with me anymore, either."

"Gordon, you're my best friend, and that hasn't changed. Maybe you could take Debbie for a double date with me and Mary," I offered, not really wanting to, but not sure what else to say.

"No, her parents won't let her go out with anyone else but Cheryl."

"Well, I'm sure someone else will want to date Cheryl, she's really fine."

"Yeah, but she still likes you. She's wondering if the thing with Mary will last, especially since Mary will be going to college when you're a senior."

"I didn't think she liked me that much."

"Yes, she does."

"Okay, I'm sorry."

"Can you call her and tell her that?"

"I already did, but she got angry and hung up on me."

"Oh, I didn't know that."

"That's why I'm surprised to hear that she still likes me."

"She likes you, but it's a love-hate thing. She hates the way you treated her."

"Oh, give me a break, Gordon. I can't help who I like—and you know I've liked Mary from the beginning."

"Yeah, no kidding, I think I know that much."

"So are we still friends or what?"

"Yeah, we're still friends—that is if I ever see you again now that you landed Mary."

"I don't know if I've landed her yet—I think I'm still reeling her in."

After the movie, we drove along the Boulevard and then stopped at Stewart Beach, where we walked on the sand for a while. I stopped and kissed her, and then she looked up at the sky and started pointing out the constellations.

"Oh, it's such a starry night; there are many constellations."

"Yes, I can see the Big Dipper," I said.

"Well, technically, that's not a constellation, it's an asterism."

"Oh, of course, I knew that—that's exactly what I meant to say. So how do you know all of this?"

"It's my hobby. I've been interested in it since I was little."

"So you're saying it's an asterism—is that what you called it?"

She smiled at me and then looked back into the sky. "Yes. Since the Big Dipper is part of the constellation Ursa Major, which is also called The Great Bear, it is technically not a constellation."

"But what is that one?" I asked pointing to another star.

"Which one?" she asked, and I positioned myself in back of her, and then held my arm up and pointed.

"It's the one that looks like it could be an animal and it has a real bright star," I said, as I slipped my hand up from her waist to the top of her stomach.

"Oh that's Leo—it's supposed to look like a lion. The star is called Regulus."

"That means 'Little King' in Latin," I said.

"Why, did you take Latin? I thought they stopped teaching it."

"I was at an old school. They change very slowly. It's a private school, but I got in for free because of some textbook deal my father made with them."

"Well, it was named by Copernicus around 1550. I didn't know it meant little lion. I wonder why he named it that."

"Probably because it hadn't grown up to be big lion." I jested, kissing the side of her neck, and then I turned around so I could kiss her on the mouth. We kissed a few times and then she turned her head away.

"Yes, and speaking of animals," she said lightheartedly, "let's slow this down a little."

"Oh, okay," I said innocently. "I'm sorry, I guess I got starry-eyed."

I drove Mary home at about 10 p.m., and there were no lights on.

"Your mother must be asleep."

"No, she's working a late shift tonight," Mary said as she opened the door, and I followed her in.

"But her car is here."

"It wouldn't start, so she walked to work."

"Really? That's too bad."

"It's not a long walk, it's only about a mile and a half."

"So what time does she get off?"

"At midnight."

"And she's walking home at that time?"

"Yes, I guess so."

"Can you call her?"

"Yes, but I can't always reach her. Sometimes I have to leave a message at the nurse's station, why?"

"Tell her I'll pick her up."

"What? You want to pick her up?"

"Well, she shouldn't have to walk home in the dark—especially at midnight. I don't think it's safe."

Mary looked away and then she turned to me and nodded. "She was a little concerned about that, but are you sure you want to do that—it will be awfully late."

"Well, we can do it together if that's okay. I'll call my parents and tell them I'll be late, and we can watch an old movie on TV or something."

Mary was quiet for a moment, and then she picked up the phone. She was able to reach her mother, and after they spoke for a while, she hung up and smiled at me. I already heard enough of the conversation to know that it would be okay.

We turned on the TV and the only movie that was on was *Dracula*. It was the original version with Bela Lugosi. I had seen it before but Mary hadn't and I wasn't really watching it because I was more interested in making out with her as we sat on the sofa. I was trying to figure out how to get that going, but as the movie progressed, Mary seemed to be upset. There was a scene where a man visiting Count Dracula's mansion cuts his finger, and Dracula moves towards the blood, as if he is going to pounce on the man. But just then, a crucifix comes out that was around his neck, and Dracula turns away quickly. I laughed at the scene, but Mary was bothered by it.

"This is absolutely evil—it's from the devil," Mary said.

"Mary, it's not true, it's just a fantasy—you know vampires don't really exist."

"Yes, of course I know that," Mary said, and she got up so suddenly that it surprised me. She walked to the TV to turn it off. "But evil does exist, and this glorifies it."

"Okay, we can watch something else. Just switch the station."

She did, and the "Tonight Show" with Johnny Carson came on.

"Oh, it's him," Mary said.

"He's okay, I think. He's not a vampire unless he got bitten recently," I said.

"Are you sure?" Mary asked, going along with my little joke.

"Yeah, but I'm not sure about this guy," I added, as Ed McMahon starting talking about a product from an advertiser. "He might be hiding a fang."

Mary laughed and hit me with a cushion from the couch. I hit her back and then I playfully pushed her down on the couch and we kissed for a long time. We continued to make out as different guests came on the show—and we were mostly ignoring it. After about an hour and a half of kissing she pulled away from me and sat up. "We've got to stop."

"Why? I thought you liked kissing me."

"I do—maybe too much. And I'm saving myself for the man I will marry."

"And who do you think that will be?"

"I don't know yet."

"You don't?" I asked, and I was about to say it would be me when she looked over at the clock and changed the subject.

"Oh, we better go to the hospital."

I thought it was too early to go, but I knew she wanted to stop making out. "Sure, we can go now."

We walked into the emergency room about fifteen minutes before 12:00 and took a seat. Mrs. Sanderson appeared briefly and she looked at a little girl who had been brought in by her mother. She had a burned hand, and Mrs. Sanderson gently took off the bandage she had on and looked at the wound. Then she gave the woman a bottle of medicine, and said something—evidently giving her some instructions, and the woman nodded and left the hospital. Then Mrs. Sanderson waved at us and walked away.

A few minutes later, a young Hispanic man was brought in by a couple of other men and he was bleeding so much that his whole shirt was covered with blood and it dripped on the floor as he slowly sat down with his companions helping him. He was heaving and when the admitting nurse saw him she disappeared behind a door, and a doctor came out quickly with an orderly and a stretcher. As they were loading him on the stretcher, the nurse cut off his shirt to reveal a gory knife wound.

I heard Mary make a gasping sound and turned to see her horror-stricken face. She got up and moved towards the door and I followed her. We got outside and we sat down on a bench near the entrance. She was crying and she closed her eyes and breathed deeply, trying to catch her breath.

"Are you okay?"

"That poor man—did you see all that blood! I could never be a nurse."

"It's okay—he'll probably be okay," I said, not certain of what to say to her to calm her. "Things like that just happen."

"I know, but I don't like to see them. That was so sad."

We sat there and I put my arm around her as she continued to sob.

"Are you sure you're okay?" I asked, wondering why she was still so upset.

"I don't do well when I see things that are bad. And life seems to be full of them. It's hard for me to accept them."

"Well, try to get it out of your mind," I said, and I hugged her and stroked her back. Her crying subsided a little, and I could see her mother coming through the double glass doors, so I let go of her. "Your mother is coming."

She looked up and then we stood up as her mother walked out of the building. Mrs. Sanderson walked to our bench and Mary hugged her mother and her sobbing seemed to increase. I thought for a moment that her mother was slightly embarrassed, but I wasn't certain. She stroked her daughter's hair and then let go of her and looked at her face. "Did you see the man who was stabbed? Is that it?"

"Yes," Mary said, sniffling. "I don't know how you can do your job."

"Well, you get used to it. Of course, it's not for everybody," she added. "Paul, thank you so much for the ride," she said, turning her attention to me.

"Oh, you're certainly welcome, Mrs. Sanderson."

"Let's get Mary home and into bed—it's awfully late."

"Sure, just follow me to my car," I said, and I began walking to the parking lot. Mary was still whimpering a little in the car, and I could tell that I needed to leave as soon as I dropped them off.

That night, lying in bed, I wondered about the way Mary had acted. I understood how she could be affected by seeing the bleeding man, but there was something about her sobbing that somehow seemed unusual to me, and when her mother held her it was almost as if she was a small child. But I assumed that I was just too insensitive to understand how she felt.

"You must keep the meter centered!" Mr. Hanson shouted in my ear. I was flying with "hood time," which is a plastic hood that is put on to cover the head so that one's eyes cannot see through the windshield—only the instruments can be seen. "Fly your heading, and keep your altitude—there are mountains due east and you will run into them if you're not careful."

Of course, there were no mountains in Galveston, but he was going to make certain that I was trained to avoid them as if there were. "All right, change your heading to 180 degrees and increase your altitude to 6,000 feet."

I did as he commanded, but the wind made it hard to maintain the correct heading. "Tighten up," he shouted, and I did so. "Actually, you are doing quite well flying instruments since this is only your second time—you are doing very well."

I needed that, I thought—Mr. Hanson was not a man to give a compliment unless he meant it, and they were few and far between his corrections. But I knew he was putting out a lot of effort to teach me, and I was grateful for that. I continued to climb, and when we reached 6,000 feet he told me to climb to 9,000. When we got to 9,000 feet I leveled off, and was getting used to switching my eyes from the different instruments, as his voice boomed again. "Watch your vertical airspeed—you're falling." I corrected it only to get another command. "Watch your attitude indicator—you're tilting—okay, that's better—keep your heading."

We flew for a while without any changes, and I was able to relax a little. "You're doing fine—so well that I'm going to see if you can pull out of a stall using instruments. Don't worry, we're high enough for me to take over if I have to."

Without a moment's more notice, he took the controls and climbed and then slowed down until the plane started to stall—which meant it stopped flying. "Okay, you're on," he said.

I tried to push the nose down and increase the speed, but it was harder to do than I thought it would be. Finally my speed picked up, and I was able to level out and fly at the same 180-degree-south heading.

"Good, now try this," he said, and he again took control and put the plane into a spin.

I was nervous because I had only practiced pulling out of a spin once and that was without the hood on. But I followed the procedure he had taught me—I pulled the throttle back to an idle, and then I stepped on the right rudder to stop the spin as I thought we were spinning to the left and I tried to counter it by depressing the right rudder. But instead of stopping it, the plane spun faster and faster, which confused me. "Try the other rudder," he said calmly, and then I did what he said, although I doubted it could be the correct instruction. But I did it, because he had told me to never question his orders. As I continued to hold the rudder down we came out of the spin. After that I neutralized the rudder and leveled the wings.

"You can take your hood off, now."

I took it off and breathed heavily. "I don't understand what happened. I thought the spin—I mean I was sure the spin was to the left, that's why I stepped on the right rudder. But it must have been spinning to the right. How could that happen?"

"It happened because when you have no point of reference, it's very difficult—in most cases impossible, to know which way you're going. That's why you have to trust your instruments—but that's hard to do in a spin."

After we landed and got back into the airplane rental office, he had me watch a portion of a short film called *Signposts Aloft*, where a man who was a gymnast sat on a rotating stool and was blindfolded. Another man spun the stool to the left and the gymnast said, "turning to the left" several times as the stool continued to spin. Then the gymnast said he had stopped, even though the stool was still spinning to the left. He was convinced it was stationary and then the stool was stopped and he said it was moving to the right. With the blindfold off, he could see how wrong he was. The film went on to explain the reason why he was wrong about the direction of his motion: the body alone, without a visual reference, can be misled due to the dynamic of the motion of fluid in the inner ear. Mr. Hanson turned off the projector before the film was over.

"Paul, you only have a few more solo hours and you can take your flight test and I waited to show you this because it is so important. Many pilots who don't have an instrument rating don't understand it. In fact, what you just saw, and what you experienced today, may save your life."

"Yes sir, I can see why. That's very fascinating. I never would have thought that could happen."

"It's much easier for people to be deceived than they think—because when you are deceived, you don't know you are. And there is also a spiritual analogy for that, but I won't go into that now."

I had begun to eat lunch with Mary at school, so Gordon and I were not seeing each other much, and that next week he called several times, but I am ashamed to say I did not return his calls. My mother had been insisting that I invite Mary over for dinner, so I finally gave in, and she came over that next weekend, on Friday night. The dining room table in the formal dining room was extravagantly and elegantly set, and there were vases with flowers on the table. I knew my mother had gone to great lengths to make it look as beautiful as possible—and it did. But for some reason it embarrassed me.

I picked up Mary and brought her to the house, and we walked into the living room, where my father was watching the news. He greeted her heartily and was very friendly. I knew part of the reason was that he was a little drunk from his wine, which always seems to make him agreeable, but I didn't think Mary would know that, because it was not obvious. After he got up to say hello to her, she looked towards the television where some scenes from the Vietnam War came on. The scenes were a little graphic, showing soldiers running with injured men to put them into helicopters.

Mary's face fell as she watched the scenes. After that the news showed protests against the war at an East Coast university.

> ...and when the leader of the SDS, Students for a Democratic Society, at Columbia University announced that they wouldn't leave, the governor called in the National Guard to carry away the rioters.

As it was playing, my mother walked in with hors d'oeuvres and placed them on the antique coffee table. We all watched for a moment, and then the television station went to a commercial and my father turned it off. "I'm so glad you're not teaching anymore," my mother said.

"When I went to Columbia, I had to study too much to protest anything. I wonder how these kids find the time."

"College is a lot easier now, isn't it? That's what you've told me," I said.

Mary was on the verge of tears and my mother walked over and helped her sit down. "What's the matter?" she asked.

"There was a boy, Ricky Jamison, and he dropped out of high school and joined the army. He kept singing that song—the one called 'Green Berets.' I think that's what got him to join. That was just six months ago. And he was killed two months ago. I can hardly believe it!" she said, and started crying.

My mother held her and comforted her a little—my mother had a gift for doing that, and Mary soon cheered up a bit.

"Well, you know he gave his life for a good reason—he was fighting communism. He must have been a very brave young man. Freedom is not free—we are only free because we are willing to fight for it," my father said.

Mary looked at my father, and I wondered if she was unhappy about what he said.

"Paul told me that your father also died defending our freedom, and I'm sure you are very proud of that," he added.

It took a few moments for Mary to answer. "Yes, I am proud of my father—I know he was a wonderful man."

It was still an awkward moment, and then my mother wisely changed the subject.

"Well, we are so happy to have you as our guest. We wanted to get to know you, since we know how much Paul thinks of you," she said, hugging Mary and smiling at her with such a broad and contagious smile that Mary also managed a smile. "But I must run into the kitchen and check the roast. Paul, take Mary to the dining room and I'll soon be out with the salad."

"Mum really decorated the dining room table," I said, but my mother didn't like what I said.

"Paul exaggerates, it was nothing," she said as we walked towards the dining room. Upon entering it and seeing all the flowers and the ornate polished silver and finely cut crystal glasses, most of which my aunt left us, Mary's eyes seem to light up.

"Oh, it's so beautiful!" Mary exclaimed, and she walked around the table, examining it. "But Mrs. Welles, I want to help you in the kitchen," she said, as my mother turned to walk away.

"Mary, you are a guest," my mother protested.

"But I'd love to help you—please let me, I'm really quite good in the kitchen," Mary insisted.

"All right, then, follow me and we'll put you to work as a scullery maid!" my mother said jokingly.

After she had left, my father looked at me for a moment as if he were studying me. "What is it, Dad?"

"She's really a nice girl. Extremely…I mean quite sensitive, but very nice."

"What do you mean, quite sensitive, but nice? You make it sound like that's a bad trait."

"No, no, you misunderstand me. It can be a fine trait."

"You're qualifying it again—you say it can be."

He was quiet for a moment, and I could tell he was trying to figure out what to say next. "Sorry, I mean it is a fine trait—that's what I really mean. And she's obviously a sweet girl."

I thought he was changing what he said and really had some reservations about her and thought she was oversensitive. I was a little concerned myself that she was, but it still irritated me that he was insinuating that, even if it was true. Besides, I thought, how could he determine that so quickly—especially since he'd been drinking? My second thought was that he was very perceptive, but at that age I didn't like the idea of him being right so much of the time.

As I was thinking about that, my mother walked back in the room with a large salad bowl, and Mary followed with some homemade dressing. After eating the salad, we had a delicious prime rib roast. Mary had asked my father some questions about his history textbooks, and when he stopped talking, my mother asked her what she wanted to do.

"I'd like to teach young children, but I also am considering being a doctor. That's what my mother wants me to do—she said she could have been, but in her day it was much harder for a woman to get into medical school, so she settled for being a nurse."

"She has the grades for it," I said.

"I'm sure she does," my mother said.

"Do you like biology?" my father asked.

"That's one of the problems. I don't like the sight of blood—it really disturbs me."

"You'll get used to it, if you continue," my mother said.

"That's what my mother says. And you would know, Mrs. Welles, because Paul said you used to be a nurse."

"You could always be a psychiatrist—then once you go through medical school there would be no more blood. And that way you could also help Paul out," my father said whimsically.

Mary laughed. "Your Dad is so funny, Paul."

"Yeah—him and Don Rickles. By the way, I have some news. I only have a few more hours to fly, and then I can take my test to get my pilot's license."

Mary hesitated before she answered. "Oh, that's nice."

"And then I can take you flying—I'm sure you'll like it."

Mary was quiet again and she wouldn't look at me.

"What's wrong? Is there something wrong?"

"Well, it's just that when I told my mother that you were learning to fly, she immediately said she wouldn't let me fly with you. You know, it's probably because of my Dad and all."

"That's perfectly understandable, Mary," my mother said.

"Yes…I do understand," I said.

"So how's that old Colonel treating you, anyway?" my father asked.

"He's…he's very good and thorough, but he is tough. He springs things on me, but it's good—I mean I need to be able to know what to do in an emergency, but sometimes he does things very suddenly."

"Paul is thinking about…oh, I forgot what I was going to say," my father said. I knew he was going to say I was thinking about being a military pilot, but with all that had been discussed that evening, he had the good sense to drop the matter. My mother also knew what he was going to say, and she changed the subject.

"Mary, everyone is finished now. Why don't you come into the kitchen and help me serve dessert."

"I'll help, Mrs. Welles, but that was such a wonderful meal and I ate so much that I don't think I can eat any more right now."

"Well, we can have a little girl talk, anyway."

"Just wait until you taste my mother's raspberry meringue pie and you might change your mind," I said, as they got up and walked into the kitchen.

After dessert was served, Mary looked over at my father for a moment and then asked him a question. "Dr. Welles, in the history I've studied, it always seems like boys join the army whether the war is important or not. I don't understand why it's so easy to get them to risk their lives. Is the glamour and adventure of war that strong?"

Perhaps the last thing my father expected was an analysis like that from Mary. His surprise showed on his face, and subsequently his pleasure in hearing such a thoughtful question showed also.

"That's a good point," he said, but before he could speak, my mother did.

"I've often wondered the same thing, especially when I think about how my father—Paul's grandfather—died at Gallipoli. They had the boys so brainwashed in that battle that they charged even when they knew they'd be shot after running fifty yards. It was as bad as the charge of the Light Brigade. But I don't think it's just the men's fault, Mary. Much of the blame has to go to the way the women swoon and carry on about the bravery of the soldiers. If young men didn't think they would be respected and desired by young women for soldiering, that might reduce the glory incentive."

"If it were only as simple as that," my father said, and smiled. "Perhaps we need that incentive so men will fight, because when they don't, nations get taken over. So I agree that war is anything but glamorous, but if glamour helps to recruit, perhaps it's not such a bad thing."

"Dear, I think Mary has had enough war talk," my mother said.

"I don't mind, Mrs. Welles," Mary said. "In fact, the one war I really can't understand was the Civil War. I don't see how people so much the same could manage to fight each other. It seems so sad that they would fight their own countrymen. How do you think that happened, Dr. Welles?"

Mary had no idea that my father was an expert on the Civil War, because I had never told her, and of course she couldn't have asked a question closer to his heart. So he began giving her a capsulized history of the motivations behind the war starting, and how it accelerated, and in his gifted way he painted a historical picture that had depth but was also easy to understand. She seemed enthralled, and asked a lot of good questions, which he was only too glad to answer. I was getting pretty bored, as I'd heard so much of it before, but I didn't let on so Mary wouldn't feel self-conscious about her questions.

When my mother began clearing the table, Mary offered to help, but my mother wouldn't hear of it. However, finally things wound down, and Mary went into the kitchen to help. My father stared at her as she walked away. "That is a special girl you have there," he said. "And I'm not talking about her looks, I'm talking about her mind."

"Yeah, but I never thought I'd like a girl who was interested in the Civil War—I guess I can never escape it!"

"Oh, get out of here!" he said jokingly.

I walked into the kitchen and Mary turned to me with a serious expression. "Your father is a genius, and he's always in such a wonderful mood."

"Thanks," I said, "but you might have to credit the mood part to Chateau de," I said, picking up a bottle in the kitchen and reading the label.

"Paul," my mother said, interrupting my reading and slightly scolding.

"I was just joking around."

"Well, you could show a little more respect," my mother said.

"Sorry," I said.

"I just wish I had him for History," Mary said. "I'd never get bored again."

CHAPTER 11

The weeks went by and Mary and I saw each other every weekend and spoke on the phone many times during the week. I knew Gordon was feeling as if I'd abandoned him, and one day at school he yelled out to me in the hallway.

"Welles!" he shouted.

I turned around and saw it was him, so I slowed down so he could catch up.

"Hi, Gordon—why did you shout?"

"Because I called your name about ten times and you didn't hear me."

"I guess I was thinking about something else."

"Yeah, and I know who it was." Falling in step with me, he added, "Look, we haven't gone racing in a long time—are you free tonight? I know Mary doesn't go out on the weekdays."

"That's true, but I've got an essay to finish, and it's due tomorrow."

"Well, maybe some other time. But I do have some other news. Debbie's parents said she could go out with me as long as there was another couple with us. It no longer has to be her cousin. And the school dance is coming up."

"Sure, if Mary wants to go—I mean her mother doesn't like dancing much, but since she'll be with me I think she'll let her go."

"Wow, you mean her mother she thinks she's safe with you! I better talk some sense into her."

That night I called Mary and set up the date with Gordon and Debbie. We had major tests coming on Monday, so on Friday Mary and I studied for the class we had together, and then we helped each other by asking questions for classes we were being tested in. We were up late studying, and I was very tired when I got home and fell asleep quickly. I was a little irritated because my father knocked on my door fairly early, and then he walked in before I answered.

"Paul, are you awake?"

"Yeah, Dad, I am now."

"I've been waiting for you to wake up, because we need to have a talk."

"Well, I was over at Mary's late…"

"Yes, I know that—I hope you had a good time," he said, in a way I thought was slightly rude.

"Your flight instructor called me. He was wondering why he hadn't heard from you, since you are so close to taking your flight test. He hasn't seen you in weeks and was wondering if something was wrong."

I sat up from the bed and rubbed my eyes. "We were studying, by the way. I mean Mary and me."

"That's nice, but what about your flight instructor?"

"Well, I haven't really had time."

"Seems to me you have plenty of time—you just spend all of it with Mary—or talking to her on the phone. And you had the time when you asked me to pay for the lessons, and with something as expensive as this, I expect you to finish what you start—even if she can't fly with you."

"Okay, I will."

"Now I know your mother already told you that we will be in Australia for most of the summer, so you need to take your test before then."

He walked to the door and then he looked back at me. "Paul, Mary is a fine girl, but life carries certain responsibilities."

Gordon had Debbie with him when he picked me up for the dance, and when we picked up Mary, he took off quickly, and Mary gasped.

"Please, Gordon, can you slow down a little?" Mary asked.

"Oh, you'll get used to it," Debbie said. "Then it will be fun."

Gordon slowed down, but I could see the marked contrast between Debbie and Mary and I was wondering how they would get along. But Mary made an effort to befriend her by asking her about herself as we drove. She also complimented her on the dress she was wearing.

We planned to eat first, so we stopped at a fast food hamburger place on the Boulevard, and by that time Mary and Debbie had become friends. I was sitting opposite Mary when I noticed a crumb on her face.

"You have a crumb on your face."

"Here?" Mary asked, touching her face below her right cheek.

"It's higher than that," I said, pointing at her face. She moved the crumb and it ended up on her chin.

"Now it's on your chin," I said, laughing.

She moved her hand over her chin, and I starting laughing again.

"Is it off yet?"

"Now it's on your neck," I said, barely able to speak because I was laughing so hard.

Mary pulled it off her neck and threw it at me.

"Guess what, Paul."

"What?"

"It's on your hair now," she said, pointing above my right eye.

"Really, right here?" I asked, my hand going to my hair. "Good, I like it there."

After a few dances, Mary and I walked to the punch bowl and Gordon and Debbie walked up. Debbie walked closer to Mary. "I'm going to the restroom—do you want to come?"

"Sure," Mary said, and they walked away.

"I'd like to hear what they say about us in there."

"I don't think Mary ever said a bad word about anyone."

"Perfect, huh?" Gordon said cynically.

"Pretty close."

"What are you going to do when she graduates?"

"Well, she's going to summer school at the University of Houston. She was going to try to work this summer, but her uncle is pretty well-off, and he offered to pay her expenses if she wanted to start in the summer instead of working, and she didn't want to pass that up. And I'm going to Australia with my parents for part of the summer."

"So you'll find out if absence really makes the heart grow fonder. I just hope she doesn't meet anyone while you're gone."

"Why would you say that?"

"I don't know. I was just joking a little."

"Well, that's not funny."

"Come on, Paul. Lighten up."

I tried to, but Gordon's words keep haunting me. I thought it was ridiculous to worry about that, because I trusted Mary and thought that nothing like that would ever happen. But I was also concerned about being gone that long. So a few days later, after my father had eaten and had a fair amount of wine, I figured he was in the best mood for a discussion. He was in his study, reading, and it took him a moment to notice I was there, because when he read, he often became totally engrossed and seemed to lose touch with reality. After a few minutes of watching him, I finally knocked on the side of the door, and he slowly looked up. I walked from the door into the study, and was a little surprised to see him reading the Bible.

"Hi, Dad. Are you reading the Bible?"

"Yes—some of the best poetry you will ever read. When God answers Job out of the whirlwind—it's powerful."

I could tell he wanted to read some of it to me, but I knew if he did we'd be there a long time, and I was anxious to talk to him.

"I'd like to read that myself, but I have something else on my mind."

He spoke again as if he hadn't heard me, and I didn't know if he had or not.

"You know, I never understood this book—is this actual truth, or symbolic? Well, God says he will confound the wisdom of the wise, so maybe I'm not that smart."

"I think you're smart, Dad."

He nodded and smiled, and finally seemed like he was out of his bubble and was willing to hear what I had to say.

"I got my pilot's license," I said and began to take it from my wallet.

"I knew you would—but I don't need to see it. I trust you. Put your wallet back."

I put it back in my rear pocket and took a breath, a little afraid to speak, but I knew I had to.

"Dad, I was wondering about something. Instead of going to Australia with you and Mum, I thought maybe I could stay here."

"Here? By yourself?" he said incredulously, and my stomach seemed to sink at his reaction.

"Well, yes, or maybe I could get a place in Houston."

"No, son. All of your Australian relatives are waiting to meet you for the first time. It would be a great let-down for them and for your mother."

"But, Dad, I thought…"

"It's not open for discussion," he said, somewhat harshly.

I felt anger rising in me and it was hard to control.

"What are you, a dictator or something?"

"Or something—I'm your father. And you are still a minor."

"Does that mean I'm your slave—that you can make me do anything you want me to do? Is that the way a father is supposed to act?" I said angrily.

"Don't talk to me that way. I'm not changing our plans for your obsession."

"My obsession? Are you talking about Mary?"

"You figure it out."

"Because I met a girl I like it's an obsession?"

He was quiet for a moment, looking down at the Bible, and then he looked up again. "You can like someone and you can even love someone, and you can also be obsessed with someone."

"I'm not obsessed."

"Well, you should hear yourself; it's always Mary, Mary, Mary. Now I think that speaks of obsession."

"Well, I guess you would know about obsession, wouldn't you? What about your obsession? I'm not drunk on wine most of the time, am I?"

His face got red when I said that and he raised his voice. "That car is in my name, and I will take it away if you keep talking like that. Now the only reason you want to stay is for Mary, and your family is more important."

"No, I'd like to stay here because I don't want to travel with a new dictator—the world got rid of one in 1945, and I don't think I want a personal one."

"Are you really comparing me to Hitler—have you sunk that low?" he said, shouting.

I knew it was wrong to say, and as I stood there, my mother walked in, concerned from hearing our loud voices.

"What in heaven's name is going on here?"

My father turned towards her and took a moment before he spoke. "Just a father-son disagreement, but nothing major, I assure you."

"Well, it certainly sounded like something major," she said, and then she looked over at me, and my father stared at me, with a look that said I should stay quiet.

"Everything is fine, Mum."

After she walked downstairs, my father spoke in a quieter tone. "If you go to your mother with this, you will spoil the trip for her. She thinks you want to go, so please don't be selfish and bother her about it. This is a trip she's wanted to go on for many years. You are her only child and she wants to show you off. Now I know you love her, so please restrain yourself."

"Sure, I'll restrain myself," I said, and I ran downstairs, and through the front door, slamming it hard. When I got to my car, I raced out of the driveway, but as I began driving I regretted what I'd said, and thought I should apologize, so I drove back to the house. He was still in his study reading and I had to clear my throat to get his attention.

"I just wanted to say I'm sorry for comparing you to Hitler."

"I'm glad you came back, your *entschuldigung* is accepted."

"My what?"

"*Entschuldigung*—it's German for apology—a little joke."

"I see."

"But since you came back, I want you to hear this poem. Alan Seeger was a contemporary of T.S. Elliot and a Harvard graduate who had a premonition about his death in World War 1—it was called the 'War to End All Wars' at that time. Let me read it—it's short."

"Okay."

I have a rendezvous with Death
At some disputed barricade,
When Spring comes back with rustling shade
And apple-blossoms fill the air—
I have a rendezvous with Death
When Spring brings back blue days and fair.

It may be he shall take my hand
And lead me into his dark land
And close my eyes and quench my breath—
It may be I shall pass him still.
I have a rendezvous with Death
On some scarred slope of battered hill,
When Spring comes round again this year
And the first meadow-flowers appear.

God knows 'twere better to be deep
Pillowed in silk and scented down,
Where love throbs out in blissful sleep,
Pulse nigh to pulse, and breath to breath,
Where hushed awakenings are dear…
But I've a rendezvous with Death
At midnight in some flaming town,

When Spring trips north again this year,
And I to my pledged word am true,
I shall not fail that rendezvous."

"He was killed in action on July 4th, 1916."

"That is a haunting poem. But Dad, I thought the U.S. didn't even enter the war until 1917."

"That's right—I'm glad you caught that. Seeger went to France and enlisted in the French Foreign Legion."

"Wow, he must have really wanted to fight. But that name Seeger—there's a musician named Pete Seeger who keeps protesting the Vietnam War—but I guess he's no relation."

"Sadly, he is. He would be Alan Seeger's nephew and he's a self-proclaimed communist."

"Funny how they could be such opposites and still be related."

"Well, you've got a similar thing with Teddy Roosevelt and Franklin D. And then there was Cain and Abel."

"Do you really think that Bible story is true?"

"I don't know, but it explains why you can get diametrically opposed personalities from the same family. Kind of ruins the Freudian view that it's all in the upbringing. Some of us just chose to do evil."

CHAPTER 12

A few weeks later I tried to talk to my father about staying home again, but he kept saying how much it would hurt my mother, so I finally gave up. Mary knew I was trying to get out of it, so it was time to tell her that I was definitely going. We talked about it while we were walking on the beach one day, after swimming in the ocean for a while. Walking and swimming were two simple things that we both liked to do.

"Will you write to me?" I asked Mary as we strolled.

"Of course, silly—but will you write to me?"

"Every day. My mother uses special envelopes that you can write on and then fold up to send. Since the envelope is the writing paper, they are very light and that makes it less expensive to send by air mail. I'll get you some before I leave, and give you the addresses of my relatives there."

"Well, I know you're a good writer, but will you really write to me often?"

"Yes, of course. Long, romantic letters, filled with poetry and my deep thoughts about our relationship."

"Wow, that sounds great. I didn't know you were so romantic. So why don't you start writing me now?"

"Well, I have to think about it a little—you know, it takes a while to get that deep."

"Yes, I would think so," she said. And as she spoke the tide came in. She walked towards it and playfully kicked some water at me, then she ran and I followed her, kicking water back at her. She slipped and fell on the beach as she ran.

"Are you okay?" I asked, and I kneeled down to help her.

"I think I am," she said, feigning pain in her right leg, and then she splashed me in the face with some water.

"Well, that was tricky, and I should punish you for that," I said, as I lay next to her, "But instead…" I pulled her up and kissed her. Then we continued walking, and all I could think about was how hard it would be to be without her for the summer. The year was ending in about a month, so I planned to spend as much time with her as I could. Her mother frowned on us getting together on weekdays, unless we were studying together for the one class we shared. So outside of school, we saw each other mostly on the weekends.

One Monday in English Composition, the class worked on an assignment as Mrs. Erickson called each one of us up to her desk to return our essays to us. After she discussed the paper with me she looked up from it and then changed the subject. "You've not only done quite well on this paper, but also on the social scene—only came this year and you've already got a popular cheerleader as a girlfriend. Congratulations."

I was surprised at her comment and was not certain what to say. "Yes, I've been fortunate to meet Mary."

"She's a very sweet girl. I'm very happy for you," she said, but then I thought I saw her make a slight facial grimace.

I left the class and Gordon saw me in the hallway. "Hey, stranger—don't I know you from somewhere?"

"Hi, Gordon. Sorry I haven't been around."

"I understand. You're trying to get in all the time you can before you go to Australia."

"Yeah, that's it."

"So do you want to double date this weekend?"

"I would, but I'm taking Mary to Houston, so she can look at the campus."

That Saturday Mary and I drove to the University of Houston and walked around the campus. We were also able to go to a dormitory and see a room which was similar to the one she would be staying in when a final room assignment was made. After that we ate lunch, and then I offered to take her to the zoo, and she agreed.

Since it was Saturday, it was very crowded and we had a difficult time parking. When we finally found a space, it was a long walk from the car to the entrance of the zoo. The place seemed almost like a madhouse to me, because children were running all around and often people were in the way as we walked.

Our first stop was an indoor facility where birds were kept. Some of them were flying around a large main area which was netted in with a wire screen, but others were caged singly or together with their own species. At the entrance of the zoo, we had passed several vendors of helium balloons, and as we stood in the main area, a child lost control of one and it traveled to the ceiling. The birds were afraid of it, and as they tried to avoid it, some of them hit the wire screen and fell a bit before recovering their flight.

I noticed that Mary seemed upset about this but was not sure why. As I looked at her, the child started screaming. "Daddy, I want my balloon, I want my balloon," he said over and over again. His pleas were very irritating, and I took Mary's hand and we moved away from that area, but we could still hear him.

"Let's see something else," Mary said, and we walked out of the exhibit. Back in the sunshine I could see that she had been crying, and she dried her eyes as we walked.

"Are you all right?"

She nodded her head "yes" but she still seemed upset and I moved us towards a bench where we sat and I put my arm around her.

"Why would anyone take a bird—something that can fly—and lock it away like that? What have those birds ever done to be imprisoned like that?"

I was quiet for a moment because I wasn't certain how to answer her. I watched the people bustling by on the walkway in front of us and struggled for an answer that might calm her. "It's just a few of them. And it's just so people can see them."

"They have movies, don't they? Can't they just make a movie about them and leave them alone?"

"Why don't we see something else?" I suggested. "Something that doesn't fly."

"Okay," she said, and we got up and started walking. Then something occurred to me and I turned to her.

"This isn't the first time you've been to a zoo, is it?"

"No, of course I've been to the zoo before."

"Okay, I was just asking."

"The last time I was here I was twelve, and I'd just joined the Girl Scouts. We came here on a field trip."

We continued walking and then stopped in front of a cage of monkeys. As we watched them swinging around, two boys who were about twelve years of age started throwing jelly beans at them.

"Don't do that!" Mary said, scolding them, in an aggressive manner which was uncharacteristic for her. In response, they looked over at her and started cursing at us. Just then a monkey took a hard biscuit out of its mouth and threw it at one of them, hitting him in the face. The other one kept cursing, and I made a fist and walked towards him and they both ran away.

"I'm glad that monkey got him," Mary said, and just then another monkey threw a biscuit which came flying out of the cage and hit the ground between us. I laughed, but Mary seemed preoccupied.

"I guess he can't tell the good guys from the bad," I said, trying to bring some humor into the situation. We continued walking and we saw a black bear and then we saw lions in the distance and walked towards them. There were cages but also a rather large area of ground with trees and boulders where they were able to roam. The open area had bars, and the cages had a second set of bars. Several lions were walking around and one was locked in a cage. I assumed he was locked in there so that the people walking by could see him close up, because the other lions were able to move away and were difficult to see. As we approached, I saw the same two boys, and they were taunting the lion.

"You're just a stupid lion, and you can't hurt me," one of the boys said, as he pressed his face against the bars. "Na, na, na, na, na," the other one said, and then he started shrieking at the lion. The lion actually growled at him, and he backed up for a moment. Then the lion sat down, his eyes looking tired and angry. "You don't scare me," the boy said, pushing his face against the bars again.

"But he's a lion, the king of the jungle!" the other boy shouted mockingly.

I knew animals could discern things from the tone of a person's voice, and from what I could tell the lion was agitated by it, but at the same time he seemed resigned to his fate.

"You've got to stop this," Mary said to me, desperately.

I moved closer to the boy who was shouting and he turned around, surprised to see me. I gave him the meanest look I could, and he nodded to his friend and they walked away. Then Mary walked as close as she could to the lion and began talking to it in a sweet voice. The lion had been near the back of the cage, but as Mary continued talking, it moved closer to her. It was not hard to see the anger that was in its eyes when the boys were mocking it, but as Mary continued talking and cooing at the lion, his eyes became peaceful. I was amazed at the effect she seemed to be having on the animal—I wondered if it was just a coincidence, and as I was considering that, the lion closed its eyes and appeared to fall asleep. Mary stood there, appearing to be entranced until I touched her arm.

"He's sleeping now," I said softly, and she turned around and put her head on my shoulder and cried a little as we walked away from the cage, trying to dodge people as they went by. Once we got away from the cage, I found a bench no one was standing around and we sat down. Suddenly she jumped up.

"I've got to get out of here," she said, and I also stood up and followed as she started walking towards the exit. As we passed the bird exhibit she quickened her pace, and then she started running and I ran to keep up with her. When we got to the street that separated the zoo from the parking lot, I slowed down, but Mary kept running and a driver had to slow down to avoid her. At that point I caught up, and I took her arm. "Would you slow down?" I yelled.

"I had to get out of there," she said, still moving fast, but not running.

"Well, we're out now."

"I know, but I just want to run until we get to the car," she said, taking off again. When we reached the car she got in quickly and put her head between her knees. I got in the driver's side and held her hand. She was hyperventilating and her body was shaking a little.

"Mary, calm down. It's okay. It's only a zoo. You need to catch your breath. Just relax."

"I hate zoos. It isn't fair. People don't have to see the animals."

"But you said you wanted to go."

"I know, I just didn't think it would bother me like this."

"Well, we just happened to be around two bad kids. Most people don't act that way." I started the car and began to drive.

"I remember hearing about the animals not having offspring because they're in captivity. That should tell people something. If someone put you in prison, you wouldn't want to have children that would suffer the same way, would you?"

"No, but please calm down. I'm concerned for your health. It may not be right, I understand that, but it's only a zoo, and there's nothing we can do about it. Please don't let it bother you too much. That won't solve the problem."

"I know," she said, and then she moved towards me and kissed me on the cheek. "At least you understand me."

I wasn't sure that was true, and she held onto my arm as we drove through Houston. She only let go once we reached the Gulf Freeway and headed back to Galveston. We listened to the radio a while, and as we passed the Clear Lake area, which was about thirty miles from Galveston, a Beach Boys song was playing.

Wouldn't it be nice if we could wake up
In the morning when the day is new
And after having spent the day together
Hold each other close the whole night through

Happy times together we've been spending
I wish that every kiss was never ending...

I was singing along with the song a little, but she was looking out the window, and I could tell that her mind was on something else.

Maybe if we think and wish and hope and pray it might come true
Baby then there wouldn't be a single thing we couldn't do
We could be married
And then we'd be happy

I sang the last part a little louder, hoping to give her a hint of how I felt, but instead of noticing, she reached over and turned the radio off. "I've got an idea for a story, do you want to hear it?"

"Sure," I said, a little surprised at her abruptness in turning off the music.

"Well, I want to tell you because I know I'll never write it but you might."

"Why wouldn't you write it?"

"I just wouldn't. I'm not a writer—I mean I can do term papers, but I can't write like you can. Remember, I read your short story for English. I think you have a gift."

"So, let's hear it."

"It will probably sound crazy, though."

"I still want to hear it—now I really want to hear it."

"Okay," she said, and looked away from me for a moment and stared out the window at the passing traffic. "It's about a man who works at the zoo, feeding and taking care of the animals. To the others who work there it's just a job, but not to him. To him it's...it's sort of a calling. You see he really loves the animals and understands them in a way few people do, and it's a joy for him to be around them. But he doesn't like the zoo, he thinks it's cruel and that the animals should run free. He knows he can't free them, so the next best thing is to work there and try to make them happier. You know what I mean?"

I nodded, and she continued. "He's not like me—he doesn't like people. No, that's not it, he doesn't dislike people, he just doesn't understand people, so he keeps to himself. It's like…like he just doesn't have anything to say to people—he just doesn't want to talk. Maybe his parents ignored him or something when he was young, and his only friend was a dog or a cat. Anyway, he spends a lot of time at the zoo, even when he's not working because he feels at home there—like he's with people who understand him. All the other employees think he's a little crazy, but he doesn't bother anyone so they don't bother him.

"Every day, though, he has to watch the animals being tormented by people—just like we did today. I mean, most of the people don't bother the animals, but some do and because of that, and because they're imprisoned, his heart aches for them—it really breaks his heart. And, as time goes on, the sadness he feels for the suffering of the animals becomes greater and more acute.

"Anyway, there is one particular lion he likes a lot. He's an old, ferocious thing, but he likes him and feels sorry for him because the lion is unhappy in captivity. One day, after watching kids taunt the lion, he walks into the cage and locks himself in with it. The lion circles him a few times and then attacks and kills him."

"So the lion kills him even though he's been nice to it?"

"Yes, because like the other wild animals, the killing is instinctive. It's part of the Fall."

"The Fall?"

"You know, the Fall of mankind—into sin. The animals react and cannot help themselves."

"So the man went into the cage thinking the animal would like him but instead he ate him?"

"No, you miss the point. The man knew the lion would kill him."

"I'm still missing the point. If he knew the lion would kill him, why would he go into the cage?"

"It was like a sacrifice—a way of making up to the lion all the injustice he had suffered. And I guess another part of it was to stop the sadness he was feeling, because the more he watched the animals suffer, the harder it became for him to bear the sadness. He thought by trying to understand them and feeling for them he could help them, but in the end it just dragged him down too deeply, and…well, that's it. Do you think anyone would understand the story?"

"I don't know," I answered honestly, and I could tell she didn't like the answer. "But I think it's very interesting," I added.

"Do you think you might write it someday?"

"I don't know if I can—it's really your story," I answered, and noticed from the corner of my eye that she was disappointed. "But maybe I'll give it a try," I lied.

We drove for the next ten minutes or so in silence. "So, let's be happy—I think it was a sad story," she said.

"I'm happy—I'm happy when I'm with you."

"That makes me glad I'm with you, then. By the way, my mother is going to keep my cat when I move to Houston, and I'm going to miss him. I hope he'll be able to adjust being without me. Do you think he will?"

"Yes, I think he'll be fine. But I need to tell you that no matter how unhappy he gets I won't let him eat me," I said, and it took her a second to get the joke, then she smiled and we both laughed a little.

As we drove towards Galveston, I thought about her. Mary and I got along well, but sometimes I felt that she was somehow playing a part—that like many popular people she seemed to almost always be nice and bubbly—some might call it phony, or "plastic." I wondered for a moment if I was seeing the real Mary and I debated with myself: was she being phony? No, she wasn't pretending, she was genuine in being nice to everyone and it was how she actually felt. I was being cynical to think otherwise.

Then another thought came to me. She was acting to fulfill an image she had of herself—one that she believed in, but also one that I thought no one could continuously maintain. And the cracks in that image did come when she told me things like she did at the zoo. Her oversensitivity only confirmed that she was a passionate, concerned person who sincerely cared about others, but it also brought out another side to her personality. And that side was one that seemed fragile, and showed me that she was susceptible to being injured by things that most people would not give a second thought to.

I thought about the rare times she became unhappy and how I was able to help her by joking and teasing her. She had a good sense of humor, and I had a dry sense of humor, and through it I tried to make her aware that her concerns about things like animals in the zoo were excessive and bordered on neurotic. She would get it when I joked with her, and she was able to laugh at herself and see my point of view, but just like most of us, the things that she was extreme about were hard for her to give up.

She was leaning on my shoulder as we drove home, and I thought she had fallen asleep, but then she sat up and looked out the window. "I guess it's always something?"

"What do you mean?"

"I mean something is always wrong with the world, and that is why Jesus had to die for us. And I need to accept the things that are wrong and do what he told me to do."

I tried to stay out of religious discussions with her, because I rarely understood what she meant, and I was also trying to hide the fact that I didn't believe like she did—in fact, I didn't know what I believed. But I was curious about her statement.

"What did he tell you?"

"He said to think on the things that are true, noble, just, pure, lovely, of good report, virtuous, and praiseworthy."

"Oh."

"And he said, My peace I give unto you, let not your heart be troubled—but I'm paraphrasing a little. I'm sure you've read that in the Bible."

I had not read the Bible much at all, so I was not certain what to say. "Well, that sounds like good advice."

"It's the best advice, because it comes from God, and I try to practice it but sometimes it's hard when I see things that upset me."

CHAPTER 13

The time passed quickly and before I knew it Mary was ready to move to Houston, and my trip to Australia was coming up. I'd always wanted to go there before, but now I didn't care about going, and I told Mary that as we packed up her things. School was out now, and I was to drive her to Houston and help carry her things to her dormitory room.

"Paul, it's really not so bad—even if you stayed I'd be in Houston and we wouldn't see much of each other. It's only a few months."

"Yeah, I know," I said, as I finished putting the rest of her clothing in the backseat. I had rigged up a bar that extended across the seat to hang her clothes on. We had already packed the trunk with other things. We reached the university and I stopped the car but I didn't get out. I could tell she was wondering why I didn't move.

"Remember that night when we were waiting to pick your mother up at the hospital because her car was at the mechanic's?"

"Oh, yes. That was very nice of you."

"You told me then that you were saving yourself for the man you were going to marry—do you remember that?"

"Yes."

"Well, I want you to save yourself for me, because I believe that I'm him. Because if you do, I could move to Houston and get a part-time job and..." I stopped talking because she was quiet.

I looked at her, waiting for her to speak, but it took a while. "Oh, that's such a nice thing to say."

"But do you feel the same way?"

"Paul, you've told me many times that your father wants you to go to an Ivy League college, and you'd always resent me if you went to college in Houston."

"But maybe you could go to school back East with me, then."

"Paul, I'm honored that you've asked me, but I know my mother would not let me marry yet—she already told me she wants me to be more mature before I make that decision."

"Okay," I said, trying not to seem dejected. "But we can be engaged—I mean without telling anyone. We could just keep it between ourselves. Do you love me, and do you want to marry me? If you say yes, then we can save ourselves for each other. I won't see another girl—I will wait for you. I'll wait until your mother feels good about you making the decision."

She looked at me for a moment, which seemed like a very long time.

"Just say yes,"

"Okay, Paul, yes. I will save myself for you, but I have to wait to commit to marriage—I wouldn't want to hide that from my mother."

"I understand. Well, I don't have a senior ring yet—and it would probably look silly for a college girl to be wearing one around her neck, anyway."

"No, that wouldn't bother me at all."

"But I do have something," I said, and I pulled the gold amulet that Mrs. Roth had given me from my pocket. I had visited a jeweler a week before and he had put a pin on it to make a broach. "Would you take this?"

I could tell that Mary was impressed by it, and she held it up to the window and it shone and reflected sunlight in several directions. "Paul, it's beautiful. So much prettier than a senior ring. Has it been in your family?"

"Sort of."

"Oh, but I couldn't take it. It looks expensive and I'm sure it's a family heirloom. I'm sure your parents wouldn't want you to give it to me."

"It was in a friend's family and they gave it to me. It was never my parents—it was given directly to me. Please take it and wear it always, so it will remind you of me."

"But I said I'm not really ready…"

"That's okay, you will be one day," I said, pinning it on her blouse.

"Oh, Paul—if you insist."

"I insist."

She looked at it, then leaned toward me and kissed me. "You are so sweet."

CHAPTER 14

We were in Australia for about two months, and we traveled a lot because my mother's relatives were spread around the country. Some were in Sydney, some were in Melbourne, and most were in West Hobart, Tasmania. I wrote regularly to Mary, but there was a lag in the mail, and the itinerary I gave her meant that I might have missed some of her letters because she would not know how long it might take for them to get there. Our last stop was Tasmania, which is an island about one hundred miles south of Melbourne. We stayed there the longest—almost a month, but I also got the fewest letters there.

My mother caught me moping one day, outside my aunt's house, and she asked what was wrong. "Are you homesick?"

"Yes, I guess. I haven't gotten a letter from Mary in three weeks, and I used to get them more often."

"Paul, mail has to come on the ferry—that's why you're getting them late. They may all come once we are back home. I've asked my sister to forward them."

"I hope you're right—I hope there's nothing wrong."

"Oh, I'm sure there isn't," she assured me. "But you don't want to make your cousins think you don't enjoy their company, do you?"

"No, I don't. I'll cheer up for them."

"Good, I appreciate that."

The last part of our vacation time really seemed to drag for me, but the trip back was not too bad because I was so happy that we were on our way. When we finally got home it was about 3 a.m. and I couldn't call Mary that late, so I tried to get to sleep. However, the jet lag and my anticipation of seeing her made it difficult. Finally I drifted off and when I awoke it was about 9 a.m. on Thursday. I called her dorm but there was no answer, so I assumed she was in a class or out somewhere. I kept calling all day and finally, at about 5 p.m., she answered.

"Hi, Mary, I'm back."

"Oh, that's wonderful, Paul. How was your trip?"

"It was fine, but I missed you. Did you miss me?"

"Of course, silly," she said, but I noticed there was something slightly different in her voice, and although I couldn't say exactly what it was, it seemed like a lack of enthusiasm.

"So, are you okay?"

"Oh, yes, of course."

"You just sound a little different."

"Well, we had a test today, and I was up last night studying, so I'm pretty tired."

"I see. Well, I thought I might drive up there to see you tonight—actually we were at the Houston airport last night but it was so late I didn't want to bother you."

"Paul, tonight would not be good for me. I'm so tired and it would be late before you could get here, and you're probably tired from your trip. What about coming up Saturday afternoon?"

I didn't answer because I was discouraged that she didn't want to see me right away. I knew she was right about me being tired, and what she suggested would have seemed reasonable to most people, but I was impatient and wanted to see her right away. I was silent for a while and she finally spoke again.

"So is Saturday afternoon okay?" she asked.

"What about tomorrow—Friday?"

"Oh, that won't work. If I'd known you were coming back I could have made time but…"

"Never mind, Saturday is fine," I said, trying to hide my disappointment.

We talked a little longer, set a time when I'd be there, and then she said she had to go and we hung up. Even though I was tired my desire to see her seemed to give me energy. As I got off the phone, my father walked in with a bag filled with mail. He had told the post office to hold it, and had just picked it all up.

"Wow, look at that!" my mother said, as she walked out to greet him. She saw that I was off the phone and turned to me. "Were you talking to Mary?"

"Yes."

"And—so how is she?"

"She's fine."

My father dumped the mail on a couch in the living room, and sighed as he realized how much he would have to go through. I stood staring at it in thought.

"Paul, is there something wrong?" my mother asked.

"No, I just...well she doesn't sound the same—I can't put my finger on it. But she said she was up late studying for a test."

"Well, in college there is a lot of that—less time for fun than in high school."

"Yeah, that's what I hear."

"Well, Dad and I are going to look through some of this mail."

"I can help."

"But did you ever sleep?"

"Yes I did some. I got up about nine."

"I think you need to get to bed. We only woke up this afternoon."

"Okay, I'll try."

I had, in fact, hardly slept for the past several days since we were flying and it was hard for me to sleep on the jet. This was especially true because smoking was allowed, and many people seated near us were smoking, and the smell of it kept waking me up. The energy I had in anticipation of driving to Houston to see Mary was dissipating, and I could barely keep my eyes open. So I went up to my bedroom, pulled off my shoes, and collapsed on the bed and fell asleep instantly.

Around ten Friday morning, my mother knocked on my door. I woke up and answered it, rubbing my eyes as I turned the knob.

"I didn't want to wake you, but I have a lot of shopping to do, and now that you've got that responsibility your father always tells me to ask you."

"Sure, that was part of the deal for the car. I'll get ready in a few minutes and we can go."

"That's good. Since we've been gone so long I have to buy a lot of fresh groceries."

As we were driving, I looked over at the list my mother was going over with a pencil. I was surprised to see it was so long.

"Mum, why don't you separate some of the items that are easy to find, like bread and milk and stuff like that, and I'll come in and help you shop."

She was surprised at the offer and hesitated before she answered. "Are you sure?"

"Yeah, I can do that much. I'll find you when I'm finished, and you can make certain I got the right things."

"Thank you, Paul," she said, as we pulled into the parking lot. She wrote a list for me, and soon we had our carts and I looked for the items she wanted. I didn't know the store, so it was taking me longer than I'd hoped, but I also knew she was a slow shopper, so I didn't think I'd finish later than her.

I had found most of the items on the list when I saw her on one of the aisles and I walked up. She was busy reading the ingredients on a box of cereal, and she didn't notice I was there. Then I saw Mrs. Erickson coming down the same aisle. She saw me and walked up to us, but my mother was still preoccupied.

"Hello Paul, how are you?" she asked, and she touched the back of my hand which was on the shopping cart.

"Fine, we've been in Australia and we just got back."

As I said that, my mother heard my voice and looked up. She saw Mrs. Erickson, and then she looked at me.

"Mum, this is Mrs. Erickson. She was the substitute teacher I had for English."

"Oh, well, it's a pleasure to meet you. I'm Ann Welles," my mother said.

"And it is a pleasure to meet you, and please call me Susan," Mrs. Erickson said, and she and my mother shook hands. "Paul said you just got back from Australia. Was it a good trip?"

"Yes, it was very nice. We saw so many relatives I hadn't seen in years."

"You have such a lovely accent. So you must be Australian?"

"Yes, and Paul was finally able to meet all his relatives there. He's wanted to do that since he was a young boy. And we had plenty of time for him to explore the areas where I grew up. He even got to snorkel at the Great Barrier Reef."

"Oh, I've heard that's beautiful. It's so wonderful that he got the chance. Paul is a very good writer—perhaps he'll write about that experience someday."

"Well, that would be interesting. But we'll find out today how good he is at shopping, since he's been generous to help me with the long list I have."

We said good-bye and I went back to my task. After going down a few more aisles, I stopped at the jam section and began to look for the flavors and brands on the list. When I looked up, Mrs. Erickson was coming down the same aisle.

"Hello, again," she said. "It's nice that you're helping your mother."

"Yeah, but it's turned out to be more complicated than I thought. I didn't know there were so many choices for these products."

"Paul, I wonder if you would be willing to help me with something. My husband is gone and I was trying to rearrange the furniture, and I have most of it done, but I just need a little help moving our couch."

"Oh, sure, I'll help."

"Thank you. Why don't you come by after you finish shopping? Here is my address," she said, writing it on a small notepad she took from her purse.

I took it from her and she walked away. When my mother and I met up again, she seemed upset.

"Mum, what's wrong?"

"It's your friend, Gordon."

"What about him?"

"I saw one of the women on the historical society—you know, she's one of the women who approached us to allow tours of our house. But your father is adamantly against that."

"But what about Gordon?"

"Yes, of course. She told me that he's in the hospital and has been there a while. I don't know how serious it is."

"Okay, I better visit him when we're finished."

After I dropped my mother off and helped bringing in the groceries, I got back in my car and drove to Mrs. Erickson's apartment, which was near the medical center and not far from where we lived. I was trying to find her apartment number when I saw her by the pool in a bikini. She smiled when she saw me and got up. She was a beautiful woman, and it was hard for me to keep my eyes off her body as I walked behind her. When we got to her apartment, she walked to the kitchen.

"Would you like something to drink? I've got juice and soft drinks."

"No, thanks," I said, feeling a little nervous.

"This is the couch," she said, and she walked towards it. "If you could just take the other end of it, we could move it together."

We moved the couch, and she sat down. Then she patted the seat next to her. "Sit and tell me a little about your vacation."

I sat down, and when I did, she moved closer to me. "What I really want to say, is that I've fallen in love with you."

"You've what?"

"I've fallen in love with you. I've tried to resist, but I can't seem to. I'd heard that you were in Australia, and I was looking forward to seeing you, and then there you were in the supermarket. I think it's fate."

"But you're married."

"Well, we're not getting along very well. And love is more important than some piece of paper, I think," she said, and she moved towards me and kissed me on the mouth.

I moved back from her a little. "But what if someone found out?"

"Well, I'd just ask them if they ever read *Tea and Sympathy* and I think they'd understand. It all started with the way you write—it wasn't physical, but you are a very handsome young man," she said, and she kissed me again. I didn't respond and she stopped and looked at me for a moment, questioningly. "Don't you find me attractive? Haven't you had...thoughts about me?"

"Yes, you're very attractive. You're beautiful. But I can't. I'm engaged," I said, which wasn't exactly true but it just came out.

She pulled back from me when I said that, and sighed. "It's Mary, isn't it? Darling Mary?"

"Yes, I mean we're committed to each other and I just don't feel right about this."

"Well, she's a lucky girl. She's really a lucky girl," she said, and she got up from the couch. "Good-bye, Paul."

"Good-bye," I said, and I left the apartment.

When I entered Gordon's room at John Sealy Hospital Gordon was in the bed with his eyes closed. I thought he might be asleep, but as soon as I got near his bed he opened his eyes wide and smiled at me.

"Don't tell me," I said, "it's some kind of con?"

His smile faded when I said that. "I wish it was, man."

"So what's wrong?"

"They think I have a brain tumor—they aren't sure yet. I just keep fainting, so I have to stay in the hospital. They keep running tests. I'll probably need brain surgery—almost for sure. But how was your trip to Australia?"

"Do you really want to talk about that?"

"Why not, I'm interested."

"It was okay. But how'd this happen to you?"

"I don't know—one day I started having headaches and then I fainted a few times. So what about you and Mary?"

"I haven't been to see her yet. I just got back last night, and I'll be going on Saturday."

"Well, you can tell me about it when you get back."

"How about you and Debbie? How's that going?"

"I don't know. She visited a few times when this first happened, but lately I haven't seen her. Actually, I've been getting to know Ruth better, because she comes by a lot and talks to me. She's a Candy Striper, so she's here a few days a week."

"What's a Candy Striper?"

"It just means she's a hospital volunteer."

"I didn't know Ruth did that."

"She just started. And she is really a nice girl. Sometimes she talks to me about Jesus, but I don't mind because she's so nice. She even brings me desserts that her mother makes. But what is that on your face, and your shirt?"

"What do you mean?"

"Move a little closer."

"It's lipstick. Have you been making out with someone besides Mary?"

"It's a long story, and I can't tell you. But a girl came on to me, and I turned her down."

"Who was it?"

"I can't tell you."

"Come on, Paul. You walk in here with lipstick all over and you won't tell me who was kissing you. That's not fair. You have to tell your friend. Look, I've got no life now—I need to hear about yours."

"It was someone we both know. Can we leave it at that?"

"Can we leave it at that? Are you kidding? That's worse than not saying anything. I've got to guess who that might be? You can't do this to me. Come on, man.

"Okay, but don't tell anyone."

"My lips are sealed. Who was she?"

"Mrs. Erickson."

"Mrs. Erickson! Are you kidding? The gorgeous Mrs. Erickson? You were making out with her? How did that happen?"

"She asked me to her apartment to help her move furniture and then she started kissing me. She said she had fallen in love with me."

"Come on, no way. Are you serious?"

"Look, you asked, and I'm telling you the truth."

"Mmm—well, her husband's in psychiatry, maybe he can straighten her out. What happened then?"

"What do you mean?"

"I mean she started kissing you and then what?"

"I turned her down, and I left her apartment."

"You did what! You turned her down? Really?"

"Yes, really."

"Man, I think you're the one who needs brain surgery instead of me."

"Gordon, I'm going to tell you a secret and please don't tell anyone."

"Another secret. Okay."

"Mary and I are sort of engaged. She asked me to keep it quiet. I said I'd save myself for her."

"Wow, I know how much you like her, but to turn down Mrs. Erickson! Man, you must really be in love."

"I am. I am. So when will they know what's wrong with you?"

"I don't know. No one knows at this point." As he was talking a nurse came in and stood there for a moment, then walked to his bed when we finished talking. "Time to draw blood, Mr. Silvers."

"You better go now, Paul. This is going to get ugly."

"Yeah, I'll see you later…Mr. Silvers."

CHAPTER 15

I was still tired from the trip, and I went to bed around ten o'clock. Around eleven I thought I heard a voice and woke up from a deep sleep, startled. My bedroom door was open and the light in the hallway was on, and as I looked around my room, I saw my mother picking something off the floor.

"Mum, what are you doing?"

"Just tidying up a bit."

"But it's eleven o'clock, and you're usually in bed by ten."

She continued doing something with my clothing.

"Now, you didn't come in here at eleven o'clock to clean up my room, did you?"

"Well, no it's...well, it's about your father."

"What, is he okay?"

"Yes, I think so. But he may not be."

"What are you talking about?"

"I'm just telling you, he may not be."

I sat up from the bed and rubbed my eyes, trying to figure out what she meant. "So there is some problem, is that it?"

She arranged something in my chest of drawers and answered slowly. "Well, there might be."

"Okay," I said, getting exasperated. "What might be wrong?"

"I'm not sure."

"Well, would you please try to tell me before I go crazy?"

"He didn't come home tonight."

"I didn't know he went anywhere. Where did he go?"

"He went out."

"Okay, but where did he go?"

"I don't know."

I sighed and looked at her for a moment, wondering what this was about.

"Mum, I know you are upset about something, but please tell me what it is. You're not making sense."

"He got a letter from his publisher today. Most of his books are not being renewed. The school boards voted them out."

"What? How could that be? They've been using them for years, why would they vote them out?"

"I don't know. It's something about them being out of date or something."

"How can history books be out of date? History doesn't change. That doesn't make sense."

"I know it doesn't, and he took it very hard."

"So where is he?" I asked, and I noticed she had a tear trickling down the left side of her face. "Mum, where is he?"

"I don't know, he said he was going out to a bar," she said in a light voice.

"But he never goes to bars, he always drinks at home."

"He's very upset. You're too young to remember but the last time he went out he…"

"Was that when he got into the wreck that hurt his back?"

"Yes, and it was very bad—he ended up in the hospital for a week."

"Do you have any idea which bar?" I asked, as I got out of bed.

"He said something about the waterfront—maybe there's a bar there. I'm not sure."

"Don't worry, I'll find him." I hugged her and she hugged me back and clung to me for a moment. She was shaking and I'd never seen her like that before. But then she let go and seemed to pull herself together although her voice wavered a little as she spoke.

"In the old days, he had a predilection for the less expensive drinking establishments. He said he liked the ambience."

"Okay, I'll get dressed and start at the sleazy bars near the piers where the ships come in. I'll look until I find the Electra," I said, referring to our Buick.

"Paul, thank you so much. I'm sorry you have to do this."

"Mum, it's fine, but I better go," I said, and she walked out. I dressed, ran down the stairs, got to my car, and was soon on a street called The Strand in a rough part of town near the docks.

I drove down that street and others as fast as I could, looking in the parking lots of various bars, but I couldn't find his car. I was frustrated, and then it occurred to me that even though I really didn't know what I believed in, maybe God could help. So I prayed to find my father's car. I drove past a few more bars, but his car was still not there, so I stopped the car for a moment, trying to figure out where I was, since I was getting lost. I started driving to the south and I found myself back in front of the first bars where I drove by when I started my search. For some reason, I decided to turn a corner, and when I did I saw the Buick parked on the street. It stood out against the mostly older cars and pickup trucks that lined the street, and across that street there was a blue and light green sign that said *Calypso Tavern*.

The place looked pretty rundown from the outside, and the inside was dark and it smelled like stale beer. As I walked in, I noticed a huge bearded man near the door who was having an animated conversation with an older man. As I passed him, his attention switched to me, and he caught up with me and grabbed me by the arm.

"Ain't you a little young to be in here, sonny?" he said in a gruff voice.

"I'm just looking for someone," I said, dividing my attention between him and the people sitting at the bar.

"No young women in this joint," he said. "Try the Greeks down the street—they got a few."

"I'm looking for a man," I said, and at that he grabbed my arm again and pulled me back a couple of feet.

"This ain't that kinda place—." he started.

"No," I said, interrupting, "I'm looking for my father. I don't want to stay."

"Your father?" he said.

"Yeah. It's an emergency. I just want to look around for a minute, and I'll come right out," I said.

"All right, but make it snappy, and don't try to buy a drink," he said, and let my arm go. I walked in and saw a lot of tired, drunk faces, but my father's wasn't among them. The bar was pretty small, and I also checked the men's room, but he wasn't there. The bearded man caught up with me, and told me I'd have to leave.

"Is there another bar around here?" I asked him.

"Popeye's is down the street to your right, but their sign is broken."

"Okay, thanks," I said, and I walked outside. It was raining now, and I walked down the street in an easterly direction but I didn't see a bar. Then I realized that I had walked past a house that had a broken sign next to it. I looked up and saw that the sign said *Popeye's*.

It was a huge, old, white wooden house with peeling paint that had been converted to a tavern, and there was a lot of noise and activity in the place. I was able to walk in unnoticed, and I meandered around, trying to see through a haze of smoke that enveloped the whole bar. At first I walked the length of the bar, where there were many burly seamen, some with tattoos on their arms, some already drunk, and others evidently trying to get drunk. He wasn't among them, so I started looking at the tables. Besides the smoke, near the tables it was so dark that it was almost like walking around in a movie theater. Again, no Dr. Welles, so I turned around and walked swiftly towards the entrance. As I did, I noticed that the bar made a right angle to the left that I hadn't seen when I entered. So I walked towards it and then I saw someone that looked like it might be him.

As I got closer, there was no doubt, it was him. A woman was on his right side with her arm on his shoulder, and an old man was sitting on his left side, and somehow they all seemed to be talking at the same time. Only a few feet away from him now, I saw the woman's hand reach around him, and slowly descend to his rear pocket. As her hand closed around his wallet and began to draw it out slowly, I grabbed her wrist. She looked up at me, startled, and then sort of shrugged her shoulders and let go of the wallet. It fell on the floor and I picked it up as my father turned around, drunker than I'd ever seen him.

"Hello, son!" he slurred heartily. "What are you doing down there?"

I handed him his wallet.

"I think you dropped this."

"Oh, well, good for you," he said, and tried to take it from me, but his hand missed. "You're a good boy. I'm going to buy you a drink."

"I don't want one, Dad."

"Sure you do—every underage kid in the world wants a drink. Bartender," he shouted. The bartender came over after a few seconds. "He'll have a . . . . what do you want?"

"Nothing, let's get out of here. Mum's worried about you."

"Oh, your mother. What have I done? Your mother is very concerned because I'm driving tonight. She told me not to drive tonight."

"Can we go, then?"

"Yes," he announced grandly. "We shall go!"

I helped him off the barstool, and he pulled out a couple of dollars, and slapped them on the counter. "My compliments to the chef!" he said to the bartender, and then I helped him to the door. It was raining harder now, and the wind was blowing. It was humid, and the rain was warm as it hit my face, and I remembered how the rain was always cold back East. We started walking down the sidewalk, with me supporting him.

"Where are we going?" he asked.

"To my car."

"We're going to ride in the three ninety-five!" he said, waving his hand in the air, and then he seemed to be thinking. "But what about my car?"

"I'll pick it up tomorrow."

As we walked towards my car, we passed the first bar I had visited and could hear music coming from it. Suddenly my father broke away from my support and started dancing.

"We used to really dance," he said, slurring even more as he moved himself in a kind of parody of dancing. "Not like you kids—you don't understand dancing. Dancing means you hold the girl close to you—you should hold her close, and thrill her that way," he said, as he flung himself out into the slippery, wet street. I ran after him, and he slipped on the curb, and a pickup truck was coming in his direction. I got to him as fast as I could and pulled him out of the way, with little time to spare.

"Whew, you saved me, Gunga Din," he said, and then went on, dramatically, with an extreme Cockney accent.

I shan't forgit the night
When I dropped be'ind the fight
With a bullet where my belt-plate should 'a' been.
I was chokin' mad with thirst,
An' the man that spied me first
Was our good old grinnin', gruntin' Gunga Din.

At that point, he seemed to lose his place, but he soon started again.

" . . . It was crawling and it stunk
But of all the drinks I've drunk
I'm the gratefullest to one from Gunga Din.
It was Din! Din! Din!

"Dad, it's Paul, not Gunga Din," I said, and I guided him and we began walking again. He looked over at me, nodding his head, to confirm what I'd said.

"You're right!" he said, then he went on:

Though I've belted you and flayed you,
By the livin' Gawd that made you,

You're a better man than I am, Gunga Din!

He had quieted down quite a bit by the time we reached the car, and I leaned him over the hood while I unlocked the passenger door. With some difficulty I got him in the car, and I breathed a sigh of relief once he was in. As I was about to start the car, he reached over and touched my hand.

"One thing," he said, with a volume I could barely hear.

"What?"

"Come a little closer—I don't want anyone to hear this," he said. I thought about explaining to him there was no one around to hear, but it seemed easier to just do as he requested, so I leaned forward.

"You won't tell your mother about that . . . that woman there, will you?" he asked, and I backed up because his breath almost knocked me out.

"I wasn't interested in her . . . she just sat down next to me and wouldn't leave me alone. I am not immoral in that way."

"I know, Dad. I know why she was near you. She was trying to steal your wallet, and I stopped her. I won't say anything. I'm just glad I found you when I did."

"You don't have to worry about me, I can take care of myself," he said, and then slumped down in his seat. I thought he was finished, and started the car, but as I pulled into the street, he sat up again. "I saw action in the Pacific—New Guinea. That's what put me in the hospital in Australia, but I made it, so don't worry about me."

As we drove through the downtown area, he was sobering up and becoming more coherent, and he looked out the window. "This is a funny little town, isn't it?" he said.

"Yeah," I answered.

"It's an island and everyone seems to know your business—sometimes I feel like I'm trapped on an island. The publishers tried to get me to change the textbooks, but I would not. I will take a teaching job and I will do what I must to support our family, but I will not lie about the history of this country. I will not sugarcoat our faults and mistakes, and I will not emphasize them over our merits. You must remember this above all—you have to have standards. No matter what anyone says, you keep your standards. Would Robert E. Lee have changed history for a buck? Would Stonewall Jackson have twisted the truth for monetary gain?"

"I doubt it," I answered.

"Well, neither will I! History is important. One must know what happened in order to avoid the same mistakes. One must know history to have a sense of pride of one's origins," he said, this time showering me a little.

"Dad, back up a little. You're spitting."

"Oh, I'm sorry . . . are we going back?"

"That's where we're going," I confirmed, and he was quiet for a few moments.

"Son, do you think we could make a detour?"

"Where to?"

"I need some time to sober up. Let's go up to the Boulevard and take a drive . . . you know, cruise for a few minutes," he said, emphasizing "cruise" since it was a word the kids used a lot.

"You want to cruise on the Boulevard with me?" I said, without thinking first.

"Oh," he said, nodding his head drunkenly. "You'd be embarrassed if we saw some of your friends, wouldn't you? It's okay, we can just go home."

"No, I wouldn't, Dad. We can go for a ride."

"Sure you would," he said unsteadily, "But you're becoming a little diplomat. I remember how it was with my parents—I felt embarrassed when they came to the school and . . ."

He looked up and noticed that we had reached the Boulevard.

"Oh, we're riding . . . cruising in your three ninety-five—I mean six—it's not a prime number, is it? How exciting this will be," he said facetiously. It was Friday night and the beach was crowded with cars with kids in them, honking and shouting at each other. After we drove for a few miles, he started frowning and got somber.

"I'm a drunk and a failure," he said, and I looked at him, surprised because I'd never heard him talk this way.

"No, you're not, Dad. Not at all," I said.

"I am," he said resolutely. "And I must tell you something about life, son. It is rarely what you expect, and never what you plan. I should have written many, many books by now."

"Don't worry about it, Dad. Everyone thinks you're a great teacher. Mary said you were a genius," I added.

"If it takes a genius to remove a corkscrew from a bottle of wine, then I am a genius. Otherwise, I'm a drunk."

"Take it easy, Dad." I noticed some girls from school I knew driving by. They looked at me, and then at him, and waved, giggling. I ignored them. "You haven't failed," I said. "I was much younger when you were teaching and I sat in on your class, and I knew your teaching was exceptional. And I've read your textbooks, and they explain history in a way that makes it interesting—the ones from most authors are boring."

"That's nice of you to say."

"It's true. And I can understand why you don't want to change your books. I'm proud to see you stand by what you believe in."

"Thank you, son," he said, and I could see he was cheering up a bit. Just then I heard a horn honk, and turned to see Jim Mahoney with another football player named Mark in the car next to me.

"Hey, little boy," Mahoney yelled. "Got a hot date with your old man tonight?"

At first I did feel embarrassed, but it was gone in a flash. I looked over at them, and then I reached over and kissed my father on the cheek, and started laughing.

"Oh, that's really nice," Mahoney shouted sarcastically. My father looked at me, trying to focus.

"Why son, you haven't kissed me since you were a little boy," he said graciously.

"Yeah, well, why don't we pull into the burger place up here and get some coffee?" I suggested, also wanting to get away from Mahoney.

"Fine idea," he said, his mood brightening.

We stopped there and Mahoney kept going.

"I'll get some coffee," I said, and began to get out of the car.

"I'll come with you," my father said, and I stopped and looked at him, a worried expression on my face, which he discerned.

"Don't worry, I'm not that drunk anymore," he said as he reached for the door handle and missed it. On a second try, he found it and began to open the door. Just then, Mahoney's car reappeared and he pulled into the parking space next to us.

"Well look at that," he said, watching my father. "He's loaded to the gills."

"Are these friends of yours?" my father asked as we got out of the car.

"No, they're football players and one is Mary's old boyfriend."

"Oh, I see."

"Don't hassle him. Maybe he'll buy us some beer," Mark suggested.

"No way," Jim said, as I walked with my father towards the door of the restaurant. He stopped and turned in their direction, and looked at Mark.

"My dear boy, I discountenance anomalistic behavior that would contribute to the delinquency of any adolescent, particularly one as appallingly minor as you obviously are," he said, and turned away as we moved closer to the door of the hamburger place.

"What do you mean?" Mark shouted out, and my father turned around.

"Are you discombobulated?" my father asked.

"What is he saying?" Mark asked.

"He put you down," Jim said, and they got out of their car and followed us in. I led my father to an empty table, and sort of pushed him into the seat. Then I went up to the serving area and ordered the coffee. Mahoney and Mark sat in the table next to us, and Mark kept looking evilly at my father.

"What did you mean out there?" he said, threateningly, and my father looked up slowly, then stood up.

"You would be well-advised to keep your bellicose propensity to yourself, even if it was fomented by my predilection for sesquipedalian loquaciousness."

Mark walked closer to my father and tried to stare him down, but my father looked right back at him and did not move. Jim moved towards Mark as Mark doubled up his fist. I moved towards Mark, ready to grab him from behind if I had to.

"Your exceeding truculence may demand that we box, and I must warn you that I was trained as a professional pugilist," my father said.

"Oh, yeah, you're a tough guy, huh?" Mark said with a threatening voice, his anger rising. Mahoney took his arm and began to pull him away.

"Besides," my father said, smiling, "if the boxing failed, I wouldn't hesitate to kick you in your pubescent gonads."

"Dad, please stop," I whispered to him, and Mark's face became beet red with anger and he moved even closer to my father, who was not backing down.

"I am not pusillanimous. I fought in World War Two!" he said.

"What are you doing?" Jim said to Mark. "You can't hit him, he's an old guy. You'd be in big trouble."

"That may prove to be the understatement of the year. It would be the beginning of many woes," my father said to Jim, as I pulled him away and tried to get him to sit down. Then I picked up the coffee and paid for it and returned to our table.

"Here's your coffee," I said, and I sat down next to him. Mark was staring at him, still angry, so I started talking to him to divert his attention so that he wouldn't see Mark's face.

"Let's go," Mahoney said, and Mark reluctantly followed him. Before they reached the door, Jim looked back at me. "Mary must have dropped you."

"You wish," I said, as he walked out and the door swung closed.

"So they think they're tough. They don't know the meaning of the word. They never met Stonewall Jackson, or Hood. Hood was a Texan. They never met Hood," he said.

"I think we could safely assume that," I said, smiling a little, but I don't think he heard me.

"The Aussies were tough, too. Did I ever tell you about the Aussies? They were good soldiers. They didn't like us because when we were in Australia we had the chocolate and the stockings and we made more money than they did, and the Australian girls liked us. So they disliked us. But I saw them fight and they fought hard. Did I ever tell you how tough they were?"

"You did, but I didn't think they were in the Civil War," I said, teasing a little, but in his condition he took it seriously.

"No, no, no, I'm talking about World War Two. Ask your mother, she'll tell you. She likes to act British since her grandparents were from England, except when it comes to remembering those Aussie soldiers. They had more heart in their little fingers than these little high school boys have just because they throw a ball around."

"Speaking of Aussies," I said, "I better make a phone call."

There was a pay phone outside, so I called my mother to tell her we were all right. She was tremendously relieved, and thanked me, and Dad and I left the burger place and drove around a while longer, until he sobered up a bit more. It was a strange evening, and bittersweet, because although I had to search for him and help him sober up, I also I saw an interesting side of him I had not really seen before. And I enjoyed the irony of our brief role reversal—I was playing the parent that night, and he was more like the child. That irony obviously did not escape him, either, because as we exited the car to walk into the house, he stopped for a moment and looked at me. "Now, things go back to normal when we walk in—this was only an interlude in idiocy for me," he said, as we walked up the long stone stairway and reached the patio, which was decorated with different colored tiles.

Before going in, he stopped and looked up at the moon for a moment, which was full. "Or maybe I should call this an interlude of lunacy," he said, smiling wistfully. "Let's sit down for a moment, as I want to ask you a question—I need your perspective as it will be different from mine."

He sat down on a bench on the porch and I sat next to him. He gazed at the moon again, and then looked at me. I could tell he was mostly sober now, because he was speaking very clearly. "What is happening in this world—in this country? I don't understand it. They want to believe a lie. It's like the blindness in Germany in the thirties—I see it creeping in, but why?"

"I don't exactly know what you mean, Dad."

"I mean they don't want my textbooks on history and social studies because they want to deny the truth. They want to say America is a fascist state and the communists will save the world. Is there any evidence or logic to that?"

"No."

"Do we have walls with barbed wire around our country to keep our people in? Oh, it's subtle, but they're changing the books. No longer are the Marines brave in Iwo Jima, now it's the disgrace of Hiroshima and the bomb. They don't teach that the Japanese considered surrender the most extremely dishonorable act in the world. That's why they mercilessly tortured our soldiers who surrendered—they were the first ones. After it was known what would happen, others fought to the death rather than surrender.

"That's why nothing but the atomic bomb would stop them—they considered surrender worse than death. And if we hadn't used it, we would have lost millions more Allied soldiers storming their beaches and islands. But the way they are teaching history now, when the kids grow up, they'll hate this country. Oh, I know we have our failings, believe me, I know that—at Yalta the Allies gave away Poland and other countries to Russia, and there were other things. But most of what they write now is lies that smear us. My question to you is, why do people so easily believe a lie?"

"They are deceived about the truth?"

"Yes, I think so, and there's even more to it than that. I think there is something basically wrong with all of us."

As he finished speaking, my mother opened the door, and she rushed over to him and hugged him. "Oh, you're okay, I'm so glad you're home."

"Yes, I'm fine," he said, with a slightly irritable voice. Then as he walked in to the foyer, he leaned over and kissed her. "Oh, I'm sorry, Ann. I'm so sorry I took off tonight like that."

"I understand, dear. It's quite all right," she said soothingly.

CHAPTER 16

On Saturday I was in a good but somewhat anxious mood as I drove to Houston. After parking in the visitors' lot on campus, I ran to Mary's building and was soon knocking on her door.

She looked different. At first I wasn't certain what the change was, but as we talked, I realized that there were a number of subtle things. First, her hair looked longer, and not as neat as it usually was; as if she wasn't brushing it as regularly. Besides that, although she usually didn't wear much makeup, it seemed that now she wasn't wearing any, or at least none that I could detect. She was also dressed differently than I was used to seeing. However, I thought that the slightly worn jeans and simple cotton top were something she was going to change out of before we left her dormitory. I sat down, prepared to wait, but all she did was rearrange some books she had been reading.

Her roommate, Sally, walked in, and Mary introduced me. Sally was made up to the hilt, and she had a bouffant hairdo, which was piled high on her head. Every hair was in place, and she was dressed in very nice clothing, making her contrast rather starkly with Mary and her new look. Mary and I talked for a little while about my trip, and then about her course in psychology, but somehow the conversation wasn't quite as easy as it usually was, and I thought maybe that was because Sally was there. I was waiting eagerly for us to leave the dorm room, but Mary made no move to leave until I suggested it. We walked out of the building to my car, and before getting in, I turned to her and kissed her, but although she kissed me back, it seemed there was some hesitation as our lips touched.

"Is there something wrong?" I asked.

"Oh no, not at all. It's just this is such a public place."

I looked and there was no one around and very few cars, since it was still summer. I got in the car and we started driving out of the parking lot. "We can eat dinner early if you want, or maybe see a movie first," I suggested.

"Well I have an idea. We can have a wonderful walk in Hermann Park, and then there's this really wonderful place in Montrose called Sand Mountain. They have folk singers there and it's lots of fun. I think you'll really like it."

"Sure, it sounds great."

"Good. Some friends of mine from school will be there, and you can meet them. I know you'll like them, they're beautiful people."

"Well, I hope I'm pretty enough for them," I said, smiling, but she didn't seem to catch the slight joke I was making.

We stopped first at Hermann Park, and I noticed that there were a lot of long-haired hippie types around. There were very few people who looked like that in Galveston, so I was surprised to see so many. Some were throwing Frisbees and others were lying around, looking a little glassy-eyed.

"There are really some weird-looking people around here," I commented, as some guys with extremely long hair and tie dyed T-shirts walked by to our right. She looked over at them.

"Oh, they're freaks. Some of them are really beautiful people, you know."

I looked at her for a moment, not sure I had heard her correctly. "Yeah, but if they get any more beautiful, they might end up in that zoo you hate," I said, again thinking I was being pretty funny, but she smiled in a way that I thought was somewhat condescending.

Both of us were quiet for a while, and then I spoke again, trying to get back the conversation the way we used to have it. "I didn't like being away from you like that. I hope it's never that long again."

"That's nice to say," she said, but then became quiet again.

"Not in the mood for talking, huh?"

"No, I'm just getting off on how beautiful the park is today, I'm sort of into it with my head."

I looked at her for a moment, not sure what to say.

"What are you talking about? When did you start talking like that?" I asked, but she didn't look my way, but just kept gazing out into the trees. Then she said, "I've always felt that way, I just started expressing it. Let's go to Sand Mountain now."

Sand Mountain was a small coffeehouse that served no alcohol and specialized in folk singers. It was located in the heart of the Montrose section of Houston, which was Houston's arty, hippie area, and I noticed a lot of them as we drove down Richmond Avenue. But the atmosphere was pleasant, and Mary told me that it was owned by a woman in her fifties who wanted a wholesome environment. She wanted it to be a safe place for young people to go and listen to folk music, which was sort of fading now that the English bands like the Beatles had become more popular.

Driving through Montrose and seeing all the hippies and freaks made me feel strange, but when we walked into Sand Mountain it felt peaceful, and I could see why Mary liked it. Mary told me that the rule was that we had to buy a drink or something to eat, and it was evident to me that Mary had been there several times before, because when the waitress took our order, she greeted her as if she knew her. I was not used to drinking coffee, but Mary ordered it so I did also—including whipped cream on the top. As we waited for our orders, a woman with a guitar started playing and singing. The place was small, and the singer was only about fifteen feet from our table, and her guitar was clear and crisp and seemed to reverberate in the room.

Her voice was strong and so loud that it sort of shocked me at first, as I had never been that close to a performer. Once she started singing, we stopped talking and listened, for this woman seemed to command our attention.

I can wash out 44 pairs of socks and have 'em hangin out on the line
I can starch & iron 2 dozens shirts 'fore you can count from 1 to 9
I can scoop up a great big dipper full of lard from the drippins can

Throw it in the skillet, go out & do my shopping, be back before it melts in the pan
'Cause I'm a woman! W-O-M-A-N, I'll say it again

I can rub & scrub this old house til it's shinin like a dime
Feed the baby, grease the car, & powder my face at the same time
Get all dressed up, go out and swing til 4 a.m. and then
Lay down at 5, jump up at 6, and start all over again
'Cause I'm a woman! W-O-M-A-N, I'll say it again

If you come to me sickly you know I'm gonna make you well
If you come to me all hexed up you know I'm gonna break the spell
If you come to me hungry you know I'm gonna fill you full of grits
If it's lovin you're likin, I'll kiss you and give you the shiverin' fits
'Cause I'm a woman! W-O-M-A-N, I'll say it again

I got a twenty-dollar gold piece says there ain't nothing I can't do
I can make a dress out of a feed bag and I can make a man out of you
'Cause I'm a woman! W-O-M-A-N, I'll say it again
'Cause I'm a woman! W-O-M-A-N, and that's all.

As she stopped and reached over for a sip of coffee, I noticed some people at the door, two guys, in their twenties, and a girl who looked to be about eighteen or nineteen. They all had long hair, and one of the males had a beard. Mary turned to see what I was looking at, and her eyes lit up.

"Oh, it's Don and my other friends," she said. "They're the ones I wanted you to meet. They walked over to the table, and Mary hugged all of them, which seemed a little unusual to me, but I didn't say anything. Then they sat down with us.

"This is Paul. He's visiting here from Galveston. This is Don, Gary, and Susie," Mary said, but as she went on with the introduction I only heard part of it, because she hadn't introduced me as her boyfriend. "Don is getting his master's degree in psychology—he was a T.A. in the class I took this summer, and he works here part time."

"What's a T.A.?" I asked, and I noticed that Don smiled in sort of a condescending manner.

"It's a teaching assistant," Mary said. "He helped teach the class—and he was really beautiful."

I looked at Don as she said that and noticed that his eyes were red. In fact, his friend's eyes were red also. Maybe, I thought, he was trying to become competition for Mary, and I analyzed his looks and concluded that he wasn't exactly "beautiful." He was average looking, I thought—not ugly, although he might have been behind the beard he wore. He was also very thin and was about four inches shorter than me. On looks alone, I figured I had nothing to fear from Don. Just as I was assessing him, he leaned over and spoke to Mary.

"I've been working on the paper I told you about on ethnology, and I've found out that some tribes must marry endogamously. Even in Hawaii, the royalty has to marry within the family. That just goes to show that it's all what you've been programmed to accept. Another boohoo for another taboo. Isn't that far out?" he said, and laughed a little.

Mary said, "Really?" obviously impressed with what he said, and suddenly his laughter spread to Gary and Susie, who joined in for no reason, for they had not even heard him speak, and soon they were all in stitches. Mary smiled as she watched them, and I suppose my look was one of sheer puzzlement, because that's how I felt. I was wondering if I'd heard him correctly—was he really saying that incest was okay? After the laughter died down, Don started talking again to Mary, but he hardly looked at me the whole time.

"Isn't this a beautiful place?" he said. "The vibrations in this place are so far out that they just make you want to laugh all the time." He held out his hand, as if he was touching the air or something. "It's a manifestation of the good vibrations from the music that's played here. It immediately allows your mind to seek a higher level. It's really beautiful."

"I better get some of that to take back to Galveston," I said, and opened up my hand and grabbed into the air. Needless to say, no one thought I was funny. But I could see that Don had an effect on Mary, and I was reacting defensively. I was already aware of how young I looked compared to her new friends, not only because I was in fact several years less in age than they were, but also because their long hair, and especially his beard, made me with my clean-cut look seem even younger. After I spoke, Don finally looked over at me.

"Perhaps when you get a little older you'll understand," he said, in a tone that I knew Mary would consider sympathetic, but that I knew to be condescending and smug.

"Boy, I sure hope so," I said, and stared back at him with a cutting look. I could tell this time he was assessing me.

"Peace, brother—it will all come together in the end," he said. "We will all come together in the end." He looked at Mary then, and she smiled, and then the woman picked up her guitar again and we stopped talking.

"Well, this next one is an oldie by Dylan," she said, and then began playing.

The line it is drawn
The curse it is cast
The slow one now
Will later be fast
As the present now
Will later be past
The order is rapidly fadin'
And the first one now
Will later be last
For the times they are a-changin'

As she sang, *the curse it is cast,* Don gave me a harsh stare and raised his eyebrows and then smiled as his head went back in a mocking gesture, and I knew I had trouble.

I nudged Mary and then whispered in her ear that I wanted to leave. I could tell she didn't, but she acquiesced, and we finally walked out. The hot evening air hit our faces as we walked on the sidewalk towards my car. I opened the door for her and watched as she got in, which I thought she did reluctantly.

"Do you really like those people?" I asked her, with all the subtlety of a freight train. She looked at me with a hurt expression.

"Of course I do, don't you? They're really beautiful people."

"Yeah, that seems to be your big adjective these days."

"Why are you being this way? Why don't you give them a chance? You only just met them."

"I'm sorry, you're right," I said, not really sorry, but not wanting to argue. "It just seemed strange when they started laughing all of a sudden. I couldn't figure it out."

"Oh," she said, as if she now completely knew why I wasn't as enthralled with them as she was. "They were just stoned."

"What do you mean, stoned? You mean on grass?"

"Yeah, probably," she said, making little of it.

"Doesn't that bother you? I mean, aren't you afraid they might ask you to take some?"

"No, not at all. Like Don says, I'm naturally high on life, I don't need grass," she said, and we drove in silence for a while, although I wanted to ask her many more questions, one of which was why she didn't introduce me as her boyfriend, but I realized that enough friction had been created between us, and it was better not to exacerbate it.

We stopped at a place called Gourmet Burger and ordered special hamburgers. She asked me about my trip and I told her about my relatives in Australia. She couldn't seem to get enough information about them, and then I realized that she was probably only asking to keep the conversation going, for I wondered if she really cared that much.

I remembered that Mary was popular because she always seemed interested in what other people were doing and that made them feel special. When she talked to you, you might think you were the only person in the room. Was I now getting that treatment? Before she always seemed to be genuine with me, but now I wondered. I remembered an advertisement about hair coloring where the question was "does she or doesn't she?" in reference to the idea that the dye job was so good no one could tell if the hair had been colored. I wondered about Mary as we sat there—does she still care for me or doesn't she?

After we finished eating, I offered to take her to a movie, or for a walk, but she said she was tired. So we drove to her dormitory, and I walked her to her room, wishing hard as I could that somehow the old feeling between us would come back, if only for a moment before I left. She unlocked the door, and we walked in. Her roommate was not there.

"Look, I hope I didn't seem too critical about Don and his friends. I guess they just took me by surprise," I said, trying my best to smooth things over.

"Oh, don't worry about it," she said, and then kissed me, and things almost seemed to be back to normal. But it was spoiled when she spoke again. "Don has a vision of things that most people don't, so he expects most of us not to understand him at first. As you get to know him better, you'll start to like him—I'm sure of it."

As she finished speaking, it was all I could do to bite my tongue and keep from saying that I didn't care about Don, or about ever becoming his friend. But I was leaving in a few minutes, and I knew if I rekindled the seed of that disagreement, I would have to leave with her angry at me, even if she didn't show it. So I didn't say anything, and we kissed again, but she pulled away this time, and I knew it was a cue for me to leave.

"I'll come back up on Saturday at the same time," I said. "That's okay, isn't it?"

"Oh, sure," she said, sounding like her old self again. "I can't wait," she said. We briefly kissed good-bye, and I walked down to my car, thankful that I'd had enough discipline not to say any more about Don.

I thought about her and the whole situation as I drove home. I knew she was impressed with Don, and I knew I was powerless to keep her away from him, so the only way to keep him from dividing us, was for me to tolerate him and not say anything else that might be considered negative about him. I probably wouldn't see him again, anyway, but if I did I'd have to be quiet, and I knew it wouldn't be easy.

I comforted myself again by thinking that I had Don beat in the looks department,—if Mary was even interested in him at all on that level. As I passed La Marque, I got a new slant on things, and realized that I was over-reacting to it all. Mary had always made a lot of friends, and people always liked her, and although Don might think Mary liked him beyond the friendship stage, I knew that she didn't and there was absolutely nothing to worry about. By the time I drove into our driveway, I had convinced myself that all was well with us. Don would have the surprise, because if he tried to make that relationship anything more than a friendship, she would surely rebuff him. Then she would be disillusioned with him and she would break it off and that would be the end of it. All I had to do was be patient.

The next Saturday Mary took me to what she called a health-food restaurant, which had recently opened. I found the food rather tasteless. Also, although it was supposed to be healthy, the people working there had pale, pasty complexions and they looked unhealthy to me. But I didn't complain, and dutifully ate my sandwich that had alfalfa sprouts and other strange things in it. After we ate we drove to the park and walked around. Then we went to the art museum across the street, and spent the rest of the afternoon looking at paintings.

After the trip to Australia, where we toured many museums, I wasn't very interested in this place, but the old warmth with Mary seemed to be solid again, and I was happy to be with her, no matter where we were. I thought we were talking more easily, and when we left the museum, I felt that things were very close to normal. That is, until she mentioned the party.

"Don's invited us to a party tonight," she said as we drove down Main Street and past Rice University. I thought for a moment before I answered.

"Oh, that's nice, but didn't you want to go to a movie?"

"I think the party would be better. Besides, movies are just part of the brainwashing that goes on in this society."

"According to Don?" I said, and regretted it as soon as the words were out. I had to control myself and not say anything about him.

"Yes, he's been studying their effect on our society in his graduate work. It's very interesting."

"Yeah, it sounds like it," I concurred, happy that my comment hadn't created any friction. "But you know, I'd just like to spend the evening with you."

"Don't you want to get to know my friends? You have to give them a chance."

"I didn't drive all the way up here to see them, Mary. I just want to be with you. They're *your* friends."

"But my friends are your friends—aren't they?" There was silence between us for a moment, and then I gave in.

"Let's go to the party."

"Good, I know you'll have a beautiful time. Some of his friends are amazing."

It was in an old, dilapidated house deep in Montrose, near the southwest freeway, and if I'd thought Don and his two friends looked a little different, they were nothing to match the "freaks" at this party. Many of the males not only had long, dirty hair, most of them were dressed in white robes, as if they were in some religious ceremony or something, and they kept muttering about how beautiful, far out, and groovy everything was.

My appearance caused a little stir—these cool cats seemed ruffled when they saw me, and their furtive, nervous glances had me wondering what the problem was. Then Don walked over to me and gave me what I considered a phony smile. He also told me the problem.

"Some of my friends think you're a narc. It's your 'straight arrow' appearance. But don't worry, I'll vouch for you."

Mary looked concerned for some reason, and I thought it was because I was somewhat of an embarrassment. Don talked to them and they calmed down. But I felt uncomfortable, especially since I didn't even want to be there in the first place. We sat in a circle on the floor, with Don and about six other people. He kept talking about how horrible the war in Vietnam was while everyone listened. I think some of them were too stoned to absorb what he said, but I have to give him credit—he was a compelling speaker. There was something about him that seemed to demand a person's attention, some type of charisma.

However, his speech was also pedantic and stilted, and he used some words incorrectly, although I knew this crowd would not know the difference, except I thought Mary would. He also often changed the subject before he'd made a point. Of course I'd had a lifetime of listening to my father, who was an excellent speaker, and by comparison, he paled. One look at Mary's face, though, and I could see she was soaking it all up and evidently not noticing the errors. She was looking at him with what I would say was adulation, and he noticed too—then he looked at me and was quiet for a moment.

"We have someone here who is still a pawn in the public school system—a young high school student. Maybe Paul can tell us how he is being indoctrinated towards capitalism and the war," he said in a way that appeared to be so genuinely friendly that I almost felt obliged to think of an answer he might like to hear had it not been for the subtle put-down of being called a "young" high school student.

"I think that's in your mind," I said. "No one tells me how to think in school."

"No, it's in your mind. You don't even know it's happening to you—but someday you will," he said, again seeking the upper hand.

"Maybe you're trying to indoctrinate me the other way."

"Maybe, but if the other way means no more war, and no more people starving in the world, don't you think it's better?"

Before I could answer he spoke again.

"You come up here on weekends, so why don't you listen to everything that's said in your school in Galveston, and then you can report back to me, and we'll analyze it. We might find some brainwashing that way—sometimes it isn't axiomatic."

"I don't report back to you. You're not my leader or anything," I countered, with anger in my voice.

"It's all right, just calm down. Hostility has been bred in you over the years, and I don't want it expressed here. We are peaceful here. We want our lives to be filled with peace and beauty." I looked over and saw Mary looking at me longingly, her face pleading with me to stay quiet.

Don took a marijuana cigarette out of a pouch he was carrying, and lit it. He took a long draw, and then reached over and handed it to me.

"Share the peace, brother. You may not know it, but I love you."

I looked at him for a moment, then took the burning cigarette and passed it to someone else in the circle. It made its way around as he spoke again. "I can understand your fear of trying it, but it's really non-addictive—irregardless of what you've been told."

He then got up and walked away while the joint was passed around. A minute or so later, I breathed and felt smoke go into my lungs. I turned around and Don had another joint in his mouth with the lit end between his teeth, and he was blowing the smoke in my direction. I started coughing from the smoke, and I got up. I suppose I took this as sort of a dare, because I decided to smoke the cigarette the next time it came around. It reached Mary, and since she didn't smoke, she passed it to me, and I took a drag on it. Suddenly I was coughing violently, and the rest of the people were laughing at me as I tried to stop. To my chagrin, I even noticed Mary smiling.

I looked over at him, angrily. "If you're so happy," I said, "Why do you need this?"

"You don't understand," he said. "We never take a substance for titillation, only for edification—enlightenment."

"You've got all the answers, don't you?" I said, and then looked over at Mary. She seemed horrified at what I'd said. Then I looked back at him and he was smiling.

"Pax," he said, and gave the peace sign with his right hand.

"Do you mean peace?" I said.

"Yes, but pax is peace in Latin," he said.

"I know that," I said, defiantly, "Why don't you just say it in English? They both mean the same thing."

"Yes, to you they would. But to me, it has more meaning that way. It's closer to the etymology of the word—its beginnings."

"I know. You don't have to explain everything to me, like I'm stupid, just because you're a little older."

"He's just trying to be nice, Paul," Mary said. "You could learn a lot from listening to him."

"Pax," Don said again. "Why don't we become water brothers?" he suggested.

"What's that?"

"It's a way that you and I can become one, by simply drinking water together."

I looked at him for a moment, trying to remember words from my Latin classes. I smiled as if I was giving him a nice answer.

"*Tu non habueris fratrem meum. Vade jump in stagno ardenti si vis aquae,*' I said, which means 'You are not my brother, go jump in the lake if you want water.'"

He smiled back, and then I realized that he probably didn't know enough Latin to understand what I said.

"What does that mean?" Mary asked me.

"It means let's get out of here. I've had enough of this," I said, and I stood up. She looked at Don and then at me and frowned.

"But, Paul. That was a very wonderful offer. It's a special thing to be a water brother. I'm sorry, Don," she said, and he nodded sympathetically.

"Don't apologize for me. Are you coming?" She looked at Don, then back at me.

"Yes, I just want to use the restroom first," she said, and then left the room. When she did, Don moved a little closer to me.

"You're really putting her on a bum trip, man. Why don't you lighten up?"

"She is my girlfriend man, and it's you who should leave her alone."

"I wouldn't be so sure. You know you're just a boy, and rather immature and unimaginative—maybe she needs someone older," he taunted, and I started getting angrier.

"You mean like a phony like you, who's in graduate school but doesn't even know that irregardless is not a word? The word is regardless." At that his condescending smile turned into a snarl.

"You better run along back to Galveston and grow up, and maybe I'll let you see Mary again," he said, and almost without thinking, I pulled back my arm and punched him with all my weight. He was smaller than me and very thin, and he went down almost instantly, blood spurting from his mouth. For a moment I thought some of his friends might come after me, but none of them moved. I'd never hit anyone that hard that I could remember, and I was surprised at the damage it did to his lip, which was split open. But my hand had also hit his teeth, which cut into my knuckles, and it was very painful. As I examined my knuckles, Mary came back into the room, and she shrieked and ran over to Don.

"What happened?" she cried.

"He attacked me. I told you he was hostile, an aggressor. Look what he did." He showed her his lip. She became even more upset as she looked at it, and then she held the back of his head and looked back up at me.

"How could you do that!" she asked incredulously, and I looked at her and for some reason I couldn't think of a reply. Then Don said something which almost got me to hit him again.

"Forgive him, for he knows not what he does," he said, and looked over at me, that constant smile back. Mary was falling for it, and she held his head closer to her bosom, and my body was shaking from trying to hold in the rage I was feeling.

"We're going," I said, and she seemed to ignore me.

"I want to make sure he's all right," she said finally. "Why don't you go without me?"

"You came with me, and you're leaving with me," I said with such authority that it surprised me and her. Then I walked over and took her hand.

"But she . . ." Don began, but stopped as I stared at him, my eyes telling him he might be on his back again if he argued with me. "Go ahead, but be careful. I'll be all right."

She got up slowly, and as she did, I could remember the many times I'd heard my father talking about history repeating itself. How dumb could I be—hadn't I learned anything when Jim Mahoney hit me?

We walked to the car in silence, but once we got in, she spoke in an uncharacteristically strident tone.

"How could you do that to someone like him? He's such a peaceful, loving person." I looked at her for a moment, and somehow knew that it wouldn't matter what I said, but I had to try.

"He threatened me first—he said he would keep you away from me."

"So you hit him because of that?"

"You should have heard the way he talked when you weren't there and you would understand why."

"No, I wouldn't. I don't believe in violence. This whole world is falling apart because of violence."

"Do you still love me?" I asked.

She breathed hard and didn't answer.

"I mean it, Mary. Do you still love me? The rest doesn't matter," I said.

"It does matter, those are my friends. Don is a . . . a genius."

"Who told you that?"

"Well . . . he did," she said, which would have made me laugh if I hadn't been so angry. "But everyone knows it. He's been helping me find myself—I'm changing, and it's because of him."

"I know."

"No, you don't—you don't understand. He knows about things, about living a life with peace and tranquility. You know how upset I get when I see bad things? Don is helping me spiritually—so I can accept everything. I'm in harmony with life now in a way I've never been. But it's more than that, he has figured out a way where everyone can live in peace forever." She stopped talking for a while, but I didn't say anything, and she started again.

"You see, the world is changing. He's not just a hippie, or a freak, he's the future. In the future everyone will love each other, and they'll be no more wars, or hunger or evil. If we can end Vietnam, it will be the last war. People will never think like that again, and Don's one of the people who is helping to bring it all about."

"So he's the new messiah?"

"No, he's just a man—but there's something special about him."

"So I gather, much more special than me."

"I didn't say that."

"You didn't have to."

We were quiet for a while as we drove. Then I broke the silence.

"Do you love me? You never answered me."

"Yes, of course I do," she said.

"Then will you stop seeing Don if I ask you?" I waited a while, but she didn't answer. "How do you feel about Don, do you love him?"

"I love him, too," she said.

"You mean you love both of us?"

"I love a lot of people."

"Great. If you say you love everyone, it means nothing to me. "Don't you see that? You said you were saving yourself for me, but you don't act like you even care about me anymore."

"I'm sorry, Paul. I do love you, but Don is guiding me spiritually and I'm becoming enlightened and it's a new way of life. If I stop seeing him now, I'll lose all of that. You know, just a few days ago we went to see a guru and—"

"I don't want to hear anything more about Don. If you don't want me, I'll go back to Galveston and I'll never talk to you again."

"I don't want that, either, but I do want you to apologize to him when you come back up."

"Never," I said, and we drove onto the campus and towards her dormitory. "Are you still my girlfriend?" I asked her. Again, she was slow answering.

"I don't know, I'm just not sure anymore since you did that. He forgave you, and you wouldn't even apologize," she said, which started me fuming again.

"Don't you see what a phony he is? He didn't forgive me, he said the words that Jesus said on the cross. He was making himself like Jesus. Doesn't that bother you at all?"

"Well what's wrong with trying to be like Jesus?"

"Do you think Jesus used illegal drugs?"

"The drugs should be legal—you just don't understand."

"No, I think you don't understand. He's trying to win you over so he can take advantage of you. He made that clear to me when you weren't around. You're an intelligent girl—can't you see through him?"

"He said you'd say that," she said, as I pulled into a parking space and stopped.

"Well, I've got to hand it to him, he thinks of everything. But I know this, all he wants is to control you, and use you, and then throw you away. But I cherish you."

When she answered, it was almost as if she had not heard what I said. "And I wanted you two to be friends." I noticed some tears in her eyes, and she opened the door.

"I'll walk up with you."

"No, I'm okay by myself," she said, with a slight harshness I'd never noticed in her voice before.

"Fine," I said, and when she got out of the car I raced out of the parking lot. As I reached the driveway, I realized I was acting immature, but I couldn't seem to get control of my anger, and my heartbreak. I drove fast all the way back to Galveston, wishing there was some way to take back what had happened, especially that silly punch that only added to his cause.

CHAPTER 17

When I got home I went directly to my room, without even saying hello to anyone. Later, when I came down for dinner, my mother asked me what was wrong before my father came to the table, but all I said was "Mary," and she let it go at that. By the next day I was thinking what a fool I'd been for losing my temper with Mary when I should have been going along with what she was saying. In the end, I reasoned, she'd probably lose interest in Don, and then I could get things back to where they were. That evening, I called her, my intention being to apologize and to show an understanding of her new interests—even if they did stem from Don. It was about eight o'clock when I reached her.

"Hi, this is Paul. Look I'm really sorry about yesterday," I said.

"That's okay, I understand."

"Good, I was afraid you wouldn't," I said, trying to think of the correct thing to say next. Why was it I never had a problem speaking to her before? In Galveston I'd never had to plan what I said.

"Don helped me with it," she said, and as I heard that my heart felt like it was sinking into my chest. "He understands you, but he's afraid of the affect you might be having on me."

Straining once again to keep any sign of belligerence out of my voice, I hesitated before speaking again. "What do you mean by that?" She didn't answer for a while. "Look, this is long distance," I added.

"I wanted to tell you in person, when I got back to Galveston."

"Tell me what?" I asked, deep inside knowing what was about to happen.

"I can't see you again for a while. Not forever or anything. I mean I want to see you again. But I need some time away from you, so I can reach the edification I'm seeking."

I was quiet—what was there to say?

"I don't want you to take this the wrong way, Paul. You and I have been the product of the same type of upbringing. It's Western, and aggressive, and war-mongering—but it's not our fault—it's just the society. I have a chance now to shed all of that, and reach a new height of enlightenment, but I can't do it with the pressures you impose. Once I've gotten there, though, I can help you, and we'll be stronger than ever, together. But you must give me this time."

Again I didn't answer. "Are you still there?" she asked.

"Yeah, I'm here. I guess Don's your new boyfriend, then?"

"No, that's exactly the type of thinking that's a problem. The possessiveness and all that. Don and I don't have that kind of relationship."

"Sure."

"Paul, you know how upset I get sometimes—when I see things that bother me, and I told you Don is helping me reach a point where I can accept everything, but it's a process. Can't you give me time for that?"

"How long?" I asked weakly.

"I don't know, but I don't want to hurt you. I wish you could understand and not get hurt."

"I wish I could too. I guess I'd better go now—my parents are going to kill me when they see this bill," I said, not even particularly angry anymore, because there was nothing left to argue about.

"Okay, thanks for understanding," she said, although I hadn't said I did. "And I know Don will be pleased when he hears about this conversation."

"Yeah, I imagine he'll be very pleased," I said, and hung the phone up quickly, without saying good-bye. Then I sat there staring at the phone, wishing I hadn't said that. Why did she have to mention pleasing Don, though? It was just too much to take. But what difference did it make, anyway? I knew our relationship was over.

I sat there for a long time, thinking about the time we'd spent together, and the things we'd talked about. How was it that I thought I knew her so well, and we got along so well, and yet something like this could happen? Soon the stress of that thought, which kept recycling in my mind, made me sick to my stomach and I ran into the bathroom and threw up.

I knew that I had to get my mind off Mary, but it was hard to do. Then it occurred to me that a person can only think of one thing at a time, so I had to think of something else. Then I remembered that I hadn't seen Gordon for about a week, and he probably felt neglected. Our last time together was short, so the next day I went to the hospital.

He was livelier this time, and I was hoping he was recovering from whatever was wrong with him.

"So, you got any sexy nurses?"

"Naa, mostly old bags—but they're nice. I don't know if that's because of my father or not."

"Anything new with your tests?"

"No, but Debbie broke up with me. Some surprise, huh?"

"I'm sorry to hear that, Gordon."

"Well, at least my parents are happy. They'd probably rather see me in the hospital than with a *shiksa*. What about Mary—it must have been great seeing her again. Did you go to Houston yesterday and last weekend?"

"Yeah, I saw her."

"You don't seem happy about it. Did something go wrong?"

"Yeah, but I don't have any problems compared to you."

"What do you mean? What happened? I really want to know."

"She doesn't want to see me anymore—or for a while, she said."

"You're kidding, why?"

"It's a long story and you wouldn't want to hear it all."

"No, I love long stories. Tell me everything."

And so I did. I started slowly, but soon I was telling him everything in detail, from the very beginning with Don to what had happened the day before.

I finally stopped talking and Gordon was quiet for a moment. "Well, we both got put down, huh?"

"Yeah, I guess."

"I'm sorry to hear that. I mean I like Debbie, but you were really serious about Mary. I mean you wanted to marry her."

"Yeah, I can't believe how quickly things have changed. Well, I guess I should get home."

"Paul, do you think me being in here has anything to do with me running those guys off the road? Is it like some kind of payback? Do you think that's how it works?"

"Man, I don't know how it works."

"Neither do I, but I'd like to find out—if there is a way."

"I'll see you later."

When I got home, I called Mary's mother. Before she always seemed nice and cheerful on the phone, but this time her voice sounded distant, and I thought she already knew what happened between me and Mary.

"So, how are you, Paul?"

"I've been better. I just got back to Houston, and I need to tell you that Mary is hanging around with some really bad people."

"Now, Paul, I know things are strained between you and Mary, but it's not right to judge the people she's with."

"I'm not judging them, I'm just telling the truth."

"Well, I know you took the breakup hard. I understand that, but you both are very young and you'll get over it."

"Do you want to hear what Don is like—what he's really like?"

"No, Paul. I'm sorry, I don't. I trust Mary implicitly and I don't want to hear any evil speaking about her or Don."

"Mrs. Sanderson, I am telling the truth—you should hear me out."

"I realize it is the truth as you see it, but I also know that Mary sounds better than ever with her new friends. And I'm sorry you didn't get along with them. I know you attacked Don and I was saddened to hear that."

"Believe me, he deserved it," I said, and I knew it was a mistake to say it as soon as the words were out.

"I have to go now," she said curtly, and she hung up before I had a chance to say anything else.

A few hours later I looked for Ruth's number and called her.

"Hello?"

"Hello, Ruth, this is Paul. How are you?"

"I'm fine—I'm blessed."

"Have you heard from Mary lately?"

"No, but Mrs. Sanderson called me because Mary said you beat up a friend of hers. Is that true?"

"I didn't beat him up, I only punched him once."

"But she said you weren't even sorry about it."

"Believe me, I am now."

"That's good. We all sin and need to repent of it."

Of course that was not why I was sorry—I was only sorry because of the problems it was causing me. But I said nothing more about it. "But Mary is with a really bad crowd."

"I know you don't like them."

"They're hippies—freaks with long hair and…"

"You shouldn't judge them by their hair," Ruth said.

"Well, they also smoke marijuana."

"Really? Well, that is bad. Does Mary know about it?"

"Yes, she knows. But they've convinced her that it shouldn't be illegal."

"Is she smoking it?"

"No, it was just them."

"Well, bad company corrupts good morals—that's for sure. I'll be praying for her, and I'll write her a letter."

"Okay, thanks."

"By the way, I have your father for history when I start at Galveston Community College in September."

"You do? Oh, that's great. I hope you like his class," I said, and I wondered why I didn't know he was teaching there, but I didn't want to let on.

"Ruth, you have really good grades—I'm sure you can get into a four-year college."

"If it wasn't for the new college, I couldn't even afford to go to college at all, and my parents don't want me to go into debt. But God provides. Just when I needed it this college opened up. And I'm sure after two years God will open up a way for me to finish and get my B.A. somewhere. I want to teach and I'll need a four-year degree for that. Isn't God good?"

"Yeah, I guess."

"Oh, I'm sorry, I was insensitive about you and Mary."

"That's okay. Just please believe me when I say she's in bad company."

"Yes, I know you're concerned."

I stayed in my room a lot for the next few weeks, mostly reading and trying to get my mind off Mary. But often I would wonder what she was doing. I also kept wondering how she could throw me over for Don. Then I remembered Ruth mentioning my father teaching. Normally I would have asked him already, but I had been so depressed thinking about Mary that I had hardly thought of anything else. I walked into his study and, as usual, it took him a while to realize I was there as he was engrossed in a book, which I noticed was a history textbook.

"Hi, Dad," I said, as he looked up.

"Ah, you have come out of your hermitage. Do you know the difference between a democracy and a democratic republic?"

"Well, we live in a democracy, which means we vote for things and it's the will of the people that rules, rather than a dictatorship. Is that right?"

"Somewhat, but that was not the question. In the Federalist papers James Madison explains that the United States is not only a democracy but also a republic. That is important because in the Federalist Paper Number 10, he clearly states that a republic must be contrasted with a democracy, because in a pure democracy there is no check on the majority to protect the weaker party or individuals. In other words, in a pure democracy, what would happen if the majority voted to take property from a certain class of people?"

"Well, I guess they could—what would stop them?"

"There would be nothing."

"So you need to have some written laws that can't be violated."

"Exactly, and that is the point. One must have a constitution which guarantees certain basic rights so that the people can't vote for things that would jeopardize the rights of others in the country. That is why we need to have a republic as well as a democracy. Voters can only vote within the permissibility of the constitution. Otherwise a democracy is a very dangerous thing—it becomes mob rule."

"So, didn't we ignore the Constitution since it allowed slavery? Wasn't that the majority voting to take advantage of Negroes?"

"It was, it was. But that was not in the Constitution. Rather, it violated our principles in the Declaration of Independence that stated that all men are born equal and have inalienable rights. In fact, in 1776, abolitionist Thomas Day said how ridiculous it was for a patriot to sign that document and still allow slavery."

"But that was corrected, right, in the Constitution? That was the nineteenth amendment."

"Yes, we make mistakes, but we try to fix them and we did. But what is so scary about the history textbooks I'm reading today is that they don't differentiate our form of government from a pure democracy. If that distinction is not made, the students will not understand our government when they mature and get in positions of power."

"I see."

"But you didn't walk in here to get a lesson on government, did you?"

"No, but I heard you were teaching at a college here—I think it's a new junior college. I mean I know you'll be teaching the maritime students at Texas A and M. So are you also teaching at the new college?"

"Well, I wasn't going to, but someone contacted me about it when we first moved here, and when some of my books were rejected, I decided to take it. By the way, I am very sorry it didn't work out with you and Mary. You never said anything, but Mum told me about it."

"Yeah, she said she told you."

"What was the reason?"

"She found someone she liked better at college."

"Well, again, I'm sorry to hear that. I liked her."

"It probably wouldn't have happened if we hadn't been separated."

"So you think going to Australia ruined your relationship with her?"

"Well, yes, I do. You can't deny that, can you?"

"I absolutely deny it. It was her choice that ruined the relationship, not the circumstances. Moreover, I think it was for the best. How else would you know if she would remain faithful to you unless she was tested—unless you were both tested? Would you rather it happened after you had invested even more time with her?"

I became instantly angry at what he said, and yet I could not deny his logic. "You know, you make a great comforter," I said, as I turned to walk out.

"I'm sorry, Paul. But you blamed Australia."

I turned around and walked back towards him, shouting. "You are so cold-hearted! Is being right the only thing important to you? You don't care whose feelings you hurt, and you don't care about anyone else, or anything else, besides your beloved bottle!" Then I ran down the stairs and out of the house.

I needed to talk to someone, but I knew Mrs. Sanderson and maybe Ruth didn't believe me about Mary, and I also owed Gordon a visit. So I drove to the hospital.

Gordon started talking as soon as I walked in his room.

"You know, I've been thinking about this guy who's trying to steal Mary, what was his name?"

"Don."

"Yeah, Don. I mean this guy is poison. If I were you, I'd go back up to Houston and try to get her back, now. Because he's just going to be putting you down all the time she's with him, and eventually you'll be completely out of the picture."

"Maybe you're right. I thought it might get better when she sees what he's really like."

"No, if she doesn't see it now, when will she see it? I think you'll lose her forever if you don't try to win her back. You can go up there like the movie where that girl was about to get married, and that guy stops her right before the ceremony, and she goes with him on a bus with a wedding dress still on."

"I don't think Don wants to marry Mary."

"Yeah, that part doesn't fit. But I think you have to try again. If you don't give it one more shot, I think you'll be sorry. She says wait until Don says it's okay for her to see you again, and we both know that will be never."

"Kind of like waiting for Godot," I said.

"Waiting for who?"

"Oh, it's a play I read in school last year. They wait for someone who never comes."

"Yeah, well, the longer you wait, the more time he's got to get what he wants. And we know what that is."

"You're right. It's worth one more try."

"Oh, I wish I could go with you. But I can't," he said, frustrated as he sat up in bed. "But visit afterwards and tell me how it goes."

"I can't wait until you're well and we can cruise again. It's seems like just the other day you and I were blasting down the Boulevard."

"Yeah, but I don't think that will happen again."

"Sure it will, when you're well. You'll get well."

Gordon shook his head no and then smiled weakly. "It's malignant, man. Too much to operate on. I could kick it anytime."

"What, are you serious?"

"I'm serious."

"Why didn't you tell me before this?"

"Because I'm trying to ignore it. But really, I don't get it. I mean, I'm only seventeen, and my life's going to be over already?"

We were both quiet for a moment, and I could see tears coming from his eyes, so I walked closer to him, and sat on the bed, and put my arm around him. "I'm sorry, Gordon."

"Look, please get out of here and go to Houston. Don't get mushy with me—I'm not dead yet."

I looked at him again, but he nodded no to me. "I mean it, get going, Welles. It may be your last chance with her."

"Okay, but I'll visit more often when I get back."

"Yeah, sure you will. Good luck."

CHAPTER 18

That next Saturday afternoon, I drove to Houston. The fall semester was supposed to start in a few days, and there was a lot more traffic on the campus. After parking in front of the dormitory, I sat in the car, thinking for a long time. For a moment, I considered turning around and just driving home, because I didn't know if I could take the rejection I might get, but finally I opened the door and walked into the building. In the lounge area there were a number of students sitting around, and I quickly passed them and took the stairs up to Mary's room and knocked on the door.

"Who is it?" a voice said.

"It's Paul," I answered, and then waited for a response. When it didn't come, I spoke again. "Look, I know I should have called you, but I just want to talk. I've driven sixty miles just to see you, please don't turn me down." I heard the lock click, and then the door opened, and there stood a girl, but it wasn't Mary. She was an attractive brunette with a well made-up face, and she looked at me for a long moment and then smiled and spoke in a pronounced Texas drawl.

"I can't imagine anyone coming sixty miles just to see me," she said, facetiously. "I just got here from Dallas the other day."

"I'm sorry, I thought you were someone else—Mary," I said, and then checked the number on the door to make sure it was correct. It was.

"I'm afraid there's no Mary here, but I think she lived here before me, because I saw her name on the register when I took the room."

"Could she be your roommate?" I asked.

"No, I already have one. Why don't you check downstairs and see if they can tell you where she went?"

"Yeah, I'll do that," I said, backing up from the door. "Sorry I bothered you."

"It's no bother. Come back some time and say hello, if you want to," she said flirtatiously. "I might like a boy who cares that much for a girl."

I went downstairs and checked as she suggested, but all anyone could tell me was that she had moved from the dorm room. One woman suggested that I ask the admissions office, but of course they were closed until Monday. I sat in the lounge, trying to figure out how to find her, when I thought of calling her mother. Using a pay phone there I tried her number, but there was no answer. It was about five o'clock, so I drove off the campus and stopped at a hamburger place to get something to eat, and then I called her again, but there was still no answer. Then I tried Mary's telephone number, even though I figured it had to be disconnected, and it was and there was no referral. Where was she? I wondered, as I got into my car and began to drive.

I didn't know much about Houston, but I had been to Hermann Park, so I headed there again, parked, and walked around. There were a lot of long-haired people milling around, and several came up to me to ask if I wanted to buy some grass or acid. Ignoring them as I walked and thought, it occurred to me that if I had any chance of finding her that evening, it would be at Sand Mountain, so I got back in the car and drove toward Richmond Avenue, in Montrose.

Sand Mountain was crowded, and it was difficult to see through the cigarette smoke, but after a few minutes of looking I was satisfied that Mary wasn't there. But I remembered that Mary said Don worked there part time, so I walked to the restroom which was near the kitchen and looked in, but I didn't see him. As I walked out to leave, I saw the couple who had accompanied Don on the night we first met there. I stopped them before they had a chance to reach a table.

"Hi," I said, as friendly as I could. "I'm Paul, a friend of Mary's . . . and Don's."

"Oh, yeah, peace, brother," the man said slowly, and I noticed that his eyes were even redder than they were at that first meeting. He smiled, then turned to walk away.

"Hey, I'm kind of in a fix. Mary asked me to bring up some of her clothes, but I lost her address and telephone number. Do you happen to have it?"

"Sure, man. It's the same as ours. Mary moved in with us."

I looked at him for a minute, then at his girlfriend. "That's right, she did mention you. Do you think you could give me the number? I've got to get that stuff over there and get back home," I said, trying to keep his waning attention.

"I'll give you the address," his girlfriend said, obviously in better shape than him. She took a pen from her purse, and I got a napkin from a table for her and she wrote it down, and handed it to me. "There is no phone number—we don't believe in phones—they're like part of the plastic world."

"Yeah, I know what you mean," I said, and took the napkin from her.

As I walked to the door, I heard her say to her boyfriend: "He's really strange."

After asking directions at a gas station, I finally found the place, which turned out to be large, sprawling wood frame house that looked like it should have been condemned many years before. I noticed that the rest of the neighborhood was in about the same shape as I parked my car and walked up the sidewalk towards it. Some of the windows had rags for curtains and some had no coverings; and through them I could see one room with colored lights and a large water-pipe with several hippie types inhaling from it. From another I heard a stereo and saw some posters reflecting from the wall, a purple or "black light" making them shine iridescently.

It took a few minutes of loud knocking before someone came, but finally a girl with jeans, a halter-top, and long, frizzy dishwater-blonde hair answered. As she opened the door, the music became louder.

Purple haze, all in my brain

Lately things they don't seem the same
Actin' funny, but I don't know why
Excuse me while I kiss the sky

She stood at the opened door but didn't say anything.

"I'm looking for Mary Sanderson," I said, wondering if she could understand me. It took her a moment, but she did answer.

"Nobody like that lives here," she said, and began to close the door.

"I think she just moved in with Don," I added.

"Oh, yeah. Well, they're not here."

"Do you know where they are? I'm supposed to bring them something."

She looked at me for a moment, probably trying to decide if she should tell me or not.

"Don is my far out friend—he's really groovy," I added, which prompted her to tell me.

"Try Love Street."

"Oh, you mean at Allen's Landing?"

"Yeah, they went to hear the band playing at Love Street. It's a groovy cover band."

"What's a cover band?"

"They play songs from other bands. Sometimes you can't tell them from the real thing."

"Oh, I see. Well, I appreciate it. Thank you."

"You are welcome," she said, playfully mimicking me because I think I sounded straight to her. "Have a far out time."

I walked back to the car, thinking could Mary have really moved in there with all those people? I thought about the girl at the door—her clothes were not only shabby, they also looked dirty.

The traffic was jam-packed around Allen's Landing, and it took me a long time to get there. There were no parking spaces nearby, so I had to drive a couple of blocks away, where I parked in a high-priced parking lot. Although it hadn't been such a long time since Gordon and I had made our first trip, the area had evidently risen a great deal in popularity, and it was crowded and hard to walk around. There were literally hundreds of people sitting and standing around, most of them with long hair, and most of them appearing to be high on something. I took a deep breath and wondered how I would find Mary in the midst of so many people. Then I remembered I was told they were going to see the band that was playing.

As I got closer, I saw a large neon sign on the second story of a building next to the park area lit up with the words 'Love Street" and music was flowing from the place. As I made my way towards it, the pungently sweet odor of burning marijuana that I'd first experienced at Don's party filled the air. On the first story and across the street were a number of head shops with drug paraphernalia, and black light gaudy-colored posters with everything from unicorns to naked women. There was an outdoor stairway to reach the Love Street club, and as I looked up I saw in a smaller, unlit sign the words "$3 Cover Charge." There were people standing on the stairs, making it difficult for me to climb them. As I ascended, the band began a rock song, and as I got closer it got louder. I paid the cover charge and walked in, and now the music was so loud it hurt my ears. I'd heard the song they were playing on the radio.

There must be some kinda way out of here
"Said the drunkard to the thief
There's too much confusion, I can't get no relief....

I actually had to squeeze by people, the place was so crowded. I walked around as much as I could, looking for Mary, but it wasn't long before I decided that there were just too many people, and it was too hard to move around to find her. Going back to where I thought the entrance was, I walked next to the dance floor, where people dancing were virtually restricted to moving up and down, and one couple was perspiring so heavily that as I walked by, I was sprayed by their sweat. The music kept pounding as I tried to get through.

No reason to get excited, the thief he kindly spoke
There are many here among us, who feel that life is but a joke.
But you and I have been through that, and this is not our fate.
So let us stop talking falsely now, the hour's getting late.

Close to the doorway, I saw her. She was bent over with her head down, on Don's shoulder, and he was slowly moving her towards the door, and another couple seemed to be with them. I pushed a few people out of way, irritating them, to try to reach them before they got any farther. As I did, I kept my eye on Mary, and could see that she was moving strangely, as if she had lost her sense of balance. Pushing harder still, and getting a punch in the side from someone as I did, I finally caught up with them. Don saw me coming, and turned Mary so she couldn't see me, but I walked in front of her.

As she held up her head, and looked at me, I backed up a little in shock. Her eyes were red, and she kept opening and closing them, and her whole face was contorted into a sort of smiling, degraded looking caricature of her normal appearance. Although it may sound melodramatic, the story of Dr. Jekyll and Mr. Hyde flashed through my mind as I watched her, speechlessly, and tried to understand what was happening. I took her arm, and Don took the other one, and we had a mild tug of war with her body as we both gravitated towards the door. He shouted something at me, but with the music going full blast, I still couldn't hear him. Then the music stopped for a while.

"What did you do to her?" I screamed at Don.

"Take is easy, man. You're putting her on a bummer," he said, as the other couple with them caught up with us.

"Wow, I can see all sorts of colors," Mary said, pulling her hands away from both of us and moving them into the air in front of her. Then the band started again with another song.

One pill makes you larger, and one pill makes you small
And the ones that mother gives you, don't do anything at all
Go ask Alice, when she's ten feet tall

Don had taken hold of Mary again, and was dragging her away from me, and now the other couple was in my way, but I was determined not to let Mary get away, as the music continued.

And if you go chasing rabbits, and you know you're going to fall
Tell 'em a hookah-smoking caterpillar has given you the call
And call Alice, when she was just small
When the men on the chessboard get up and tell you where to go
And you've just had some kind of mushroom, and your mind is
moving low...

It was so hot inside the club that even the humid Houston air outside seemed cool by comparison. I followed them down the stairs and caught up with them. Don was holding Mary's left hand and I took the other one again. The other couple gave me strange, stoned looks, but didn't say anything. I looked at Mary again, and although her face wasn't back to normal, it looked better to me than in the club. Had I imagined it looking so grotesque? We walked along the grass in front of the building, and I moved quickly to get ahead of Don. I was finally able put my face directly in front of Mary, and her eyes focused and she recognized me.

"Paul. How'd you get here? . . . You look so...so different, you look so young."

"What did he do to you?" I asked, looking over at Don.

"It's wonderful, I took some acid."

"What?" I shouted.

"It's okay. Don's helping me. He studied with Timothy Leary."

I stared at Don. "You son of a..."

"Go home, man. You're giving her a bum trip."

"I'm staying with her, so forget it," I said, as I walked along with them, not even knowing where they were going. Then I turned my attention back to Mary.

"Why would you take acid? You said you'd never take drugs."

"It's only for edifi...edifi..."

"Edification, yeah, I know, I heard it before when you said Don said you were naturally high."

"Yes, well I am, but this is important," she said seriously. "This is different. It's mind-expanding. Don's tripping too."

"The blind leading the blind?" I said, turning to him, and he looked at me darkly.

"I can handle it," he said, and I noticed we were walking into the park area where the largest crowd was. A few seconds later, Don let go of Mary, and I saw him talking to two tough looking, bearded men. They didn't look like students, but it was clear he knew them pretty well, and they looked as he pointed in my direction. I turned my attention back to Mary.

"Mary, people have killed themselves on this stuff. Please come with me and I'll take care of you until it wears off."

"Don dropped acid with Timothy Leary—he's the best one to guide me on this fabulous trip. I can see all types of colors in the sky," she said, looking up. "The stars are all colored and they're vibrating!"

Soon Don was back, and he pulled Mary to the side, turning her head away from me, and someone grabbed me by the hair and arm from the rear, and pulled me backwards.

"What!" I screamed, but Mary didn't hear me. As I tried to turn around, I saw that it was the two guys he was talking to. One of them had me by the wrist, and his grip was too powerful for me to break, but as I was trying to, the other one punched me in the back of the neck, and I fell to the ground. The music seemed to pulsate in my head as it emanated from the club.

I tried to get up, but then the other man pulled his hand back to hit me and I decided to stay on the grass. Lots of people were around, but even the ones who saw me didn't seem to care what was going on.

"They're gone now," the man who hit me said to the other one. "As soon as you get up, you better start running," he said to me. So I got up and ran, my head pounding from the punch.

When I reached my car, I got in and locked the door, and then sat for a moment, trying to get my thoughts together. I decided to drive back to the house she had moved to and wait for them to come home. But two hours later, they still hadn't come home, and I fell asleep with my body stretched across the console and my head on the passenger bucket seat.

At about six a.m., the sun woke me up, and I sat up feeling cramps in my body from the unusual position. After stretching a little, I got out of the car and walked up to the house and knocked. If I'd thought it took a long time to answer the first time, it was nothing compared to this time. Both knuckles reddened from the knocking, and I started kicking the door instead. Don finally answered it.

"You better go home," he said.

"I want to see Mary."

"Well, you can't," he said, and slammed the door in my face.

"Then I'm calling the cops," I shouted at the top of my lungs, hoping he could hear me through the thick old door. He did, because it opened again.

"Why don't you just leave her alone? She doesn't want to see you," he said.

"Just let her tell me that for herself, and I'll never bother you again."

"Now, are you going to stick to that?" he said, pointing his finger in my face.

"Yes. And keep that finger to yourself, or I'll break it off," I added as he walked away from the door. A few minutes later, Mary walked up. She looked pretty bad, but she was coherent.

"What do you want, Paul?" she said drowsily.

"I just want to talk to you. Will you come and sit in my car with me for a second?"

"Okay," she said, and we slowly walked from the porch towards it. I opened the door for her, and then got in myself.

"Why did you take that acid last night? Why would you do that? Did he force you?" She looked at me for a moment, and sighed in a way that implied that I'd never understand.

"No, Don would never do that. LSD has helped a lot of people break out of old thinking. I knew I had to get a different view of the world, and that was only my second trip, and already I'm seeing and understanding things I never did before," she said.

"Like what?"

"Oh, so much. Don's a pantheist, and they believe that life is in everything. See, there really isn't pain and stuff, it's just like a big illusion. We can control our own reality, and I'm learning to do that."

"But I thought you believed in Jesus. You said he used to talk to you. Did he stop?"

Her face showed guilt as I finished and she had to think for a while before answering. "I still do, but Don's gone beyond that."

"Yeah, I just wonder how far he will go. He also said he didn't want to make it with you, and now you're living together."

"You're wrong," she said, bothered by what I said. "We haven't done anything. I'm pure, and that's one of the things Don loves about me. He wants me to stay pure. He has a platonic love for me that goes beyond anything that you and . . . I mean it's a special love."

"Better than what we had, you were going to say," I said, but she didn't answer. "And just like he said you didn't need drugs, he says he wants you pure. Do you really believe that?"

"I better get back in," she said.

"There's nothing I can say, is there?"

"You just don't understand, Paul," she said, opening the door.

"Would you mind giving me my broach back?" It took her a moment to remember what I was talking about.

"Yes, I will. I'll find it and give it back to you, but I just moved and everything is still in boxes."

"Be careful," I said, as she walked away, and then tears started falling involuntarily from my eyes. I had been taught not to cry, but I couldn't seem to control it, and I held my hand over my face so she wouldn't see, but it didn't matter because she never looked back. Suddenly my body seemed to convulse with tears, and I felt ashamed of myself. A hippie couple walked by and the man stopped by the passenger window which was partially open.

"I've got the best, Michoacán. Ten dollars a lid, man. You'll love it."

"Go to hell!" I shouted, and then I started the car and stepped hard on the accelerator, and he jumped back quickly as the car spun out and the tires squealed. I raced up Westheimer Road to the freeway and soon I was on my way back to Galveston. I kept recycling the whole event as I drove, so finally I turned on the radio to get my mind off it. A Beach Boys song came on.

...where is the girl I used to know
How could you lose that happy glow
Oh, Caroline no
Who took that look away
I remember how you used to say
You'd never change, but that's not true

Oh, Caroline you
Break my heart
I want to go and cry
It's so sad to watch a sweet thing die
Oh, Caroline why

Could I ever find in you again
Things that made me love you so much then
Could we ever bring 'em back once they have gone
Oh, Caroline no

I turned the radio off. The song was making things worse, and I told myself that I had to be strong and not think about Mary. By the time I reached the bridge which joined Galveston to the mainland, I had finally accepted the fact that she was out of my life. My pride was terribly shattered, and I promised myself I would never contact her again.

As I reached the top of the porch stairs, my mother opened the door. She had a worried, yet scolding look on her face, but she didn't say anything as I walked in. But my father had something to say and he shouted as he walked out of his study.

"Where in the world have you been? We almost called the police, and we were going to in the next few hours."

"I'm sorry," I said softly.

"You're sorry? You don't sound very sorry. You've broken our trust!"

"You could have at least called," my mother added.

"No, I couldn't, because I fell asleep in the car. I was trying to find Mary and she was out with Don until late last night, so I went to the house she was living in and sat there, but I fell asleep, and just woke up this morning. So I talked to her and then I came home. I'm didn't mean to upset anyone."

That calmed them down a little, and when my father started to speak again, my mother gave him a look and he thought better of it.

"It sounds like it didn't work out—you did tell us you were going to see her, but we never expected you to stay out all night."

"I know. I didn't either. And it didn't work out. The relationship is over—that's clear now. I gave it one last try, and that's all I'm going to do. I'm finished with it now, and I won't contact her again."

My mother came over and hugged me. "I'm sorry, I know you really liked that girl."

"It was more than that. I proposed to her and she said she'd save herself for me, so I hoped we'd get married. I wasn't interested in any other girls—I thought she was the one."

"There will be another one, son. And you will find happiness," my father said.

"Yeah, well, I'm really tired, so I think I'll just go to bed now, if that's all right."

"I can make you some breakfast, dear. Would you like that?"

"No thanks."

"Later then, when you wake up. I'll make your favorite—waffles."

"Yeah, thanks Mum."

CHAPTER 19

I suppose it was from the relief of the stress of wondering about our relationship, but I slept deeply all day and all night. I finally woke up at about ten the next morning, and I took a long, leisurely shower. I was feeling better, but my mind was still playing some of the scenes from Houston over again. I remembered first meeting Don and thinking he was trouble. But I never thought that he could brainwash Mary the way he did, and it still astounded me. However, it wasn't just brainwashing—I had thought Mary cared about me as deeply as I cared about her. I smiled wryly as I looked in the mirror and combed my hair—how could I have been so stupid? That thought didn't seem to dissipate my sadness, and it went beyond the actual break-up; now I was really worried about what would happen to Mary. I knew she was naïve and I knew that Don would take advantage of her and use her if he could.

As I walked down the stairs, the phone rang and it was Gordon.

"What happened?" he asked. "Did you see her?"

"Yeah, I'll come by later and tell you about it. I've got to visit her mother now."

Mrs. Sanderson was in her car and was about to drive away when I drove up. I walked up to her window and she rolled it down, but I could tell she was not pleased to see me. But she was polite and she waited for me to speak.

"Mrs. Sanderson, there's something I have to tell you."

"What is that, Paul?"

"Mary is really in trouble now…"

"Paul, we've had this conversation before, and I refuse to have it again. Now I know you're hurt, Paul, but your heart will mend," she said, cutting me off and rolling up her window.

"But she's on drugs now!" I shouted.

With that she stared at me and rolled her window down again.

"Paul, I really am losing respect for you. Lying about Mary will not win her back," she said, and she rolled the window back up and drove away quickly.

"Mrs. Sanderson, I'm telling the truth!" I shouted after her, although I knew she couldn't hear me.

I wanted to see Gordon, so I drove towards the hospital, and as I stopped at a light, I noticed she was in the car in front of me. She looked in her rear view mirror several times and I realized she probably thought I was following her, and that probably made my claims seem even more preposterous.

Gordon seemed happier than the last time I saw him. He was sitting up on his bed and reading a book, which he closed and put under his covers when he saw me at the door.

"So what happened, did you win her back?"

"No, it's over—absolutely over. By the way, is that a dirty book you hid when I walked in?"

"It's not dirty. You mean she wasn't even happy that you spent the time to go up there and try?"

"No—not at all. I'll tell you the whole story later. I don't want to think about it anymore right now. I've been trying to get her out of my head."

"Okay, one question—did you tell her about Don? Did you tell her what you thought of him?"

"Oh, yes. But you see, she thinks Don is almost like Jesus Christ, and I can't exactly compete with that."

"Yeah, I know you can't. It's funny you should mention that. Ruth was here the other day, and she told me things about Jesus I never knew."

"Really? I think that's the first time I've heard you use his name when it wasn't a cuss word."

Gordon nodded. "Yeah, I've done that. That was wrong—very wrong. And I was also wrong about Mrs. Erickson. I made fun of you, but you should have turned her down—it would have been a sin."

"A sin? I never heard you talk like this before. I turned her down because I love Mary."

"Whatever. But let me read something to you and you tell me what you think it means."

"Okay."

He pulled the book out and it was a Bible. Then he turned to a place he had bookmarked, and looked up at me. "Now, you need to know that this was written about 912 B.C. They've found scrolls that pre-date Jesus, so it's a prophecy you can't deny."

"Come on, Gordon, you're not going to really read the Bible to me, are you?" I asked. I was not interested, and I turned to leave, but he spoke in a loud voice.

"Please don't, Paul. This may be the most important thing I've ever read. Now I'm your best friend—I mean we are best friends, right?"

"Yes, Gordon, we definitely are."

"Your best friend is lying here, and I'm going to die any minute. So would you please listen?"

Of course I couldn't say no after he said that, and he knew it.

"I just want you to tell me who you think this is being written about, okay?"

"Sure, Gordon, fire away."

"Okay, this is Isaiah fifty-three:

1 *Who hath believed our report? and to whom is the arm of the LORD revealed?*

2 *For he shall grow up before him as a tender plant, and as a root out of a dry ground: he hath no form nor comeliness; and when we shall see him, there is no beauty that we should desire him.*

3 *He is despised and rejected of men; a man of sorrows, and acquainted with grief: and we hid as it were our faces from him; he was despised, and we esteemed him not.*

4 *Surely he hath borne our griefs, and carried our sorrows: yet we did esteem him stricken, smitten of God, and afflicted.*

5 *But he was wounded for our transgressions, he was bruised for our iniquities: the chastisement of our peace was upon him; and with his stripes we are healed.*

6 *All we like sheep have gone astray; we have turned every one to his own way; and the LORD hath laid on him the iniquity of us all.*

7 *He was oppressed, and he was afflicted, yet he opened not his mouth: he is brought as a lamb to the slaughter, and as a sheep before her shearers is dumb, so he openeth not his mouth.*
8 *He was taken from prison and from judgment: and who shall declare his generation? for he was cut off out of the land of the living: for the transgression of my people was he stricken.*

9 *And he made his grave with the wicked, and with the rich in his death; because he had done no violence, neither was any deceit in his mouth.*

10 *Yet it pleased the LORD to bruise him; he hath put him to grief: when thou shalt make his soul an offering for sin, he shall see his seed, he shall prolong his days, and the pleasure of the LORD shall prosper in his hand.*

11 *He shall see of the travail of his soul, and shall be satisfied: by his knowledge shall my righteous servant justify many; for he shall bear their iniquities.*

12 *Therefore will I divide him a portion with the great, and he shall divide the spoil with the strong; because he hath poured out his soul unto death: and he was numbered*

with the transgressors; and he bare the sin of many, and made intercession for the transgressors.

"So, Paul, who do you think that's talking about?"

"Well, it sounds like Jesus, Gordon."

"And since it was said before Jesus ever walked the earth, what do you think about that?"

"I think that…well, I don't know what I think, but I've got to get going."

"So I've given you something to think about instead of Mary. But I'm real sorry about the way it turned out."

"I know you are, Gordon, and I appreciate your friendship," I said, and as I turned to go, Ruth walked in.

"Oh, Paul—it's good to see you."

"I just read Isaiah 53 to him," Gordon said.

"I see."

"Well, I need to get going," I said, not wanting to talk to her about Mary again.

"Okay, we'll be praying that you…"

I closed the door as she was speaking and rushed out of the hospital. I didn't know why I was in such a hurry, but for some reason I felt that I had to get out of there.

After the break-up, I lost interest in almost everything, and it showed. I normally sat by myself at lunch time, because I really didn't feel like talking to anyone. But one day, Curt and R.J., the friends of Gordon I'd met, came over and sat down with me.

"Welles, every day you just sit here and you look miserable," Curt said.

"You look like a mannequin in a store window—like you're half dead," R.J. added.

"Okay, guys, why are you hassling me?"

"We're not, we're not. We just want you to cheer up."

"I don't think that's going to happen."

"Well, come out with us Friday night. We're going to this little town, La Marque, and the girls there think Galveston guys are great. They think the boys in their town are hicks, but they think we're cool."

"It might just be your Grand Prix they like," Curt said, needling.

"Okay, Robinson, we can always take your old piece of junk."

"Thanks. Okay, come on, Paul, go with us."

"I don't know."

"Well, I do know. You need to get out, man, and I know you're good at hustling. So I'll pick you up at seven."

"Okay, I'll try it."

That Friday they came by in R.J.'s Grand Prix, and we drove about fifteen miles to La Marque. After driving down the main drag, R.J. turned off and stopped at a rundown house in a poor-looking neighborhood. R.J. honked and a man came out and passed him a paper bag, and R.J. gave him some money. We drove down the street and stopped and then he pulled two six-packs of malt liquor out of the bag and handed one can to Curt and one to me. I tried to refuse it, but he insisted.

"Welles, you've got to loosen up. You'll be a crumpled old man by the time you graduate at this rate," R.J. said.

"R.J. is right—you only have so many years to be a juvenile delinquent," Curt said as he took a swallow of his malt liquor. He then took my can, opened it, and gave it back to me.

I took a sip, and then he started the car, and soon we were back on the drag.

"Hey, man, I almost forgot to tell you. I know someone who has it bad for you," Curt said.

"What do you mean?"

"I mean Cheryl—the girl you used to see. She's friends with my little sister and when they found out you were going with us tonight, Cheryl said she wanted you to know that she misses you. I think that's kinda sweet—she misses you," he said with a slight mocking in his voice.

"You've gotta call her, Welles, she is fine," R.J. said, and then he took a long swallow and added, "She's finer than Mary."

"Don't talk about Mary," I said, with anger in my voice.

"Sorry, man, I shouldn't have brought her up."

"Man, you gotta catch up," Curt said, handing me another beer.

I took it, and by the time I finished the second malt liquor I did feel a lot better.

"Well, hello, beautiful," R.J. said, looking at a girl in a car driving next to us. She couldn't hear him, but she was smiling at us, and the girl driving also was looking our way. "There are only two, so someone will be blue," R.J. said.

"That's okay, you guys can have them," I said, and he motioned for them to pull over and they did. The girls were very friendly, and one got in the front with R.J. and the other sat between Curt and me. They drank malt liquor with us, and then we parked in a parking lot in back of a closed bank building, and R.J. starting making out with his girl, but the one in the back was resisting Curt. Finally he stopped trying, and soon she was pushing up against me, and then she kissed me. The malt liquor was doing its job, because I was no longer thinking about Mary, and we made out until they said they had to go home.

Soon we were driving back to Galveston.

"Next time, make sure there are three girls," Curt said. "Welles stole my girl," he said, but in a way that showed he was only kidding.

"I told you to leave me at home," I said.

"See, I said you'd have fun tonight," R.J. said.

"I've got some peppermints," Curt said, and he reached back and gave me a couple as we drove up to my house. It was late and the lights were off, except for the porch light.

"You sure that house isn't haunted?" R.J. said.

"No, not sure yet."

"Yeah, that's what I figured. We'll be at the races tomorrow on Pelican. Why don't you bring your car and give it a try?"

"Okay, I'll think about it," I said, and as I got out of the car, I was a little wobbly, and they both laughed at me.

"Sober up, man!" Curt shouted at me, in a voice so loud I was concerned someone in the neighborhood might hear, and then they drove off with tires squealing and I climbed the stairs and opened the front door as quietly as I could because I was coming home later than I was supposed to.

The next day, which was a Saturday, both of the boys came by unexpectedly and knocked on the door. My mother answered and then I walked to the front door and introduced them. Then we went up to my room.

"Man, you could have a girl in this place and your parents wouldn't even know," Curt said.

"How about a tour?" R.J. said.

"Okay, follow me upstairs, first," I said.

The top floor was an old ballroom and there was also a higher circular area that was built, I was told, so that the women of the house could look out for the ships coming in because their relatives might be on them. If they saw the ship, then they could take a horse-drawn carriage to the dock to meet them. After that I continued the tour and the last place we stopped was the basement. My father had many wine bottles stored down there, and R.J. took an interest in them.

"Yeah, yeah, yeah—man. This is quite a collection," he said, as he picked up some of them and read the labels. "Good stuff, too—cabernet sauvignon, pinot noir, white chardonnay—all from France. This is pretty pricey stuff. Do your parents let you drink it?"

"Of course not, I'm not old enough."

"Just wondering—they have a lot to sip down here."

"My mother doesn't drink at all. It's my father's."

"I doubt he'd miss a bottle or two…"

As he was speaking we heard someone on the stairs and when we looked up it was my father. R.J. was startled and was afraid Dad had heard him, but I knew he hadn't because he was too far away.

"Oh, hello, boys," my father said congenially.

"Hi, Dad. I was just giving my friends a tour of the house."

"Well, don't get lost," my father said jokingly, and he walked towards his collection of wines as we went back up to the main floor.

"How do you know so much about wine?" I asked R.J.

"My father is a connoisseur like yours—but he only stores a few bottles. Of course your basement might be as large as my whole house."

"Mine buys it wholesale from someplace, and he gets a better price."

"Yeah, I guess he would," Curt added. "I'll mention that to my Dad."

"What does your father do?" I asked.

"He's a maritime lawyer. Mostly handles cases when longshoremen get hurt and sue the shipping company. Or when the shipping companies are hurting and they start suing each other. There used to be more shipping in Galveston, but after they dredged the Houston ship channel, a lot of it moved there, so he spends a lot of time there."

"That's how R.J. talked him into the car," Curt said.

"What do you mean?"

"Well, my mother drives a station wagon, and since he was gone so much I talked him into leaving me the Grand Prix, and he bought a new Cadillac."

"R.J. kept leaving brochures and pictures of Cadillacs around until his father got the itch."

"So where are we going?"

"Pelican Island. Have you ever raced your Chevy?" R.J. asked.

"No."

"Well, let's have some fun."

"Okay, I'll meet you there."

"By the way, did you ever call Cheryl? My sister said she still wants to hear from you."

"If he doesn't call her, I will," R.J. offered.

"She likes Welles, not you," Curt said.

"Hey, man, I'm an acquired taste. If she gave me a chance…"

"Fat chance," Curt said.

"Okay, okay. I'll call her tonight, when we get back," I said.

"Well, I've got something new both of you will like," R.J. said, and he pulled out a marijuana cigarette and lit it, then took a drag and passed it to Curt.

"Is this pot?" Curt asked.

"The best," R.J. answered. "You know, when the Beatles say, 'I'd love to turn you on,' that's what they're talking about."

Curt took a drag and passed it to me, and I passed it back to R.J.

"What's the matter, Welles? Don't you want to try it?"

"I already tried it once," I said, and I remembered how I'd coughed when Don challenged me to smoke it.

"Come on, man," R.J. said.

"No, thanks. Maybe some other time."

"All right then," he said, and he took another rolled joint from his pocket and put it in my top shirt pocket. "Yours to try when you get in the mood."

I didn't want it, but I took it anyway so I wouldn't offend him.

We raced that day, and I noticed he didn't do as well after smoking the pot. When I got home I called Cheryl. She sounded happy to hear from me, but I wasn't sure what to say to her and the conversation was a little awkward.

"So, how is school?" I asked.

"It's okay. How are you doing?"

"I—well, I'd like to see you again, if you want to see me."

"If I want to—yes, I want to and I'm so happy you called."

"Well, would you like to go out this Friday? We could see a movie, or something else."

"Yes, Paul, I'd love to go," she said, enthusiastically.

"That's great."

"But, Paul, aren't you seeing Mary Sanderson? I thought she was your girlfriend now."

"No, we're not seeing each other anymore."

"Oh, I didn't know that. Well, I'd like to see a movie playing at the Martini theater. It's called *Barefoot in the Park*, and it's supposed to be really funny. But I'd like to meet you there, because right now my parents would still prefer that I double date."

"Okay, I can meet you."

"The movie starts at eight o'clock. Go ahead and buy a ticket and I'll meet you by the entrance."

"That sounds great."

"And I'm so happy you called and I can't wait to see you again, Paul."

"Yes, me too."

As the week went by, I started really looking forward to my date with Cheryl. She was very pretty, and it seemed to me that I'd been foolish to give up the relationship I had with her so quickly for Mary, now that it was clear that it was over with Mary. Curt and R.J. kept teasing me about it at school, but I could also tell that they were happy that I was finally going to see someone else. I thought maybe seeing Cheryl would help me forget Mary, and that this might be a turning point.

I spent a lot of time in front of the mirror on Friday trying to get my hair to look just right, but it was not cooperative. English Leather was popular, so I splashed a generous amount on my neck and hands and drove to the theater.

I bought two tickets, and walked in, but she wasn't there yet. I thought the best place to watch for her was from the doorway, where the usher was taking the tickets, since I'd have to give her the ticket I bought her. I was about fifteen minutes early, so it didn't surprise me that she wasn't there. But time passed and then the movie was about to start and she still hadn't shown up. About five minutes after eight, I started wondering if I had missed her and thought she might be in the theater already. So I walked in and tried to find her. She wasn't on the lower level, so I walked up to the balcony. Some couples were up there making out, and I could tell they were not pleased as I walked the aisles, checking every seat for Cheryl.

I walked back to the front of the theater, and she was still not there and it was now eight fifteen. Well, maybe she was late because she couldn't get a ride or something I thought, and I waited another ten minutes. At eight twenty-five, I decided to call her and went to the pay phone. I couldn't remember her number, so I looked it up. It only rang a few times and she answered it.

"Hello?"

"Cheryl, is that you?"

"Yes."

"I'm at the theater and I've been waiting for you. Is there a problem?"

"Yes, there is."

"Oh, I see. What is it?"

"You're the problem."

"What do you mean?"

"I mean you dropped me for Mary so fast it made my head spin. And now you think I'd ever like you again?"

"What? You said you wanted to go out. And Curt said your sister told him you wanted to see me again. That's why I called you."

"Oh, I know. I thought that would work," she said, laughing.

"And now you know what it's like to get put down. You fell for it."

"Yeah, I guess I did."

"Hope you like the movie," she said, and she hung up the phone.

CHAPTER 20

We were cruising the Boulevard the next day, which was Saturday afternoon, and I told Curt and R.J. about it. Curt was mad and called her a name, but R.J. seemed more reflective about it.

"What is the line, 'hell hath no fury as a woman scorned?' I mean she went to a lot of trouble to pull that off. You have to admire her ingenuity."

"No, I don't," I said.

Something happened to me after the incident with Cheryl—I started to sink into a deep depression. First Mary had dropped me, and then Cheryl was nasty to me. I could not completely fault her for being angry, but standing me up on the date seemed a little extreme. And so to keep the depression at bay, I began a new phase in my high school life in the days that followed. I went out drinking with my friends and racing at Pelican Island and Cherry Hill almost every weekend. Soon it tended to drown out my thoughts about Mary, but I also lost interest in school and just about everything else. I also felt cold towards girls, even though several showed interest in me. Curt talked me into stealing wine bottles from my father, and I took one about every two weeks, figuring he wouldn't know what he had since there were many bottles in the basement.

My hair had also gotten long, and I wasn't as concerned about my appearance as I had been. One Saturday I came home late after racing at Pelican Island. It was about two in the morning and I was supposed to be home by one. I saw a light on upstairs as I drove up and parked. But when I walked in the house, I didn't see anyone. Then I went to the kitchen and began taking some cold chicken and other food out of the refrigerator. I was starting to eat when suddenly my father appeared.

"Hi, Dad—you startled me."

"I did? Well, do you have enough food there?" he asked, looking at the array of dishes I had placed on the table.

"Yeah, I think so."

I continued eating, but it was disconcerting the way he kept watching me. Finally I stopped and looked up at him. "Do you want something?"

"Maybe a little father-and-son talk."

"It's kind of late, isn't it? Could we do it in the morning?"

"No, we need to talk now," he said, with a firmness in his voice I rarely heard. Before I could protest, he continued talking. "You've always been an A student, but now you're getting C's in some classes. At this rate, you won't be able to get into any of the good colleges we talked about, including Columbia, even with my contacts."

I shrugged my shoulders. "I'm not really worried about that."

"Yes, that's obvious. And it is also obvious that you've become a thief and a lawbreaker."

"Come on, Dad, what are you talking about?"

"You've been racing your car and speeding."

"What?"

"Don't deny it, I was in the audience at Pelican Island last week."

"You were? What, are you spying on me now?"

"Yes, I'm spying on you like James Bond."

"Oh, that's funny. I'm going to bed now," I said, getting up from my seat."

"Not if you want to keep that car, because I'm still talking."

I sat down again.

"I often smell liquor or beer on you, and your mother smells it when she washes your clothes. You're too young to drink, so that is also breaking the law."

He looked at me for a moment and then sighed. "And worst of all, you've been stealing wine from me."

"Oh, well, I might have borrowed some bottles from you. I'm sorry, I'll pay you back."

"I doubt that. But it's still stealing and you've been taught better. You've been taught right from wrong."

I looked away from him as I answered. "But it's in the family—I mean, is that really stealing?"

"Just as if you stole it from a store."

"Okay, I guess you're right."

"I know I'm right. And you also stopped your flight lessons."

"I got my license."

"Yes, but your instructor told me that you need to get an instrument rating if you want to fly for the military."

"I know, but I don't think I want to do that after all."

"After I spent all that money?"

"It's just that I'm kind of against the war."

"So you're for communism now, is that it?"

"I don't know. I don't really care about it."

"Yes, I know, but what I don't know is how much more of your nihilistic existentialism I can take."

"I don't know what that means, Dad."

"It means you act like your life means nothing and the world means nothing. Is that how you feel?

"Yeah, I guess."

"And you probably don't think that laws are important. Like some of my students at the community college. They think that free love and marijuana, and anarchy are just fine. Just like the hippies who keep disrupting and protesting at the colleges where others are simply trying to learn. Is that how you feel?"

He kept staring at me until I had to answer. "I don't know. Maybe. I'm not worried about it."

"Even if they break the law—if they throw a firebomb or start a violent riot?"

"Maybe it depends on if they have a good reason."

"So if you have a good reason, you can break the law—is that it? You know I think you fit right into this town, 'The Free State of Galveston.'"

"Dad, Galveston is a city, not a state."

"Correct, but they whimsically acquired that appellation for themselves many years ago. I never finished telling you about the history of Galveston. In the roaring twenties it was a haven of illegal activity. Celebrities from all over visited for illegal liquor and gambling and prostitution. A couple of crime families ran most of the town, and it became very rich. The "free state" moniker stood for the belief many citizens had that Galveston was above the law. They said they were free from what they thought were the repressive mores and laws that governed the rest of Texas. People looked the other way and allowed all kinds of vice, because the merchants got wealthy from it. You know where the Balinese room is, don't you?"

"Yes."

"Well, it used to host gambling and prostitution. And when someone called the sheriff to raid it, he wouldn't. Later he said he couldn't because it was a private club and he wasn't a member. Of course he could have gotten a search warrant, but he was probably getting paid off not to interfere. Anyway, that's its sordid past and why they called it the 'Free State of Galveston.'"

"That's interesting, Dad. But can I go to bed now, I'm really tired."

"Sure, the history lesson is over. But the ethics lesson isn't. Change your ways, and, by the way, get a haircut, you're starting to embarrass me."

Gordon was still in the hospital, and I had seen less and less of him, but the next day I got a call from Ruth.

"Paul, I saw Gordon yesterday and he told me not to tell you, but he really misses you and hopes you'll visit him. I just thought you'd like to know."

"Yeah, okay. I'll try to see him this week."

"Please don't tell him I told you, okay?"

"No, I won't say anything. How's he doing, anyway?"

"Poorly. Again, don't tell him I said anything, but I talked to his doctor and his chances are not good. You know it's inoperable, don't you?"

"Yeah, he told me but I was hoping…well, okay, thanks for letting me know."

I should have seen him right away, but I didn't, and the next Saturday afternoon Curt and R.J. picked me up and we cruised the Boulevard. We were driving slowly, looking for girls, and suddenly a car full of college boys raced by us, and then they pulled right in front of us, causing R.J. to slam on his brakes. He had been drinking a large soft drink in a cup from a hamburger place, and some of it spilled on his seat. They were in a fairly new Plymouth Satellite with a 426 symbol on the side, meaning they had a 426-cubic-inch motor, which was probably much faster than his Pontiac Grand Prix.

R.J. raced up next to them. "You're driving like a bunch of …." he shouted at them, and then he threw the contents of his fountain drink, which was mostly ice, through the passenger-side window and it splashed all over their interior. We raced away and they followed and chased us down the Boulevard. All I could think of was my episode with Gordon, but I stayed quiet, hoping we would lose them. But their car did turn out to be faster, and after we turned off the Boulevard, they pulled in front of our car to stop us. R.J. threw the Grand Prix into reverse and we got away, but they kept following.

"I can't lose them with speed, but I think I can with…" he stopped talking as he drove into an intersection where the light was changing. He gunned the car and went through as the light went from yellow to red, but the Plymouth ran the red light and was gaining on us. Soon we were barreling down alleys and after a few more minutes it seemed that we had lost them. However, R.J. was not going to slow down until he was sure, and he made a fast corner, skidding as he turned, only to see a dog run out in front of us. He tried to maneuver to miss it, and lost control of the car and we careened against three other cars, smashing them all on the left side, to the point that they appeared to be totaled. And the Grand Prix definitely was. He was able to glide it to the curb in front of the cars he'd wrecked, and it stopped there and would not start again.

"That stupid dog!" he shouted, and then he looked over at Curt who was riding shotgun. His door was caved in, and he was holding his arm in pain. "Are you okay?"

"No," Curt said emphatically.

"What about you, Welles?"

"I'm okay," I said, getting out of the car on the driver's side as I spoke.

R.J. opened his door. "Come on, Curt, slide over here. Can you do that?"

"Yeah, I can do that, driving genius," he said, angrily.

"Okay, we need a plan. I'll leave my keys in the car, and we need to get out of here. Did anyone see us?" he asked, looking around.

We all looked and the street was vacant. "Okay, let's get out of here," R.J. said, and he tried to help Curt walk, but Curt pushed his arm away.

"I'm okay, I can walk without your help," he said.

"Hey, man, I'm sorry."

"You ought to be. You're driving like a maniac."

"Look, we can argue later, we need to get out of here. The Martini Theater is just a few blocks away. Let's go buy some tickets and we'll say we were watching the movie and someone stole my car—that the keys fell out of my pocket on the seat."

We walked to the theater and the marquee said the movie was *Blowup*. R.J. walked up to the window to buy a ticket. "Get your money out, guys."

"You're paying for the tickets, man, it's your mess," Curt said.

"Yeah, I guess I should."

He gave us our tickets and we walked into the theater. The movie was just ending and people were walking out.

"We need to find out what this movie was about," R.J. said, and then he walked up to a woman who had walked out and was looking for her keys.

"Ma'am, I was wondering if you could tell us what this movie is about."

She looked at him, a puzzled look on her face. "Well, I have to think about that—I'm not really certain."

R.J. shook his head and then a man walked by and he asked him. The man hesitated and then answered slowly. "I think it was about what is actually reality and what isn't."

A couple of teenagers came out of the theater and R.J. approached them. "Hey, guys, what was the movie about?"

"Well, there was this photographer and he took a picture and made a blowup of it."

"Don't care what it was about, but there were naked girls in it. It was really cool," the other one said.

"Man, I give up, no one seems to know what this stupid movie is about," R. J. said.

"Why don't we just watch it.? I'd like to see the girls." Curt suggested.

"Because that would mean we were not in there when the car was stolen. We need to walk out of the theater, then I'll come back, sort of panicked, and I'll use the pay phone and call the police."

"I need to get home," Curt said.

"Sure, both of you can go home. I'll take care of it."

"Good. Curt, I don't live too far away. We can walk to my house and I'll give you a ride."

"Thanks, Paul."

After I dropped Curt off, I remembered that I needed to visit Gordon, so I drove to the hospital. I was surprised when I walked in his room, because he seemed so animated. If fact, he was so energetic that I wondered if he was better.

"You look like you're feeling better," I said, after we talked a little.

"No, I'm dying. But I'm also living."

"What does that mean?"

"It means God has given me new life. I'm a new creation, and I'd like to tell you about it."

I didn't want to hear it, but I couldn't refuse him so I nodded and he talked excitedly.

"I finally asked him," Gordon said.

"Asked him what? Asked who?"

"Yeshua."

"Who's that?"

"That's Hebrew for Jesus. I asked him to forgive me and he did and my life has changed."

"Oh...well, that's good."

"Paul, do you remember when I asked you what it was all about—when I was first in the hospital?"

"Yeah, I guess."

"Well, I know what it's about now. We all have sinned and we need to trust Jesus for salvation. He forgave me and he wants to forgive you. Would you like to ask him?"

"No, I don't think so."

"Why not? You've sinned like I have."

"Yeah, I guess I have but it's not logical to me. I mean, I just don't believe it, but I'm happy for you."

"Look, Paul, it's the truth. The truth is we are a fallen race and we are blind to that fact. Sin blinds us. Do you believe that?"

"That may be true," I said, thinking of how Mary seemed blind to her situation. "But the dying on the cross and stuff—it's not logical to me. And I've done some good things too—don't they count for anything? Are you saying I'll go to hell when I die—is that what you are saying?"

"Precisely, that's what I'm saying. But your logic is off, and I'll show you why."

"Gordon, do we have to talk about this now?"

"Yeah, we do, because I may be dead tomorrow, so please hear me out. Do that much for your dying friend, will you?"

"Yes, okay. Go ahead."

"All right, let's say a person stole a car, and robbed a bank and he got caught. Then he goes before the judge and it turns out he gave the money to charity and was known for doing good things. What would the judge do?"

"What do you mean?"

"Well, would he let him off, because of the good stuff he did?"

"No, I guess not."

"That's right. He couldn't let him off because he still broke the law and he would have to be punished. So we will be punished for the wrong we've done even if we did good things, also. Do you get the point?"

"Yeah, but I don't believe in hell and all that stuff anyway because like I said it's not logical. It doesn't make sense to me."

"Okay, let me show you why you're the one who's not logical. Let's pretend that we are on a different planet and we're looking at people on earth. Most of the people on earth say they don't know what happens when they die. But a small group, some Christians, say they do. They say there's a heaven and a hell, and without forgiveness from Jesus everyone will be judged for every bad thing they've done and will go to hell for eternity and it's a terrible place. But they promise that Jesus will reveal himself to them if they will repent and ask him, but most of the earthlings won't do it. They spend all their lives doing other things, but they won't even spend a few minutes asking Jesus to reveal himself. Now, who is illogical?"

"What do you mean?"

"I mean since they don't know what happens when they die, if they were logical they would at least try and see if it's true. They could ask Jesus, but they don't. Now, is that logical?"

"No, but you said something about Jesus revealing himself. What do you mean by that?"

"Well, it's a spiritual experience. If you repent and turn your life over to him, he opens your eyes to the truth. He cleanses you from sin even though you don't deserve it. In Genesis man lost touch with God when he sinned, but when you ask Jesus into your heart, the relationship is restored.

That's what happened to me. And now I'm not blinded by sin any more. So do you want to do it?"

"Do what?"

"Ask Jesus."

"Maybe some other time, I've got to get going now."

"Paul—don't wait too long—it can happen anytime."

"What can happen?"

"You can die—especially with the guys you hang out with—the way they drive."

"The way *they* drive. Are you kidding me? What about the way you drive?"

"I'm changed now. I see things differently. That was wrong—we should all drive safely."

"Boy, you're starting to sound like my parents."

"I know I drove like a maniac. And I was guilty about those guys on the beach."

"Gordon, keep your voice down."

"But I've been forgiven. Jesus had mercy on me."

"Okay, Gordon. I'm happy for you, but I have to go now."

"Thanks for coming, Paul. Come back again soon, will you? I'll be praying for you. That's okay, isn't it, if I pray for you?"

"Yeah, sure, I guess. I'll be back soon. I will."

CHAPTER 21

Several weeks later, I was sleeping late into the afternoon on a Saturday after drinking with my friends on Friday night. I was having a dream and in that dream the phone rang, but I was not able to answer it. Then I woke up and realized that it was actually ringing, but I was so tired and hung over that I didn't want to answer it. I also knew that my mother would answer it, so I continued to lie in bed. However, it rang and rang, so I finally got up and walked into my parents' bedroom, where the closest phone was.

The voice on the other end was very weak, and it was also familiar, but I couldn't identify it.

"Hello?"

"Hello," I answered

"Paul, is that you?"

"Yes," I said, and then I realized it was her.

"This is Mary," she said, almost inaudibly, and there was a long pause before either of us spoke again. Of course it was her voice, I thought, but I'd never heard it sound so lifeless. It was as if all her vibrancy and energy was missing. It sounded like someone who had given up on everything, which was so unlike Mary that it was hard to believe it was actually her.

"Mary . . . it's nice to hear from you," I said slowly, with my voice a little weak from having been asleep. "Are you okay?"

"Okay? Yes, I'm okay," she said, obviously having difficulty saying what she wanted to. "I'm just calling to say that I'm sorry for the way I treated you when you were up here. I'm truly sorry. I realize it was wrong and that I hurt you."

"That's okay," I said, hardly believing my ears, but nevertheless happy to hear what I was hearing.

"So I hope we can still be friends—if you can forgive me."

"Yes, of course I forgive you. Are you still seeing Don?"

"No, not at all. Seeing him was a big mistake. I know that now."

"Are you still living in that house with him?"
"Oh, no, I moved."
"Where to?"
"A garage apartment."
"Can I get the address?"
"Paul, this is not a good time for us to see each other. I'm sorry."
"Mary, you called to apologize, and I accept that. But in case I'm ever in Houston, may I have your address and your phone number?"
"Okay, Paul," she said, and then she gave it to me, although I could tell she didn't want to.
"Are you okay? You sound very unhappy?"
"I need to go now, and I am sorry."
"Okay," I said, trying to figure out a way to keep her on the phone.
"I must go. Good-bye then." She hung up before I could say anything else.

After a few minutes I tried to call her back, but the phone was busy. I kept trying for about ten minutes but I still couldn't get through. The call left me in a daze. Always, deep down, I'd believed that I would be with her again, and that the story wasn't over for the two of us, but this was so unexpected. She was through with Don, and she had moved out of that old house, so something must have happened to make her realize he was a jerk, I thought. She'd finally come to her senses, and it wouldn't be long before we'd be back together again. The only thing that worried me was her voice, which sounded so distressed, and what the reason might be that she didn't want to see me.

The thought of being with Mary again sort of electrified me. My mother had been outside in a garden she started, and she was just walking in the house as I started down the stairs. She went to the kitchen and started taking items out of the refrigerator to prepare some food, as I walked in. My father was sitting at the kitchen table. I sat down at the table he stared at me for a moment.

"You certainly seem chipper. Who was that on the phone?"

"It was Mary."

"Mary! Really," my mother said, but neither of them looked particularly happy about it. "What did she want?"

"She wanted to apologize for how she treated me. I'm thinking about going up there."

At that my mother frowned, and glanced over at my father. "Paul, why don't you think about it before you go?"

"I *am* thinking about it. But she sounded very unhappy and I think she may need someone to talk to."

"I just don't want you to get hurt again. And what about that boy she was seeing, the one you didn't like?"

"I asked her about him. She told me she got rid of him."

"She got rid of him?" my father said, slightly amused.

"You know what I mean. It's over between them. She just came to her senses, that's all."

"I wish you'd come to yours," my father said.

"What does that mean?" I said defensively, and he looked up from his plate.

"Nothing, son. I'm glad she called you—I know it's what you've been hoping for," he added, but I didn't think he was sincere. Unlike a lot of people, he rarely said things that he didn't really mean to comfort people, and when he tried to, he seemed phony.

After I ate, I went back upstairs and showered and then sat down in a chair in my bedroom to do some homework. I was behind in some subjects, and I began reading a textbook for biology. Then I realized that although I was registering the words, I was not getting the meaning because she was on my mind. I pushed her out of my mind and started reading again. Things were going alright for about an hour when suddenly she came back in my mind—like an avalanche.

I put the book down for a few minutes, and I picked it up again. But as hard as I tried, I couldn't seem to get her out of my mind. I knew she said it was not a good time to visit, but she did call me, I reasoned, so she must be thinking about me, just as I was thinking about her. She sounded so upset and I thought I could probably comfort her. Yes, I should do that. She only said that she didn't want to see me, because she didn't want to impose. But actually she must be aching to see me as I was to see her.

Convincing myself, I got dressed to go. I put on some older jeans—similar to the type I'd seen Don and his friends wearing. With that and my longer hair, I thought I'd seem much cooler and more attractive to her than the last time she'd seen me. Then I remembered the joint that R.J. had given me. I had hidden it in a plastic bag under my bed, and I pulled up the mattress and retrieved it. I didn't really want to smoke it, but I thought it would show Mary that I was now "with it."

Once in Houston, I asked directions and found Mary's apartment. It was also in the Montrose area, but it was a nicer neighborhood than her former place. The garage apartment was separated from the main house by about thirty feet. As I climbed the steps, I had a feeling of lightheadedness, and for just a moment I had a strange sensation—that I wasn't supposed to be there. I stopped on the stairs and I looked up at the door, a little frightened by the lingering feeling. I shrugged it off and continued up until I reached the door and then knocked.

I could hear some activity going on in the tiny place, and it seemed like a long wait before she opened the door. She was startled to see me, and I knew she wasn't happy about it, but she tried to smile.

"What are you doing here Paul?"

"I know you said not to come, but you sounded so sad and I thought maybe I could cheer you up."

"Okay—well, come in."

I looked at her as I walked in. I thought that she looked a lot older than me now, and I almost felt embarrassed because of it. Then I noticed her hair. The last time I had seen her in Houston she had been growing it out and it was very long—but now it was shorter than I had ever seen it. Her eyes were red, and I knew she'd been crying, but beyond that temporary condition, there was something else about her face that had changed, although it was still very pretty. Even with her attempt to smile she seemed withdrawn and sad.

"Please, have a seat."

"Thanks. It's been so long since I've seen you," I said, and I followed her over to the only seat in the place, which was a small couch.

"Can I get you something to drink?" she offered. "How about some orange juice?"

"Sure, that would be great." She walked over to the bar-sized refrigerator and took out a container and poured from it. I took the glass from her, and could feel her hand trembling.

"Are you okay?" I said, but she ignored the question.

"Paul, I'm really not in the mood for company."

"Okay, I'm sorry I just showed up. I'll leave now," I said, standing up.

She seemed to feel guilty and motioned for me to sit down again. "It's alright—please stay awhile. I treated you pretty badly, didn't I?"

"Yeah, I guess you did. But don't worry about that now," I said, sitting down again. I couldn't think of what to say next.

"Your hair is getting long, isn't it?"

"Uh huh, does it look better?"

"No, I like it shorter. I like it the way it used to be," she said, and closed her eyes. "I just wish that things could be the way they used to be."

"They will be, Mary," I said, and she smiled slightly at me, as if she knew something I didn't.

"You were right about Don. I just don't understand why I couldn't see through him," she said, a trace of that same wistful smile still on her face. Again she closed her eyes and became melancholy. I wanted to bring her out of it, but I didn't know how—her behavior was new to me, and it was sort of frightening.

"Well, look, I might be able to cheer you up a little," I said, and reached into my pocket and pulled out the joint. "Why don't we smoke this?" I offered. She looked at it and her face contorted and she suddenly became erratic, and slapped the cigarette out of my hand.

"No, no, no!" she said in a loud, scolding tone.

"What's the matter?" I asked, confused. "I thought you liked grass."

"I don't want grass, or anything else. It's wrong, it's all wrong. All it will do is ruin you."

"Okay, okay."

"Don't become like the rest—I'm telling you!"

"I won't. I'm sorry I brought it," I said, surprised at her sudden outburst. "I really didn't want it—I thought you would."

"My counselor told me not to be around anything."

"Your counselor?" I said, and she looked up and sighed.

"Yes, I go to a place for drug abusers—the psychologist said I have an addictive personality."

"I'm sorry, I didn't know—really, Mary, I'm sorry," I said and moved closer to her and took her hand. At first she pulled away, but then she took it also, and squeezed it hard, but I felt she was grasping it in desperation, not intimacy.

"I really thought the drugs were helping me . . . because of Don. He said they were a way to enlightenment and . . ." she trailed off, on the verge of crying.

"I know, I remember what he said. It hasn't been that long."

"It seems like a long, long time," she said, in a sort of childlike tone. "If I could go back and change things I'd give anything." Her tone was a little frantic and she turned away and looked out the window.

"But they can. Things can be just like they were."

"I wish they could," she said, still looking out the window, and I thought she was trying not to look at me. Her behavior was worrying me, because she seemed distant, but I didn't know what to say, and we were both quiet for a while.

"Don fooled me. What he said was right, was wrong. What he said was good, was bad. What he said was happy, later was to be sad," she added in that same childlike voice.

"Well, Don is gone," I said, smiling at my own little rhyme, but she didn't seem to notice. "Mary, what's wrong? Please tell me."

I could tell she didn't want to answer, but then it came out. "I'm pregnant."

"What? It was Don, wasn't it? And he said he wanted you pure!" I was getting angry. Then I cursed him.

"Paul, please don't talk like that. That's the way he talks."

"Okay, I'm sorry. But he's the lowest."

"Yes, he always lied," she said, faintly. She was looking at me now, but her eyes didn't seem to be focused on me.

"Where is he now?" I asked, but she didn't answer.

"I said, where is he now?"

"I'm not sure it was him," she answered in a monotone, but then stopped speaking.

"What do you mean?"

"He drugged me and I passed out. When I woke up, I knew I'd been raped, but I don't know exactly what happened…I don't know who."

"You don't know who? What do you mean?"

"I mean what I said."

"Okay, I'm sorry I asked."

"I might as well tell you," she said, and she resumed looking stoically out the window again, then took a deep breath. "There were these two guys at a party we had one night and Don owed them some money for some stuff—some grass, and I think he was in trouble over it. One of them liked me, and he wouldn't leave me alone and—and I think Don put something in my drink."

"I'm going to find him and he will pay for this," I said angrily.

"No, I don't want you to," she said. "It wouldn't do any good, and he's got some dangerous friends."

"I'm not afraid of them."

"Would you drop it? I don't care about getting him back—it won't change anything." She looked over at me longingly. "I don't want revenge. Please don't make it worse."

"When did you find out you were pregnant?"

"A few weeks ago. By then I'd already moved out." She looked around the apartment as if she were searching for what to say next. "So, I've ruined my life, and I'm sure you hate me now."

"I don't hate you, and things can be like they used to. We're going to get married, and we'll say that the baby is mine."

She looked over at me but said nothing, but I could see she was thinking about what I said. Finally I said something.

"Didn't you hear me? It's going to be okay."

"Yes, I heard you."

"So, doesn't that sound like a good solution?"

"No. I don't want to ruin your life, too."

"It wouldn't, I want to do it," I assured her. "No one would ever have to know. It will be our secret."

"No, you would always resent me, your parents would resent me, and I'd have to tell the truth. It just wouldn't work."

"It will work," I said, with more confidence than I actually felt, and I sat down next to her and took her hand. I moved closer to her and put my arm around her and I felt her stiffen. But I didn't take the hint—I moved even closer and she moved away.

"I don't want to do anything, okay?" she said, pushing me away a little.

"Okay," I said, feeling defensive. We sat for a while, but then I reached over to kiss her, and she turned her head away.

"Paul would you stop?" she said, moving away from me as much as she could.

"I was just going to kiss you, is there something wrong with that?" I asked, at first in an apologetic tone, but then it changed, and it was as if the words were coming out of my mouth without my control, but they were harsh. "Look, we're going to get married, right?" She looked at me with a somewhat startled glance, probably because of my tone of voice, and answered slowly,

"I didn't say that."

"I know, but it will fix everything. Don't you love me?"

"Not when you're this pushy," she said, standing up.

"What does that mean? You either love me or you don't. And if we're going to get married, is a kiss some big deal? I mean, you've always had your way with me. Do you know what you've done to me, putting me down like that after I thought you loved me? I've been crazy over you . . . I've done crazy things, and then you finally call, I come running up here like a yoyo on a string, offer to marry you and get you out this trouble, and you won't even kiss me!"

"I asked you not to come."

"Did you really think I could stay away?"

"So, what are you trying to say?" she said, her face looking strange to me as she spoke. "That I owe you something?"

"No, but—well, I thought you would at least want to kiss me—instead you act like I'm repulsive or something."

"It's not that. Would you try to understand?"

"Why don't you try to understand *me*? It's hard to take the idea of you being with someone else, but now I'm back, just like a loyal little puppy, and you're making me feel like I've done something wrong."

It was dusk now, and with no lights on in the apartment, I could only see some of her face, which in the reduced light looked more like it used to.

"I think it would be better if you left."

I looked at her with disbelief. "Are you kidding? You want me to go right now?" She got up and walked into the kitchen without saying anything else.

"Even after I proposed to you? Didn't that mean anything to you?"

"I really wish you'd leave."

"I can't believe you're saying this."

"I'm not going to give you what you want."

"You mean a kiss? You're got to be kidding!"

"One thing leads to another—I found that out with Don." she said, her voice a little lower, but her teeth clenched.

"I'm not like Don and you know it. I just want to marry you."

"I'm sorry, Paul, but I have to say no."

"Oh, I see, you said you loved me but you really hate me."

"I don't hate you, but you only see yourself," she said, her voice rising.

"Yeah, I guess I'm a lot like you that way," I said, losing my temper, even though deep down inside I knew that with what she'd been through, I wasn't acting right. But the thought was drowned out by anger. "Don't worry, I'm going. But I do want something from you." She didn't ask what. "I'd like that broach back—the one that I gave you to symbolize our love, remember?"

"I think I have it." She walked over to her dresser and looked through the top drawer.

"You sure you didn't sell it and give the money to Don for dope?" As the words came out I knew they were cruel, but I couldn't seem to stop.

"Here it is," she said, handing it to me as if she didn't hear my comment. Then she picked up the joint and gave it to me.

"Mary, I'm sorry," I said, touching her arm. "Let's start over, I shouldn't have said that. I'm really sorry."

She pulled away. "Keep your hands off me. I mean it!"

I looked at her for a moment, finally realizing that she was not going to change her mind. "Okay, I will," I said, and rushed out the door and ran down the stairs, thinking deep down that this couldn't be happening. Weren't we made for each other? So why was it happening?

I threw the joint on the grass as I ran to the car. Then I started it, and floored the accelerator, tires squealing as I raced down the street. Why would she say she didn't want to marry me when it was the one solution that made sense? Approaching the corner, I braked a little, and slid around it at about thirty miles per hour—driving fast had become a release for me when I was angry, but then I started to slow down and think about what had happened.

Why should she be so upset about just kissing me? Was that too much to ask? I wasn't like Don. She knew I loved her—I wasn't just using her. But did she really know that, I began to wonder? After going through what she had, how could she be sure of anything? Instead of going directly to the freeway, I drove around Montrose for a while, and finally I stopped the car on the side of the street to think. Should I go back to her apartment and apologize? But what for? And what if she told me to get out again? I didn't think I could take hearing that again. No, I'd just go back to Galveston. This was absolutely the end of it, and I had to accept that.

Finally making the decision to go home, I headed to the freeway, but after driving on it for about twenty minutes, I took an off ramp and pulled into a vacant area, and thought some more about what had happened. Every time I thought about going back to Galveston, I felt a deep grieving in the pit of my stomach, and I started thinking that Mary might be in some grave danger. Part of me thought that was silly and illogical, but the other part kept me frustrated. I wondered if I was imagining something, just due to my guilt.

I finally made a decision to go back, so I got back on the freeway and drove until I found the first chance to turn around and go back to Houston. But when I got back to the city, this time I took a different exit, and I got lost. I stopped at a gas station and they headed me towards Montrose but they didn't know her street. I thought I could find it when I got to the Montrose area, and I kept speeding down different streets but nothing looked familiar. Finally, unable to find it, I turned a corner and pulled over and took a deep breath. "God, where is the street?" I shouted out loud. Then I looked up and read the sign of the cross street in front of me. I saw that it was her street. I raced down it until I reached her apartment.

The first thing I noticed was that the lights were off, and I figured I was a real fool for coming back, and that she'd obviously gone out. But I'd driven all this way, so I thought I'd at least climb the stairs and knock. When I reached the top of the stairs, an indescribable feeling of dread came over me. I knocked, but there was no answer. I knocked again and waited, and then I tried the door.

It was open, so I said her name a couple of times but there was no answer. I wondered if I should just leave, but having driven all the way back, I hated to do that and decided I'd just wait for her. As I walked into the dark apartment and looked for a light switch, a car drove by and its lights shone through the window, showing the outline of Mary on the bed. She was sleeping, so I thought I should leave, but then I noticed that she was in the clothes she was wearing when I left. That seemed strange, but should I wake her, I wondered? Or, now that I knew she was all right, should I just leave and not bother her? If I did wake her she might be upset with me, and she might be angry that I just walked in on her.

Considering these things, I stood there watching her for a while, wondering what she would say if she woke up and found me there. She had to want my help, and if I apologized, maybe she'd come around and we could get back on good terms again. I walked a little closer to her—she was sleeping on her stomach, and had not moved since I had come into the room, which seemed strange to me. Then I saw an empty bottle of sleeping pills on the bed next to her.

I found the light switch and turned it on, and then I rushed back to her and turned her over, and I knew she was dead. I couldn't believe what was happening, and I stood there a moment, in shock. I put my head on her chest to see if I could hear a heartbeat, even though I instinctively knew there would be none. My mind was racing and trying to figure out what to do. Should I call the police first, or just take her to the hospital? Maybe I was wrong and she was still alive.

Just then I heard a siren, and soon there were heavy footsteps on the stairway. I opened the door and two medics came in and went right to her body. They examined her for a moment, touching her neck to find a pulse, and then one of them shook his head. "She's dead, isn't she?" I asked.

"Who are you?" one of them asked.

"I'm a…a friend. I just came over a minute ago."

"What's your name?"

"Paul Welles," I said, and he wrote it down.

"We got a call from her mother. She said her daughter called her and said that she took some pills. Is that why you're here?"

"No, I just happened to stop by," I said stoically, unable to accept what was happening.

The phone rang and they took the stretcher they brought up with them over to the bed and lifted her on to it. It kept ringing, so I finally picked it up, but I didn't say anything. I recognized her mother's voice.

"Mary—Mary is that you? Is the ambulance there yet?"

I didn't answer. Instead I gave the phone to the paramedic who was next to me, and he began talking to Mrs. Sanderson. I could hear her asking if Mary was alright, but the paramedic was not giving her a straight answer. Her voice became frantic, and she demanded an answer, but I didn't hear what he said after that because I ran down the stairs. As I started my car, I saw them taking her out of the apartment on a stretcher.

I almost lost control of my car as I skidded around several corners. I ran through one light and sent pedestrians scurrying for cover. Finally I got control of myself. Was I now going to make things even worse by running someone over, I wondered as I slowed down. I had been on Montrose Boulevard, so I turned off onto a small street and pulled over to the side and shut my engine off. Was she really dead? Did this really happen? Was I the reason she did it—yes, I was the reason. It was too much for me to accept—it was just too unbelievable. And yet, I knew it was true. She was dead and I was responsible. I pushed her when I should have just been her friend.

The feeling I had now was terrible, and it was tearing me up, but then I started thinking about Don. The more I thought about him, the more I was able to drown my guilt with anger. I would avenge her death—that's all that was left and that was all I could do. I would find him and…I didn't know what I'd do, but I would find him and he would pay for what he had done.

I remembered where the house he was living in was, and it was only a few miles away. When I reached it there seemed to be less activity than before. One window had a normal light in it, and another had a black light, and I could see iridescent black light posters from the street as I drove up. I parked and then walked onto the porch and knocked, and a feeling of being in a bad dream enveloped me. After a few minutes there was still no answer, so I knocked again, louder, and followed that by kicking the door as hard as I could. Finally, a bearded freaked out-looking guy opened the door, and tried to focus his eyes on me.

"Wow, man. What's all the racket about?" he said in a slow voice.

"Well, man, I wanted you to answer the door," I said sarcastically, and he began to close it, but I put my foot in and walked in. He looked at me with his drugged eyes, and was about to say something when I beat him to it.

"I'm looking for Don. Where is he?"

"Who?" he said.

"Don," I shouted at him. "You know, Don and Mary. Mary used to live here."

"Sorry, brother," he said, and turned away from me. I followed him a few steps, then grabbed his arm and pushed him up against the wall.

"Wow, man. I'm not into violence," he said, looking at me sheepishly.

"I'm not either, but I'm going to get into it if you don't tell me where he is. He did something bad to my girlfriend."

"Wow, that's really a bummer. But this place is just a crash pad for me. I don't know anyone."

"Well, I'll just look myself," I said, and I let go of him.

"That's cool, man, look for yourself," he said, and scampered away. I walked into the first room on my right, and switched on the light. It used to be a dining room, and I could see the kitchen beyond it, where there was a mess of trash and dirty plates that looked as if they hadn't been washed in months. The dining room had a few sleeping bags on the floor, but there was no one there. As I backed out of the room, my foggy-minded host walked into it and lay down on one of the sleeping bags. "Wow, I hope you find him, man," he said, his tone trying to placate me.

There was no one in any of the other downstairs rooms, so I climbed the stairs and I looked around on the second story. Someone about my age was sleeping in one of the bedrooms, but he only slightly moved when I turned on the light, so I switched it off and walked to the next one, which proved to be empty. A bathroom was next to it, but I could see from the hallway that no one was there, so I walked to the last bedroom, which had the black light on in it, and some music playing.

I was trembling a little as I opened the door, partially afraid that I would find Don, and that a violent part of me would be unleashed and do something I'd later regret. That thought flickered through my mind as I opened it and walked in. There was a guy and two girls in the room, lying on a king-sized mattress that was on the floor. One of the girls was kissing him and the other girl was lying under the covers next to them on the bed, her eyes open, staring in my direction. I could hear the music clearly now, as Janis Joplin sang.

No, no, no it just can't be
No it just can't be
There's got to be some kind of answer.
No it just can't be
And everywhere I look, there's none around
No it just can't be
Whoa, it can't be
No it just can't be, oh no...

"Do you know who Don is?"

"No, but I'd like to know who you are," the girl under the covers said.

I stood there for a moment, a little dazed, as the scene with Mary lying lifeless flashed into my mind. Finally I snapped out of it, and backed up, out of the room. The girl who'd talked to me called out, "Hey, man, don't leave. Come in and join us."

I closed the door and ran back down the stairs and then out of the house and to my car. I drove around for a few minutes, and I remembered that Don worked at Sand Mountain part time, and I drove there. The place was busy, but I found a table and sat down. The waitress who walked up recognized me. "Well, you haven't been here for a while, what will it be?"

"Well, I'm actually looking for Don," I said.

"But you've got to order—you know that's the rule. So what will it be?"

"Okay, I'll have a Coke. But is Don here? I want to score some weed and he said he had some."

She looked at me for a while and then answered slowly. "Let me get you your Coke and we'll see."

"But I just want to know if he's here."

"I don't know—I'll have to check," she said, and walked away.

I wondered why she wouldn't know since it was a small place. Then a man with a long ponytail started playing an acoustic guitar and I looked around the room to see if Don was there. It was a long time before the waitress came back with the Coke.

"Well, is Don here?"

"Oh, no, he left. He was here."

"Do you know where he went?" I asked, getting up from my seat.

"No. Christie does, but she's on a break."

"Well, can I talk to her?"

"Yeah, sure, man. She'll be back in a little while. Just sit down and be cool and we'll find Don for you."

I did as she asked, and watched the performer as I drank my Coke. I wanted to get up and walk back to the kitchen, but

I was afraid they'd tell me to leave and I'd never find Don. The first waitress came by a few more times, telling me to wait. I'd drained my glass and was eating the ice when another girl came out. I hadn't seen her before, but she seemed nicer than the first one. "Hi, I'm Christie," she said, and she touched my hand in a way that made me think she was flirting. "You're looking for Don?"

"Yeah, I need to score. Do you know where he is?"

"Yeah, sure. He went to Love Street. He just left about half an hour ago."

"Okay, thanks," I said and I left as quickly as I could.

CHAPTER 22

The traffic got thicker as I drove in downtown Houston and closer to Allen's Landing. The department stores were open until nine or nine-thirty in the evening, and were jammed with shoppers.

Eventually I got to Love Street, but I couldn't find a place to park, so I drove a few blocks away and searched for one. Every available space on either side of the street was taken, along with some that weren't intended to be parking spaces, so I kept driving farther and farther away until I finally found one. It was a fairly long walk to the Landing, and as I got closer the pedestrian traffic became denser, and I realized that looking for Don would probably be akin to looking for the proverbial needle in a haystack. But I was determined to find him, and I would look until I did.

If I'd thought that the landing area was crowded the night I saw Mary there, it didn't come close to this night. There were people all over, smoking grass and offering to sell it and other substances. The line to get in the club was a very long line and it ran from the entrance, which was upstairs, all the way down the stairs and then continued in a serpentine pattern throughout the park. I turned to a guy who looked straighter than some of the others.

"Why is it so crowded tonight? It wasn't like this when I was here before."

"It's the Fever Tree, man."

"The what?"

"The Fever Tree—the band. They're really far out. They made it big and now they're back here, where they started. They're from Texas."

I tried to figure out how I could find Don in the crowd. So I went to the end of the landing, where it descends into the water, and I kept walking along the perimeter looking for him. I thought if I kept circling methodically I might find him. But after covering most of the area without success, I walked towards the club. Then I walked along the long line until I got

284

to the stairs. He wasn't in the line, so I went to the headshops along the street looking for him. Not finding him there, I thought he must be in the club, so I walked back to the line, and then I pushed my way up the stairs to get into the club, squeezing through people and hearing a number of protests and groans as I got to the head of the line.

When I got there, there was a doorman taking a cover charge. He was a large ox of a man with gold rings on almost all his fingers, and he frowned at me as I attempted to explain that I had to find someone and that it was an emergency. He wasn't buying any of it, and he told me to go back to the end of the line. About that time a few of those in line grabbed my shirt to pull me back. So I turned around and walked back down the stairs.

As I walked to the sidewalk I heard music coming from the club—a song I had heard on the radio.

Out there it's summertime
Milk and honey days
Oh, San Francisco girls with
San Francisco ways...

I was about to sit down on the grass next to the sidewalk when I thought I saw the waitress, Christie, walking towards me. As she got closer I was certain it was her. Good, I thought, she'll lead me to Don. The music seemed to get louder as she approached.

Don't try to stop me girl, you can't have your way
Don't try to stop me girl, nothin' you can say
Live like you wanna live and stay where you wanna stay
I just gotta go and get back to the Bay

She had been running and she stopped to catch her breath for a moment before she spoke. "Oh, I'm so glad I found you."
"Did you come to see Don?"

"No, I came to warn you. They said you were a narc but I don't believe it. For one thing you're too young."

"I'm not a narc, Christie."

"They told me to tell you that Don had come here, but he was at Sand Mountain the whole time."

"Okay, thanks, I'll go back there."

"No, he's gone now. But I found out he put something in your Coke."

"In my Coke?"

"Yeah, he put a lot of acid in it—a whole lot—ten times more than you need for a trip. He was bragging about it."

"You mean LSD? But I don't feel anything."

"You will—believe me, you will. You need to get to a hospital."

"But I feel fine and I need to find Don. It's important. Do you know where he is?"

"No, but you need to get to a crash pad or something."

"Do you have his new address?"

"No, but you can come with me. You can crash at my apartment," she said kindly.

"I can't, but thanks for the offer, and thanks for telling me. I feel okay. Maybe it won't affect me. I'll go back to his old house—someone there must know where he lives now."

"I wouldn't worry about scoring any grass."

"I'm not trying to score. He raped my girlfriend."

Christie looked at me as if she didn't believe me.

"Not really, did he?"

"Yes, really. He got her pregnant and she committed suicide tonight."

"Man, you are already tripping."

"No, I'm not," I said, and I walked away from her, but she followed me. She grabbed my arm and I turned and stopped.

"I don't know what he did, but I'm telling you with that much acid you need to crash somewhere." She took a pen out of her purse and wrote her address and phone number on it and gave it to me. "If you need help, call me."

"Yeah, thanks. I've got to go," I said, and I started walking away again.

So you love me girl, you're just in my way
Don't try to stop me girl, I'm movin' out today
Do what you wanna do and play what you wanna play
I just gotta go and get back to the Bay

As I walked away I could still hear the music, but now it seemed to crescendo in an unusual way—different from any music I'd ever heard before. I turned around and Christie was gone. As I walked along the street I realized that I was a little disoriented. Then a voice roared in my head: *You killed her!* It kept repeating in my mind until I finally stopped walking and suddenly I was on the curb, crying. I shouted "Stop" and the voice stopped. I got up and started walking again, and then I didn't remember anything. As I walked it was as if I were floating.

I knew I'd been upset but didn't remember why. What in the world had I been in such a stew about? I felt very good now as I walked down the sidewalk, glancing in the store windows. One was a jewelry store that had a display that seemed magnificent, and I stood there for a long time, staring at the watches and diamond rings and other jewels. Bright light was reflecting from them, and somehow they looked too shiny and effervescent to be real, and I decided that they must be magic. Houston was a magical place, I thought, and just then the reflecting light seemed to get brighter, and I turned away to save my eyes.

After I'd walked quite a while, I found myself standing in front of Foley's, a huge department store that sold all sorts of merchandise. I'd gone there once before, with Mary. As I thought of that, the pain of her death came back in my mind and seemed to vibrate through my whole body. It was like a dagger in my head, and I felt faint and staggered over to rest against the side of the building.

The store was open late, and there were numerous people walking in and out of the automatic entrance doors. As I started to feel better, I lifted my head and watched them, then my mind seemed to shift to another place again and made me wonder all over again what I was doing there. I tried to think, but somehow I just couldn't get back to where I was, and as I sat there wondering, a voice came up from somewhere: *Mary is dead, and you killed her*. "No, she isn't!" I mouthed the words. "It's not true—it's just a dream—a nightmare." But then the words from the poem my father quoted came into my mind like an audible voice.

Yet each man kills the thing he loves
By each let this be heard,
Some do it with a bitter look,
Some with a flattering word,
The coward does it with a kiss,
The brave man with a sword!

I wondered how that whole stanza could come back in my mind, because I only heard it once, and I wondered what it meant, because my father never explained it. The voice continued.

You killed the thing you loved…you killed the thing you loved.

No, she's not dead, I thought. That's a lie. The people around me were moving quickly in and out of the store, and as I tried to push the voice out of my mind, I saw a girl with long brown hair walk into the store. From the back, I could pick out Mary from a million girls I thought, and I knew that was her. She turned after entering the store, and then I saw her profile, and that cinched it. It's her, I thought, but a voice from somewhere said, *No it's not, she's dead.*

I followed her into the store, but she was moving fast and for a few moments I lost her, and I looked around wildly in the crowd, searching out that long hair. Turning around a couple of times, I saw the back of her—she was looking at some clothing, and I walked towards her. She didn't see me and began walking again, and I followed, closing the gap between us. She is alive, I thought. She's alive and everything is going to be okay. I had almost caught up with her when she went into a changing room. I yelled "Mary," after her, but she didn't turn around, and instead she closed the door without looking at me.

"Mary," I said, against the door, but heard nothing in return. "Mary, it's me . . . Paul." A saleslady approached me with a frown on her face.

"Can I help you?" she asked, but as confused as I was I still knew what her tone really meant.

"No. I'm waiting for my girlfriend."

"Oh, which one is she?"

"It doesn't matter, I'm just waiting," I said, and a customer approached her, and she turned away from me. I walked closer to the changing room, and shouted through the door this time. "Mary, are you coming out? Come on, I can't wait all night."

Again the saleslady was at my side, but she didn't say anything. A second later, the door to the dressing room opened and a girl walked out, and as I turned around, again her back was to me. "That's her," I said defiantly to the saleslady and walked towards the girl.

"Where have you been?" I said, and she turned around and backed up as she did. Of course it wasn't her, but whoever it was, I must've scared her, because she dropped the dress she was holding and ran from that area of the store. I followed, trying to apologize, but soon I lost her in the crowd, and I found myself near an escalator. Stepping on to it, I rode it up, with people all around me.

As we ascended, I began to feel as if I were glowing—glowing with brightness and power. My face was warm with the sun's energy, I thought, and I was a sun god from another place, far, far, away. As I listened to people speaking next to me, their language became unintelligible, and I knew that they were different from me—for they were the natives of this planet.

My beginnings were on a bright, shiny place, where people could fly effortlessly through space and meander as they wished through the course of the past, present, and future. I'd only been sent to this planet to study its inhabitants for a period of time, and soon I would be home. Home was that great, golden, shining city where people who were like me were, and as I considered that, a wave of nostalgia for the place came over me. After all, I'd been here long enough and it was time to go home.

I was on the fifth floor now, and I continued riding the escalator to the top, where I was certain that I could get a ride back to my home—my planet. My people would find all this very amusing, and the bright sun there would purify and cleanse all the negativity I felt inside. It would all wash away into the sunset, and the music would play and fill my soul—making it lighter and happier. How could one really live for any amount of time on this world? Then I heard a voice in back of me, and I turned around. There was no one there, but I still heard the voice, which said,

Water falls on satin wings
Music rests on newer things
Seems the song might drown away,
Except for water's washing way.

I turned around completely, but again there was no one to be found save a few shoppers who were too far away to have spoken. Closing my eyes, I felt the sun of my own planet bathe my face, and I knew that it would be a short time before I was back, and I heard the voice again.

We are the star people, sun people
Time and light our tools
Our ears grow long and pointed

But we know beauty in a special way.
And as we fly the skies in gleaming brightness
Collecting moonbeams between the glittering stars
Our lives grow meaningful and glorious
And the energy we know extends throughout the universe.

All I had to do was get to the top and I knew I'd be out of this dimension of existence. I'd always known there was another place, somewhere happy and perfect where I belonged—I knew it all the time, but they hadn't let me become completely aware of it, so that my experience on earth would be without interference. Now, though, the game was over. The great riddle would soon become a simple axiom, and I would soar through time and space in that place where I truly belonged.

Almost to the top floor now, I knew that my skin was glowing more than before, and I hoped no one would notice. Inside, deep inside, I could feel my body gaining a great, overpowering strength, and I loosened my grip on the rail of the escalator, afraid that with this new power I might squeeze the material it was made of too hard and ruin it. Turning around briefly, I took a look at the people in front and behind me and felt sadness for them. If only they knew what I knew, and if only they could go where I was going. Someday, perhaps, they would know something better, also. And when I got back to my planet, I would see to it that something would be done to help them. Surely there would be a way—somehow.

Arriving at the top floor now, I stepped off the escalator, and moved towards some shelves filled with radios and stereos and other similar merchandise. Examining these objects I thought they seemed to glitter in a special way, so I knew they were not of this planet. Nothing glittered that way normally on Earth and colors were not that rich, so they must be from my planet, and I would take them back with me when I left. I walked over to a large stereo display and looked at the controls. A salesman approached me. "Can I help you, sir?" I looked over at him, and used the intense power of my eyes to drive him away.

"I need no help from you," I said, and then thought better of it. "But I don't mean to hurt your feelings. Someday you will learn, also."

"What?" he said, and I turned away from him and started turning the knobs and flipping the switches on the stereo receivers. By setting them where they should be, they would know I was here, and soon I would be off, I thought.

"What are you doing?" he asked.

"I'm going home," I said to him, solemnly, and resumed my work with the controls.

"That's fine, but would you leave the stereos alone?"

"No, I must use them."

"You're crazy," he said, and walked away from me. I turned knobs until the radio came on and a song by the Moody Blues was playing.

> *Nights in white satin*
> *Never reaching the end*
> *Letters I've written*
> *Never meaning to send*

I remembered the song and now I was listening to the lyrics carefully, because I believed it was a message to me from my planet.

> *Beauty I've always missed*
> *With these eyes before*

Yes, that was the message. I'd always missed the beauty of these things on planet earth. But now I could see them clearly. And this message had to be understood by the whole earth! So I turned the sound up louder and louder, and soon the clerk ran back towards me. He was angry, and I moved away from the stereos. But it took him a while to figure out which one was playing.

Just what the truth is
I can't say any more
'Cause I love you
Yes I love you
Oh how I love you

As he turned it off, the light of the room seemed to diminish, and everything seemed to move away from me. I felt faint and walked over to the wall and leaned against it. The lyrics stayed in my mind—"Just what the truth is I can't say any more."

What was the truth—could I say what it was anymore? No, I couldn't quite seem to think correctly, and it was the acid. Just then it all came flooding back again. I wasn't going anywhere, and I wasn't anyone special—I was just one of those people I was feeling sorry for a moment ago. Mary was dead—that was the truth, and there was no way in the world that I would ever see her again. How could I have followed that girl in the store? How could I have believed it was her? Who was I trying to fool? What was trying to fool me?

I closed my eyes and opened them again, and the light of the room was back to normal, but the crowd seemed thicker, and the noise from all the voices seemed to get louder and louder. I felt sick to my stomach, and claustrophobic, and I pushed off against the wall and ran to the escalator, and rode it down. On the next floor, the din increased, and there were even more people who seemed to crowd me, and I knew I had to get out as fast as I could. Pushing through the shoppers, I ran down the escalator, one floor after another, until I reached the first floor. Once there, I looked around for the door to the outside, but the store was large, and it was not easy to find one. I ran down aisle after aisle until I saw an exit. Rushing through the glass doors, I got out to the sidewalk and tripped and fell, and I lay there, panting from the run.

Slowly, I got up. I was still near the entrance, and people were coming and going, so I walked down the sidewalk away from it, and as I did, I bent over, because I knew I'd be sick any minute. Suddenly I heard a voice near me, and for a moment I didn't know if I was imagining it or not. Then I saw a black man sitting near me, up against the building. As I focused my eyes, I saw that he had no legs and was selling pencils.

"Don't you do that here. I sits here every day," he said, looking at me with a frown.

He had startled me, but I also seemed to feel better. I was no longer nauseous. It was as if my mind was cycling back on forth between reality and fantasy, and it was hard for me to tell the difference. I walked several more blocks and saw the name of another store—Sakowitz. I remembered that my mother had visited the store when my parents went to Houston, and she commented on how expensive it was. I remembered her words, "ridiculously expensive."

Suddenly my curiosity was aroused and I walked into the store. It was beautifully decorated and as I walked through it I stopped and looked at the jewelry counter where there were exquisite diamond rings and expensive watches. But the radiance from the jewelry was beyond anything I had ever experienced—much greater than the store window I had looked in from the street. As I moved my head, the light seemed to dance on the gold and the diamonds and the shine was so magnificent that I had to avert my eyes.

The jewelry counter was a square with clerks in the middle, but they were all waiting on people. I continued to walk around with wonder as I reveled in seeing beauty I had never experienced before. A woman who was probably about thirty was trying on a diamond-encrusted watch, and I stopped as she fastened it on her wrist. "That is an exquisite watch and it looks beautiful on you," I heard myself saying. I had surprised her as she had not seen me, and at first she looked up at me and stepped away. Then, she smiled. "Well, thank you. I think I'll take it."

I continued around the counter until I had marveled at everything. Something was saying in a small voice that the

LSD was affecting me, but I was trying to drown that out, because now I was enjoying the discovery of what seemed to be a new world—one that was shiny and brilliant and beautiful. Then Christie's words came back to me. *You need to get to a hospital.* But no, I didn't. I actually felt very good now—better than ever.

I turned around from the jewelry counter and crossed over to the women's furs. There were beautiful full mink coats as well as stoles, and the coats were so luxurious, I just had to touch them. So I stroked one, and then I touched another one. They were incredibly soft—softer than anything I had ever touched, I thought. But the clerk walking towards me did not seem very friendly, and it was obvious he didn't like me touching the furs. "May I help you, sir?" he asked very condescendingly, as he moved the fur I was stroking away from me.

I didn't like his tone. Besides, wasn't he just a poorly paid clerk? Why should he be so stuck up just because he worked in an expensive store? Well, I'd show him, I thought, and I put on the accent I remembered Bela Lugosi had in *Dracula*, lifted my head up, and looked down my nose at him. "My name is Prince Salaran," I said. "And I am visiting America with my mother, and I am seeking a gift for her. She is Queen Salaran—perhaps you have heard of her?"

Suddenly the clerk's attitude changed. "Yes, perhaps I have. So what type of mink did you have in mind for your mother…Prince?"

"Salaran."

"Prince Salaran—yes, of course."

"Our country is small, and we have no stores like this one," I added.

"Yes, well, Sakowitz is a very special store, and I sure we can find something suitable for your mother."

"I hope so. The problem is that she loves furs, but she has so many I don't know what she would want to add to her collection."

"Yes, I see how that could be a problem."

"And of course you know what the climate is like in our country."

"The climate?"

"Yes, it's so warm, so when can she wear furs? Only when we go to New York for the United Nations."

"Oh, I see."

"So if it is possible, please find me a fine fur that is not too heavy. But I will ask my mother before I buy it."

"Is your mother here then?"

"She is in the store somewhere, and while you are looking for the perfect fur, I will shop for myself. But please tell me where the men's department is. I'm tired of looking like an American teenager, but my bodyguard thought it would be safer to dress this way."

"Of course, but let me find someone to take care of you," the clerk said, and then scurried off and soon returned with a chubby, balding man who led me to the men's department. I studied the suits there, and picked out a few, and the clerk called a store tailor. He had me stand on a platform before a three sided mirror and he pinned up the suits to make the necessary alterations.

"So, how do you like America?" the salesman asked as the tailor worked.

"I find it quite likable, except that your country is—well, you are preventing us from buying the weapons we need to protect ourselves from the Russians. Your government would rather give us a treaty to protect us. But what would happen if the Russians moved quickly? I don't think your military would be fast enough, as most of the army is stationed in Germany."

"Oh, I see—that does sound like a problem."

"Our country has the budget for the McDonnell Douglas F-4, Phantom II, but we have been denied. I don't think that is fair, do you?"

The salesman took a moment to answer. "No, probably not. Not if you need help against the Russians."

"I have finished," the tailor said.

"How long will it take to get these?" I asked.

"They should be ready in two weeks," the tailor said.

"No, we cannot wait that long. We are leaving before then."

The salesman then said something to the tailor I could not hear.

"When are you leaving?" he asked me.

"Four days. I have four days."

The salesman again talked to the tailor and then he looked at me, triumphantly. "Then you will have them in four days."

As I stepped off the platform I started feeling woozy, and my head started aching. "I must change. Send these to the Hilton, Room 203 when they are ready." I walked into the changing room and put my own clothes back on. When I walked out the salesman asked me for payment information, but I interrupted him.

"Oh, I see Mother," I said, as I spotted a wealthy-looking woman walking across the store. I rushed over and caught up with the woman, walked beside her for a while, and then I walked out of the store.

My head was still aching and my ears seemed to be ringing as I walked down the street. I stopped and shook my head, but it still felt very strange and then my neck starting moving spasmodically. It twisted uncontrollably to the right and then to the left over and over. I didn't want anyone to see me, so I slipped into an alley. There I started feeling sick again and this time I vomited, and hoped that maybe some of the LSD left my body. I thought then that the first thing I should have done when Christie told me the Coke was spiked was to put my finger down my throat and try to vomit. But I'd never done that before and it didn't occur to me.

Now depression really began to set in, and all I could do was replay the scene of Mary lying dead on the bed. The LSD had temporarily taken my memory of what had happened away, but I felt that there would be no respite from it again. My neck stopped twitching, and I walked back into the street.

Some stores were closing now, and the traffic was beginning to diminish. Now that I was thinking clearer, I realized that I had to find my car, but as I tried to remember where it was, everything was blank. Yes, I had to admit that I had absolutely no idea where I'd parked, so I began walking back towards Foley's. From there I walked in the direction of Allen's Landing, looking at the parked vehicles, just hoping that I'd see mine. I tried to concentrate and bring back the memory of the location, because I had read somewhere that memories stay in your subconscious. But it didn't work, and I couldn't even remember how long I'd walked to reach Foleys from where I'd parked.

Covering every street more than once, I continued my search for hours, and finally I felt I just couldn't walk another step. I wasn't sure if the drug had made me tired, but I knew I had to rest. There was nowhere else to go, so I entered an alley between two tall buildings and sat down with my back against the wall of one of them. I let my head hang forward, because the concrete was too hard to let it lie against that, and I thought to myself that I was lucky I wasn't back in Connecticut, where I would surely freeze to death if I stayed out at night in the winter.

Alternately sleeping and waking, my mind drifted back to that day in the high school auditorium when Sergeant Ricstetter of the Houston Police Department had visited us. He'd been right! That dumb redneck, who reduced everything to a simple right or wrong, had been right, I thought. The drugs had destroyed Mary. They were only destructive—there was nothing good about them.

Soon I was sleeping deeply and having a dream in which Mary was still alive, and we were talking to each other about something. We were in an apartment I'd never seen before, and she got up and walked into the kitchen. Just then I felt a pain in my side, and then another, and I woke up and opened my eyes. Before me there were about six Mexican kids, most of whom were teenagers, but one was very young—maybe twelve. They were all wearing long, pointed shoes made of an orange-colored leather, and they had jackets on with some type of gang insignia on it. I held my head up further and the one closest to me kicked me again, but this time I moved out of the way.

"What do you want?" I said.

"Get up, mon," he said with a thick accent. I looked around for a moment, then did as he demanded.

"Give me your watch," he said, and I looked at him, and then at my watch, and I noticed that it was around two o'clock. "*Now*, mon," he said, and the others moved in closer to me, and he doubled up his fist, and then opened his hand and rubbed it. I took the watch off, and handed it to him. "Now the wallet," he said, with his head lolling back indolently, and I took it out of my back pocket but decided I would make a run for it. I pushed him out of the way, and moved as fast as I could, but I was still unsteady and no match for them. One of them tackled me and I slid on the pavement, tearing my clothes and scratching my arms and face as I landed. As I tried to get up, they made a punching bag out of me, hitting and kicking me all over my body. One of the pointy shoes hit my eyebrow and blood started spurting. I had dropped my wallet and one of them picked it up and took the money out and threw it down. There was about twelve dollars in it.

"What you got in your pockets?" the first boy asked.

"Nothing, you got all the money," I answered, weakly. I'd actually forgotten that the broach was in one of my pockets. He stuck his hand in both of my front pockets and found the broach. My car keys were also in that pocket, but he didn't dig any further. He looked at it and smiled.

There was blood in my eye, and I rubbed it away to see, and then struggled to get up. "That broach will bring you bad luck—it's cursed!" I shouted after them as they walked away, laughing at me. After I spoke one of the older ones said something to the young one, and he walked back and eyed me for a moment, evidently trying to muster the courage to hit me. He finally kicked me in the leg, and I wanted to grab him and hit him back, but I knew the others would walk back and hurt me if I did. He seemed to squeal with delight at being able to hit me and get away with it, and ran back to the others, and soon they were gone. Slumping back down to the pavement, I found the aches and throbbing pain had a curiously comforting effect on me, and I fell back to sleep with my head between my legs.

I was sleeping when the morning sun glared down between those two buildings. It hit my face and penetrated my eyelids so quickly that it took me a few moments to realize that it was the sun and to remember where I was. Dried blood kept me from opening one of my eyes immediately, but after a few seconds I managed to scrape it with my fingernail and peel it off. My watch was gone, so I didn't know what time it was, but it seemed early, and I didn't hear any cars driving by. My head throbbed when I stood up, and I looked down and saw my empty wallet a few yards away. I was grateful they didn't keep it, and that I also had my car keys. I walked slowly towards the wallet, picked it up, and then walked to the street.

It was Sunday and everything was closed, and the streets were empty except for an occasional car. In the daylight I hoped I could find my car, but as I walked my head pounded with each step I took. My side ached and my chest was sore, and since walking was so painful, I knew I needed to get some help to find my car. I had no money to use a pay phone but I thought if I could find someone maybe I could beg a dime for the phone. There was no one walking on the street, so I started walking in a direction that I hoped would take me away from the downtown area, where there might be a house. After walking a number of blocks, I was still in a commercial area, but I saw a large, ornate church several blocks away that looked old enough to have predated the other downtown buildings.

I tried to ignore my pain and walked as quickly as I could towards it. When I got to the front door, I could hear organ music. I opened the door and there were people sitting in the service, all of them dressed very nicely, and the choir was signing a hymn. I wanted to ask to use the phone, but I didn't want to interrupt, so I walked towards the back pew to sit down. Just as I was about to take a seat a man standing at the back of the church walked up to me and signaled for me to get up. When I didn't respond quickly enough for him, he took my arm and started pulling me back towards the entrance. I pushed his hand away from my arm, and walked out of the church with him following. When I got outside, he gave me a disgusted look.

"You don't come into God's house looking like that!"

"I got mugged, and I need to call home. Can't I just use the church phone?"

"You are a dirty hippie and you got what you deserved. Now get out of here before I call the police," he shouted, and then he walked back into the church and slammed the door.

I kept walking and happened to see my reflection in a store window, and it shocked me. My eyebrow wound had bled a lot, and my face and clothing were covered with dried blood and dirt from when I was knocked down. My hair was also stiff with blood, and it was a mess. But there was no place to wash so I just kept walking away from town and was soon in a poor neighborhood. The houses were small and old and most needed maintenance. I was a little afraid to knock on a door after seeing the way I looked, so I sat down on the sidewalk to rest. For a moment I seemed to fall asleep, and then I heard a woman's voice.

"Oh, my Lord, what happened to you, child?" she asked, and I looked up to see a heavy black woman and her husband. They had stopped their car in front of the sidewalk I was sitting on.

"I...I got beat up and robbed," I said.

"Oh, you poor thing," she said, looking at my face.

"Son, why don't you get in the car? We're going to church and we'll get you cleaned up there," he offered.

"Oh, I'd really appreciate that."

"I'm just wonderin' if he needs to go to the hospital," the woman said.

"No, I think I'm all right. I look worse than I feel."

"I sure hope so, honey, because you look terrible," she said.

The man helped me get into the backseat of the 1950 Buick he was driving, which was old but also in such immaculate condition that I was concerned I might soil it with my dirty clothes. I told him my concern but he just chuckled and continued to help me in. "I'm Brother Roy, and this is my wife, Sister Sarah," the man said, and he shook my hand.

"Paul Welles," I said, not sure of what all the brother and sister stuff was about.

We drove for about ten minutes and they stopped in front of a small, old church which was constructed of wood and painted white. The neighborhood seemed poorer than the one they had found me in, and the service must not have started, I thought, because there were a lot of people standing outside the church, talking to each other. Brother Roy got out of the car and talked to several other men, and they rushed over to the car and helped me out of it. They all seemed concerned, and I couldn't help thinking of how different they were acting compared to the first church.

We walked into the church and into an area which appeared to be a room converted to a kitchen. I sat down and several of the women found some cloths, which they soaked in warm water, and then wrung out, which they cleaned my face with.

"God was looking out for you, child," Sister Sarah said, as she tried to clean up my hair by dampening it with warm water and brushing it out with a hairbrush.

"Yes, I believe so."

"Do you believe in Jesus?" Sister Sarah asked, as she was working.

"Well, I...I think so," I said, not wanting to disappoint them with my answer.

"Oh, you don't believe, or you'd know for sure," Brother Roy said from behind me. But I didn't know he was there, and his booming voice startled me. He realized he'd startled me and walked around and kneeled down in front of me. "But you can know Jesus," he said, smiling. As he finished speaking, a large man in a three-piece suit walked over to me and took my hand.

"I'm Pastor Samuel."

"Paul Welles."

"Well, Brother Paul, I'm so glad you could join us today. We'll see you in the service."

CHAPTER 23

The service was unlike any I had ever been in before. It started with the choir singing and then everyone joined in as hymns were sung. But the pastor's deep, melodic voice could be heard above everyone else's, and he sounded like a professional singer. Then he started preaching, and talked about how the Apostle Paul began by hating Jesus and everyone who followed him, but ended up loving Jesus so much that he was willing to suffer for him joyfully and in fact suffered for him all his life.

At the end of the preaching, he suddenly began singing again, and asking questions in song, which the choir answered. "And why did Paul love Jesus?" he sang. The choir sang back, "Because Jesus first loved Paul." This went on for about five minutes, and then he stopped preaching, and an older man stood up and spoke in a foreign language. I noticed that it sounded somewhat like Hebrew, which I only recognized because Gordon had spoken Hebrew one time when he told me he used to go to Hebrew school after school when he was younger. It seemed so strange to me that I was hearing Hebrew that I wondered if the LSD was still affecting me.

Then another person stood up and began speaking, "Thus saith the Lord, 'Are you concerned about your life in this world—what you must endure? I tell you, my son endured much more for you, and it was no small thing what he did for you on the cross. Take up your own cross and live for him and one day you will inherit the kingdom. Abide in him, and you will overcome the world.'"

After that another hymn was sung, and the music slowed down, and the pastor sang praises to God. Then everyone got quiet, and no one seemed to move at all. Suddenly Sister Sarah, who was sitting next to me, began to speak. "God has a message for this child, this white boy: 'Do you think you are here by chance? I tell you, no. Behold, I stand at the door and knock. If you open your heart, I will come in. I stand at the door and knock.'"

"Come up here, young man," the pastor said, and he signaled with his hand for me to come. I hesitantly stood up and then walked toward him. There was a chair at the front and he motioned for me to sit there. "Now some of you gather around and let's anoint him with oil," he said, and about ten people walked up as he took out a vial of oil and made the sign of a cross on my forehead with it. "The Bible says in James 5:14 and Mark 16:17:

Is any sick among you? let him call for the elders of the church; and let them pray over him, anointing him with oil in the name of the Lord: 15 And the prayer of faith shall save the sick, and the Lord shall raise him up; and if he have committed sins, they shall be forgiven him.

And these signs shall follow them that believe; In my name shall they cast out devils; they shall speak with new tongues; 18 They shall take up serpents; and if they drink any deadly thing, it shall not hurt them; they shall lay hands on the sick, and they shall recover."

At that point it seemed like the whole church came up and I felt many hands on me. People were praising and crying out to God for me, and I heard others speaking in foreign languages. I seemed to feel warmth in my body, but I wasn't sure if I was imagining it. What I wasn't imagining was the compassion with which these people prayed—they prayed like they expected God to really hear them, I thought, as the prayers ended, and people walked back to their seats.

When we got in his car, Brother Roy asked me where I wanted to go, and I told him I wanted to find my car. I suggested we start at Allen's Landing and drive on streets away from it until we found the car. But Sister Sarah interrupted me by praying. "Lord, you know where this child's car is—please lead us to it, in Jesus' name, amen."

We drove towards town, and Roy turned onto a side street, and my car was there.

"That's my car!" I shouted, surprised.

"What did you expect, boy? We prayed," Roy said.

"Yes, I know. I really appreciate it," I said, and I opened the door.

"You think you'll be all right? We can still take you to a doctor," Sarah said.

"No, I feel a lot better since the pastor prayed," I said, wanting to get in my car and get home. We said our good-byes and I started up my car. As I began driving I realized that I did feel better—and that somehow I had forgotten about Mary. But now it was coming back to me. What had I done! I knew what I had done, I had killed her by the way I acted. I pushed her to suicide and I deserved to die.

I started driving home, but I couldn't get the picture of Mary lying dead out of my mind. That was bad enough, but I was about halfway to Galveston when I started having flashbacks from the night before. I had heard that people that take LSD sometimes have them, but these were coming so quickly and unexpectedly that it was interfering with my driving, and I slowed the car down on the highway, looking for a place to pull over. After a few miles, there was a wide shoulder and I was about to pull over, when I heard a police siren. I looked in my rearview mirror and the police car was barreling down on me, so I pulled over quickly to let it go by. But instead it pulled over in back of me.

At first I didn't recognize him, but as I took my license out of my wallet and looked up, I knew it was Bob, the brawny cop who pulled us over when Gordon and Benjy and I were driving back from Houston. I held my head down, hoping he wouldn't recognize me.

"Do you know why I pulled you over, boy?"

"No sir," I said, still looking down.

"You were going too slow on the freeway and that's dangerous."

"Sir, I was pulling over—that's why I was going slow."

"But you were going slow for a long time."

"That's because there was no shoulder," I retorted.

"Oh, you're a smart aleck—is that it?"

"No sir, I was just explaining."

"Look at me when I talk to you," he demanded, and I looked up.

"Get out of the car."

"Why? For going too slow?"

I got out slowly, since my body ached. I could tell he was impatient and maybe he thought I was doing it to irritate him. He stared at me and then read my license.

"From Galveston—I remember you. You're the punk who said the judge was your uncle. You lied to me."

"What are you talking about?"

"You know what I'm talking about, boy. Now put your hands up against the car and spread 'em."

As I turned to do as he told me, he hit me on the side with his nightstick, and I fell to the ground.

"Looks like someone already got to you," he said, noticing my wounds as I looked up at him in the sunshine. "Now I need to finish the job. Bad boys get punished for lying," he said, and he hit me on the side of my face, which make my head spin with pain.

"Sir, please don't hit me anymore. I'm already hurt and I can't take it. And my girlfriend just committed suicide and I was mugged, and I need to get home."

"Oh, you're good, and your uncle is the judge, right? Well, punk, you're gonna wish you committed suicide when I get through with you."

He swung at me again, but I managed to get up and run from him, and I ran to the side of the road where there was a large drainage ditch. I was moving slowly and he came at me again, but I remembered an old western where a cowboy was in a fight and he threw dust in the opponent's face. So I took a handful of loose dirt and threw it into his face. It worked—he swung at me again but I was able to get out of the way. He was fuming with anger and as he rubbed his eyes, I stood up and ran at him as hard as I could and pushed him back and he fell into a deep drainage ditch behind him. He landed with a heavy thud, and I heard him groan. I ran to my car and took off.

I knew I was really in trouble now, because he would radio ahead, so I drove as fast as I could, hoping to get to Galveston before I got caught. I figured every policeman in Galveston would be looking for me after he called in an all-points bulletin on me.

I didn't know what to do, but I remembered that when criminals were on the lam the police often caught them because they would try to contact their relatives, so I knew I couldn't go back to my house. Instead I thought I'd see Gordon and tell him what happened. So I drove to the hospital and walked to his room.

The room was empty, but some of his things were still there. There were several envelopes with names on them, and one had my name on it. I picked it up and put it in my pocket, and as I did a nurse walked in. I had seen her before when I'd visited him, and the look in her eyes told me what I was afraid to ask about. "He's dead, isn't he?"

She nodded sadly, but said nothing. I ran from the hospital and when I reached the car, I started crying. I had always been taught not to cry, since it was sign of a sissy and not a man, but now I couldn't seem to stop crying. Everything was terrible—my whole life was ruined and there was no reason to live. Mary was dead, Gordon was dead, and soon I'd be arrested for assaulting a policeman. Who would believe me when I told them that he was trying to beat me to death? I would be a convicted felon and that would disgrace my family. I deserved to die—Mary would still be alive if I had acted the way I should have. I was her last hope and I failed her. But how would I do it? If everyone knew I'd committed suicide that would also bring shame on my family, so it had to look like an accident.

I thought of wrecking my car, but what if I survived the crash? I couldn't risk being an invalid for the rest of my life—

that would be worse than dying and someone would have to take care of me. It had to be something certain, and something that at least could have been an accident. Then I thought of it. I'd go up in a plane and then crash it. I'd radio in and tell them I was having engine trouble, and then I'd crash, and they would have to conclude that it was an accident. That would be perfect, but there was a problem—I would have to reserve a plane and that would take some time, and I figured I didn't have much time before the police arrested me.

I drove to the airport, hoping there would be a plane I could rent. This was my only honorable way out, I thought. My parents would think I'd crashed, and the police could do nothing to me because I'd be dead. Maybe my father would figure it out; he seemed to see through my schemes. But what did it matter? He wouldn't know for sure, and what could he do anyway? I thought of my mother and I saw her crying. She wasn't much of a crier like some women—I only saw her cry a few times, and those were serious situations. Something tugged at my heart about how sad she would be. I had to get my mind off her so I could go through with it.

When I arrived at the airport, I looked around to see if any policemen were there, and saw none. I walked into the office to rent a plane, but no one was there. There were a few Cessna 150s parked in the front, so if they weren't reserved, I had a chance of renting one. A man walked in, and then the woman I normally saw in the office walked out the back door. She smiled at him while she waited on him but didn't notice me. After he had handed her a flight plan and his credit card, she told him she would have the plane fueled. She called one of the employees on her radio and told him to fuel the plane. Then she noticed me, and did a double take. "Paul, is that you?"

"Yes, I'd like to rent a plane."

"But what happened? You look like you've been in a wreck. I think you need to go to the hospital."

"No, I'm fine—really. I just want to rent a plane."

"Oh, I'm sorry, we're all booked up today."

"Okay, thanks anyway."

I walked out of the office and watched the employee taxi the plane over to the fuel pumps. He got out, and then walked over to another plane that was being fueled, about thirty feet away.

I walked up to the plane, and when he turned his back I got into the Cessna and started it. He looked over at me, shocked, but I started taxiing to the runway before he could do anything. As I taxied I noticed my face in the mirror. I had a large bruise on it from where the policeman had hit me, and I looked worse than I thought. I could see why the woman at the flight desk was concerned.

I noticed it didn't have much fuel, but I didn't need much for what I planned to do. The airport was small and there was no control tower. I checked the windsock to see which way it was blowing. Sometimes the runway was turned around when the wind blew in the opposite direction. The planes always took off going into the wind for maximum lift. Soon I was in the air and flying towards the ocean. Someone was frantically speaking on the radio to me, so I turned it off. I was over the Gulf of Mexico, flying along the coast. The sun was bright and I had to squint to see as I normally wore sunglasses when I was flying. They were in my car but I had forgotten them. I tried to figure out if I should crash into the beach or the water. The sand was a sure thing for a quick death, but there were people there, walking, and I was afraid I'd hurt someone when the plane went down.

Just then I felt like someone was saying, "Don't do this, son." There was no audible voice—it was just a feeling. I was probably still hallucinating, I thought. But then it came again, and the thought that it was God came into my mind. "If you are real, show me," I said out loud. "Show me and I'll stop. Just somehow confirm it's you if you really exist."

At that moment I remembered the envelope I picked up in Gordon's hospital room. I trimmed out the plane to fly without much assistance, and took it out of my pocket. It was a farewell card, and I opened it and read what Gordon had written:

Paul—Jesus says to you "Behold I stand at the door and knock." Open your heart to him so we can see each other again. Your friend, forever. Gordon.

I read it twice. It was God talking to me. They were the same words that Sister Sarah said God was saying to me, and it was impossible for anyone but God to have set this up. As I realized this, I knew I had to land the plane, but now the fuel gauge was below the empty line, and unlike automobiles, plane fuel gauges are generally accurate. I turned the plane towards the airport, but after a few miles, it began to sputter, and I had to land. "God, if this is you, help me!" I shouted, and then the plane started to stall and I had to descend to get the speed back up and keep it gliding.

I aimed at the beach, and soon I was over a long stretch of sand, but there were people there, and I didn't how much more I could glide before setting the plane down. As I descended and got closer to them, they saw the plane and started running out of the way. I glided past them to a clear area, but there was also a strong wind blowing south from the ocean and I had to tilt the Cessna into the wind to land. I made contact with the sand with my right wheel, and then put down the left wheel.

The sand was soft and suddenly I was fishtailing all over the beach. The sand got even softer and the plane jarred forward, and my head hit the side of the cabin as it came to rest. When I regained consciousness the police were there, and one of them was trying to open the cabin door, which was locked. As I unlocked it an ambulance drove up, with lights flashing, and two paramedics got out. They had some discussion with a policeman and then the paramedics put me on a stretcher. They took me to John Sealy Hospital, and after a doctor examined me, I was put in a room. Then they x-rayed me and told me that I had some fractured ribs. Someone must have called my parents, because they showed up later, and when they came in, my father's face was red from anger. "What in the world is going on! The police have been to our house three times looking for you."

"I know."

"You know? Is that any kind of answer? You assaulted a policeman, stole an airplane, and all you can say is 'I know'? Do you realize what you've done! If you're a convicted felon you will never get a good job, or get into an ivy-league college. I couldn't get you in even with my connections."

I didn't answer and he shook his head. "I said, do you know what you've done!"

My mother looked over at him, her eyes pleading for him to settle down. It took me a moment to speak, because they had given me a painkiller and it was starting to take effect.

"I was going to kill myself in the airplane," I said quietly. "I was going to crash it into the beach because I know I've ruined my life—and Mary's, and everyone else's."

My mother came over and took my hand. "Oh, Paul, I'm so glad you're alive," she said.

My father looked at me for a while before answering. "I didn't know that."

"Mary's dead and Gordon's dead."

"We know," my mother said.

"I killed Mary."

"You what?" my father said.

"I killed her. But I think God has forgiven me."

"Paul, she died of an overdose, it's been on the news. You didn't kill her," my mother said.

"So what are you talking about? You understand that you didn't kill her, don't you?" my father asked.

"No, I did kill her," I said, and they both looked at each other. "I was mean to her when she needed help. I was selfish and that's why she did it."

"Paul, no one makes anyone do that. It's their choice," my mother insisted.

"I was going to crash the plane, but then I had been at this black church in Houston, and a woman had a message from

God that Jesus was saying I should open the door for him. And when I was in the plane, I read a card that Gordon left for me and it said the same thing. So I knew it was God talking to me. So I gave my heart to Jesus."

My parents stopped looking at me and looked at each other in a way I could tell they thought I was spouting gibberish.

"You just need to rest, son," my father said, his anger subsiding.

"Yes, just rest, honey, and don't try to talk. We'll sort it all out later," my mother said, still holding my hand with one of her hands and patting it with the other hand.

The drug was making me sleepier and the last thing I remember was closing my eyes.

"Paul…Paul, can you hear me?"

I kept hearing a voice, but I thought it was in a dream I was having. In the dream I kept looking for my car in Houston, walking down street after street, without finding it. Finally, I saw it, but someone else was driving it, and it raced past me quickly. Then I heard a voice calling me, and I turned around to see who it was, and it was Mary. She looked like she did when I saw her with Don at Allen's Landing and she was high—her hair was unkempt and her eyes seemed woozy. She was smiling at me and was trying to take my hand. I tried to take her hand but the more I stretched it out to her, the farther she drifted from me. Finally I couldn't see her anymore, and then I heard my name being called again, but I knew it wasn't her voice this time. It was someone else's—it was a familiar voice, but I couldn't identify it. Suddenly I opened my eyes, and saw Ruth's face looking down on me.

"Paul, are you all right?"

"Ruth—it's you."

"Yes, are you alright?"

"I think so," I said, as my head began to clear.

"Can I get you anything?"

"No thanks. Are my parents still here?" I asked, thinking that I had only been asleep for a short time.

"No, they were here this morning, but you were still sleeping. They waited for you to wake up, but you never did, so they left."

"How long have I been asleep?"

"I'm not sure—you got here two days ago."

"Two days ago!"

"You're getting medication from the IV, and it's causing you to sleep," she explained.

"Do you know about Mary?"

"Yes, everyone knows. It's been in the newspaper."

"I killed her."

"No you didn't. She committed suicide."

"No, I did it. Do you want to know what happened?"

"Yes."

I explained everything—from the call I got from Mary to what happened after that, and she listened quietly. When I stopped speaking she smiled.

"Paul, what Gordon said to you is from the Bible. Jesus said he is knocking on the door of each person's heart, but most won't open up for him. You did, and that's why you know who he is now—your spirit is alive to God now. That's what it means to be born again."

"So that's what happened. But you said it was in the newspaper about Mary. Do you still have it? Can you bring it to me?"

"It was in yesterday's, but I think there are some in the waiting room. I'll try to find it," she said, and she left the room.

I closed my eyes again. My head had a dull ache, and I was struggling to think clearly. A few minutes later, she came back into the room.

"Here it is—there was a story yesterday and a short one today," she said, and she put them on the bed. "You can read them when you feel better."

"I want to read them now. Please crank up the bed so I can sit up."

"I don't know if Dr. Epstein would want me to do that."

"Come on, Ruth."

"Okay, I guess it would be alright."

She turned the handle and the back of the bed tilted up. I read the papers and realized that Mary's funeral was going to be held at her church in a few hours. I knew I had to get out of the hospital, but I didn't say anything to Ruth.

"Oh, I need to get up," I said, but then I realized the IV she mentioned was attached to the back of my hand.

"You probably ought to just rest."

"But I need to use the restroom."

"Okay, I'll get the nurse," Ruth said, and she left the room.

While she was gone I figured out how to unplug the IV, and I sat up and looked around. There was another bed in the room, but it was made and not occupied. I wanted to stand up, but it took me a moment because my head was cloudy. Finally I slipped out of the bed and hobbled over to the restroom. Before I got there, the nurse came in with Ruth following. The nurse seemed to shout at me as she approached me. "You can't go anywhere, Mr. Welles. You are under arrest and cannot leave the room."

"I was just going to the restroom," I said.

"Okay, but you can't leave the room."

When I walked out of the restroom, Ruth was there and she helped me into bed.

"I'm sorry, Paul," she said.

"It's not your fault. I'm the one who killed Mary."

"You didn't. She killed herself."

"Yeah, with a little help from her friend."

"Paul, don't think that way. You're not to blame. I think she had it planned before you ever visited."

"How do you know? You weren't there."

"You told me what happened, and you are not responsible."

"Where are my clothes? Do you know?"

"Why do you want your clothes?"

"I left a phone number in my pocket. I was supposed to call someone."

"Paul, I wouldn't worry about calling anyone now."

"No, it's important," I said, and a doctor came in and introduced himself as Dr. Epstein. He was a different doctor from the one who first saw me, and he motioned for Ruth to leave.

"Before I tape your ribs, I'm going to touch you in different places and you tell me how bad the pain is on a scale of 1 to 10, okay?"

He continued to examine me while another man walked in and stood at the back of the room. I knew he was a doctor because he was wearing a long white coat like the other doctors. He quietly observed me as Dr. Epstein finished the pain check and then tested my reflexes and examined my wounds. I was getting tired of the other doctor staring at me and I finally said something.

"Why are you looking at me like that?"

"Like what?" he replied.

"Like I'm a rat in an experiment or something. I mean, you're too old to be an intern in training, so why are you here?"

He was very surprised at my question, but also seemed impressed.

"This is Dr. Roth, he's a psychiatrist," Dr. Epstein said.

"I'm sorry to disappoint you, but I'm not crazy."

"Well, you've been through a lot. We can talk about it."

"I'd prefer not to," I said, hoping that by being rude he might leave sooner.

"Your parents are very concerned, Paul. You told them that you were suicidal when you stole the plane. Is that true? Were you going to crash the plane? Is that why you took the plane?"

"No, I just wanted to fly. I should have checked it out with the rental office first. That was a mistake…I forgot to."

"So that was the only reason—you just wanted to take a spin in the plane? Weren't you hurting from your wounds?"

"Yeah, but I still wanted to fly," I answered, trying to figure out a way to get him out of the room so I could get to Mary's funeral.

"So you had no intention of hurting yourself?"

"That's right."

"Then why did you tell them you were going to crash the plane?"

"I lied. I was just trying to get their attention."

Dr. Epstein stepped back from my bed. "You're doing alright. I'll leave you two," he said, and walked out.

"Have you always tried to get attention that way? Have you threatened to hurt yourself in the past? Is there a pattern of that behavior in your life?"

I didn't answer, so he continued after a long pause.

"Paul, do you feel that your parents don't give you enough attention? Do you think they don't take you seriously?"

I looked at him but didn't answer.

"You need to talk to me if you want to get better," he added.

"Look, two people close to me just died. Do you think that might have something to do with what I did? Did that occur to you?"

"Of course, Paul, but your parents also mentioned that you said some religious things, but you have never been religious before. As I said, they are very concerned about you and that is why I am here."

"Your title in Latin is *psychiatria*, and it means a healing of the soul. Did you know that?"

"Yes, son, I know that," he said condescendingly, but I wondered if he did.

"Good. Then I'll tell you that there is only one person who can heal the soul, and that's Jesus Christ. He came into my soul when I was flying, and now you'll really think I'm crazy…because you're Jewish and you probably have a low opinion of Jesus."

He looked at me for a while, and I could see that he was not certain of what to say next. Then he tried to smile. "You're obviously a very intelligent young man. And you're right; anyone going through what you have would need something to…to believe in. We'll talk again when you feel better—after you have rested more." And he got up and left the room.

CHAPTER 24

As soon as the door closed I unplugged the IV, but I tried to get up too fast and fell back down on the bed, feeling faint. When I felt better, I got up again and looked for my clothes, hoping they were in the room somewhere. I found them in a drawer with my shoes, and even though there was blood on them, I quickly put them on. I was about to put on my shoes when I heard someone outside my door, so I got back into bed and pulled the covers up to my neck.

The door opened, and an orderly looked in, emptied the trash in the trash can, and then left. I got out of bed and put on my shoes, and opened the door a little and peeked down the hallway. There was a nurse walking by, so I closed the door and waited a little while. I opened it again and walked out as quickly as I could, and looked for the elevator. I found it, but I figured someone might see me while I was waiting for it, so I went to the staircase and began to walk down. My head started throbbing, and by the time I got down several flights of stairs, I was dizzy; but I knew I had to get out of the hospital before they discovered I was gone.

The sunlight blinded me as I walked out of an exit door, so I stopped for a moment while my eyes adjusted. It was too early for the funeral, and I knew I had to see Mrs. Sanderson—I had to tell her what I'd done to Mary. She had to know the truth, and I had to ask her to forgive me. So I started walking to her apartment, which was about a mile from the hospital.

Her car was parked on the street, so I thought she was probably home. Part of me wanted to keep walking, but I forced myself to go to the front door and knock. She answered the door and just stared at me for a moment. "Paul, you're hurt. Come in."

"I'm okay, there's just blood on my shirt from before—I'm okay now."

"But there are cuts and bruises on your face."

"Mrs. Sanderson, I have to tell you the truth about what happened to Mary."

"Paul, I know what happened. Mary called me after she took the pills, and she repented for all that she'd done. I know she was pregnant and I know she got involved in drugs."

"Did she tell you that I'd been there?"

"No, she didn't mention you. She told me she was sorry she took the pills, and I called an ambulance, but it was too late by the time they arrived. But I know she's in heaven because she asked God to forgive her, and that's my consolation. She regretted taking the pills—she regretted everything, but it was too late."

Up to this time Mrs. Sanderson was remarkably composed, but now she started to sob. I wanted to tell her that I was the reason Mary did what she did, but I just couldn't seem to say anything about it.

"I loved Mary," I said.

"I know you did, Paul. And I know you were trying to help her when you told me she was in trouble—that those people were so wicked. But I thought you were just jealous and...and I wish I'd listened to you. But I just never thought what happened could happen...I thought she was stronger...stronger in the faith."

She wiped her eyes and looked up at me, and I knew it was time to leave.

"Paul, I have to get ready for the funeral."

"I'm sorry, Mrs. Sanderson. I'm really sorry."

I walked back into the sunshine and towards her church. I was trying to figure out where I could get some clean clothes, or at least a shirt, because I didn't want to go to Mary's funeral looking like I did. I thought about going home, and slipping into the back door and grabbing a shirt from the laundry room without anyone seeing me. But then I remembered my parents said the police had been to our house three times. When I got near Mary's church, I stopped at a house across the street and sat down in back of a hedge of bushes so no one could see me.

My idea was to wait there until the funeral began and then cross the street.

After about thirty minutes, cars started driving into the parking lot, and I realized how strange I would look at her funeral with blood all over my shirt and pants. Suddenly I heard a noise above me, and I looked up to see someone closing a second-story window in the house above me. The person could clearly see me, so I thought I should move, but just as I got up a police car drove up. Two policemen got out and grabbed me and put handcuffs on me. Then they turned me around and looked at me and started laughing.

"So this is the punk who beat up the League City cop?" one of them said as he smiled at me.

"Why, he doesn't look too dangerous."

"Nah, wouldn't make a pimple on the criminal's…"

"Are you going to arrest me, or just mock me?"

The first cop's eyes flashed with anger and he moved so his face was right in front of mine and he made a fist and pushed against my chest. "So you're a wise guy, huh, boy?"

I tried to back away from him. "Don't do that. My father teaches at the community college. And there's a woman in the window up there who's been watching. You won't get away with it."

He looked up at the window, and then took a deep breath.

"Did you really think you could escape by coming here?" the first policeman said, again with a mocking tone.

"I wasn't trying to escape. I just wanted to go to a funeral," I answered, as he hustled me into the police cruiser. When we got to the police station they emptied my pockets and put me in something they called the drunk tank. I soon found out why it was called that. There were three disheveled men already there who stunk from liquor and body odor. One was lying on the floor and snoring, one was lying on the floor awake, and the last one sat in a corner and kept nodding his head like he was listening to music or something. The one in the corner asked me if I had a cigarette, and when I told him I didn't, he snarled at me.

After a few hours I was ushered into a room with a desk and chairs and was told to wait there. It wasn't long until a deputy unlocked the door and my parents came in.

"Why do you keep making things worse?" my father asked, angry but also perplexed.

"I was just trying to go to Mary's funeral. I wasn't trying to run away."

"How would they know that?" he asked, staring at me for a moment with exasperation. "Anyway, we've hired a lawyer, but we can't get you out today because you left the hospital. He said we should be able to post bond tomorrow."

"Oh, Paul, you look like you're hurting," my mother said, examining the cuts on my face. "Are you okay? We tried to get them to take you back to the hospital, but they wouldn't let us—even though your ribs are fractured. So please stay really still, and if the pain becomes unbearable, that may mean that…"

"Mum, I'm alright."

"Son, don't do anything else. Please. Just stay here and be quiet and don't provoke anyone, okay?" my father said. Then he lowered his voice to a whisper. "You've got to be careful with these policemen. They know you hurt their colleague, so don't give them an excuse. It's 'yes sir,' and 'no sir,' okay?"

"Yeah, Dad, I understand."

That night more people were put in the cell, which was a rectangle about 15 by 20 feet. It seemed like every time I was about to doze off, a door opened and slammed and someone else came in. By midnight there were about nine people and someone always seemed to be making noise. The toilet in the corner became clogged and wouldn't flush and the odor from it was overwhelming. I gave up on sleeping and decided that I would try to pray. I had said bedtime prayers before as a young child, but those were memorized words my parents gave me. Now, for the first time, I tried to pray to God to help me with the mess I was in. I hadn't tried very long when I fell asleep, and the next thing I knew it was morning and my name was being called.

A deputy ushered me into a room where my parents were waiting. "What's going on, am I free?" I asked as we walked towards them.

"No. You have a bail hearing in thirty minutes," he said flatly, and my mother rushed towards me and hugged me.

"Are you alright?"

"Yes, I'm okay," I said, and then I noticed a man dressed in a nice suit, standing with my father. My father looked at me disdainfully and then introduced me to the lawyer they had hired, a Mr. Benton. He was about fifty years old, with gray hair and a large stomach.

"This hearing is only for the assault and resisting arrest charge," he said. Your father got the airplane theft charge dropped."

"Well, I didn't really do it," my father said. "You can thank your old flight instructor for that. He went to bat for you when he heard what happened."

"Oh, thank God," I said.

"Well it also cost me something, too." My mother looked at him disapprovingly when he said that.

"When you go before the judge, he's going to ask you how you plead, and you need to say *nolo contendere*," Mr. Benton said.

"I will not," I said.

"It means no contest," Mr. Benton said.

"I know what it means, I was an honors Latin student," I said defensively.

"Well, Latin or not, you need to plead like I tell you if you want them to go easy on you," Mr. Benton said in a gruff, intimidating manner.

"I will plead not guilty because he attacked me. I was only defending myself and that's the truth."

"You'll have a hard time proving that. That's been tried with the police before, and it's never been successful. It's just your word against his. You need to plead no contest."

"Mr. Benton is a top criminal lawyer, Paul. You need to listen to him—he understands the system," my father added.

"I'm not going to tell a lie."

"You're a first-time offender, and I think I can get you off without jail time if you do what I say, Mr. Benton said. "I've been doing this for over twenty years, and without evidence you will lose. That policeman had bruises and cuts where you hit him—it has all been documented and photographed."

"His injuries were from falling into a ditch. I ran at him because he was hitting me with a stick for no reason at all."

"And considering all that happened with your girlfriend and her death, I think we have a good case as to why you attacked him," Mr. Benton went on.

"Are you deaf? I said I did not attack him. You don't believe me?"

Mr. Benton smiled slightly. "It doesn't matter what I believe. I'm amoral. I'm just trying to keep you out of jail. You will have a record, which is not so bad. But they'll make mincemeat out of you if you go to prison. Trust me, I know."

My mother took my hand and I could see that she'd been crying. "Please take his advice, Paul."

"Would you have me lie?" I asked her, but she didn't answer.

"Just say how sorry you are—that girl's death is your ace in the hole. But you need to show true sorrow over what you did. Say you lost your head because you were so distraught."

"I'll say nothing but the truth, and if I go to prison, I go to prison. I have to answer to God for what I say. I became a Christian the other day, and I can't lie now. I just can't."

"You can use that—the Christian angle. I like that. You can add that to it. Show you have truly repented for you've done—but save that for the trial. That will definitely help, and the way you just said it, with such sincerity, that was very good. But the judge won't believe that he attacked you, and even if he did, he really can't rule against the cop without evidence. The cop's pretty banged up. He's on medical leave."

"Paul, please listen to Mr. Benton. He knows what's best," my father said.

The deputy escorted us to the courthouse and we sat down. When my name was called, I stood before the judge. His first question was, "How do you plead?"

"Not guilty, your honor," I said, and I heard Mr. Benton sigh.

The judge looked at me with a perplexed look on his face. "Are you saying that you did not assault Officer Robert Hammond?"

"No sir—I did push him in the ditch, but it was self-defense. He was beating me with a stick."

"And was that because you assaulted him, first?"

"No, your honor, he told me to get out of the car and he hit me first."

"For no reason?"

"That's correct, your honor. Well, not exactly. He had stopped my friend and me for speeding many months ago and he was angry when he saw me again."

"Son, your story does not make sense to me. Why was he angry at you?"

"The first time he stopped us, he roughed us up a little, and I lied to him and said my uncle was a judge he knew. He got nervous when he heard that, and he let us go. So when he stopped me the second time, he had found out that the judge was not my uncle."

"So you lied to him, is that it?"

"Yes, I guess I did."

"You guess or you know you lied?"

"I know it."

"You stand here accusing a police officer of assault and with the same breath you admit to lying to him. Is that right?"

"I suppose so...your honor. But it was *vi mendacii*."

"It was what?"

"*Vi mendacii*—it's Latin for lying under compulsion. He was roughing us up, and I said what I could to protect us."

"You're a flight risk. You escaped from the hospital."

"Your honor, I was going to come back. I just wanted to go to my girlfriend's funeral."

The judge seemed to soften a little after I said that, but then he declared the bail and it was a lot of money.

The deputy escorted me out with my father on my other side, who kept looking at me and I could tell he was irritated.

"Paul, what were you thinking? You don't teach a judge Latin."

"I thought he'd know what it meant."

Mr. Benton also looked at me with distaste. "That was almost more of a trial than a bail hearing, and your bail was probably twice as high as it would have been if you'd listened to me. If you'd only done what I told you…" he shook his head, exasperated.

"I had good intentions—I was just trying to tell the truth."

"The road to hell is paved with good intentions."

"Well, I think God will reward me for telling the truth."

"Yeah, with a prison term," Benton added.

"How serious is it, Mr. Benton? Do you really think that Paul could go to jail at his age? He's never been in trouble before," my mother asked, somewhat frantically.

"I'll do everything I can to keep him out, if he'll do what I tell him."

"We'll have a talk with him about that when we get home," my father said solemnly as the deputy led me away from them. "I'll pay the bail and we'll be back for you."

When we got home, my mother called our family doctor and he came and examined me. After he left I closed my bedroom door and tried to rest. The doctor had prescribed something for my pain and my mother came in with a glass of orange juice and some pills. She tried to get me to take them, but I refused.

"Paul, please take these pills. They will help with the pain."

"I don't want help with the pain."

"You must be hurting, now take them, please."

"I'm hurting and I deserve to hurt—after what I did to Mary."

"So you're going to punish yourself? I thought you said that God forgave you."

"Yes, I guess he did, but I haven't forgiven myself."

She looked over at a sandwich she had brought me earlier. "So, you're not touching your food either?"

"I'm not hungry."

"You need to eat to heal."

"I don't want to eat and I don't want to heal," I said, raising my voice.

She looked at me, wanting to say something else, but thinking better of it, she turned around and walked towards the door. I felt guilty and wanted to say something more to her. As she opened the door I managed to. "Mum, thanks for everything." She turned around, nodded, and closed the door.

My head throbbed after raising my voice, and I lay back down on my pillow, but that seemed to make my head hurt worse. I kept thinking about Mary, and it got me so upset that I reached for the juice and the two pills she had left and swallowed them. The pills were effective and I fell asleep quickly, and slept from that afternoon to the next morning, when my mother came into my room again. She had cooked a large breakfast for me, and she put the tray down next to my bed.

"You have to be hungry now, Paul. You haven't eaten for a long time."

I nodded and she left the room, and I tried to get back to sleep, but now all I could think about was how much I'd let everyone down. I'd let Mary down, and my parents, and brought disgrace on the family. I looked over at the tray and saw that there were two more pills on the tray she left. I took them with some orange juice, but left the rest of the food alone. Soon I was asleep again.

I was dreaming about something when I felt someone shaking me. At first it was part of the dream, and then I opened my eyes and my mother was standing over my bed.

"What is it?"

"There's someone here to see you."

I looked at the clock and realized I'd been sleeping for about twelve hours. I felt groggy as I pushed myself up against the headboard.

"Who is it?"

"Your friend Ruth. She's downstairs and I told her I'd see if you wanted a visitor."

"Um...okay."

My mother walked out and soon returned with Ruth.

"Hi, Paul, how are you feeling?"

"I'm okay."

"Here Ruth, have a seat," my mother said, and she brought a chair up to my bedside.

"I'm sorry you weren't able to get to Mary's funeral. I know you tried very hard," Ruth said.

"Yeah, and it got me in more trouble."

"I know. It was wrong but it was also...well, it was valiant."

For a moment no one spoke, and then my mother realized that she was probably stopping the conversation.

"I'll leave you two," she said, and walked out of the room but left the door open.

"Paul, your mother tells me you're not eating."

"Oh no, is that why you came—did she call you?"

"No, I just wanted to come. I brought you a Bible—it's the American Standard Version which might be easier to read than the King James," she said, as she put the book on my bed.

"Thank you. I know I need to read it—God showed me that when I had my experience with Jesus."

"You also need to pray."

"I've done some of that."

"Have you prayed for Don?"

I looked up at her angrily. "Yeah, I prayed that God would kill him and send him to hell."

"Paul, that's wrong."

"Why? Doesn't he belong there?"

"You don't understand. You can't be a Christian and not forgive everyone. It's a requirement."

"Can't I forgive him after I find him and beat him up?"

"Oh, Paul."

"Okay, I get it. But I don't know if I can. I told you what he did to Mary."

"I understand and that's why I brought another book with me. It's called *The Hiding Place*. The woman who wrote it, Corrie Ten Boom, was in a concentration camp in World War Two. They did the most terrible things to her and her sister, but she forgave them."

I picked up the book and looked at it.

"That must have been hard."

"Yes it was. We need Christ's help to forgive. But you have to be willing to be made willing. Are you?"

"I don't know."

"Well, ask God to make you willing—it's the first step. By the way, your mother is one of the nicest people I've ever met."

"Yeah, I think so. Thank you."

"And you said you were sorry that you'd been selfish that night with Mary."

"Ruth, I really don't want to talk about it anymore. The guilt is driving me crazy."

"Okay, but what about being selfish now? Your mother was crying when I came over, and your father is also distraught. If you would just eat some food it would make them so much happier."

"I see what you mean. You're right."

"Here," Ruth said, and she passed the tray of food over to me, and I took a bite of the scrambled eggs, which were a little cold. "Paul, you said you had guilt, so you also have to forgive yourself."

"That might be harder than Don. Mary called me for help, and I let her down. She loved me, but the way I acted broke her heart."

Ruth looked down and was quiet. Then she started to say something, but thought better of it and kept quiet.

"Anyway, I'll get what I deserve—I'll be a convicted felon before this is all through. I guess that's punishment for what I've done."

"Paul, you told me you were innocent—that you didn't attack him."

"That's true. But there were no witnesses, and my lawyer says you can't win when it's your word against a cop."

"There was another witness."

"Who?"

"God is on the throne and he is the other witness."

"Yeah, if I could only get him to testify."

"He has many ways of fixing this, and I'll be praying that the truth comes out. I have faith he will not let us down."

"I hope you're right."

As I was speaking my mother walked into the room.

"Oh, lovely, you're eating," she exclaimed. "But let me make some fresh food for you."

"It's fine, Mum."

"Are you sure?"

"Yes, it's good."

"Well, I'd better be going," Ruth said, and she got up. "I'll be praying for you."

"That's so kind of you," my mother said, and she walked with her down the stairs.

CHAPTER 25

A few days later, my father came into my room. He seemed uncomfortable as he sat down next to my bed and noticed that I was reading the Bible.

"Reading your Bible again, I see."

Then he noticed that I had some books from his library in a stack next to my bed. He seemed happier as he read the title of the one on top, which had a bookmarker in it.

"Oh, you're reading *Christ in the Camp*. That was written in 1887. That will give you a real flavor for religion in the Civil War."

"Yes, I like it. There are a lot of letters reprinted from soldiers to their families."

"I'm sorry, but I have some bad news for you. The prosecutor wants you tried as an adult because it was an assault on a police officer, even though you're seventeen. They made a motion for it, and if it's granted, it will mean stricter punishment."

"I see."

He looked at me for a moment with incredulity.

"Did you hear what I said? Do you realize how much trouble you're in?"

"Yes, I do, Dad. But I'm trusting God, because I'm innocent. That cop starting hitting me for no reason, and I was already hurting from being mugged."

"Yes, you told us. But innocent people go to jail sometimes. The justice system isn't perfect."

"But God is."

At that he got exasperated. "Will you quit with the God stuff—enough is enough."

"Sorry, that's just how I think now."

"Yes, I know, and I can't figure out why. Tell me why."

At that point my mother came into the room, but then she realized we were having a conversation.

"Oh, is this a father-son talk or...?"

"It's fine, Ann. Sit down with us. I just asked Paul why he's gotten religious all of a sudden. So, what happened? Explain it to me."

"Well, in Jeremiah 29:13 God says, 'And you shall seek me, and find me when you shall search for me with all your heart.'"

"I didn't ask for a sermon," he interrupted, irritated.

"You asked the reason, Dad, and I'm trying to explain."

"Give him a chance, dear."

"Okay. Go ahead."

"What happened to me is the same thing that happened, I think, to Oscar Wilde. Do you remember when you quoted part of that poem to me that he wrote when he was in jail? And he kept talking about Jesus? And you were wondering about it?"

"Yes."

"And it's the same thing that happened to Gordon right before he died. And in this book of yours I'm reading, Stonewall Jackson had his arm blown off and he said he wouldn't even want it replaced unless it was God's will. He also didn't allow any profanity among the soldiers, and he prayed with them regularly."

"Yes, I know he was religious. That was before we knew much about science. Let's get back to what happened to you."

"Well, I sought God with all my heart. I gave my life to him and had a spiritual experience with Jesus when I asked him to forgive me for all my sins."

"And what was that like?"

"It was…well, it was like turning a light on in a dark room. I knew the Bible was true, I knew that heaven and hell were real and that Jesus is God…"

"Paul, that book was written thousands of years ago by a number of authors. Isn't there a chance someone was misquoted?"

"That's the natural way of thinking. But when you come to God, he shows you that it's his word in the original languages, although the translations do have flaws. In fact, I think I'll study Greek and Hebrew so I can read it in those languages."

"Oh, you have really gone off the deep end…," he began angrily, but my mother looked at him with pleading eyes, and he calmed down and was quiet for a while.

"Okay, but one more question. If you've found God and all, and it's so wonderful, why are you so melancholy most of the time?"

"William, two of his friends just died. He's still grieving," my mother said.

I looked at him for a moment. "Mum's right. I am happy that I've been forgiven, but I'm still the reason Mary died, and it is hard to get over it."

As the days passed, I talked to Ruth on the phone quite a bit, mostly with questions about the Bible. She came by one day with more books, and I met her in one of the drawing rooms downstairs. I was dressed this time, although I was still moving slowly.

"You must be feeling better," she said.

"Yeah, I've got to get better for them so they can lock me up," I said, whimsically.

Ruth answered in a very serious tone. "Don't say that. I'm praying, remember. I'm praying for a miracle."

"Well, I need one, because they want to try me as an adult."

Her face fell when she heard that. "What does that mean?"

"It means I'd go to prison with the adult population instead of to a juvenile facility."

I could tell that upset her, but then she took a deep breath and tried to smile. "I've brought you some books." She gave me "The Pursuit of God" by A.W. Tozer, and "The Cross and the Switchblade" by David Wilkerson.

"So, are you well enough to go to church now?"

"I'm getting there, but the one my parents go to doesn't believe anything. It's a social club."

"Then come to mine."

"I'd like to, but I don't know if I should since Mrs. Sanderson goes there. I saw her before the funeral and she was nice to me, but I might bring back bad memories."

"So she knows you're a Christian now?"

"No, I didn't tell her. She was getting ready to leave."

"Paul, she'll be so pleased to hear this. She's been trying to find something good that may have come from all this, and when she finds out you got saved it will make her so happy. Can I tell her?"

"Sure."

I was sleeping late the next morning when the phone rang and woke me up. By the time I reached for it, someone else answered it. So I put on my robe and walked downstairs. My mother smiled when she saw me.

"So what would you like for breakfast?" she asked cheerfully.

"A couple of eggs and toast would be great."

"Coming right up. Why don't you sit at the kitchen table and we can talk?" she said, and I followed her into the kitchen. "You know, Ruth is really an exceptional young lady." She served me some orange juice, and then my father came in with a perplexed smile on his face.

"I have good news."

"Oh, really?" my mother said, taking eggs out of the refrigerator.

"That was our lawyer. It looks like the charges will be dropped against Paul. That policeman was just charged with assault. Turns out he beat up a college student whose father is a state senator, but they were keeping it out of the news. But then there was an older complaint that came up and then a new one was filed from someone else a few days ago. So Benton figures they won't want another one to defend, and he asked the district attorney to drop the charges and it seems like he will. Boy, are we lucky."

I put down my juice glass, a little stunned. "It's not luck—it's an answer to prayer! Ruth said that God was a witness to what happened, and he would help me. She prayed for this."

"Well, whatever, let's wait until we get the final answer."

"We have the answer. It's a miracle from God," I said.

"Yes, well thank God if it does come through because then you'll be able to go to a good college."

"Dad, is college all you care about?"

"No, but...well, it is important."

Ruth had told me she had classes at the community college, so I waited until around two o'clock to call her.

"What a wonderful answer to prayer," she said.

"Yes, it is."

"But you seem so unhappy still. This is a reason to rejoice."

"Yeah I know. I read *The Hiding Place*, and I did forgive Don," I said, changing the subject. "Sometimes I feel something rising up in me when I think of him, but then I ask God to help and I resist it."

"But you still sound so sad."

"I am sad. Maybe I should have been punished that way. I mean, I can't believe what I did to Mary."

"Paul, you forgave Don, and you need to forgive yourself. You can't spend your whole life blaming yourself for Mary."

"Yeah, well, I should go."

"Paul, wait a minute. It's important that I talk to you in person. Tomorrow is Saturday so I've got Candy Stripers in the morning, but I'd like to visit in the afternoon."

"Okay, I'll see you then."

Ruth seemed jittery when she came into the house. My parents had gone to the library—since they both liked to read they probably spent more time there than anywhere else when they weren't home. Ruth sat on a chair that faced our couch and I sat on the couch.

"I've been struggling about telling you this, Paul."

"Telling me what? What is it?"

"Well, it's about Mary and I wanted you to have the best memory of her you could have. But there is something you have to know."

"Really? Okay, I'm ready."

She looked at me for a moment, and then sighed.

"I think that you think she would have married you and everything would have been fine if…what happened hadn't happened. Is that what you think?"

"I don't know, Ruth. It wouldn't have been perfect, but yes, I guess so. I mean we loved each other."

"I can't let you go on with this guilt. Do you remember how Mary never wanted to offend anyone? She always went out of her way to be nice to everyone."

"Yes."

"Well, she wanted to break up with you earlier on. I mean she thought you were really cute and smart and fun to be with and all of that, but she told me that she just never really felt it for you."

"What? Are you kidding?"

"No, I mean it. She appreciated the fact that you liked her so much, and she hoped her feelings would change. I told her that it was wrong to string you along, but she was so afraid of hurting you that she just kept seeing you."

I took a breath and looked at her, not sure of what to say. My mind started spinning very quickly, as I thought about the times I was with Mary. "Go on."

"We were writing each other regularly when you were driving up to see her in Houston. She kept wanting to tell you, but she just couldn't seem to."

"So all that time, when she said she wanted to see me, she didn't mean it? I mean she even wrote me letters when I was in Australia."

"No, I think she meant some of it. She really liked you, she just didn't…"

"Love me?"

"Oh, I don't know what to say—well, yes, that's it. She wanted to be your friend, but she didn't want more than that. It was hard for her, because she knew you liked her so much, and you sort of overwhelmed her. No boy had ever shown her so much attention."

"That's why she fell so quickly for Don. She never wanted to continue our relationship. I see it now."

"Paul, the point I'm trying to make—the point is that I don't think you broke her heart that night. There's a good chance she would have done what she did anyway. So stop blaming yourself."

"Well, I was still rotten to her."

"Maybe, but you didn't make her commit suicide. You don't even have that power."

"So she wanted to break up with me—I mean, when did that happen? We were so happy together."

"I'm sorry, Paul."

"Come on, answer me. Let's have the whole truth. When did she change her mind about me?"

"Paul, she was never sure about the relationship. But you came on so strong—you liked her so much that she yielded. And she thought that it might develop into something more for her. But it never did. She talked to me about it from the beginning."

"Wow!"

"I'm sorry, Paul, and I never would have said anything—I wanted you to have fond memories of your time with her, but I couldn't let you suffer with guilt for something you didn't do."

"Well, I still feel bad about what I did, but this puts it in a different light. That's for sure."

"I'm sorry to be the bearer of this news."

"No, don't say that. I mean, at least I know the truth. I didn't think anyone would be that malleable. She could have just turned me down."

"She had a problem in that area. It's not just you, she never really liked Jim—but everyone said she should like him because he was captain of the football team, and all."

"Maybe she didn't like Don, either. He was very pushy."

"Mary didn't have a father, and I think somehow that made her susceptible to men with strong personalities."

"Yeah, I get the picture...I get it now. If she'd just told me..."

"It's hard for you to understand because you're so straightforward. I mean she liked the attention she got from you—and she really respected you."

I stood up and walked towards the window. I could see some pigeons in a tree in front of the house and I watched them for a moment, trying to process everything Ruth was telling me. My mind kept seeing scenes of when we were together. Why was my perception so lacking? Just then the sunshine from the window caught my eye, and I remembered back to when I was lying on the bed and the amulet was reflecting the sun. I remembered I had said *I want Mary more than anything*, and right after that her cat died.

"Maybe I should go now."

"Oh, I'm sorry. I was lost in thought. Ruth do you think that an object—like an amulet, can have power—like evil power to make someone like you?"

"What do you mean?"

"Oh, nothing.

"But Mary did like you."

"Yeah a little. I just wonder how I could have been such a fool." Then a song I'd heard on the radio many times came into my mind and I sang it in a low voice. "*Everybody plays the fool sometime. There's no exception to the rule.*"

"I'm sorry it's been so hard for you," she said, and she got up and walked over to me and touched my arm in a consoling way. "When Jesus said we must forgive others, he also meant ourselves. I hope this at least makes it easier for you."

"It probably does. I think maybe she got mad at me that night because she didn't really want to marry me."

"I'll see myself out."

"Ruth, wait a minute. I want to ask you something. I read in the Bible that God says 'vengeance is mine.' I understand that we're not supposed to hate anyone. And I've forgiven Don. But the Bible also says in Romans 13:4 that even though we don't seek retribution, the government has that responsibility. It says that they are the revenger. So I think that's like the police. Is that how you understand it?"

"I suppose so."

"So I think I have a responsibility to turn Don in."

Ruth thought for a moment before answering. "Yes, I agree. And I thought about this before. But I don't know you how you can prove anything. There are no witnesses."

"I've got an idea. He's probably still using drugs, and the cop who spoke at the school said marijuana is a felony."

That night I spent most of the evening reading. Around eleven I was about to go to sleep when I heard a crashing sound. I rushed downstairs, trying to figure out where it was coming from. I heard more noise, which sounded like glass breaking, so I walked over to one of the fireplaces and grabbed an iron tool for poking logs. Just then my mother showed up, and I could tell that she had also been sleeping.

"I think someone's breaking in. It sounds like it's down in the basement," I said in a low tone.

I walked slowly down the basement stairway with her behind me. I waved for her to stay back, but she wouldn't. As I got close to the bottom I heard some more noise, and I also recognized my father's voice. Then I saw him lying on his chest with several broken bottles of wine scattered around. He was semi-conscious, and when my mother saw him she was startled, but she stayed composed, which I attributed to her nursing training.

My father started moving, and she tried to help him up. "Oh, William, what happened?" she asked. He answered slowly with slurred speech. He was obviously very drunk.

"I just came down for a couple bottles but I slipped," he said, happily. "Nothing to worry about," he added, but as he tried to get up he pushed his hand on some broken glass and cut his palm in several places. My mother tried to pick him up but she couldn't.

"Come on, Dad," I said, lifting him.

"Oh, Paul—your ribs!"

"I'm okay, Mum."

"But you can puncture a lung."

"Mum they're only fractured, not broken."

"But they can break…"

I helped him up the stairs and into the kitchen, where he sat down as my mother tended his cut hand. He also had a bruise on his face and on his right arm from his fall. He was still quite drunk, and he kept falling in and out of sleep. When she determined she could do no more for him, I helped him to a daybed in one of the downstairs rooms, and he dropped into it and fell fast asleep almost immediately.

After that we walked back into the kitchen and she began cleaning up where she had used our first aid kit. I could tell she was not only upset about him, but she also seemed ashamed.

"I'm sorry you had to see him like that," she said.

"Mum, I know he's got a drinking problem. That's no secret."

"I know, but…it's just such a terrible example for you. I hope you see it as something to avoid and not to emulate. I know you were drinking his wine."

"That was before. I'm not the same now. I'll never drink again. I want my mind clear."

She looked at me for a moment, and then nodded her head in agreement. "That's good."

"So did something bring this on? He usually doesn't get drunk like that."

"Yes. Well, you know about the textbooks. We lost most of the royalties. And now we really can't live very well on his salary. The community college pay is very low and the Texas A and M job was only one class, and it was temporary. With all the bad news, he keeps drinking more and more."

"I didn't know things were that bad."

"He doesn't want to move, he likes it here. He loves this historical house. I don't really—I think it's a pain to keep up, and it's so big it's hard to keep clean. Anyway we're going to have to move again because there are no four-year colleges nearby."

"Where will we go?"

"Well, he thought about Rice University or the University of Houston, but there are no openings."

"Good, I don't want to live in Houston."

"Yes, I imagine it holds bad memories. He's looking at a few places. One of his old colleagues is a dean at San Diego State College. So we may move to California. I know he'd like to move back East, but my health won't tolerate it. So he's searching for colleges in warmer climates."

On Tuesday, I woke up and walked down the stairs and heard my parents talking. I stopped on the staircase when I realized I was the subject of their conversation.

"I think he's just traded one obsession for another. First it was Mary and now it's Jesus."

"William, please don't be cynical about Paul. I see a change in him that I like, so if religion is the reason, I'm all for it."

I moved on the step and the banister made a sound and they became quiet, so I thought they heard me. I continued walking down as if I hadn't heard anything, and entered the living room.

"Paul, have a seat. This morning Mr. Benton said the charges were actually dropped."

"Oh, thank you, Lord!" I exclaimed.

"Yes, thank God. How are you feeling, Paul?" my mother asked.

"I'm much better. I'm ready to go back to school now, and the doc said I could go on Wednesday."

"Are your ribs still hurting?"

"Not much—not much at all."

"Well, you must stay out of P.E.," my mother cautioned.

"Actually, I'm already out of it," I said, and she didn't asked me why, but it was because of Gordon's letter.

"I'd like you to do something for me next weekend. Now that you can travel out of the city, I need you to drop me off in Houston," my father said.

"Sure, Dad. Where are you going?"

"The VA hospital."

"The hospital? What's wrong?"

"My drinking is what's wrong—it's gotten to be too much. They have something they call 'the cure' where they dry you out. I need to stay in the hospital for ten days for it. I was waiting until you could travel out of the city—before, your bail prevented you from leaving."

"What about teaching?"

"I'm taking some time off. I only have classes on Tuesday and Thursday, so we can leave on Friday morning and I won't miss much. I'm also thinking about going to Alcoholics Anonymous, but I don't think anyone can be anonymous in this little town."

"Mum told me we may be moving."

"Yes, I'm looking. There are a few possibilities. Now I'd also like you to do something else for me."

"Okay."

"Get rid of all the wine in the basement when I'm gone."

"Is it okay if I sell it?"

"Sell it, throw it away, I don't care. Just get rid of it."

"I'll do it. I've got a friend whose father may want it."

"Sure, sell it if you can. It's all right for someone who can handle it. I obviously can't."

CHAPTER 26

After I dropped my father off at the VA hospital on Friday morning, I went to the police station and asked for Sergeant Ricstetter. They asked me if I had an appointment, and I realized I should have called first. However, he was there, and after a long wait I was ushered into a large room where there were many people working at desks. I sat in a chair next to his.

"What can I do for you, son?"

"I saw you when you spoke to my class in Galveston about drugs. And you said if we ever knew about anyone selling them, we should tell the police."

"Yes, I did. So do you know someone?" he asked in his twangy Texas accent.

"Yes, his name is Don and he goes to the University of Houston."

"How do you know he's selling drugs?"

"I was up here with my friend who was going to college here and...well, I know, believe me, I know."

"What's his last name?"

"I don't know."

"Well, son, there are a lot of people named Don."

"Yes, of course. I'll get his full name."

"You do that and get back with me."

"Sergeant, what is the penalty for selling marijuana? You said it was a felony when you talked to us."

"Yes, it still is a felony in Texas—thank God. It's a minimum of two years to life. The difference is the quantity and whether he's using or just selling. He could easily get ten years if he's selling."

"So if I get the information, what do you do?"

"Send an undercover officer to buy it from him, but I would need your complaint. Otherwise, we'll get accused of entrapment. But if we have a citizen who says he's selling drugs, we have a reason to make the buy."

"Does that mean that I'll testify against him?"

"Probably not. All I need is the signed complaint, which gives us probable cause. The evidence will be the drugs he sells us and the testimony of the officers involved. We usually have two officers on each case. But he will know that you signed the complaint if you're worried about that."

"Not in the least. I'll also testify if it's needed."

"That's good. I wish there were more like you. If this drug problem continues, twenty years from now half the country will be on the stuff. Here is my card. Call me when you get the information. Again, I'm glad to see a young man who cares about this."

"Well Sergeant, I had an experience with Jesus and that's why I'm here."

When I said that, his face beamed. "Well now, son, that's the best experience any of us can have, isn't it?"

Since Don worked at Sand Mountain, I thought I could get his name by going there, but that might tip him off, and I didn't want his guard up. So I drove to the University of Houston. With over thirty thousand students, it was a big place, but I remembered that Don was a teaching assistant in the Psychology Department. I asked around until I found it, and then I walked into the building. A woman at the counter, who appeared to be a student, looked up and asked if she could help me. I stood there for a moment, trying to figure out something I could say which would not make him suspicious if it got back to him.

"I…I had Don as a T.A. in a psychology class last summer, and I wanted to send him something, but I don't have his address."

"Don?"

"Yes—I don't think I remember his last name."

"Well we don't give out addresses."

"Okay, but can I mail it to him at the university address?"

"No, that's only for professors. We don't accept mail for TA's."

"Do you know who I'm talking about? Could I just get his last name, please?"

"You said Don, is that right?"

"Yes."

"Okay, let me look," she said and she went to a desk and got what looked like a directory. "The only Don we have is Donald A. Riker who is a grad student. Is that him?"

"Yes, that must be—if that's the only one you have."

"It is, and he did assist in a class this summer."

"Great, thank you."

I walked down the hallway, feeling jubilant. I had his name now—it had to be him, I thought. But how could I be sure? No, I wasn't sure, and if I went back to the police and it was the wrong person, that would be a mess. I turned around and walked back to the same room I'd been in. The woman looked up at me, questioningly.

"Is there something else?"

"Just one more thing. Do you have a class roster of students who took that class—there is another student I met but I can't remember her last name."

"No, we can't give that out."

"Oh, I see."

"But you might find it around the corner. Those grades are still posted for Psychology 101. All names are there."

"Oh, thanks again. You've been so nice."

I rushed around the corner and found the list for Psychology 101 and quickly went to the end of the list. There it was, Sanderson, Mary. This was the class, and it had to be the same Don. I found a pay phone and called Sergeant Ricstetter. After he took the information, he started questioning me. He wanted to know how I knew Don, since I lived in Galveston. I ended up telling him the whole story, and he was quiet for a moment.

"I'm sorry to hear that. Come back to the station in about two hours and sign the complaint and we'll get him. We'll get him."

I hadn't eaten lunch, so I decided to go to the cafeteria. I bought a sandwich and sat down to eat, and then I saw him. He was a long way across the large room, and it was only the side of his face, but I was sure it was him. A pretty girl with long black hair was sitting with him, and he was talking to her and laughing, and touching her arm from time to time. Suddenly rage boiled up in me and I wanted to hurt him. I wanted to kill him—to slowly beat him to death. I imagined waiting for him and grabbing him from the back and choking him. I truly thought I had forgiven him, but now I hated him worse than before, and all I could think of was revenge.

He turned slightly, and I was concerned he would see me. I tried to push the anger away. I called on God to help me, but it seemed overwhelming. I realized that if he saw me it might alert him, so I picked up my sandwich and turned my back to his table and slowly walked out of the cafeteria. My heart was pounding as I got outside, and I was breathing erratically. I tried to control it, and slowly I normalized. I walked quickly to my car and drove off the campus. When I was halfway to the police station, I pulled over and tried to eat my sandwich, but I couldn't. I was still too upset. I got to the station early, but Sergeant Ricstetter was also finished early, and I signed the complaint and left.

When I got home, Ruth called.

"Paul, I talked to Mrs. Sanderson and she would be very happy if you came to our church."

I didn't answer for a few moments.

"Paul, are you there?"

"I can't go to church. I can't be a Christian. I saw Don and I wanted to kill him."

"Paul, stop talking this way. You are a Christian. You asked Jesus into your heart."

"Corrie Ten Boom forgave the Nazis but I can't forgive Don."

"And Corrie Ten Boom had been a Christian since she was a little girl. You just got saved."

"You don't understand. I wanted to choke him slowly. I wanted him to suffer and pay for what he did."

"Did you talk to him?"

"No. It was a coincidence. I just happened to see him in the cafeteria. I got out quickly because I didn't want him to suspect anything. The police are on the case now."

"Paul, it was no coincidence. God arranged it so you could see what was going on in your own heart."

"But I had forgiven him. I really thought I had."

"The Bible says the heart is deceitful and desperately wicked. But you *can* forgive him."

"No, it's too hard. I can't do it."

"You must do it. You can't go to heaven if you don't."

"Then I'll go to hell."

"Don't talk that way. I'm coming over and we can pray through this thing."

"No, Ruth, it's useless."

"You're wrong. You can do all things through Christ who strengthens you. That's in Philippians. I'm coming in about twenty minutes," she said and hung up before I could say anything else.

I was surprised because she was normally not aggressive, but as I hung up, I remembered a story I heard on television about a couple whose daughter was raped and murdered, and they visited the man who did it in prison and befriended him. I had always wondered how they did it.

I was actually glad to see her when she came over. I answered the door and my mother walked out at the same time.

"Is there a room where we can pray?" Ruth asked.

"Yeah, I guess. There are lots of rooms."

"Paul and I are going to pray for a while."

"I think that would be wonderful. You can use the east drawing room," my mother said, walking towards it.

"Thank you, Mrs. Welles," Ruth said, as she entered the room. "Would you like to stay and pray with us?"

"Well, I do have some dishes to do…"

"Okay, thanks for letting us use the room."

"Oh, that's fine," my mother said, and she walked away.

I started to close the double doors to the room, but Ruth stopped me.

"I don't want anyone to get the wrong idea," she said.

"Oh, I see."

We started praying for me to be able to forgive Don. Ruth stopped after about thirty minutes.

"Let's do this every day for a while. Maybe we can make this our prayer room."

"Yes, I'd like that—I need it."

As the week went by, I was able to get rid of my virulent anger when I thought of Don. The following week he was arrested for distributing marijuana, LSD, and methamphetamine. Sergeant Ricstetter said catching him was easy—he sold the drugs to two undercover agents and was immediately arrested. The bail was high and the week after that he was still in jail, waiting for his trial. Our prayer sessions were more sporadic now, and Ruth came over when I told her about Don.

"Can you finally forgive him now?"

"Yes, I have, but I hope it's not just because he got caught."

"Paul, no one gets away with anything. We'll all appear before God to give an accounting. I'm just glad I've been forgiven."

"Yeah, I am too."

"He would get punished eventually. But getting caught is God's mercy."

"You mean for us?"

"No, for him."

"I don't get it."

"By getting punished here, he might start to understand God's justice. That might bring him to God. By the way, how is your father doing?"

"He's stopped drinking, but now I know why he drank. He gets upset about a lot of things and he's grumpy most of the time. He used to be more amiable."

"I'm praying for him. Should I tell him that when I see him?"

"Oh, no. Please don't. He gets mad at me if I mention anything about God."

"We'll keep praying—he'll change."

"My mother is more open, but she sort of goes back and forth."

"I understand. She's trying to decide. Well, I need to get home," Ruth said, getting up from the couch.

"Ruth, remember I told you that my father was looking for a job?"

"Yes, you said you would be moving to San Diego."

"Well we are moving—in a few weeks."

"My, that is quick."

"Well something happened, a professor died, so they need my father right away, and the junior college has a replacement, so they're letting him out of his contract. They knew he would have to leave eventually."

"Oh, that's nice. I'm happy for him," she said, but I could tell it bothered her a little.

"I'm going to miss you, and our praying together."

"I'll miss you too, Paul."

"Would you like it if I wrote to you?" I asked.

"Yes, I'd love that."

"Ruth, I've missed you even between our prayer sessions. I've never told you that, but it's the truth. I don't think I could ever find a girl who is as kind as you are."

"That's nice," she said, and then she frowned and dropped her head and turned away, and I was afraid I was making a mistake. But I'd gone this far, so I decided to continue.

"I was hoping that you felt the same way. I mean I'll be moving, but if you do, I mean if you feel the same way, perhaps we can see each other again."

She finally looked up with a distressed look and I got ready for her to turn me down.

"Oh, Paul, I started out just wanting to help you with your Christian walk, but then I started liking you. But it seemed so inappropriate with the loss of Mary that I never wanted you to know. I felt like I was a traitor to her. But now that you're telling me this...well I would like to see you again. I hope we can. But I don't know, California is such a long way."

"The Bible says that with God all things are possible. Do you believe that?"

"Yes, of course."

"Well this is more possible than you might think. Instead of San Diego, his new job is at the University of Texas, and he's okay with me going there instead of back East for school. Anyway, Austin's not that far away."

"Paul, that's wonderful! And it just so happens that I've applied to transfer to UT, and if I get a scholarship we'll both be there."

"I have a feeling you'll get the scholarship, and this gives us something special to pray for."

Books by John Lifflander (J.B. Lifflander)

Novels
The Free State of Galveston
Disguised for Love: The Strickland Sisters
Journey in the Great Depression
Lemuel, What My Son?

Christian Teaching
The Power of the Sacrifice
Pursuing the Word
Into His Marvelous Light—Christian Poetry

Technical
Fundamentals of Industrial Valuation, IAAO 2007
Analyzing Complex Appraisals for Business Professionals, McGraw Hill, 2016
(Co-authored with Shannon Pratt)